THE BORZOI BOOK OF French Folk Tales

Selected and Edited by PAUL DELARUE

ARNO PRESS
A New York Times Company
New York • 1980

Editorial Supervision: Rita Lawn

Reprint Edition 1980 by Arno Press Inc.
© Alfred A. Knopf, Inc. 1956
Reprinted by permission of Alfred A. Knopf, Inc.

FOLKLORE OF THE WORLD
ISBN for complete set: 0-405-13300-6
See last pages of this volume for titles.

Manufactured in the United States of America

Library of Congress Cataloging in Publication Data

Delarue, Paul, ed.
 The Borzoi book of French folk tales.

 (Folklore of the world)
 Translated from the French by Austin E. Fife.
 Reprint of the ed. published by Knopf, New York.
 1. Tales, French. I. Title. II. Series:
Folklore of the world (New York)
[GR161.D42 1980]   398.2'0944   80-743
ISBN 0-405-13309-X

THE BORZOI BOOK OF French Folk Tales

*This is a volume
in the Arno Press collection*

FOLKLORE OF THE WORLD

Advisory Editor
Richard M. Dorson

Editorial Board
Dan Ben-Amos
Alan Dundes

*See last page of this volume
for a complete list of titles*

THE BORZOI BOOK OF
French Folk Tales

THE BORZOI BOOK OF French Folk Tales

Selected and Edited by PAUL DELARUE
Translated by Austin E. Fife
Illustrated by Warren Chappell

New York
Alfred·A·Knopf
1956

© *Alfred A. Knopf, Inc.*, 1956

THIS IS A BORZOI BOOK,
PUBLISHED BY ALFRED A. KNOPF, INC.

Copyright 1956 by Alfred A. Knopf, Inc. All rights reserved. No part of this book may be reproduced in any form without permission in writing from the publisher, except by a reviewer who may quote brief passages and reproduce not more than three illustrations in a review to be printed in a magazine or newspaper. Manufactured in the United States of America. Published simultaneously in Canada by McClelland and Stewart Limited.

FIRST EDITION

CONTENTS

INTRODUCTION · *The French Folk Tale*   ix

PART I · *Tales of the Supernatural*

1 · The Three May Peaches   3
2 · Jean, the Soldier, and Eulalie, the Devil's Daughter   10
3 · The Giant Goulaffre   20
4 · The White Dove   36
5 · The Devil and the Two Little Girls   42
6 and 7 · The Story of John-of-the-Bear, and The Story of Cricket (soldiers' versions)   45
8 · King Fortunatus's Golden Wig   70
9 · Father Roquelaure   86
10 · The Lost Children   97
11 · The Godchild of the Fairy in the Tower   103
12 · Petit Jean and the Frog   108
13 · The Gilded Fox   119
14 · The Love of Three Oranges   126
15 · The Doctor and His Pupil   135
16 · Little Johnny Sheep-Dung   140
17 · The Three Dogs and the Dragon   147
18 · The Self-Propelled Carriage   157
19 · The Old Woman in the Well   164
20 · The Little Girl's Sieve   167

Contents

21 · Father Big-Nose	170
22 · The Serpent and the Grape-Grower's Daughter	177
23 · The Three Stags	182
24 · The Miller's Three Sons	187
25 · The Marriage of Mother Crumb	201
26 · Father Louison and the Mother of the Wind	204
27 · Grain-of-Millet	217
28 · The Little Sardine	226
29 · The Story of Grandmother	230
30 · The Sharpshooter	233
31 · Georgic and Merlin	237
32 · The Little Blacksmith	249
33 · La Ramée and the Phantom	252
34 · The Woman with Three Children	257
35 · The Kid	263
36 · How Kiot-Jean Married Jacqueline	267
37 · Half-Man	272
38 · The Three Blue Stones	276

PART II · *Animal Tales*

1 · The Journey to Toulouse of the Animals That Had Colds	285
2 · The Lion That Learned to Swing—The Fox That Learned How to Pick Cherries—The Wolf That Learned How to Split Wood	288
3 · The Sow and the Wolf	292
4 · The Three Pullets	297
5 · The Goat and Her Kids	300
6 · Brother Mazaraud	304
7 · A Lovely Dream and a Fateful Journey	309
8 · Half-Chick	312

Contents

PART III *Humorous Tales*

1 · Turlendu	319
2 · The Fantastic Adventures of Cadiou the Tailor	322
3 · The Miraculous Doctor	332
4 · The Mole of Jarnages	338
5 · The Shepherd Who Got the King's Daughter	343
6 · Simple-Minded Jeanne	347
7 · Jean-Baptiste's Swaps	352
8 · Circular Tale	355
Sources and Commentary	359

Introduction:
THE FRENCH FOLK TALE

WHEN ONE SPEAKS of French folk tales in uninformed circles in France or abroad, one thinks immediately of Perrault's tales, which are known now by almost all children of the civilized world. Scarcely less known are other tales composed by great ladies of the same period and of the century that followed, *"Finette l'Adroite Princesse"* by Mlle Lhéritier, *"La Belle aux Cheveux d'or"* and *"L'Oiseau bleu"* by Mme d'Aulnoy, *"La Belle et la Bête"* by Mme Leprince de Beaumont.

If, for many people, these are tales which particularly represent the French folk tale, it must be asserted that until about 1860 scarcely any others were known. Whereas the Grimm brothers' two volumes of tales, published in 1812–15, had by 1856 run through seven constantly improved and enriched editions, and in most other European countries, after the example of the Grimm brothers, enthusiastic collectors had endowed their countries with national collections composed of material gathered directly among the people, the French folk tale was still represented only by Perrault's collections and by those of his imitators. The sum total of these had been assembled

Introduction

in that corpus of French folk tales the *Cabinet des Fées,* whose forty-one volumes appeared simultaneously at Geneva and at Amsterdam from 1785 to 1789. And it may justly be said of the French tale that "it smells of eau de cologne and of iris powder."

But if all the tales of Perrault, except *"Riquet à la Houppe,"* were of folk origin, only a small number of those published by his successors were actually noted among the people—those that I have cited above and a few others that one could count on the fingers of one hand. And how the literary texts of these perfumed tales departed from the oral tales of peasants and nursemaids, of artisans and servants!

Perrault, who departed the least from the folk manner, none the less eliminated those characteristics which he judged in bad taste, puerile, or too primitive, and which might shock the taste of the cultivated class to which his work was addressed, the upper middle class and aristocracy. This will be seen by comparing his versions of "Little Red Ridinghood" and of "Bluebeard"[1] with the characteristic folk versions given in this collection. What interested his readers far more than the voice of the rustic muse were affected words, gallant remarks, allusions to style, to costumes, to furnishings of the period: the sisters of Cinderella have mirrors in which they can see themselves from head to foot, send for the hairdresser to arrange their double rows of curls, buy beauty spots from the most reputable dealer, and so on; Bluebeard takes his guests to the country like a rich bourgeois of the period: "all they did was take walks, go hunting and fishing, dance and celebrate, take tea"; and Perrault complacently enumerates the furniture and the beautiful dishes in the household of the "woman-killer." The precepts, in verse, which are haphazardly soldered onto the tales have for

---

[1] Tales No. 29, "The Story of Grandmother," and No. 4, "The White Dove."

Introduction

Perrault as much importance as the stories, and he remembers them in the title he chose for his collection, *Histoires ou Contes du temps passé avec des Moralités* (*Stories or Tales of Past Days with Precepts*).

The women who, in imitation of Perrault, wrote tales depart even more from the folk expression. The least elevated people therein are gentlemen, the shepherds and shepherdesses are disguised princes and princesses, kings have the majesty of the one that reigned at Versailles,[2] and this whole society speaks a court language, a language of the salons, with the gallant and euphuistic phraseology of the epoch. There is as great a distance between these personages and those of the folk tale as there is between the ladies of the court who played at farmer's wife in the Petit Trianon at Versailles, and the authentic country girls who live in cottages and work in the fields.

It is not among these authors of the classic centuries that one must look for the true appearance of the French folk tale, whose traits disengaged themselves one by one as progress was made on collections which, timidly undertaken between 1860 and 1870, became extremely fruitful between the two wars of 1870 and 1914.

Serious research really began in 1870. In learned journals, the *Revue celtique* and the *Revue des langues romanes,* both founded in 1870, *Romania* in 1872, *Mélusine* in 1877, eminent specialists, scholars of the romance languages, Celtic scholars, linguists, ethnographers, speak of the interest of oral literature, and these journals opened their columns to investigators, who published therein their faithfully reported documents. Later, new journals came into being in which the materials of the folk tale accumulated: the *Revue des traditions populaires,* which, thanks to the indefatigable zeal of Paul Sébillot, lived for thirty-four years (1886–1919); other journals that were less exacting in the choice of their collaborators and of

[2] Louis XV.

Introduction

published texts: *La Tradition* (1887–1907), the *Revue du Traditionnisme français et étranger* (1898–1914). Editors founded series of works on folklore in which the best specialists published their collections, *Les Littératures de toutes les nations* (Éditions Maisonneuve, 47 volumes from 1883 to 1903), *Contes et Chansons populaires* (Éditions Leroux, 44 volumes from 1881 to 1930). In addition to these collections other works kept appearing, and in that "golden age" of the French folk tale which extends from 1870 to the First World War there is not a province of France which investigators failed to endow with a collection of tales. It would be too long to enumerate the many works that appeared and I refer those who are interested to the bibliography of them made by my friend A. van Gennep in Volume IV of his *Manuel de Folklore français* (1938, pp. 654–715), where he critically examines about five hundred works.

This labor of assembling materials is accompanied by masterly studies by such men as Gaidoz, Cosquin, and Sébillot. Since I cannot summarize it here, I shall merely refer the reader to the authoritative work of Professor Stith Thompson: *The Folktale* (New York: Dryden Press; 1946), pp. 392–4, in which the learned specialist calls that period "the golden age of folklore study in France."

This golden age of research on the French folk tale came to an end with the First World War. The death of Cosquin (1918), that of Sébillot (April 1919), the disappearance of the *Revue des traditions populaires* (December 1919), struck a rough blow to this type of studies. On the other hand, Bédier, in his remarkable work on the *Fabliaux,* turned the work of Cosquin to derision and denied to comparative studies on the folk tale the possibility of arriving at conclusions about the national birthplace and the migrations of different themes. Surpassing the skepticism of their master, his students even denied

Introduction

collections mentioned earlier, and also those of folklorists who died before their manuscripts were published or who lacked the material means to have them circulated. The number of tales classified is approximately ten thousand.

But the analyses of tales contained in such catalogues cannot replace the texts themselves; each is a work of art in which the individual genius of the teller and the social milieu partake. A French publisher has asked me to direct a collection of *Contes merveilleux des provinces de France* (*Supernatural Tales of the Provinces of France*) which would give for each province the best tales that are as yet unpublished, having remained in manuscript or having been collected recently by collectors whose activity I have noted above, and to achieve thus a scientific collection that might present to the French, not sophisticated tales reworked by writers, but authentic tales as they are in the mouths of the people, with a precise indication of their source. This work is in the process of realization.[4]

Finally, tales, if they have an æsthetic value by themselves, have also a documentary value for the investigator. A national folklore journal, *Arts et Traditions populaires* (Paris: Presses Universitaires), has appeared regularly since January 1, 1953, with the financial support of the Centre National de la Recherche Scientifique, and presents studies of the folk tale. In short, there is currently taking place in France a true rebirth of studies on traditional folk literature.

But when we speak of French folk tales, do we understand thereby tales that are unique to France or to countries speaking the French language?

It is known that the Cinderella of Perrault has sisters with white skin, brown skin, yellow skin, and black skin,

---

[4] Already published are: Achille Millien and Paul Delarue: *Contes du Nivernais et du Morvan;* Geneviève Massignon: *Contes de l'Ouest;* Antonin Perbosc: *Contes de Gascogne.* A dozen other volumes are in preparation. Éditions Erasme, 31 quai de Bourbon, Paris 10.

Introduction

under many skies, and yet they are quite recognizable in spite of their costumes and their various names. Adaptations to extremely different milieus and embellishments added by storytellers of all countries reveal, underneath, a common fabric. There are very pretty versions in all European, Asiatic, and North African countries, and an American Chinese scholar, Jameson, has recently made known to us a Chinese Cinderella of the ninth century who gets her golden slippers not from a fairy, but from a marvelous fish, and who loses one of them, not in escaping from a ball, but on coming back from a festival in a neighboring region.

Similarly, the story of *Peau d'Ane* (*The Ass's Skin*), which Perrault gave us in 1694 in a versified form, the story of *La Belle aux Cheveux d'or* (*The Girl with the Golden Hair*), of which Mme d'Aulnoy gave us a lovely version in 1698, the story of *La Belle et la Bête* (*Beauty and the Beast*), which Mme Beaumont published in 1757 in a children's magazine, each represents little more than one of the innumerable variations told in diverse forms throughout a great portion of the European continent.

Most of the folk tales told in France belong to that great family of tales which is well known all over Europe, in western Asia as far as India, and in North Africa; and these tales have through the past centuries followed colonists, soldiers, seamen, and missionaries of Europe into the French, English, Spanish, and Portuguese colonies founded beyond the seas. Hence, with a very few exceptions, they may not be supposed to belong to France alone.

But in France as in the other countries they have through the course of the centuries been subjected to the influence of the physical and human environment, of the particular genius of the race; and they have acquired characteristics that are unique. A comparison with the tales of neighboring countries will make this appear more clearly.

Introduction

The German tale has held in memory the old Hercynian forest with its somber features full of mysteries and evil deeds and its population of fantastic beings; it is almost always in the deepest part of the wood, in that terrifying forest where Snow White buries herself, that the heroines and heroes have their trials and adventures; supernatural personages abound there: all sorts of dwarfs, giants, menacing pixies of the ponds and springs, wild men, swan women, men of iron, mysterious old men in forest abodes, the horse's head that talks, a griffin, and so on; the German tale is still laden with the mystery and the poetry of primitive ages.

I do not speak of the English tale, which for a long time has scarcely persisted at all, save in the adorable nursery tales. But the Celtic tale, which here and there survives in lower Brittany and in the Highlands of Scotland, and is still so alive in Ireland, is quite different. Its miraculous content is located in an enchanted world, which is sometimes incoherent and extravagant, where the mysterious elements that are luminous and very sweet are intermixed with violent combats, or else seasoned with underlying humor as if the teller were making fun of himself. Old Celtic tales and certain modern ones are full of yearnings toward the land of peace and eternal youth, which knows neither evil nor death, a land that used to be reached beyond the seas by a glass boat.

The tale of the Mediterranean countries, as it is found in Spain, Italy, and Greece, makes one think of the capricious reflections of the sea that bathes them and the clear light of the sky that illuminates them. The sun in these tales is often an active personage, and he lends his name to young men in order to transmit beauty. The gracious fantasy of the Mediterranean tale is expressed in themes and motifs that are unique and also by poetic moments that surprise and delight. It introduces heroines whose femininity strikes a contrast with the ruggedness

Introduction

of their Nordic counterparts; readily mischievous and teasing, they are occasionally impassioned and assume roles that elsewhere befit only males: in a tale well known throughout the entire Mediterranean basin, the theme of "The Sleeping Beauty" is reversed, and a princess, thanks to her patience, awakens a prince who has long been plunged in lethargic sleep.[5]

The French tale unfolds in a more varied and more familiar world, one which corresponds to the greater diversity of a land in which maritime and continental zones, mountain and plain, forest, cultivated fields, prairies and vineyards, are blended into a harmonious whole. The supernatural element is simplified, curtailed, disciplined—it becomes almost reasonable—whereas elsewhere Bluebeard is a cannibalistic monster or a creature of fantastic appearance, in France he becomes a country squire or a bourgeois. The mother of the little girl that corresponds to Grimm's Snow White learns that her daughter is prettier than she, not by looking in a magic mirror, but by listening to the compliments of two soldiers.[6] Fantastic beings, so varied elsewhere, are nearly always either fairies or ogres. The French have a tendency to substitute for an action based on magic forces a dramatic development founded on human emotions, to eliminate whatever is cruel, bloody, or a survival of barbaric periods; the motif, very prevalent elsewhere, of the suitors' heads that have been cut off in the conquest of a beautiful girl and which are thereafter mounted on stakes at the castle door (found in French tales of the Middle Ages) has disappeared from our folk tales. The French story is all action, direct, without accessory details, without description, without lyricism; the style is sober and unadorned.

---

[5] I have developed the characteristics of the Mediterranean tale by giving concrete examples in: P. Delarue: *Incarnat, Blanc et Or, et autres contes méditerranéens* (Paris: Erasme; 1955), pp. 7–13.

[6] Sébillot: *Contes de Haute Bretagne*, I, No. 21, p. 146, "Les Bas enchantés."

Introduction

French storytellers subject traditional stories to their own classical, logical, even rational taste; but the tales are not thereby despoiled of their poetry. It will be seen, I hope, in the very first tales of this collection, that this poetry is light, sweet, tender, familiar, smiling, occasionally moving, and makes one think of conversation inspired by the sparkling wines of our countryside.

PAUL DELARUE

Part I
TALES OF THE SUPERNATURAL

I

THE
THREE
MAY PEACHES

There was once a king of Ardenne who had a very pretty daughter. But the princess was ill and doctors hadn't succeeded in healing her. The king was disconsolate. Finally his attention was called to an old healer who lived in the depths of the forest: she knew the properties of all plants and the remedies for all sicknesses. The king summoned her. After examining the sick girl carefully, she shook her head three times and declared: "The princess will get well when she has eaten the three most beautiful May peaches of the kingdom of Ardenne. But then she will have to get married within a week or else she will have a relapse."

Shortly, on all the roads of Ardenne one could see young men, baskets on their arms, going to the palace of the king to try their luck. Already many boys, most of them noblemen, had presented their fruit, but not one had succeeded in healing the princess, so that finally there were few left to come and the king began once more to worry.

In a neighboring village lived a fine woman who had three boys. Two were tall and strong, but the third was short, and people took him to be a little simple-minded.

The oldest of these boys decided to go and see the king's daughter too, so his mother put the three most beautiful May peaches from her garden in a basket, nicely wrapped up in a napkin, and he set out. Shortly he met an old woman, who asked him: "What have you got in your basket, my boy?" "Rabbit dung, old woman." "Well, then, rabbit dung it shall be, my boy." And he went on his way to the court. They let him enter, and he presented his basket, but when the king opened the napkin, he found nothing but rabbit dung. The boy, amazed, was put out of the castle and returned home shameful, for he didn't dare tell what had happened to him.

The second boy wanted to go in his turn, and the mother chose with even more care the three most beautiful May peaches in her garden and wrapped them in the very finest napkin that she had. The boy set out. Soon he met the old woman. "What have you got in your basket, my boy?" "Horse turds, old woman." "Horse turds it shall be, my boy." And when he presented his basket, the king found three big horse turds. He was furious and had the poor boy thrown out. And he returned home like a beaten dog, not daring to say what had happened to him.

The third boy wanted to go too, but his mother was opposed to it, thinking that he had no chance of succeeding where his brothers had failed. He insisted, however, and so he picked three May peaches without even selecting the best ones and wrapped them in the first rag that he could find. Then he set out. Soon he met the old woman. "What have you got in your basket, my boy?" "The three most beautiful May peaches from my garden, grandmother, so that I may marry the king's daughter." "Then you shall carry the three most beautiful May peaches, my boy, and you shall marry the king's daughter." And then the old woman, who was a fairy, gave him a whistle: "Take this whistle, my boy. If you get into trouble because of the king's whims, it might be useful." In his turn he presented his basket to the king, who, on his guard now, unfolded the rag with his fingertips. He uttered a great cry, for surely before him he beheld the

The Three May Peaches

three most beautiful May peaches of the kingdom. And he took them at once to his daughter to have her eat them without delay. At the first peach she jumped from her bed; at the second, she began to sing; and at the third, she began to dance.

Everybody at court was happy to learn of the healing of the princess. But when the king had looked the boy

over carefully, he said that he couldn't give such a beautiful daughter to a little peasant boy with such a puny appearance. Rather he would have her marry within the week one of the lords of his court.

To get rid of the boy, he told him: "You have passed the first test to obtain the princess, but you must undergo a second. I am going to give you a hundred rabbits to herd for four days. If you don't bring them back to me every night, all of them, you shan't have my daughter."

So the next day they gave him a hundred rabbits to take grazing in the woods. But scarcely outside the castle the rabbits scattered out in every direction and the boy ran all day long to try to prevent them from getting lost. But if he succeeded in assembling two or three of them, he lost

(5)

them at once when he went to get others. When the hour had come to take them back he began to cry.

All of a sudden he remembered his silver whistle. He blew it and all the rabbits raised their heads; a second note and all the rabbits started to come together; a third, and all of them formed into ranks behind him. So, taking the lead, he brought them back to the castle like a commander bringing back his troops. "Sire, count them yourself," he said to the king. The king counted. There were indeed a hundred.

The next day, when the boy had gone out with his rabbits, the king thought for a long time, and when evening came he disguised his daughter as a servant and sent her out in the herder's direction to buy one of his animals from him. "Now," he thought, "he won't be able to bring a hundred back."

But the boy recognized the princess, and when she asked him to grant her one of his rabbits for a good price he replied: "They are not for sale, but to be earned."

"How?"

"Give me a kiss and you shall have a rabbit."

The princess, delighted to have it for so little, put the rabbit in her apron and went back to the castle. But the hour had come to reassemble the flock. Just as the princess was going to pass through the gates of the castle a first note of the whistle was heard and the rabbit stuck its head out of her apron. At the second note it jumped to the ground in spite of all of its mistress's efforts, and at the third, it was taking its place in the ranks of rabbits that were already assembled behind their guardian, and once more the little shepherd boy brought back a hundred rabbits like a commander bringing back his troops.

The king was astounded. The next day he sent his wife, disguised as a cook, to buy a rabbit from the herder. She was supposed to offer him a purse full of money, but at

The Three May Peaches

the first words the boy recognized her and he replied: "My rabbits are not for sale, but to be earned."

"What do you mean?"

"All you have to do is turn three somersaults on the grass and you will have a rabbit."

The queen was a bit annoyed, but as there was no one to see her except the herder, and as she thought that he had not recognized her, she accepted the proposal. With a little difficulty, for she was no longer young, she turned three somersaults and got her rabbit. As soon as she was back in the castle she gave it to the king who double-locked it in an inner chamber. The king rubbed his hands joyfully: this time the presumptuous fellow wouldn't bring back a hundred rabbits.

The hour came to return. The shepherd got out his silver whistle. At the first note the rabbit jumped to an upper window of the chamber; at the second, it leaped across the moat of the castle; and at the third, it was re-taking its place among the ranks of rabbits that had already assembled behind their guardian. And the boy brought back one hundred rabbits once more, like a commander bringing back his troops.

The king was furious. The next day he decided to go early himself to get a rabbit, to put it in a stew. Disguised as a merchant riding an ass, he went to the herder and offered him a sack of gold for a single rabbit.

"They are not for sale, but to be earned."

"What do you mean?"

"All you have to do is to kiss your ass's behind three times and you will have a rabbit."

And the boy was already raising the ass's tail, pointing out to the merchant the place to kiss. The king was greatly disturbed, but as there was no one there to see him except the little herder, who he felt had not recognized him, he did it. Then he returned quickly to the castle at a trot. The rabbit was taken into the kitchen and skinned and

French Folk Tales

put in the casserole on the fire. The old king was jubilant as he sat before the hearth where the animal was cooking. This time the hundred rabbits wouldn't be there; he was sure of it.

Came the hour to return. At the first note of the whistle the rabbit jumped from the casserole. At the second, it slipped into its skin, which had been left on the kitchen table; and at the third, it ran between the king's legs, upsetting him as he tried to stop it. It dashed down the stairs, through the fields, and arrived just in time to take its place among the ranks of the rabbits who had already assembled behind their guardian to return. And the boy brought them back another time, all hundred of them, like a commander bringing back his troops.

He had won the second trial.

But the king was stubborn and still didn't want to give him his daughter: "There's only one more test. In public you will have to fill three sacks of truths for me. If you succeed you shall marry my daughter."

And the king organized a big festival to which all the grandees of the court were invited. And then at the end of the meal he had the boy come. The boy had the king, the queen, and the princess sit down side by side, and he stood before them with three sacks.

Then he said to the princess: "Three days ago you came to find me in the forest, disguised as a servant, in order to get a rabbit. And I gave you one for a kiss. Is that true?"

"It's true," said the princess.

"First truth, into my sack, hop." And he tied the first sack.

Then he said to the queen: "Two days ago you came to find me in the woods disguised as a cook in order to have a rabbit. And I gave you one after you had turned three somersaults on the grass. Is it true?"

"It's true," said the queen.

The Three May Peaches

"Second truth, into my sack, hop." And he tied the second sack.

Then, addressing the king: "Yesterday you came to find me in the wood, disguised as a merchant, riding an ass, in order to get a rabbit. And I gave you one for kissing three time—"

"Enough, enough!" said the king. "You don't need to fill the third sack. You shall have the princess."

And the marriage took place before the eight days specified by the old healer had passed by, to the great joy of the boy, and also of the princess, who found that her husband was not lacking in wit.

As he was a boy from my country, I was invited to the wedding, and I dressed up in my most beautiful clothes to go to it. I had a dress of spiderweb, a hat of butter, and shoes of glass. But as I went through the forest I tore my dress, and when I crossed the field the sun melted my hat, and when I passed over the ice my shoes crumbled. And there you have the story out of my bag.

2

JEAN, THE SOLDIER, AND EULALIE, THE DEVIL'S DAUGHTER

There was once a soldier by the name of Jean who was coming back from military service, having finished the period of his enlistment. He had been walking for a long time and he was very tired. As the sun was going down, he knocked at the door of a thatched house and asked to spend the night.

"I can't entertain you here," said the beautiful young woman who had come to open up to him. "My father eats people. Go farther on, for there's danger here for you."

"I don't care; I'm dying of fatigue. Whether I die or not, I prefer to stay here."

"Well, come in, my father isn't here. I'll hide you as best I can."

The soldier liked it at the Evil One's house. When he had rested for an hour the Devil returned.

"I smell fresh meat," he said, entering and rolling his eyes. "There's a Christian here." And he went toward the corner where his daughter had hidden the soldier.

"Father, don't get angry; it's a poor soldier who asked for lodging and who is resting as he passes by."

"A soldier! I shall eat him tomorrow for my lunch."

The next day when he woke up, he ran straight to the wretched fellow, who thought that his last hour had come, but the girl threw herself into her father's arms and said: "Father, don't eat him so soon. You have work to be

Jean, the Soldier, and the Devil's Daughter

done; let him do it; keep him busy serving you for a while."

"Well, then, I desire that before evening and without any other instrument than his hands he polish the andirons, the poker, and the pothook until they are as shiny as silver. Do you understand, Christian? Otherwise, tomorrow I shall eat you." And he went away.

It wasn't an easy thing to clean with one's fingernails objects covered with so much rust, soot, and smoke.

"Mademoiselle," said the soldier, "you might just as well have let me be eaten immediately."

"Listen! Will you promise to take me away with you and to marry me? For I am indeed tired of staying here."

"I promise you."

"Don't worry, then. I'll do the work for you."

It can be seen at once that if the girl hadn't pleased the soldier at the very first instant, he had at least not made a bad impression on her.

At the end of the day all she had to say was: "By virtue of my wand, may my father's order be executed." And the pothook, the andirons, and the poker became at once like silver.

The old man arrived and saw the hearth all sparkling: "Aha, Christian, you've worked well!"

"Do you think so, my master? It's because I got an education during my travels."

At sunrise the Devil reappeared. "You got out of it yesterday, Christian, but that's not all. Before evening all my horses' trappings must be as shiny as gold or you will be eaten."

These trappings had not been cleaned for a thousand years, perhaps, and the soldier felt discouraged. "You see, mademoiselle," he said to the young woman, "that you have saved me in vain. It's starting all over again."

"Will you keep your promise to take me away and to marry me?"

(11)

"Yes, you may be sure of it."

"Don't worry, then. I'll do your work for you." And before evening, as she had done the day before, she used the power of her wand.

The old man, on coming home, found his horses' trappings as shiny as gold. "Christian," he said, "you've worked well, but that's not all. There are other things to do. I'll tell you tomorrow."

Meanwhile the beautiful Eulalie (that was the name of the young woman) made the soldier understand that it would be wise to flee as quickly as possible. They decided to leave that very night. They slept in rooms that adjoined the one occupied by the old man and his wife. My lovely Eulalie made two enchanted pies that could talk and answer for the two fugitives, one for her and the other for the soldier. She put them on the beds and held herself in readiness to leave the house with the young man.

All of a sudden the old man's wife, even more shrewd and more dangerous than he, said: "I'm dreaming! I'm dreaming!"

"What are you dreaming?" asked the old man.

"I'm dreaming that the soldier is going to take my daughter away."

"Beautiful Eulalie!" shouted the father.

"Yes, Father?"

"Evil Christian!"

"Yes, master?"

"You see that they're in their beds," he said to his wife. "Let's let them sleep."

A moment later: "I'm dreaming! I'm dreaming!" cried the woman.

"What are you dreaming?"

"I'm dreaming that the Christian has run away with my daughter."

"Beautiful Eulalie!"

Jean, the Soldier, and the Devil's Daughter

"Yes, Father?"
"Evil Christian!"
"Yes, master?"

This time the pies were answering in their stead, for the two young people had already left the house.

"You see that they're still in their rooms. Leave them alone."

A little later the old woman resumed: "I'm dreaming! I'm dreaming!"

"What are you dreaming?"

"I'm dreaming that the Christian is already far from here with my daughter."

"Beautiful Eulalie!"
"Yes, Father?"
"Evil Christian!"
"Yes, master?"

The pies replied feebly for their voices grew weaker as the fugitives got farther away.

"They're asleep," said the old man. "Let's do the same."

But his wife still worried and woke up again.

"Beautiful Eulalie! Evil Christian!—They're asleep," said the old man.

"No. They're gone! Get up and pursue them."

He ran to the adjoining rooms and found them empty. A few minutes sufficed for him to saddle his horse and to mount.

The beautiful Eulalie, fleeing in all haste, kept saying: "My friend Jean, my tender friend! Can you see anyone coming?"

"I can see a horseman galloping and galloping."

"It's my father. By the virtue of my wand, let's transform ourselves, you into a pear on a pear tree, and I into an old woman who wants to knock it down."

It was high time. The horseman was arriving.

"Good woman, have you seen a young man and a girl pass?"

"Ah, sir, I'm having a lot of trouble knocking down this pear."

"I asked you if you haven't seen a young man and a young girl pass by?"

"You're right! I love pears!"

He grew impatient and went home. His wife was waiting for him.

"Did you see them?"

"No. I saw a deaf old woman under a pear tree."

"And you didn't understand that it was your daughter?"

"I'll set out again. This time they won't escape me."

And the beautiful Eulalie, fleeing with her companion, kept asking him: "My friend Jean, my tender friend! Can you see anyone coming?"

"I can see a horseman galloping and galloping."

"It's my father again. By the virtue of my wand, be you a gardener in a garden, and I a rose on a rosebush."

"Gardener," said the old man, "haven't you seen a young man and a girl pass by here?"

Jean, the Soldier, and the Devil's Daughter

"Sir, I don't sell onion seed."
"That's not what I asked you."
"I sell carrot seeds."
"Stupid!" said the old man, going back to his home.
"Well, where are they?" asked his wife.
"I found a gardener in a garden and a rose on a rosebush."
"The rose was our daughter and the gardener the evil Christian. Go back quickly."

And the lovely Eulalie, still fleeing with her companion, kept saying to him: "My friend Jean, my tender friend! Can you see anyone coming?"
"I can see a horseman galloping and galloping."
"My father again! By the virtue of my wand, let's transform ourselves, I into a chapel and you into a priest."

And he arrives.
"Mr. Priest, have you seen a young man and a girl pass by?"
"Dominus vobiscum!"
"Are you deaf?"
"Alleluia!"

He spurs his horse and goes back to his wife.
"This time did you see them?"
"I saw a priest in a chapel and I couldn't get a sensible word out of him."
"But the chapel was she and the priest was he! Stay here! I will go catch them."

And the beautiful Eulalie, who was still fleeing with her companion, kept asking him: "My friend Jean, my tender friend! Can you see anyone coming?"
"I see a carriage coming, flying."
"Ah, it's my mother. By the virtue of my wand, you will be a pond and I a duckling on the water."

Already the Devil's wife was on the edge of the pond. She had her wand too. She broke some bread crumbs and called: "Duckling! Pretty duckling! Come here." The duckling approached, took the bread, and the Devil's wife, leaning over, stretched out her wand. All of a sudden the duck threw herself upon the wand and dived into the water, carrying it away.

"Give me back my wand!" cried her mother, unarmed. "Lovely Eulalie! My daughter! Don't deprive me of my power." She wore herself out in useless supplications. Then she went away, crying and wailing.

"This time," said the beautiful Eulalie, "we are beyond danger. Is your country far from here?"

"No, we're more than half way."

"Listen carefully to the counsel I have to give you. When we arrive at your parents', don't let anybody kiss you; otherwise you will lose your memory and you will forget me."

"Don't worry. How could I forget you? As soon as we arrive we'll get married."

It was a great joy for the mother of the soldier to see a son come home from whom she had been awaiting news so long. She threw herself into his arms, but he withdrew, and as she insisted on kissing him, he pushed her away, which caused her great pain. After the meal she got him to go to bed to rest. As soon as she saw him asleep she leaned over his bed and kissed him with the prolonged kiss of a mother's heart.

When he awoke, the soldier had forgotten everything. He didn't recognize the beautiful Eulalie, who, rejected by him, was forced to leave the house. But she didn't leave the country. At some distance from there by virtue of her wand she built a castle, moved in, and lived there quietly all alone.

Near the castle there was a big rural estate with lots of employees and servants. Three of them who saw the lovely girl from time to time at her window decided to make her acquaintance. They decided that the eldest

Jean, the Soldier, and the Devil's Daughter

should present himself first at the castle, then the second, and finally the youngest. So the eldest came one evening and was so well received that he asked to spend the night in the castle.

"Ah," said the girl to the suitor, "I have forgotten something. Please cover my fire with cinders."

Immediately the boy set himself to the task.

She seized her wand. "May it uncover itself each time you cover it, until dawn!"

No sooner had he covered the fire than it uncovered itself. All night long the boy kept re-covering the coals until his fingers were half roasted, and at daybreak he went sorrowfully away.

"Do you like that girl?" the other two asked him.

"Very much. Don't fail to go there, too."

That evening it was the second boy's turn. He was well received and treated in the same way as the other. But, as it was raining, the beautiful girl said to him: "The rain that is beating against the windowpane will stop us from sleeping. Go close the shutters."

And as soon as he had gone she seized her wand and said: "May they open each time you close them, until dawn!"

And she went away to bed. The closed shutters kept opening and the young man kept pushing them back. All night he was forced to work in the rain. He was frozen and trembling when he went back to his comrades.

"Are you satisfied?" they asked him.

"Very satisfied."

"Well," said the youngest, "it's my turn to go this evening."

And he had the same luck as the others. At the hour of retiring the girl asked him to go bolt the door, and as soon as he had his hand on the bolt she seized her wand. "May it be unbolted each time you bolt it, until dawn!"

(17)

And she went off to bed. Each time he pushed the bolt, it went back, and he worked thus until morning at such a pace that his hand was all sore.

When he went back to his two companions they asked him: "Are you satisfied?"

"No reason to be," he replied. "I spent the night bolting the door, which kept unbolting itself."

"And I covering the fire, which kept uncovering itself."

"And I closing the shutters, which kept opening."

And all three of them came to an agreement to wreak their vengeance on the girl.

A few days afterward the marriage of Jean the soldier was announced. He was marrying a young woman of the country. The three boys, who had been invited to the marriage, went to find him. "Why shouldn't you invite the girl of the castle? She would make one more lovely girl to dance with."

"I shall be happy to invite her this very day."

The rejected suitors thought they would take advantage of the wedding to punish her for their misfortune. The morning of the marriage she arrived at lunch time, as beautiful as the day. They sat down to the table. Since a seat remained unoccupied beside the husband, she took it. She had prepared two pies that could talk, one for her and the other for the soldier. She put them on the table and the two of them were the only ones who could hear.

One said: "My friend Jean, my tender friend! Do you remember my father's house where I received you when you were dying of fatigue?"

"No, I don't remember," said the other.

"Do you remember the andirons, the poker, and the pothook that were cleaned?"

"No, I don't remember."

"Do you remember the trappings that were brilliant as gold?"

"No, I don't remember."

Jean, the Soldier, and the Devil's Daughter

"Do you remember our flight, the dangers that we were subjected to?"

"No, I don't remember."

"I had told you: 'Don't let anybody kiss you!' Do you remember?"

"Yes, I remember."

"And your promise, do you remember?"

"Yes, I remember."

Immediately the soldier left the table and went to find his mother. "Mother, I have lost the key to my cupboard. I have ordered a new one, but I have just found the old one. Which one shall I take?"

"The first one, since you're familiar with it."

"Well, I had promised to marry that girl who saved my life. I had lost her, and now I have found her. So she's the one that I shall keep."

And the soldier married her. The wedding lasted a whole week, as long as they could find any food in the country. There were six hurdy-gurdies and six musettes.[1]

Everyone danced, timid, and bold,
Even Mother Barbichon,
Who leaped like a goat
Though eighty-five years old.

---

[1] The French *musette* differs from the bagpipe in that the air sack is filled by a bellows pumped with the arm rather than by a blowstem. (TRANSLATOR.)

3

THE GIANT GOULAFFRE

There was once a poor woman who lived alone with her son. Every day the mother and her son went to beg from door to door at the farmhouses and manors, receiving here a piece of barley bread, there a buckwheat cake, and somewhere else a few potatoes. They lived thus from the charity of good people. The son was called Allanic and the mother Godic or Marguerite When Allanic reached the age of fourteen or fifteen, as he was sturdy and in good health, and because nevertheless he continued to beg with his mother, often peasants said to her:

"It's high time, Marguerite, that this young strapling work like us to earn his bread. You have nourished him long enough while he does nothing. It's his turn now to help you. See how strong he is and how healthy! Aren't you ashamed, lazybones, to remain such a burden to your old mother?"

Every day he was subjected to similar reproaches, and every day he and his mother went back home in the evening with a lighter store of alms.

Seeing this, Allanic said to his mother: "I want to go to France, Mother, to try to earn my living and to help you in my turn."

Godic was sorrowful at her son's decision, but she understood nevertheless that she couldn't keep him always, and she didn't oppose his departure.

The Giant Goulaffre

So Allanic departed on a beautiful spring morning, taking along on the end of a stick a piece of rye bread with six pancakes, and quite proud to have in his pocket six coins that his mother had given him. He wandered at random, as God willed. About noon he noticed along the road that he was following a spring of fresh clear water that was shaded by a clump of trees. He stopped to rest a bit, to eat a piece of bread, with a pancake. While he was thus eating his frugal meal, seated in the shade, another traveler, who scarcely appeared to be any richer than he, approached the spring to get a drink. Allanic offered him a pancake. They started a conversation and shortly they were friends.

"Where are you going, friend?" said Allanic.

"Well, I'm just walking straight ahead; that's all I know. How about you?"

"I'm going to France to try to earn my living."

"Let's travel together, if you're willing."

"That suits me. What's your trade?"

"I'm a dancer, and my name is Fistilou."

"Wonderful, for I'm a musician and I am called Allanic."

"But what instrument do you play? I don't see you carrying one."

"Ha! An instrument is no trouble for me; I'll find one when I need it. Look, there's a field that's full of them. So many straws—two or three times as many instruments."

"What do you mean? You're joking, aren't you?"

"No, I'm not joking. I'll prove it to you at once."

And, jumping over the fence that surrounded the field of rye, Allanic cut a stalk and in an instant he had made a reed pipe like those seen in the hands of little shepherd boys in springtime. He began to play it with uncommon skill and facility. Fistilou, hearing him, began to dance, to leap, to throw his hat in the air, and cry: "Iou, iou, hou, hou!" as the men from Cornwall do.

So there they are, the best of friends, on their way, chatting, laughing, dreaming of abundant receipts. Towards evening they arrive in a city whose name I don't remember. They were shortly on the square, which was surrounded with houses on all sides, a place where there were lots of people walking about. Allanic began to play his reed pipe, Fistilou to dance, to leap, to throw his hat in the air, crying: "Iou, iou, hou, hou!" And people came running from all directions so that a crowd was formed, everybody pressing against another in order to see them. Never had the inhabitants of that city heard such music nor seen such dancing. Coins of all sizes were showered upon them, and they made a magnificent collection, five or six crowns at least. They repeated their performance the next day, and their receipts were still excellent. They were beside themselves with joy.

But Fistilou then came up with an unfortunate idea. He thought that as they earned so much money with a mere reed pipe, if they had a violin they would earn ten times as much. So they bought a violin and Allanic began to saw on it in a way that would peel even the least sensitive ears. But no matter, they found that it was charming, and they dreamed of marvelous successes. So they went to another city to try their new method. As soon as they arrived they began to play and dance on the public square. But they were indeed surprised to see that the inhabitants of this city, far from running to the place where they were, fled running and holding their ears, and instead of coins this time they received nothing but curses and stones, so that they had to leave the city as fast as they could.

"Decidedly those people didn't like lovely music," they said to themselves when they were out of reach of the stones. "We'll have to go back to the reed."

Allanic cut a reed pipe in the first field of rye that they came upon, and they continued on their way, but less

The Giant Goulaffre

joyfully than the evening before, for already they were penniless.

Soon they were in front of a castle surrounded with high walls. "We must try the effect of our music and our dancing here," they said to one another.

But they didn't know how to get in. They could see a door with a knocker, but this knocker was placed so high that they couldn't reach it.

"You stand against the door," said Fistilou to Allanic. "I'll climb on your shoulders and so I shall reach the knocker."

So they did. The door opened at once and they entered into a garden where they saw two beautiful girls taking a walk. They were daughters of the giant Goulaffre, who lived in this castle. Allanic began to play his reed pipe, Fistilou to dance and to jump. The two girls hastened to watch them. They had never gone out of their garden and so they had never seen anything like this, and the music of the one and the jumps and cries of the other amused them a great deal. Their mother, a giant ten feet high, came too, and they begged her to keep these two men in the castle to amuse them, as they never went out.

"But, my children, what about your father?"

"They're so amusing and so nice that our father will like them too and he will let them live."

"I'm not sure of it, but they may stay all the same since you like them."

And so the giant's two daughters were very happy. When the dinner hour came they rang the bell and the giant came home. Our two friends had been hidden in a big chest, but the giant, on coming into the dining-room, shouted:

"I smell the smell of a Christian and I want to eat him!"

"That's something I've got to see!" replied his wife. "Eat my two nephews who have come to see me, two boys who are so charming and whom our daughters like so much because of their talents, and whom you will like too!"

"Make your nephews come so that I can see them!"

They had our two companions come out of the chest, trembling and dying of fright.

"Your nephews are mighty small, woman. What can they do?"

"Dance and play music delightfully."

"All right, but let's eat first, for I am very hungry. Then we shall see."

And they sat down to the table. First they served a soup in a staved-in barrel. Then they brought in a roasted Christian on a platter. The giant Goulaffre cut him up and kept for himself the biggest piece. And then the giant's wife divided what remained between her and her two daughters. They also gave a foot to each of the two strangers. They were very sad, looked at each other wide-eyed, and didn't eat.

"Well, little fellows, you're not hungry?" said the giant.

"No, sire, we're not hungry."

"But it's very good!" Taking the two feet that they had on their plates, he swallowed them in a single mouthful.

When the meal had come to an end: "Let's see your talents now, children. Try to entertain me a bit."

And Allanic began to play his reed pipe and Fistilou to dance, to jump, and to throw his hat in the air, shouting: "Iou, iou, hou, hou!"

The giant gave forth peals of laughter and was greatly amused, as were his wife and his two daughters. Goulaffre said to them at the end of an hour of this activity:

"Go to bed now with my daughters and tomorrow I shall see what I'm going to do with you."

Then the giant took them to their room, gave red nightcaps to Allanic and to Fistilou, and white caps to his daughters. Then he went away. The two girls didn't delay in falling asleep and began to snore, making the panes

The Giant Goulaffre

of the windows shake in their frames. But Allanic and Fistilou were not sleepy. They soon heard noise in the room beneath them. It was the giant and his wife quarreling. Allanic sprang from his bed, put his ear to the floor, and here's what he heard:

"I tell you, woman, I'm going to eat them tomorrow morning for breakfast!"

"Wait a few days anyway. You'll enjoy their music and their dancing. And our daughters, these poor girls who never have any diversion—haven't you noticed how happy they are? Save them for their sake."

"There's no use talking. I must eat them tomorrow morning. Where is my cutlass?"

And a moment later they heard the step of the giant on the stairway. Then Allanic ran to his bed, changed his red cap for the white cap of the giant's daughter who was still sleeping, and told Fistilou to do the same. Then they turned their faces to the wall and pretended to sleep. Goulaffre came into the room at once, holding in one hand a lantern and in the other a great cutlass. He approached the first bed and with one blow he cut off the head in the red cap. Running to the second bed, he did the same thing, and then, letting the heads roll upon the floor, he went downstairs carrying the bodies of his two daughters under his arm, and he put them on the kitchen table without examining them.

When he came back into his bedroom he said to his wife: "It's done. What an excellent breakfast tomorrow morning!"

"Provided that you haven't made a mistake in your haste," said the giant's wife.

"How do you suppose I could have made a mistake? I can tell the difference between a red cap and a white cap, can't I?"

And then they went peacefully to sleep.

As for Allanic and Fistilou, as soon as the giant had left

their room they went down into the garden, using their sheets, and took in the fresh air!

The next morning Goulaffre had his wife get up early to prepare his breakfast, but when she came into the kitchen and recognized her daughters, she cried so hard that she shook the castle. Goulaffre hastened out on hearing her, and added his own cries and bellows to those of the wife. He ran to his daughters' room, thinking he would still find his guests there, but all he found was a paper on which was written (Fistilou knew how to read and write a bit):

"Fistilou and his friend Allanic thank the giant, Goulaffre, for the hospitality he has accorded them, and they promise to come back to see him."

The giant, howling with anger, put on his seven-league boots and started in search of the fugitives. They were already far from the castle, but Goulaffre soon caught up with them. Seeing a great leg with enormous boots pass over their heads, they said to one another: "Here's the giant!" They hid under a great stone, and Goulaffre passed without seeing them.

When they thought that he was far away they came out from their hiding-place and went on their way. Toward sunset they arrived on a great plain that was scattered over with enormous blocks of granite, some of which were by themselves and others balanced upon one another. Among the latter they saw two great boots, then farther on in the depths of a somber cave something red and shiny that resembled those ancient window panels that were called "bull's-eyes." They approached on tiptoe and recognized that it was Goulaffre who, tired from following them (for seven-league boots are very tiring), had stopped there to rest awhile. The red and shiny object that they saw in the depths of the cave was his one eye. He was sleeping heavily, and they remained silent a few moments, analyzing the situation.

The Giant Goulaffre

Then Allanic said: "If only we could take off his seven-league boots, then we could laugh at him."

"Yes, but suppose he wakes up," replied Fistilou.

"He sleeps too heavily for that; listen to the way he snores. Let's try it and see."

They took off one of his boots without his moving. But as they were pulling with all their might on the second one, the giant moved, and they thought they were lost Happily he didn't wake up, and they were able to take that one off too. Then Allanic put the two boots on and was getting ready to leave when the other said:

"What about me? Are you going to leave me here?"

"Climb on my back, quick!"

And there they go, one carrying the other.

When Goulaffre woke up and saw that he no longer had his boots, he howled enough to terrify the wild animals for three leagues round about. He had to go back to his castle without boots, and when he arrived his feet were all bloody.

Meanwhile Allanic and Fistilou had arrived in Paris. They went and knocked at the king's palace to ask for work, and they were taken on as stable boys.

The king's son loved the hunt passionately. But it seems that with him it was a more or less unfortunate passion and that his gamebag was frequently empty when he came back, so that Fistilou said one day to his comrades:

"My friend Allanic could take in a single day as much game as the young prince does in the whole year."

The remark was reported to the prince and he had Allanic called and took him hunting the very next day. Allanic didn't forget to take his seven-league boots in his gamebag because, as they were magic boots, they increased or decreased in size as desired. He was given a good gun, the first that he had ever held in his hands, and the prince and he went to a great forest where game of all sorts was abundant. Under pretext of paying the honors of the day to his companion, Allanic let him shoot all of the game animals, hares, deer, foxes, and as he was of a rare clumsiness he missed everything. About noon they sat down on the moss at the foot of an oak to eat a pasty and to drink a glass of wine.

Then Allanic said to the prince: "You rest a bit, prince, while I walk off a little way in that direction. In an hour at most I'll come back to join you."

"All right," said the prince, "and I hope you're more lucky than I."

A few paces from there Allanic put on his seven-league boots and in less than an hour he had taken so much game of all kinds that he had to get a cart at a neighboring farm to bring it back to the palace.

"And how were you able in so little time to make such a kill?" the prince asked him, seeing him come back with his cart loaded.

The Giant Goulaffre

"It's luck, my prince, and a little skill too; but you know there are days when one feels truly bewitched he has such bad luck, and apparently this is one of those days for you."

The prince seemed satisfied with the explanation and they went back to the palace, where people were much surprised to see them come back with such a quantity of game. From that day on, Allanic was welcome to the king, and especially to the prince, with whom he went hunting almost every day.

Fistilou, jealous of this favor, tried to stir up new embarrassments for his old friend. He told the stable boys and others about their visit to the castle of the giant Goulaffre, and the manner in which they had been able to come out of it without harm. He also spoke of the giant's seven-league boots, by means of which Allanic performed such magnificent hunts. These reports came quickly to the king's ears and he had Allanic come before him and spoke to him thus:

"They tell me that you have been to the castle of the giant Goulaffre, and that you came out without harm?"

"Nothing is more true, sire."

"Ah, what a wretch, what a monster, this Goulaffre! And how he has harmed me! He stole my crescent, an incomparable marvel, and my golden cage, which was my only joy. If only I could avenge myself upon him and recover my crescent and my golden cage! But since you have already been to his house and since you have come back from it without harm, you could go back there again!"

"To be burned alive here or to be eaten by Goulaffre doesn't make any difference to me, and as such is the situation, I will undertake the adventure."

So Allanic departed, and as he knew the way, and had his seven-league boots, he arrived easily in front of the giant's castle. Workmen were repairing the roof. He hid in the woods to await night. About ten o'clock, when it was very dark, the crescent was hung on the highest tower, and immediately everything was lighted up for several leagues round about. The workmen, on withdrawing at the close of the day, had left their ladders against the walls of the castle. About midnight Allanic came out of the forest and, by means of these ladders, climbed to the platform of the tower, took down the crescent, put it in a bag that he had brought along, and departed without staying, as they say, "to look for the sheep's five feet."

At the darkness that suddenly fell, the giant came out to know the cause, and he saw Allanic departing, carrying away the crescent on his back. He shouted, howled like a ferocious animal. He wanted to pursue the thief, but, alas, he no longer had his seven-league boots!

When Allanic arrived in Paris with his crescent, he hung it at once from the highest tower of the royal palace, and the whole city, a moment before plunged in darkness, was suddenly lighted as in full day. The inhabitants got up and hastened toward the palace whence came the light and saw that their king had once more found his crescent, and they were all happy. The king was beside himself with joy. He directed that a great festival be held, to which were invited the princes, princesses, generals, and all the grandees of the kingdom, and he presented Allanic to them as the restorer of the crescent and ordered them to honor him as his own best friend. The festival and entertainments lasted for two whole weeks throughout the city.

When he had admired his crescent for three months, the old king began to regret more than ever his golden cage, and each day his joy was more dissipated and he became sadder and sadder.

Allanic noticed it, as everybody did, and he said to himself: "Things are going badly. The king will never be

The Giant Goulaffre

consoled for the loss of his golden cage, and one of these days he will direct me, I fear, to go get it for him."

And, as a matter of fact, shortly thereafter the king called him to his chamber and said to him: "Allanic, you see that I am languishing from sadness. It's the loss of my golden cage that is the cause of it. If I don't see it again in my palace, I shall die without delay. You stole Goulaffre's seven-league boots; you have also repossessed my crescent; you must go now and bring back my cage."

"Ah, sire, what you're asking me no man in the world can do. Think that this cage is suspended from four chains above the giant's bed! How can I go into his room and cut the four chains of gold without awaking him? It's impossible!"

"Well, you brought me back my crescent; you must also bring me back my golden cage or you shall die."

"You want to send me to a certain death. To die here or there matters little, and I prefer to try the adventure. Have manufactured for me scissors capable of cutting the golden chains as if they were threads of linen or hemp, and then I will depart."

They found an artisan sufficiently skillful to make the required scissors, and Allanic departed. When he arrived near the castle he saw with pleasure that the roofers had not yet finished their work and that their ladders were still leaning against the wall. About midnight he got into Goulaffre's bedroom by breaking a window. The giant was sleeping so soundly that he heard nothing. The room was lighted. Allanic saw the golden cage above Goulaffre's forehead. He put one of his feet on the bedstead, the other against the wall, and with a snip of his scissors he cut one golden chain! The giant didn't move. Then he cut a second chain, snip! The giant moved. Then a third, snip! The giant turned over in his bed, but he didn't wake up. Finally the fourth chain was cut, but, alas, the cage fell

French Folk Tales

on Goulaffre's face and awakened him. He seized Allanic by the waist, recognized him, and shouted:

"Ah! It's you, little monster! This time you won't escape me! And your business is clear. I shall eat you for breakfast this very morning."

"Alas, I see very well that I have no more hope and that I am done for. Moreover, I recognize that I have deserved my destiny by all the harm that I have done you. But in what sauce do you intend to eat me, I beg you?"

"On a spit I will put you in the fire, alive."

"I see that you don't know anything about good cooking. Do as I tell you and you will have the most delicious morsel that you have ever eaten."

"Well, tell me about it."

"Put me in a sack; then go to the wood, uproot a tree of medium size, and come and beat me with the trunk of the tree until I am reduced to a pulp in the sack. Then you put it all in your big kettle with a little butter, salt, and pepper. Then you make a good fire underneath. I'm telling you, you'll have there a morsel to make you lick your fingers for twenty-four hours!"

"By Jove, you're right. That must be very good, and I am resolved to do as you say."

So the giant put Allanic in a sack. Then he went to the wood to uproot a beech tree to beat him with. As soon as he had gone out, Allanic began to shout with all his might for help. The giant's wife came.

"Who's there? Who's crying like that?" she asked.

"Alas, my good lady, a poor man who has never done anybody any harm."

"Who put you in this sack?"

"Your husband."

"Why?"

"For a few pieces of dry wood that I took in the forest."

"Why steal wood from us like that?"

"To cook potatoes for my children and my wife's din-

The Giant Goulaffre

ner. I'm so poor. I've got six children, and nothing but my own toil and the charity of my good friends to sustain me. Have pity on me, and on my poor wife, and my poor children, who are dying of hunger at home. Help me to get out of here. Your husband will believe that I escaped by myself."

The giant's wife was moved. She untied the strings of the sack, and Allanic came out at a bound. Then he shoved her in, in his place. He ran to the giant's room and took the cage of gold and departed.

Goulaffre arrived shortly with the uprooted tree. He began to beat the sack.

"Stop, wretch, it's your wife!" she cried, in the bag.

But Goulaffre didn't listen to her, and he struck like a deaf man. At the end of a half-hour, when he couldn't hear her crying any more, he opened the bag. "My wife!" he shouted, recognizing her clothing. And he began to tear his hair out and to howl like a wild animal.

Meanwhile Allanic had arrived in Paris with the cage of gold. The old king, who was so sad before, became gay and joyful once more in possession of his cage. He passed whole days looking at that marvelous thing. But at the end of a few months his happiness began to vanish again, little by little.

"What's he going to ask me to do now?" Allanic asked himself, worried.

Finally the king told him one day: "I shan't live happy until you have brought me here, into this very palace, the giant Goulaffre himself."

"Ah, sire, you require the impossible! And after all that I have done for you, won't you leave me a moment of peace?"

"I tell you, you must bring him to me or you shall die."

"Yes, I see now that it is my death that you desire. But at least you will give me all that I ask you for, to try this impossible task?"

"Ask anything you wish. I will refuse you nothing."

"Well, have built for me a massive golden carriage, all garnished inside with sharp points, and having a single door, which will close automatically on whoever enters the carriage without his being able to open it, no matter what strength he may have. I will need more than twenty sturdy horses to hitch to it."

"You shall have all that," replied the king.

They found skillful blacksmiths and locksmiths, and in a short time the carriage was constructed according to the desired specifications. They hitched twenty-four magnificent horses to it, and Allanic climbed on the seat, dressed as a coachman, and departed. When he arrived in the wood that surrounded the castle, he saw the giant walking about, waving his hands, and uttering savage cries. Allanic came toward him and asked him respectfully:

"My lord, what is the subject of such great sorrow?"

"Ah," he replied, "I am the unhappiest of giants. A runt by the name of Allanic caused me to kill my two daughters and my wife. And, moreover, he stole my seven-league boots, my crescent, and my golden cage. If only I had him! But I don't know where to find him, nor in what country he lives."

Allanic said: "But I know him very well, and I have sufficient reason to complain of him, so that it would be a great pleasure to be able to avenge myself for all the injury that he has done me. Get into my carriage, sire, and I shall see that you find him without delay."

Goulaffre didn't recognize Allanic disguised as the coachman of a noble house, so he got in the carriage without hesitation. Immediately the door closed upon him with a great noise, and the coachman whipped his horses, who departed at a gallop. The poor giant, jostled in his prison, torn by the spikes that entered his body from all sides, uttered formidable cries and did his best to open

The Giant Goulaffre

the door and to break the carriage. But it was in vain. All—men and animals—were terrified by his cries of rage as he passed by.

They arrived at Paris, but as soon as the giant was brought into the courtyard of the palace, they didn't know what to do with him. Everybody trembled on hearing him howl and roar in his prison. A council was assembled to deliberate on what was to be done. No one was able to give reasonable advice; fear dominated everything.

Then Allanic said: "I will take the carriage to the middle of a great plain and have heaped around it fifty wagonloads of oak and as many wagonloads of kindling; then we will set fire to it, and Goulaffre will be burned alive and reduced to cinders in the midst of this hell's fire without being able to harm anybody."

They followed his advice and thus they got rid of the terrible Goulaffre. Allanic then married the king's daughter and, as he was good-natured, he named Fistilou his commander-in-chief, though he had tried to do him a great deal of harm.

For a whole month there were public celebrations and unceasing festivals. I was young at the time and was taken to the palace kitchen to turn the spit, and that is how I was able to learn the story of Allanic and the giant Goulaffre, and to tell all the details as they happened.

4

THE WHITE DOVE

A PRINCE AND HIS LADY lived in their palace with two children, a son and a daughter. When the young prince was twenty he got married and lived in the family castle, as is proper. The girl, on the other hand, had extravagant ideas. She systematically refused all marriage proposals, having sworn that she would marry no one save a prince who had a blue beard.

Now, one day the trumpet of the guard announced the arrival of a magnificent carriage. It was a giant, who was reputed to be a great hunter, and this giant had a blue beard. He accepted hospitality, as was the custom. The girl was presented to him, and he pleased the capricious child. The marriage was celebrated the following day and the father gave a hunting party in which the son-in-law distinguished himself.

Then came the day for departure; the giant was taking his wife away to his distant castle.

The mother, who loved her daughter a great deal, confided in her: "What dowry can I give you, my child? Gold? But where you're going you'll have a castle and treasures. Horses? The giant has marvelous horses. I'm going to give you these three birds, the pride of my aviary, the black dove, the white dove, and the red dove. Thus we shall have news from you, for you will be far away. Listen carefully: when you are in good health and living compatibly with your husband, you will send the red one;

when you are ill, you will send the white one; but if discord or misfortune should befall, send at once the black dove."

Of course the father and mother accompanied the young wife to her new domain, but they returned as is customary at the end of a few days. Bluebeard had but one occupation and but one passion: hunting, to which he devoted himself all day long.

One day, taking leave of his wife, he gave her a bunch of keys.

"Wife, here are nine keys. Each of them opens one chamber. But I forbid you to use the ninth and go into the room at the end of the hall."

"Good, my lord."

He assembled his dogs and left on horseback. Meanwhile his wife made an inventory of the castle. All women are curious; the lady of the manor went into the eight chambers, but that didn't suffice her. Her fingers wanted to turn the ninth key in the lock.

"Anyhow, I'm going to visit the last chamber."

The key turned; the door opened. The princess saw a great basin filled with blood. She raised her eyes. The key slipped from her fingers because above the receptacle she saw, swinging in the half-darkness, eight corpses of women, all hanging by chains from hooks in the ceiling.

She had enough strength to pick up the key and to close the door. But she rubbed the key in vain: the bloodstain persisted. Anxiously she awaited her husband's return, her anxiety turning into terror.

"Woman, that key!"

"I'll give it to you presently, my lord."

"Bring my keys at once."

Against her will she had to bring the nine keys.

"Haaaa! You counted the corpses, I see. You shall die too! Go up and put on your loveliest robes, and in one hour—an hour and a half at the outside—you will be hanged on a hook with the others! Go and adorn yourself for the last time!"

The poor woman, her heart failing her, nevertheless had the courage to climb to the tower. She sent to her father the black dove.

"Black dove, go quickly and tell them that I must die in an hour. And you, white dove, stay on the roof."

The unhappy woman went back to her chamber, where she was supposed to adorn herself for the last time. From time to time the window opened and she questioned the bird:

"My white dove, see'st thou aught on the way?"

Her husband, downstairs, had lighted a great fire and was boiling oil in an enormous caldron. He blew up the fire, threw logs into the brazier, then he stirred the liquid with a big wooden branch, and from time to time he

The White Dove

shook the house with his cries. The strokes of his stirring-stick beat time like a clock.

> "Down, down, down,
> Dress and come down!"

And the lady upstairs replied:

> "Let me put on, I pray,
> The shift of a bride
> In this hour, woe betide.
> White Dove, see'st thou aught on the way?"

"I see the Sun and the Wind."
Below, the oil was burning now.

> "Down, down, down,
> Dress and come down!"

> "Let me put on, I pray,
> The bodice of a bride
> In this moment, woe betide.
> White Dove, see'st thou aught on the way?"

"I see the Sun and the Wind."
"Down, down, down," went the sinister stick, "dress and come down!"

> "Let me put on, I pray,
> The skirt of a bride
> In this hour, woe betide.
> White Dove, see'st thou aught on the way?"

"I see the Sun and the Wind."

> "Down, down, down,
> Dress and come down!"

> "Let me put on, I pray,
> The gown of a bride
> In this hour, woe betide.
> White Dove, see'st thou aught on the way?"

"A cloud of dust on the horizon."

> "Down, down, down,
> My oil is boiling.
> Are you finally coming down?"

> "Let me put on, I pray,
> The hose of a bride
> In this moment, woe betide.
> White Dove, see'st thou aught on the way?"

"I see two knights very far away in a cloud of dust."
Below, the oil was boiling in the caldron.

> "Down, down, down,
> I'll come up if you don't come down!"

"Let me arrange, I pray,
The cap of a bride
In this minute, woe betide.
White Dove, my white one, see'st thou aught on the way?"

"Two knights are halfway along the road."

> "Down, down, down,"
> And the oil kept boiling.
> "I order you to come down!"

> "I'm coming, I'm coming,
> With the bouquet of a bride
> At thy order, woe betide.
> White Dove, see'st thou aught on the way?"

"The horses are there!"

Bang! Bang! The husband was counting off the steps of the staircase.

Bluebeard had naturally put the great wooden bar across the portals. The knights were already against them, but

The White Dove

the door was barricaded. What could they do? They backed their horses up against the obstacle to break it down. The portals gave way. The visitors entered on horseback, sabers in their fists.

"What are you doing, son-in-law?" cried the prince.

"You arrived in the nick of time," replied the giant, without being discountenanced. "It's perfect. My wife is all dressed for dinner. Let's have a feast."

They enjoyed a hearty meal where meat and wine were not lacking. Finally Bluebeard fell into a deep sleep. Had he drunk too much? Or else had someone poured a sleeping-powder into his wine? In any case, he fell to snoring with his mouth wide open. With the aid of a funnel his guests poured a big dipper of boiling oil into his throat. He choked to death. Then they washed the key with that oil, and the bloodstain disappeared.

This done, all three took leave without delay. They inherited rightfully all of the domains of the deceased, so they had two castles. It's a very sad truth that in this world some have too much wealth whereas others, of which I am one, haven't enough.

I've gone as far as my fields extend,
So my tale is at the end.

THE DEVIL AND THE TWO LITTLE GIRLS

There were once two little girls. The elder was called Marie and the younger Marguerite. One day as they were going to school they amused themselves by picking strawberries and flowers in a wood beside the road, and they ended by getting lost. After having tried to find their way for a long time, they arrived at a little house and went in to ask for directions.

They found there a little old woman who told them she didn't know the way out of the wood. But she offered them food and a place to sleep while waiting for her husband to come back and build up the fire. The poor little girls, without understanding what she meant, began heartily to eat the food, which they were not familiar with, but they were so hungry that they didn't ask what it was.

When they had finished, the old woman shut them up in a little room that was poorly lighted and waited for her husband—that is to say, for the Devil. He arrived shortly and asked if there was anything new.

"Indeed there is," said the Devil's wife. "You may heat the stove. There are two lovely girls shut up in that room."

"There's wood in it already. Open it, so that I can light it."

He blew into the stove and the wood immediately be-

The Devil and the Two Little Girls

gan to flame. Then he told his wife to bring the little girls to him, and while the stove was heating he took Marie, the elder, and began to pull her clothing off, one piece at a time. Marguerite, the younger, went toward the door.

He took Marie's bonnet off and, putting it in the stove, said to her: "Who bought you this lovely bonnet?"

"My father bought it, and my mother gave it to me. Look, little sister Marguerite, and see if there's anyone coming."

"I see only a little road all lighted up by the sun."

The Devil took off her shoes. "Who bought these beautiful shoes for you?"

"My father bought them for me, and my mother gave them to me. Look, sister Marguerite, and see if there's anyone coming."

"I see only a woman and a little white man very far away on the silver road."

The Devil took off her bodice. "Who bought you this beautiful bodice?"

"My father bought it for me, and my mother gave it to

me. Look then, sister Marguerite, and see if there's anyone coming."

"All I can see is a woman and a little white man very far away on a silver road."

The Devil took off her dress. "Who bought you this lovely dress?"

"My father bought it for me, and my mother gave it to me. Look, sister Marguerite, and see if there's anyone coming."

"I do see a little woman with a little white man closer on the silver road."

The Devil took off her other outer garments. "Who gave you these white petticoats and this lovely corset?"

"My father bought them for me, and my mother gave them to me. Look, sister Marguerite, and see if there's anyone coming."

"I see a little lady coming with a little white man, and they're very close on the silver road."

The Devil took off her hose. "Who bought you these lovely stockings?"

"My father bought them for me, and my mother gave them to me. Look, sister Marguerite, and see if there's anyone coming."

"I see a little lady with a little white man almost here on the silver road."

The Devil was getting ready to take off her shift, but the little woman, who was the Holy Virgin, and the little man, who was the Good Lord, came in and, taking the Devil and his wife, threw them into the oven that they had warmed for the two little girls. Then having withdrawn from the fire the clothing that the Devil had thrown there to burn, they dressed little Marie and took the two sisters back to their parents.

6 and 7

THE STORY OF JOHN-OF-THE-BEAR AND THE STORY OF CRICKET

(*soldiers' versions*)

WHAT IS LACKING in a collected story in order for it to be restored to its living form is the reconstruction of the environment, of the *ambiance* in which it is told, the reproduction of the time-honored dialogues that introduce it, and reactions of the listeners, the analysis of the impressions left in their minds when the voice of the teller is silenced. I give below two tales restored to the atmosphere of barracks full of soldiers by an author, an officer, who knew the mentality of the soldiers admirably, who has faithfully observed it and rendered it in a work long since forgotten in France, the first one that in the past century gave faithful versions of our folk tales. It was at a time when soldiers were, to a large extent, illiterate; before the last third of the last century their literature was an oral literature supplied them by a few gifted storytellers in hours of rest and in the evening after curfew. Soldiers, moreover, have played an important role in the diffusion of tales, and that explains why so often the hero is called *La Ramée, Pipette, La Chique,* which were among the most popular surnames of our foot-soldiers of the *ancien régime*. At the moment when the story begins, the drum has just beaten curfew, and the sergeant of the guard is angry because one barracks, still very noisy, has failed to extinguish the candle.

The setting

"Put the candle out! Do you hear me up there?"

And the order was reinforced by an energetic curse.

"If you make me come up, it will annoy me and tire me, but for you it will be bad luck. Put the candle out!"

Thus shouted, but in vain, a sergeant of the guard at the St. Raphaël garrison in Bordeaux.

The roomful of men he had so vigorously ordered to extinguish the light hadn't heard the beating of curfew because they were cutting up, laughing loudly and long. Their heads had been warmed by that good wine which is sold to soldiers at six sous the bottle under the pompous name of Bordeaux wine. Hence it was in vain for the sergeant to shout himself hoarse. He was forced to climb the two stories, cursing his legs, his three stripes, and his twenty-five years of service which made a tour of guard duty so painful to him.

When he had arrived at the third story with his lantern, however, he entered the disobedient quarters and succeeded in re-establishing silence there for a moment by taking possession of the candle and putting it out. Then after cursing at his leisure, and threatening to take the soldier in charge of the quarters to the guardhouse, he finished his round in that area.

The appearance of the sergeant arrested the joyous outbursts of the gathering for only a moment. Half the soldiers had hastily gone to bed on the sergeant's arrival, and the others were obliged to do the same.

But they weren't planning on going to sleep so soon. One poor devil had just gone out for a moment.

"Well, friends," says the jokester of the quarters, "we've got to catch that fellow. Wait a moment and you're going

John-of-the-Bear

to laugh." Our man gets up and fills one of his shoes with water, balancing it on the door which had been left half open by the other. He, on coming back, pushes the door brusquely, the shoe falls on his forehead, and its contents shower him from head to foot. He gets mad, but who can he take it out on? Everybody is pretending to be asleep. He goes over and gets in bed and at the moment that he is getting into it the staves which support it give way, and there he is on the floor. Then a great racket, bursts of laughter, and the poor boy, seeing that he is dealing with all of the occupants of the quarters, can't get even, but he promises himself that he won't put up with it and that some other time he will have his turn.

When the laughter has calmed down, it is necessary to search for a way to spend the long hours of the evening. Invitations pass from one to another to talk and to tell one of these new and marvelous stories in which the hero is always an old soldier who ends up by marrying a princess. The right to speak is given unanimously to the one who knows "John-of-the-Bear," a tale that he has narrated at least thirty times, and one that the whole quarters knows by heart. It is the best of his repertoire and no one knows better than he how to interlace in his discourse the flowers of rhetoric which blossom in the heart of the barracks. Everybody agrees that he should talk.

The prelude
First took place the usual introduction of which each word is repeated by the teller and by the listeners, who give him this proof of attention:
The narrator: "Cric!"
Listeners: "Crac!"
The narrator: "Wooden shoe!"
Listeners: "Spoon in the pot!"
The narrator: "Legging strap!"
Listeners: "Walk with it!"

The narrator: "Walk today, walk tomorrow; by dint of walking you go a long way. I go through a forest where there is no wood, through a river where there is no water, through a village where there is no house. I knock at a door and everybody answers me. The more I tell you, the more I shall lie to you. I'm not paid to tell you the truth."

The tale of John-of-the-Bear

There was once in the forest of Ardennes a woodman who lived peacefully with his wife, who had not been able to bear him a child. One day when this quite pretty country girl was in the forest busy gathering wood, she was taken by a monstrous bear; this bear took her into his cave, and when he came out to get provisions he was careful to close his den with a huge stone so that the woman couldn't come out. At the end of five or six months she was pregnant, and at last she gave birth to a handsome boy who in three or four months walked alone and who could speak and run at a year.

The woman, who had a missal, raised him in the Catholic religion; she kept telling him that she was in prison and that she wanted to get out, but she and her son couldn't move the stone. But the little boy began to be able to move it, and finally at the end of five or six years he was strong enough and his mother told him: "Tomorrow when the bear has gone for provisions we'll both go out." No sooner said than done: the boy, who was now grown up, moved the stone aside so that his mother and he escaped. The woman went back to her husband and told him what had happened to her.

The little boy gave promise of a high degree of intelligence; they sent him to school. But when he was ten years of age he was beating up all of his comrades, who had named him John-of-the-Bear because he was very hairy, and every time they gave him this name he thrashed them. So the schoolmaster notified his parents that they

John-of-the-Bear

would have to punish their son, who was hated by everybody.

Then John-of-the-Bear told his parents that he didn't want to go to school any more, but wanted to learn a trade.

"And what trade do you want to learn?" his father asked him.

"Blacksmith."

"Very well."

For two years they had him serve as an apprentice to a blacksmith. At the end of the two years his master asked him how much he expected to be paid.

"You will pay me nothing, but when I am tired of staying with you, you will give me an iron cane as large as I want."

The blacksmith having accepted the bargain, the boy remained with him for five years. At the end of five years, having grown tired of this kind of life, he went to his master to tell him that he wanted to leave, but that before doing so he was going to make his cane. The master told him to take iron from the storehouse. There was eight hundred pounds of it there, which he used to make his cane, but he still didn't have enough to make the head, so he went back to his master to ask for more iron.

"What! There isn't any more in the storehouse? There was eight hundred pounds!"

"I need a little more to make the head."

And so he gave him two hundred pounds to make the head, and when it was made he took leave of his master, who felt the loss of his iron more than the loss of his journeyman.

He came to tell his parents of his intention to travel, and his father having given him some money, he set out with his cane. On the way he met a man who was making withies out of hundred-year-old oak trees.

"What are you making there, my friend?" asked John-of-the-Bear.

Twistoak replied that he was making bands to tie his sticks with.

"You are very good to work so hard. Come with me. We will be able to live without doing anything."

"All right. Let's go," replied Twistoak.

A little way from there they met a man who was amusing himself raising boulders with a pair of pincers, and at each try he raised one and broke it.

"Good lord! What's your name, friend?"

"My name is Cutmountain."

"Let's go seek our fortune. If you want to come with us, come along."

Cutmountain followed them.

As they were going into a forest, night came upon them. After having walked for three hours in the darkness, John-of-the-Bear said:

"Good heavens! Where can we go? One of us must climb a tree to see if he can't see something."

Twistoak climbed. He saw a light and told John-of-the-Bear, who explained to him that he should throw his hat in the direction whence he saw the light coming and then come down. Twistoak came down and found his hat, and all three of them set out in the direction where he had seen the light. After having walked for some time they found themselves in front of a castle. Arriving at the gate, it opened of itself, and John-of-the-Bear said:

"By heavens, they're certainly trusting in this house!"

After going through the yard, they entered a great parlor, where there was a nice fire.

"By heavens," said John-of-the-Bear, "here's a place to get warm; but if there was something to eat, it would be all the better."

Immediately a table with three places was set in front of the fire. John-of-the-Bear said:

John-of-the-Bear

"Good! There are three of us, so it must be for us."

They ate a hearty meal and after dinner it was time to go to bed. At once a door opened; they went into a magnificent bedroom where there were three beds, and without ceremony they went to sleep and slept like angels.

An interlude

An imperious "Hush!" imposed silence at this moment upon one of the listeners who hadn't been able to hold back a cough. From the moment that the narrator had begun his fantastic story not a breath had been heard in the room, not the slightest movement. It was a deep silence, and uninterrupted. The soldiers' imagination took delight in seeing this rough kind of energy go from success to success, because for the soldier happiness consists in sensual pleasures and the sweetness of physical life. The narrator resumed:

Continuation of the story of John-of-the-Bear

The next day they were quite surprised to find magnificent clothes instead of the rags they had taken off the evening before. Then John-of-the-Bear said with great wisdom:

"It's awfully nice here. We must stay."

Cutmountain added: "We dined well last night, but will they give us breakfast this morning?"

And the table reappeared with a breakfast including meat and prepared in the most careful manner.

"After breakfast it would be nice to smoke a pipe."

Poof! And there were three pipes of excellent Maryland tobacco on the table.

After three days of this life they began to feel bored. John-of-the-Bear said: "Two of us must go hunting while the third stays here in order to be present if the owner of the house should come back."

It was agreed that Cutmountain would stay that day and that the two others would go hunting. They assigned him the task of ringing the bell at dinner time. No sooner had they gone hunting than Cutmountain, having sat down in front of the fire to warm himself, saw a little man come out of the chimney, and as soon as he was in the parlor, he expanded to extraordinary stature, carrying a walking-stick that increased in size with him. He set upon Cutmountain and thrashed him soundly. Then he went out the door that opened on the courtyard. Our poor Cutmountain, sorely wounded, his body broken, beaten to a pulp, dragged himself to his bed and forgot to ring the bell to call his comrades.

John-of-the-Bear said to his companion: "What time do you think it is now?"

"I don't know, but judging from my stomach, it seems that the bell should have rung."

They set out toward the castle. On arriving they saw Cutmountain in bed and asked him if it wasn't dinner time and why he hadn't rung the bell.

"Excuse me, my friend, I got thirsty. I wanted to go

down to the cellar, and I fell down the stairs, and I think I have dislocated my arms and legs."

"Well, get up. We're going to eat."

"No," he said. "I'm not hungry."

John-of-the-Bear and Twistoak went and sat down at the table to eat. After dinner they rubbed Cutmountain with soap and brandy. The next day he felt better and was able to go hunting with John-of-the-Bear.

Twistoak stayed in the house, having been instructed to ring the bell and not to forget as Cutmountain had done. Twistoak, alone, sat down to smoke his pipe in front of the fire, and no sooner had he done so than the little fellow arrived by the same route. He expanded in the same manner and assailed poor Twistoak just as he had done Cutmountain.

The latter, who had received his ration the evening before, noting that his comrade hadn't rung the bell, said to himself: "I'm not the only one; he's got it too."

And then he said to John-of-the-Bear: "I think it's past time. He's neglected the signal."

John-of-the-Bear answered: "By heaven, he's probably done the same as you. He probably went down to the cellar too fast."

So they went back to the castle, and Twistoak was in bed.

"So you wanted to go down to the cellar too!"

"No, but I wanted to go get some wood to put in the fire, and the bundle fell on my back."

John-of-the-Bear said: "It's my turn to stay tomorrow, but I shan't go to get wood nor to the cellar, since to have all you want here, all you have to do is wish."

They sat down to the table, as usual, and then they went to rub Twistoak.

The next day Twistoak and Cutmountain went hunting in their turn, leaving John-of-the-Bear all alone, and he had promised to ring the bell.

John-of-the-Bear, having only his cane, which he never abandoned, began to smoke his pipe in front of the hearth and he soon heard a noise.

"Ah!" he said, "I think there's something queer."

He got up from his chair and saw a little giant coming out of the fireplace, and before he had time to expand to full size John-of-the-Bear had already given him a few blows with his little stick, which as we know weighed a thousand pounds. The giant, who didn't expect this kind of a reward, took Jack Scram as his attorney and, seeing that John-of-the-Bear was after him, he jumped into a well. John-of-the-Bear, who hadn't been able to catch him, threw his cane at him, saying: "Rascal! You won't come out soon!"

And he stood guard while he waited for his comrades to come and pay a visit to the well.

While all this was going on, Twistoak, turning to Cutmountain, said: "By the way, the bell isn't ringing. But, you know, I think it's time to go and eat."

So saying he scratched his ear, though that wasn't the place where he was itching.

"I think so too."

"But tell me, did you really fall on the cellar stairway yesterday?" he asked the other as they were going back to the castle.

"Well, what about you? Did wood really fall on your back?"

"Don't worry. I'm sure he'll get his dose too."

"Well, to tell the truth, it was a giant that beat me."

"And me too," said the other.

On arriving they were quite surprised to see John-of-the-Bear seated on the edge of the well and shouting as loud as he could: "Over here, over here, my friends! I've got him!"

John-of-the-Bear

And speaking to Twistoak he said: "Go quickly and get some ropes and a big basket."

And when he came back, John-of-the-Bear said to Cutmountain: "You're going to go down in this basket. Here's a little bell. When you reach the bottom and find the giant —for I'm sure I killed him with a blow of my cane—you can put him in the basket and then ring for us to pull him out."

Cutmountain got in the basket, but when he was down a few hundred feet, fear overcame him and he rang and was pulled back out. John-of-the-Bear asked him where the giant was.

"I didn't see anything," he said. "My head was in a spin."

John-of-the-Bear said to Twistoak: "Well, you try."

So Twistoak got in the basket and went down much farther than the other, for he touched the head of the cane, but having rung, he was pulled back out, and John-of-the-Bear said:

"I guess I'll have to go get him myself."

Whereupon, having got into the basket, he was lowered by the two others. Arriving at the bottom, he took his cane; then, seeing the light of day in this underground place, he set out to continue his search, for he hadn't found the giant's body. And on the way he met a nice old woman and he said to her:

"My good woman, I'm looking for a big cur who gave my comrades a good beating."

This good woman told him that it was a giant who held the three daughters of the king of Spain in slavery; one was in a castle of steel guarded by tigers, the second in a castle of silver guarded by leopards, and the third in a castle of gold guarded by lions that were the size of elephants. She beseeched him to go back because he would risk getting himself devoured if he went farther. But John-of-the-Bear, trusting his strength and his cane, swore to the old woman that he wouldn't go back until he had found the giant and liberated the three princesses.

Then the old woman said: "Here, my brave fellow—for you are brave!—take this little jar of salve and if you chance to be bitten by one of these wild animals that you are going to attack, all you have to do is rub yourself and you will be healed at once. Good luck!"

So John-of-the-Bear set out in the underworld. Upon approaching the castle of steel he saw tigers, who immediately threw themselves upon him. He killed the first one with a blow of his cane. As for the second, he shoved his arm down its throat so that his fingers came out the rear and he caught him by the tail, and he turned the animal inside out like a wool sock, which angered the tiger somewhat. What enraged the tiger even more was that now he couldn't bite because all of his teeth were on the outside. John-of-the-Bear, having no more adversaries to combat, entered the steel castle, where all were asleep.

An interlude

"Cric, crac!"

No one responded immediately to this signal, for the whole room was sleeping except the narrator and the unfortunate companion who was on the floor as a result of the prank played upon him an hour before.

"All right," he thought, getting up. "Here's the moment for me to get even."

He took a string and passed it through the eyes of the barracks-bag straps which were hanging on the shelf above the beds, and gave it a jerk; all the sacks fell at the same time on the stomachs and heads of all his comrades, who awoke with a start, crying like men possessed of the devil, and vying with each other as they complained of eyes, noses, and the whole body being bruised. You may imagine that the one who was the cause of this disagreeable awakening began to shout louder than the others,

John-of-the-Bear

for he feared the moment of vengeance; but the next day they noticed that he was the only one who didn't have black eyes or contusions on his face, and the trickster was thus discovered.

"By the way, my good Auvergnat, you certainly ought to finish the tale you started telling us a little while ago," said the soldiers when all had been set in order.

"By heavens, it's pleasant to tell you something that puts you to sleep immediately. You listen to me a bit and then I'm left alone to sell my merchandise like Saint John preaching in the desert."

"Ah, too bad; your pride is hurt?"

"Well, let's agree on one thing, that the first one to go to sleep will buy me a drink tomorrow."

"All right, all right," cried all his comrades.

And the Auvergnat said: "At what point in the story were we?"

"Wait a minute, Auvergnat. You were at the point where John-of-the-Bear was going into the castle of steel," said the one who hadn't gone to sleep in order to get even.

"That's true. Well, I'll start there, or if you wish I'll begin all over again."

"No, no, start at the steel castle."

Continuation of the story of John-of-the-Bear
"Cric!"
"Crac!"
"We're off!"
"Forward march!"
And he began:

Having overpowered and exterminated the two tigers, John-of-the-Bear entered the steel castle, and there he saw a pretty little sleeping princess, and he found her so beautiful and to his liking that he didn't dare wake her up. But he was brave enough to take her pretty little hand and give it a kiss. The princess woke up at that very instant and she was surprised to see a man beside her, for she had seen no one for three years. John-of-the-Bear, aware of her fright, told her what he had just done and informed her that she was free. The princess flew into his arms, telling him that if she had the good fortune to see her father again, the first thing she would tell him would be that she wanted to marry her liberator, but that in the meantime she had two sisters that he must try to deliver. John-of-the-Bear, without delay, asked her to point out the road to the castle of silver, and immediately the princess said to him: "I'll show you the way." And as she preceded him to climb to the top of the tower, John-of-the-Bear was more occupied, I assure you, looking at her pretty legs and calves than he was counting the steps of the stairway.

Having seen the castle, he decided to put her in safe keeping. They went down from the tower, and John-of-the-Bear had her lead the way to the underground. There he put the princess in the basket. Before leaving John-of-the-Bear she gave him a steel ball, urging him to keep it, for it might be useful to him. As for him, he directed her to send the basket back down for her sisters.

Imagine the surprise of Twistoak and Cutmountain, who thought they were hoisting the giant or their friend, when a princess they had never seen in their lives came up!

Twistoak wanted to have her and he flung himself into her arms saying: "For me!"

Cutmountain also said: "No! For me!"

And while each was pulling her his way, she tried to explain to them that she had two sisters who were being delivered at that moment, and she tried to make them understand that when they came, the six of them could all make arrangements together.

And while they were pulling that poor girl from one side to the other to determine which one would have her,

John-of-the-Bear

John-of-the-Bear was carrying on a determined battle against the leopards. He had already killed three, but the fourth grabbed hold of his thigh and he just barely had time to cut off the morsel that the leopard held in his mouth. Then, while the leopard was devouring the beefsteak, with a blow of his cane John-of-the-Bear laid him out dead. Then he made use of his little jar, and when he had rubbed himself with a bit of the salve, he was immediately healed.

Having gone into the castle, he found in the parlor a princess who was still prettier than her sister. A bit more bold than with the other, he kissed her and she woke up with a start. He told her that she was free and then, as this lovely princess wanted to speak to him of her sisters, he told her that he had already delivered the one who was in the castle of steel, and that now all she had to do was to show him the way to the other castle, which she did. John-of-the-Bear took her to the underground, put her in the basket to go and rejoin her sister. The princess pulled a ball of silver from her bag and gave it to her liberator, telling him to keep it.

When John-of-the-Bear had rung, the basket went up,

but scarcely had it arrived above when the comrades resumed the same discussion saying:

"Ah, look here, this one's mine!"

The other replied: "But you want to have both of them! You wanted the first one! Now this one is mine!"

While they were arguing like ragpickers, our poor John-of-the-Bear had gone into combat with the lions, a combat that lasted for three hours, for there were six of the most terrible lions against him. He laid them out as was his custom and entered the castle, as he had the other two. But he was still more surprised, for he thought indeed that he was looking at an angel, so much more beautiful was this princess than the other two. He didn't dare awaken her by kissing her, so he contented himself with knocking on the floor with his cane. The princess, waking up, said to him:

"Ah, my sweet friend, pray what have you come to do? I am guarded by six of the most terrible lions that have ever been seen and if they smell you here you are a lost man; they will devour you."

"Have no worry, my lovely princess, the six lions are dead, and before succeeding in coming this far I have already delivered your two sisters."

Then they set out for the underground passage and on the way the princess saw the six lifeless lions stretched out on the ground, and the leopards, and the tigers which had guarded the three castles. She took a golden ball from her bag and, giving it to John-of-the-Bear, she told him to keep it.

Having arrived at the basket, John-of-the-Bear put her in, and having rung, he advised her to send the basket back down again. She went up. Our two gallants again began to argue over the beautiful girl, finding her still better than her sisters, and each wanted to have the booty. The basket came back down, John-of-the-Bear got in with his cane. But the two perfidious friends had come to an

John-of-the-Bear

agreement that as soon as he had come within a certain distance of the rim they would let go of the rope and let him fall back again to the bottom of the well, in order to deny him forever the chance to come back up, and that's exactly what they did.

John-of-the-Bear's body, having fallen from so high, was bruised and broken; all his limbs were shattered. So he had to take recourse to the little jar. As soon as he was well he went back into the underground passage to look for the good old woman. After having walked for half an hour he had the good fortune to meet her; he told her of the treachery that he had been the victim of and how he had fallen back into the well.

The old woman said to him: "It was very difficult to deliver the three princesses but it's still more difficult to get out of the well again. The only means," she added, "is to make use of an eagle which inhabits these parts and who alone will be able to lift you out; but each time that it squawks, you must give him a big piece of flesh. However, since your comrades have been mean enough to want to kill you, I want to save you."

Having spoken thus, the old woman took him into a barn where there was a bull, two calves, and four sheep; she loaded all of them upon the eagle, aided by John-of-the-Bear, who had no sooner gotten on than the bird took flight. The eagle squawked so often that John-of-the-Bear just barely had time to cut and give him the required pieces of meat. He still had a good bit of distance to make when all he had left was a single sheep; then he said to himself:

"If you squawk once more I'm done for; we both go back down again."

Finally the sheep had been eaten and John-of-the-Bear was just on the point of coming out of the well when the cursed animal squawked again! There was no escaping it, she was going to go back down. John-of-the-Bear didn't hesitate nor did he try to drive a bargain: he cut a piece of flesh from his own thigh and put it in the eagle's beak. At almost the same instant he grabbed the edge of the well.

"Squawk!"

"Ah!"

But squawk or no squawk, John-of-the-Bear was saved. He rubbed his thigh and that's all there was to it! This proves to you that you must have courage in critical moments. He went into the castle, expecting to find the princesses there and his comrades who had played such a nasty trick on him, but he found no one.

"Ah," said he, "you rascals! You've outsmarted me!"

But, knowing that the three princesses were the daughters of the king of Spain, he set out for Madrid.

During the time that our poor devil John-of-the-Bear was down underground, the two good-for-nothings had made the princesses promise to tell their father, the king, that they had been delivered by them. The princesses feebly consented, and as soon as they had arrived, they presented to the king as their liberators these two jokesters. The king, who had promised his daughters to whoever might bring them back to him, told them to choose two princesses. But the eldest, who had been retained in the golden castle and who was her father's favorite, begged him not to speak of marriage before a year and a day, because within herself she hoped to find her true liberator, and the king granted her wish. At the same time he gave orders to all of the grocers of the kingdom to bring him all of the Marseille soap that they had in their stores in order to cleanse Twistoak and Cutmountain, who had never during their lifetime been inside a palace. After having been well groomed, they were dressed up as princes and given beautiful white shirts which made them resemble a fly that had fallen in the milk, and finally

John-of-the-Bear

costumes embroidered with lace, which suited them like an apron on a cow, and swords on their sides, and pairs of cuffs, which suited them as they might a Lorraine sardine.[1]

Well, let's let them take a walk, play the matador in the palace with the princesses; and let us return to our poor John-of-the-Bear. Upon his arrival in the capital of Spain, which was long before the French arrived in that country, he took his lodgings in a little inn, where he learned from his host that the princesses were in the palace with their liberators, and that shortly they were going to marry them.

From the moment of his arrival in Madrid he went walking daily to the royal palace to see if he might discover one of these princesses. One day when he was taking his usual walk he saw the eldest of the princesses at a crossroad and, having recognized her, he took the three balls which he still possessed and he rolled them one after another down the garden path. The princess, having seen the balls and recognized her liberator, went at once to find her father, and she told him that he who had really delivered them was in Madrid, that she had just seen him in the gardens. The king, attempting to find him the sooner, took three balls similar to the other three, all six inimitable, and he had it announced in the city that anyone who could make for him three balls exactly like the ones he possessed would have one of his daughters in marriage, or be hanged if he attempted to make them and didn't succeed.

John-of-the-Bear, having learned of this, took the three balls to the king, who examined them and had his daughters come to present him to them. The princesses recognized John-of-the-Bear as the one who had really delivered them, and then the king said:

---

[1] There is humor to be derived from the fact that Lorraine is not a coastal French province but well inland. (TRANSLATOR.)

"So then, my daughters, those you brought back to us weren't really your liberators?"

The princesses confessed that Twistoak and Cutmountain had told them to do what they had done under pain of death. The eldest added that it was for this motive that she had asked for a delay of one year, hoping that her true liberator might appear. Then John-of-the-Bear began to speak, and he told the king that his two comrades were traitors who had wanted to assassinate him by letting him fall back into the well, which was more than six thousand feet deep.

So the king gave him his eldest daughter in marriage, and as they were going into the church to receive the nuptial benediction, our friends Twistoak and Cutmountain were being hanged before the cathedral doors on some brand-new gallows that were twenty-five feet high. I leave it to you to imagine what a good time they had at that lovely wedding.

As for me, since I wanted to eat a piece bigger than the others, a cook gave me such a kick that I was hurled to this very spot, and thus my story ends.

New interlude

"By heavens, I'm not sorry, because that story is very long," said one of the soldiers, half asleep.

"Well, that's the way you are!" said the storyteller in an angry tone. "I guess I'll have to tell you stories from Voltaire."

"Ah! From Voltaire! He's sharp there with his Voltaire. Voltaire didn't write anything but tragedies for the French."

"Bah! You think so, mister scholar. I tell you that Voltaire wrote stories, and that this is one of them."

"By Jove, I think you're right, because there were two volumes of them in my uncle's house."

"And that's where you read it?"

Cricket

"Well, not exactly, because I don't know how to read. But I know it's his; the drummer of the 4th Company of the First Battalion told me so the other day."

"In that case there's no reason to have any doubt about it. Your authority is unimpeachable."

Yet the soldiers had developed a liking for these fantastic tales. Sleep didn't dog them now. So they begged the teller to give them one more of his stories. Swigs of brandy were promised by way of inducement. Some of them, it is true, might have preferred some story from our old Imperial campaigns, some episode told in a military manner concerning the European wars, but the barrack room was composed only of young soldiers of which the oldest had memories of military service which went back only to the last war in Spain. Hence their experience was not teeming with remarkable happenings; their adventures and their battles scarcely whet one's curiosity and certainly don't strike the imagination. There is nothing colossal, gigantic, of diademed glory which embellishes and lends poetry to the military exploits of the Empire and of the Republic.

Hence they were constrained, after having talked for some time about the monks, about the soldiers of the faith, about the convents, and all those ragamuffins of Spain, and of the pretty women of Valencia, Granada, Seville, and Madrid, and after having told of two or three skirmishes with the Spanish troops—after all these things they had to return to the domain of the miraculous, of the fantastic, to the realm of the supernatural. The storyteller, Picquenot, hence let himself be vanquished by the promise of brandy, and in the midst of a general silence he began his story.

"Cric!"
"Crac!"
"Wooden shoe!"
"Spoon in the pot!"

"Legging strap!"
"Walk with it!"
"Walk today, walk tomorrow, by dint of walking you go a long way!

The tale of Cricket

It is good, my friends, to tell you of an old soldier who had served in the time when Jesus Christ was a corporal in the Hundred Swiss Guards. The poor man's name was Cricket and he had become so unhappy that he no longer knew which way to turn. One day when he was thinking about his misery he said:

"Oh, my lord, how miserable I am! I'm going to die of hunger. But if before dying I could only have three good meals, I should go to sleep happy."

Thereupon he heard someone say that a diamond had been stolen from a princess.

"That's my business!" he said to himself.

And he went to the castle, saying that he wanted to find this diamond and that if they would leave him alone he would succeed, but that he needed three days; this was in order to have time, as you may imagine, to get his three good meals.

When he had eaten the first meal, a servant came to take away the dirty dishes, and Cricket said, striking his belly: "Good! There's one."

Frightened, the servant went to tell his comrades: "We are done for, for this man is a sorcerer."

The next day it was another servant who waited on him, and Cricket, when he had finished eating, shouted, laughing:

"What do I care about anything else? That makes two!"

The third servant was obliged to wait on Cricket the next day; the others didn't dare to appear since they thought they had been found out.

Cricket

When Cricket finished eating, he said: "There, you are satisfied. That makes all three of them."

The servant ran to find his comrades, and he told them, quite horrified: "Let's get together as much money as we can between us to give to this sorcerer; otherwise we are lost."

So they came back to find Cricket and they gave him sixty louis, and in addition they gave him the diamond they had stolen.

"Take it easy," said Cricket. "I'll take care of everything."

He took the diamond and put it in a pellet of bread which he threw into the farmyard, where there were some ducks and turkeys; a gobbler having swallowed it, Cricket went at once to find the princess and begged her to have the animal killed: "For," he said, "he's the one who stole the diamond."

You see that Cricket was not a dunce; there is nothing as clever and imaginative as an old soldier when he has to get out of difficulties. The diamond was thus recovered and the princess, beside herself with joy, asked Cricket if he wanted to stay in the castle, offering to give him an abundance of money, a well-served table, a nice fire, an excellent bed—in short, all that he might desire—and assuring him that he would be looked upon as a friend of the household, an assurance that is always very agreeable to receive from the mouth of a pretty woman, and especially from a princess who is talking to a soldier. Cricket accepted. It was too attractive an offer to be rejected.

"Well, I should think so," said a recruit who hadn't missed a syllable of the story.

But the prince, having returned from the army and learning that there was a sorcerer in his castle, and knowing particularly that his wife was entertaining him there as a friend of the household, appeared to get angry about it, and he wanted to put the sorcerer to a test.

"Good!" said the recruit, still delighted and attentive. "They're going to refresh themselves with a duel."
"Silence!" shouted the storyteller.

The prince did better. One evening he had a cricket brought to him, and he put it on the table between two plates; then when he was seated and when Cricket, who had sat down next to the princess, was making eyes at her, planning to eat a big dinner, and was voluptuously unfolding his napkin and drinking a glass of wine such as you have never drunk, the prince said to him:
"Sorcerer" (for he had no other name for him), "what's in that? If you can't guess you shall die."
The poor soldier was quite at a loss, as you may imagine. Who could have guessed that a prince might amuse himself by putting a cricket between two plates? Fearful that he might not guess, and seeing his fortune and his life leaving him all at once, the soldier cried out mournfully:

Cricket

"Ah, my poor Cricket! You are lost!"

The prince believed that he had really guessed the contents of the plates, and the soldier remained attached to the castle and to the person of the princess as an aide-de-camp.

After the story

"Well," said the recruit, "I wanted him to marry the princess!"

"Stupid. It was exactly the same thing!"

Meanwhile silence was established; there was nobody awake except the recruit, on which the tales had produced the same effect as mocha coffee does. All of the rest of the soldiers in the barrack room had gone to sleep, and although the recruit still wanted to hear the story of the campaigns of Carpentras, the classical story of *La Ramée,* and the still more marvelous one of the king of France, he had to put off this pleasure until the next day. He ended by going to sleep dreaming of princesses married by adventurers, and of old soldiers who become the friends of the household in castles, and of aides-de-camp of kings and of their wives.

As for the storyteller, he closed his eyes, having his imagination softly cradled by the prospect of little glasses of brandy which his memory and his storytelling art had earned for him. It is just that talent be recompensed and that he should drink, especially when the talent wears a saber and epaulets.

8

KING FORTUNATUS'S GOLDEN WIG

THERE WERE ONCE in the region of Lannois in lower Brittany a boy and a girl who were in love, and so they decided to get married, which is only natural. After their marriage they went to live in the country, and there they lived happy for several years, until they began to regret the fact that they had no children. Then unhappiness came into the household and misunderstandings occurred, which became more and more frequent. The husband decided that this manner of life could not long continue, so he went to find a man who was known for his wisdom and who was said to be a sorcerer to advise him about his troubles.

"I'll get you out of your difficulties," he said, "but it will be for a few years only. Come with me into the garden."

And he took him to a tree that bore three apples, a green one, a yellow one, and a red one.

"Choose the one you want and eat it," he said.

The husband took the white apple[1] in his hand and ate it.

Then the sage said to him: "You have chosen the apple that will permit you to have a son within a year, and you and your wife will be the happiest of parents. The day

---

[1] The French text has the adjective "white" despite the fact that no white apple was mentioned previously (TRANSLATOR.)

King Fortunatus's Golden Wig

your son is fifteen he will leave the house, never to return, and he will refuse to take anything away with him, in spite of your insistence. When this happens you must simply tell him: 'My son, take what you find in the ruined hut at the end of the path.'"

The husband went back home as happy as the sun and announced the good news to his wife, but he was careful not to tell her about the predictions of the sage. In a short time his wife gave birth to a boy who was so beautiful and so strong that you would have taken him to be a year old. The parents spared nothing so that their child might be reared and educated properly. But as the boy advanced in age, the father withered away. His wife, observing his torment, asked him what was wrong.

"What troubles me," he said, "will, alas, trouble you in a short time."

The child was approaching the age fixed by the sage. The evening before he was to be fifteen he went to find his parents.

"Tomorrow it will be fifteen years," he said, "that I have been in this house. You have made me happy and you haven't left me ignorant of anything that a child like myself is capable of learning. I thank you from the depths of my heart, but I have to tell you that tomorrow I must leave."

Although the father and mother had taken precautions that he shouldn't know his age, they became aware that it was to no avail because the day when their son was to depart had been revealed to him.

"Take gold and silver for your trip," his mother said to him.

"Mother, I shan't take a single penny. When you gave birth to me I was completely naked; leaving you, I shall take nothing but my clothing."

The next day at daybreak he got dressed, kissed his father and mother, and said farewell.

"You must eat something before leaving," said his mother.

"I shall eat nothing," he said. "I'm not hungry."

The father was getting ready to cross the threshold to walk a short way with him.

The child said: "Father, you mustn't come any farther. Go back to my mother and let me leave alone for the place to which I must go."

"Son, since you won't take anything, at least take what you find in the wretched little ruined hut at the end of the path."

"I shall see," said the child. "Good-by, good-by!"

And he left. When he was at the end of the path, as he was passing by the hut, he recalled what his father had said.

"Well," he said, "I had never noticed this hut. What can be inside it?"

He pushed the door open and saw a bridled and saddled horse.

"By heaven," he said, "this horse is certainly destined for me. I'm going to take him and mount."

So he rode away penniless, having neither eaten nor drunk, and he neither stopped nor rested.

One day as he was crossing a broad prairie he heard a noise in the air which made him raise his eyes. He saw two crows fighting, with feathers flying in all directions. He watched them a moment to know the reason for their quarrel, and he saw an object fall to the earth that they had dropped.

"I must know what it is," he said.

"It would be better if you never knew," said the horse, "and it would be better for you to leave as quickly as possible in the opposite direction."

"Well!" said the young man. "You know how to talk, too?"

King Fortunatus's Golden Wig

"Yes, certainly," said the horse, "as well as you do and perhaps even better."

"Good! But no matter; I shan't leave here without having seen what the crows dropped."

"You'll be sorry," said the horse, "but it will be too late. Too bad for you, my friend."

Our young man arrived at the place where the object had fallen and when he saw that it was a golden wig he took it, laughing, and said:

"It will be useful to me some day, even if only to disguise myself on Mardi gras."

"Leave this wig," said the horse, "or otherwise, believe me, you will repent of it."

"Never! I shall take it away with me," said the young man.

Turning it around and around in every direction he saw written in golden letters inside:

> KING FORTUNATUS'S GOLDEN WIG

The boy unceremoniously put the king's wig in his pocket and went on his way.

When he had crossed a vast forest his horse spoke to him again: "Young man, I wish to stay in this wood. Build me a hut of branches, leave me, and depart alone. Near by is a big city where an old king lives. Go to his palace and ask for work, and no matter what work you are offered, accept it, and if you get into difficulties, come and find me and I will tell you what to do."

Our boy followed the horse's advice and went to the king's intendant to ask for work. They took him as a stable boy and gave him two horses to care for, but as he was a very fine boy and as his horses were soon the fattest ones in the king's stables, he provoked the jealousy of the other stable boys, and they ultimately said that he must be stealing their horses' oats to give to his, but no matter how much they watched him they never found anything to reproach him for.

The first night that he slept in the stables, in a hut fixed up near his horses, he was awakened by a light that illuminated the room, and on examining what was giving forth such a light, he saw that it was the wig that he had brought along. Having fallen from his pocket, it was lighting up the room as the sun would have done at midday.

"And to think that my horse tried to get me to leave this wig behind!" he said to himself. "It's a good thing that I picked it up. Henceforth I shall be able to save the money that they give me to buy candles."

The next evening he suspended King Fortunatus's golden wig on the main beam of the stable, which was thereafter better lighted than the king's palace. A month or two passed thus and then came Carnival. What did our young man do? He put on his finest suit and the wig and went to take a stroll about the city. He disseminated such light that the streets were illuminated as he went by, and everybody wondered who this great prince could be. When the king was advised of it he grew worried, sent for him, begged him to come with him to the palace, and asked him who he was and from what country he came.

"My name is Jean," replied the boy. "I was born in a far-away country and I came to live here some time ago."

And Jean smiled on seeing that the king did not recognize him.

"You are so handsome," the king said to him, "that you must be the son of some great king."

"Oh, you think, then," replied Jean, "that only the children of kings can be handsome? Change that idea, sire. Others can be as handsome as they are, no matter what their social status or their fortune; there are, as a

King Fortunatus's Golden Wig

matter of fact, stable boys who are as handsome as kings, if not more so."

"Stable boys," said the king, "are not dressed as you are and don't have a wig like the one that you are wearing."

"And yet," said Jean, "I am your stable boy and you must be blind not to have recognized me."

"What?" said the king. "You are Jean, my stable boy? And where did you find this wig?"

And taking it from the boy's head he looked at it, turned it about, and read in the inside:

> KING FORTUNATUS'S GOLDEN WIG

"Ha, ha, ha," said the king. "You have the wig of the famous King Fortunatus, he who has the loveliest daughter on earth. And how did you get it?"

"I found it in a field where two crows that were fighting let it fall."

"Well," said the king, "I shall henceforth be the owner of this wig."

The stable boys, upon learning this, went to tell the king that Jean knew King Fortunatus very well and that he had said several times that, if he had wanted to, he could have had his daughter in marriage.

The king sent for Jean.

"So, you have boasted that you wanted to marry King Fortunatus's daughter?"

"What liar has told you such a thing? I know neither the king nor his daughter."

"You have said so, and I know it. And if you don't bring me back the king's daughter, you shall be beaten."

Heavy at heart, Jean went to the forest to find his horse, which was waiting for him in the hut of branches.

"Aha," said the horse, seeing him. "I knew that you would shortly come to see me."

Jean told him about the king's whims.

"Didn't I advise you to leave that wig alone?" said the horse. "But what's done is done, and I want to help you. Go ask the king to equip for you promptly three fine ships, one to be laden with quarters of beef, another with millet, and the third with oats; and we shall leave with them."

Jean went and asked the king to prepare the three ships, and when they were ready Jean took his horse and departed with them. The sea was calm and the wind good, and after a good crossing they arrived at the mouth of a river that the horse had them sail into.

"We are entering the land of lions," he said to Jean. "Have quarters of beef thrown on each bank all along the way; otherwise the famished lions will pounce upon us."

The king of the lions was well satisfied and came to find Jean.

"You're a good boy and you have rendered us a great service. You deserve a reward. Pull a hair from my mane and save it carefully. When you need me, all you have to do is to take the hair in your hand and call me. I will come at once with my band."

Jean continued up the river with his three boats.

A little farther on, the horse said: "We are arriving in the land of ants. We must throw millet on each side; otherwise the ants will come and devour us."

The ants dashed upon the millet and ate it immediately, not wasting a single kernel, and the king of the ants was well pleased and came to find Jean and said to him:

"You're a good boy and you have rendered us a service. You deserve a reward. Take one of my hind feet and keep it carefully. When you need me, all you have to do is to press it in your hand and call me and I will come at once with all the ants."

Jean went on his way with the three boats, and a little later the horse said to him:

King Fortunatus's Golden Wig

"We are arriving in the land of geese. Now throw oats."

And the king of the geese came to find Jean and told him: "You're a good boy and you have rendered us a service. You deserve a reward. Take one of the feathers from my tail and preserve it carefully. When you need me, all you'll have to do is to take it in your hand and call me. I will come immediately, followed by all my geese."

Jean went on his way and soon he arrived in the city of King Fortunatus. He went at once to the palace of the king.

"Sire," he said to the king, "I have come to get your daughter, to take her to the King of Brittany. He has heard that she has no equal for beauty and he wants to marry her."

"We shall see, we shall see," said King Fortunatus. "She will leave with you if you succeed in doing what I am going to tell you. For the moment, go drink, eat, and rest, for you must be hungry and tired after so long a journey. Tomorrow morning we shall see."

The next day when he awoke, Jean went to find the king, who took him to his granary.

"You shall have three tasks to perform before taking my daughter away. Here is the first: my granary is filled with seeds of all varieties, which must be sorted and separated into different heaps between sunrise and sunset."

"If that's the kind of jobs you have for me, it won't be difficult to obtain your daughter," said Jean.

"We shall see, my boy; we shall see," said the king, who withdrew laughing.

Jean lay down at once on a heap of grain to take a nap, and when it struck noon, the maid who was bringing his meal had to wake him up.

"If you work like that, you will soon be punished," she told him.

Jean told her to be quiet, ate heartily, and then lay down on his back to resume his nap. The sun was just going to go down when he awoke.

"Aha," he said, "it's time to do something if I don't want to ruin this business."

And, taking the foot of the king of the ants in his hand, he said:

"King of the Ants! Come to my help with all your ants, and separate all of these seeds, putting each kind in a different pile."

The ants arrived at once from everywhere and began to separate the seeds quicker than I can tell you. There was one who came for a moment to look at Jean in anger, because it hadn't been able to find a single grain to carry, for the other ants had done all of the work.

King Fortunatus came at sunset, and seeing the work ended, he scratched his head, though he didn't have any itch.

"This work was just plain fun," said Jean.

"You'll have more tomorrow," said the king.

The next morning he took Jean to the edge of a pond

King Fortunatus's Golden Wig

that was as big as a sea and gave him a shell with a hole in it.

"You must remove all the water in this pond with this shell, and you must put all of the fish that are large enough to eat in one basin, and the little fish in another basin."

"It won't be difficult," said Jean, "and I still expect to win your daughter."

"We shall see, my boy; we shall see," said the king, and Jean looked at the shell for a moment.

"That's just the tool for such a job, but from now till sunset there's time for me to have a nap."

When the servant brought him his meal at noon, she had to wake him up.

"This is a strange man," she said. "All he does is sleep, and still he finds a way of doing his work."

Jean ate, lay down again, continued his nap, and woke up about an hour before sunset.

"It's time for me to do something."

And, taking the goose feather in his hand, he said:

"King of the Geese! Come to my aid with all your geese to empty this pond, to put in one basin the fish that are big enough to eat, and in another those that are too small."

And in an instant the geese blackened the sky, each taking a beakful of water or a fish, and they soon finished the work.

King Fortunatus arrived at sunset, and seeing that the job was completed, he scratched his head and his chin, though neither itched.

"This work was child's play," said Jean.

"You'll have more tomorrow, my boy; you'll have more," said the king, who within himself was beginning to worry.

The next day he took Jean into a vast forest and gave him some wooden tools: a shovel, a saw, and an ax.

"With these instruments," he said, "you must cut down this forest, cut, split, and cord the logs, and cut the rest into fagots before night."

"Nothing is simpler," said Jean. "I'm sure now that I shall have your daughter."

"We shall see, my boy; we shall see."

As soon as the king had departed, Jean took the tools and, striking them against a tree, broke them to bits.

"Now I can go to sleep," he said. "What a stupid king, to think that I am going to break my back doing this work for him!"

And he slept as he had the day before.

When he saw that the sun was low: "It's time to go to it," he said.

Taking the lion's hair from his pocket, "King of the Lions," he said, "come to my help with all of your animals to cut down, split, and cord all these trees, and to bundle the rest as fagots."

An instant afterward, the king of the lions came to Jean.

"That's all? It's already done, and well done."

King Fortunatus arrived as the sun was going down. He scratched his head an instant, and then his nose and his chin, and declared: "Decidedly you are a master, my boy! You have earned my daughter and you may take her away."

That evening Jean, all happy at having fulfilled the tests, ate like two, drank like six, and then slept like a barrel.

The next day the daughter of King Fortunatus came to find him before their departure, and said to him: "I must go with you since you have earned me, but before your master marries me I shall give him something to worry about and impose on him some very difficult tasks, and upon his men too."

And when the boats had set out in the direction of Brittany, she began to cry, saying:

King Fortunatus's Golden Wig

"Farewell, my father! Farewell, people of my country! Farewell, my lovely castle, which is suspended with four golden chains and supported by four lions. What use henceforth the golden keys that closed you up?"

And, saying these words, she threw the keys into the sea.

The boats arrived shortly in Brittany, and when the king saw the beautiful princess he was ravished and he immediately made a proposal of marriage.

"I think that before marrying me you will find time long. I don't want to be your wife if I don't have here my lovely castle that's suspended from four golden chains and supported by four lions."

"But how do you expect me to bring your castle here?"

"He who came to get me can go to get my castle."

The king summoned Jean.

"Jean, here's another job; you must go get King Fortunatus's daughter's golden castle for me."

"But how can I do such a thing?"

"You must go! If not, you will die in three days. That's all I have to say."

Jean, his head hanging, went to find his horse and told him about his mission.

"Ah, that golden wig!" said the horse. "Didn't I advise you to leave it alone? For it is from there that all of your trouble comes. But what's done is done, and I still want to help you."

They departed the next day, and when they were near King Fortunatus's city the horse told Jean to take the hair in hand and call the king of the lions.

The beasts arrived with their king, who asked what was to be done.

"Kill the four lions that carry the golden castle attached by the four chains, and attach the four chains to my ship," replied Jean.

It was quickly done. Jean towed the castle behind his

vessel. On his arrival he tied it solidly to the shore and went to notify the king. The king couldn't believe his eyes and notified the princess, who was no less surprised.

"There is no longer anything to stand in the way of our marriage," the king told her.

"What do you expect me to do with a castle for which I no longer have the keys?" asked the princess. "I threw them in the depths of the sea, I don't know where, when Jean was bringing me back. Go get them for me."

"I've never seen such an obstinate girl," thought the king, who was careful not to say so aloud. "But I must marry her and Jean's the only one who can get me out of difficulties."

This time Jean was angry, but the king wouldn't listen to him.

"Bring me back the keys in three days or I shall have your skin."

Jean went back to his horse.

"Oh, the evil golden wig! You see where it has brought us? But I will try to help you one more time."

The next day they set out again on the high seas, and the horse said to Jean:

"Load all the cannon aboard and have them shoot from both sides without stopping until the king of the fish comes to ask what you want."

Jean had the cannon fired so that the earth, the sky, and the sea trembled. The king of the fish appeared:

"Well, Jean, what harm have we done to you for you to disturb us as you're doing?"

"I'll leave you in peace," said Jean, "if you can bring me back the golden keys that King Fortunatus's daughter let fall into the sea."

"I'll go and look," said the king of the fish, "I'll go and look."

And he convoked his subjects, who assembled around

King Fortunatus's Golden Wig

him in vast numbers. Not one had seen the keys, but the sand eel was not among them.

"Where can this dallier be?" asked the king. "He never arrives with the others."

"He's coming," said a fish. "His body is so long that it looks as if he were dragging a whole cliff behind him."

He appeared at last, dragging something.

"Why do you come so late?" the king asked him.

"Well, I'm just building my dwelling. I was looking for materials and look at the strange thing I have found!"

The king of the fish looked. It was the famous keys. He brought them at once to Jean, who thanked him sincerely.

When the King of Brittany received the keys he was at the height of joy.

"Jean, you have always got me out of trouble. What do you want as a reward?"

"That you leave me in peace at home, for I'm tired of chasing the high seas looking for impossible things."

"I want to give you a handsome reward."

The king brought the princess's golden keys.

"This time there's nothing to prevent our marriage."

"That is to say, there's only one thing left that I need before becoming your wife: that Jean be burned alive on the city square."

"The devil!" said the king. "You know he has rendered me many services!"

"That's too bad," said the princess. "If you want to marry me you must consent to execute him."

"Since I must, I must," said the king. "No man will prevent me from having you as a bride."

And he had Jean come to see him.

"It's to receive my reward," Jean said to himself.

He went to the king with his head high, but he came back with his head low. He was to prepare to be burned alive in two days.

(83)

"That's the way kings are," he said. "Is it worth risking death to oblige people of that sort? Have they got stones inside of them instead of a heart?"

Jean went back to his horse to tell him of the king's decision.

"It's all because of the golden wig," said the horse. "You insisted on bringing it back; from it all your trouble comes. But what's done is done. I want to help you again. But it will be the last time, for thereafter you will no longer need me. But we must act quickly. Go back to your stable. Find, as fast as you can, a bottle, a curry comb, and a brush, and come back to me."

Jean went and came back running toward his dear horse, who said to him:

"Curry me well; brush me well. Collect carefully all the dust that falls from my skin and put it in the bottle."

When Jean had done what the horse had told him, the bottle was far from full.

"Pour water in to finish filling it up," said the horse. "Now go find the king and tell him that you want to dig your hole in the pyre that has been set up to burn you. When you are in that hole, wash your entire body with water from the bottle and also wash the shirt they put on you to burn you in. Then you can tell the king to start the fire whenever he wants to."

Point by point Jean followed the instructions of the horse, and when he told the king to light the fire, the flames hastened so rapidly over the wood that the pyre was consumed in less time than I take to tell it.

And just as everybody had grown sad concerning poor Jean's death, out he jumped from the ashes and appeared more handsome than he had ever been! Everybody in attendance was astonished.

The princess felt overcome with love for Jean and said to the king: "If you were as handsome as this fellow I should be happy to marry you."

King Fortunatus's Golden Wig

"If I did as Jean," said the king, "wouldn't I also become as handsome as he?"

"I certainly think so," said the princess.

The king had a new pyre built and installed himself in a hole as Jean had done. The fire was lighted, and in an instant the king was burned; flesh, skin, bones, and all the rest were reduced to cinders, and somewhat less than nothing remained of him.

And that's how they made a handsome king of him.

Then the princess said to Jean: "You're the one who has had all the trouble. You are the one who deserves to be king and I shall be queen."

And the marriage was celebrated without delay. Ah, my friends, what a wedding! Never has there been such a wedding. Hogs ran in the streets, roasted alive with mustard under their tails, a fork and a knife planted in their hams. Anybody who wanted could cut pieces off. I was busy in the kitchen drawing wine. I drank so much that it went to my head. I wanted, no matter what, to kiss the cook, but she called her husband. The man got angry and threw me out, giving me a great kick in the seat of the trousers, and I landed here to tell you this story.

9

FATHER ROQUELAURE

There was once a queen who lived a widow with an only son, the Prince Emilien. When he was old enough to be married his mother said to him:

"My son, I am old and haven't much more time to be with you. So that you can reign suitably, you should marry a girl of your own rank. You need but choose one of the princesses of the neighboring kingdoms. I'm sure that none of them will refuse you."

"Mother," replied the prince, "I am very happy with you, and I've got time enough to think about marriage, so don't talk to me about it now; it's useless."

The queen came back to the subject every day. She took so much to heart this desire of seeing her son married, and the son's refusals were so persistent, that she fell sick and died.

The young man mourned the loss of his mother greatly. He began to govern his kingdom, but without any thought of getting married. One day he was passing in front of the home of a painter who had just established himself in the capital. His eyes fell upon a portrait exposed in the window. It was that of a marvelously beautiful girl. He looked at it with an emotion that he had never felt before and he ended by going into the house.

"Where does that portrait come from?" he asked the painter.

"Your Majesty, it is of the Princess Emilienne."

"Where does she live?"

Father Roquelaure

"Far from here in an almost inaccessible country. The princess is shut up day and night in a massive golden castle, guarded by a fairy who has the face of a demon and who keeps watch over her at the gates of the castle among ferocious animals that are all sorcerers."

"What road does one take to get to this castle?"

"I don't know. Those who have been to it have only been able to do so on the order or by permission of the fairy, and she has been careful not to reveal to them the route by which they arrived."

The prince went sadly back to his palace. He lost his sleep and appetite, having only one thought, one desire, one ambition: to discover the mysterious castle and marry the beautiful princess.

Among his servants there was one by the name of Jean whom he liked a great deal and whom he took into his confidence because of numerous proofs of devotion he had received from him.

"Jean," he said one day, "I am very unhappy and I feel that I shall shortly die if, with your help, I am not soon satisfied."

"What's it all about, Your Excellency?" asked the faithful Jean.

The prince revealed everything to him: his love for the Princess Emilienne, his desire to marry her, his determination to go out into the world in search of her despite all difficulties.

"You know, Your Excellency, that I am yours in life and in death. I will follow you wherever you go."

"Well, Jean, my decision is irrevocable. Keep the secret and make all the necessary preparations so that we may leave as soon as possible."

Jean had a great cart built, carpeted and covered with skin. On a dark night he hitched to it the two strongest horses in the stable. He put weapons in it and provisions for traveling, and the two companions left in search of adventure without making more noise than escaping thieves.

They set out on a road that went through an immense forest. The heavy carriage had already been rolling for a long time in the ruts when the horses stopped to get their breath. It was agreed that the prince and Jean would take turns keeping watch; the prince was sleeping, and the servant, seated in the motionless cart, was sadly thinking of the difficulties of such a trip. All of a sudden he heard somewhat far-off the noise of voices, some thirty people speaking at the same time:

"What's new, Father Roquelaure?" they were saying.

"And you, my children?" replied a heavy voice that resounded in the midst of the others like the largest bell of the church above the bells of our cows.

"Nothing, nothing, Father Roquelaure."

"Well, I know something."

"Tell it, Father Roquelaure."

"The Prince Emilien has fallen in love with the Princess Emilienne and he has just departed to go in search of her."

"Will he find her, Father Roquelaure?"

"Not easily, my children. Imagine, tomorrow he will arrive on the banks of the river, and there's no bridge!"

"What will he do, Father Roquelaure?"

"All he will have to do is rub the hubs of his wheels with moss from an oak tree. At once a bridge will be formed, permit him to cross over, and immediately disappear. He will be able to go on his way toward the princess, for he is on the right road."

"And will he find her, Father Roquelaure?"

"Not easily, my children."

"Why, Father Roquelaure?"

"The princess is guarded by a fairy who commands a hundred sorcerers disguised as ferocious animals. The only recourse that he will have will be to win the fairy over by offering her a distaff wrapped with a string of diamonds,

Father Roquelaure

and then pour a sleeping-potion into her glass. During her sleep he will carry the princess away."

"And will he succeed, Father Roquelaure?"

"Not easily, my children, for the fairy will wake up, and, angry at having been deceived, she will send all her sorcerers out after the kidnapper. And these sorcerers will take diverse forms. They will use all possible deceits. Thus the horses of the prince will refuse to go on, and immediately there will appear on the road carriages of all kinds whose coachmen will invite the prince and the princess to mount. It will be necessary to dash upon these coachmen, kill them, and break up their carriages. Then the princess will be overcome with thirst and she'll have to endure a real torture; she will ask for drink and there will be near her vendors of refreshing drinks, but she mustn't drink. It will be necessary to dash upon them, scatter on the earth their beverages, which are poison, then flee as rapidly as possible. A little farther on, the prince will arrive at the edge of a pond. There he'll see a man struggling and crying for help, and his first impulse will be to go to the help of the drowning man, but instead of taking him from the water he must take a pole and push him back to the bottom of the pond."

"Why, Father Roquelaure?"

"My children, all these things will be artifices invented by the fairy to overcome the prince and to repossess the princess. If they escape these dangers they will arrive at the edge of the river. The prince will merely have to rub moss from an oak tree on the wheel of the carriage for the bridge to reappear and he will be able to cross."

"Will he get the princess this time, Father Roquelaure?"

"Yes, my children, he will have her if he does what I have just said. But you know that the secret of my words must be kept:

> *He who makes this secret known*
> *Shall become a marble stone!"*

Silence was restored in the forest and Jean pressed the horses on. He had heard all, understood all; grieved that he couldn't confide it to his master, he was happy thinking that he was sure of the outcome of this perilous enterprise, and he took steps to act according to the words of Father Roquelaure.

At daybreak the travelers came out of the forest. In front of them stretched a vast plain, but the river separated them from it. Jean took the moss he had gathered, and scarcely had he rubbed the wheels of the carriage than a bridge was formed on the water inviting them to cross. They crossed without difficulty and continued on their way. The prince, wholly given over to reveries and to lovers' worries, did nothing, leaving everything up to his servant.

After long hours of travel they saw sparkling beneath the setting sun a castle that was all of gold.

"Prince," said Jean, "I think that we are reaching our goal."

"No matter what the perils that await me," said the prince, "I want to present myself without delay and without fear to the princess."

"Leave it to me, prince."

And as they arrived in front of the door of the castle where the fairy, speaking to her animals, seemed ready to have them devoured, Jean took a beautiful distaff of gold wrapped with diamonds which he had procured upon the advice of Father Roquelaure, and, approaching the fairy:

"Madame," he said, "here is a little present that the king, my master, with whom I am traveling, asks me to offer you."

The old fairy was delighted with so brilliant a gift. She appeased the animals, who stood back to let the prince and his servant pass, and she introduced the strangers into the hall where the princess was. She was a hundred times more beautiful than her portrait. The prince was delighted

Father Roquelaure

with her and she seemed sensitive to his attentions. A magnificent meal was served; at dessert Jean found a way to pour the sleeping-potion into the fairy's glass. After dinner the prince and Jean were taken to their apartments.

"Well, my prince," said Jean, "what do you intend to do?"

"I don't know. And you? Have you a plan?"

"Yes. I hope that we shall succeed. In an hour everybody in the castle will be asleep. I'll harness the horses, to whom I have given good rations of oats. Meanwhile, prince, you must get the princess. She asks nothing better, I am sure, than to leave this castle, which is a prison for her."

Thus things happened: at the stroke of midnight the princess and the prince were getting into the carriage and Jean was urging the horses forward at full speed. They galloped for some time, and then all of a sudden the horses stopped, and neither shouts nor whip could detach their feet from the ground, where they seemed to have taken root. The prince lost patience; the princess cried; Jean alone kept his composure.

"Prince," shouted the Princess Emilienne, "here are some empty carriages and coachmen offering their services."

As a matter of fact there were several beautiful carriages with fractious horses attached, and the coachmen politely offering the travelers to take them wherever they wanted to go.

"Let's get out, princess," said the king. "We'll get in one of these carriages."

But at the same moment Jean took a weapon in hand, dashed upon the coachmen, and killed them one after another and shattered their carriages. Then he got back in his cart, and his horses set out.

"Why did he kill these men who offered us their services?" asked the princess.

"I don't understand," replied the prince.

The sun had come up and the heat was already great.

"How thirsty I am!" said the princess. "Haven't you anything that I can drink?"

"Nothing, but it won't be long before we reach some spring."

"I shan't be able to wait until then. This thirst is consuming me. I'm stifling!"

"Who wants something to drink! Who wants something to drink! Good fresh beverages!" cried a voice near the cart.

"Here's some spring water! Who wants to drink? Who wants to drink?"

There had appeared around the carriage ten or more men who were thus offering their remedies for thirst. You would have thought that they had come up out of the ground.

"Stop!" said the princess to Jean, "and bring me something to drink."

Jean stopped, but only to jump down from the carriage, hurl himself on the beverage-vendors, and kill them

Father Roquelaure

without pity, tipping over their pitchers full of beverages.

"What are you doing?" cried the princess, indignant. "Give me something to drink. That man has taken it upon himself to displease me," she said to the prince, who, stupefied at Jean's conduct, remained without an answer.

But the princess's thirst had calmed. The carriage was rolling peacefully until it came to a stop near a pond, from which cries of distress were coming.

"Do you hear those cries?" asked the princess.

"Ah, it's a man who's drowning," said Prince Emilien. "I am going to help him."

Jean had already found a long pole and was running toward the drowning man.

"Good, Jean. Extend the stick to him. He's taking it; he's got it. Pull him out!"

Instead of pulling, Jean pushed the drowning man back with all his strength so that he was soon quiet and disappeared into the water.

"Prince, you've got an evil servant there," said the princess.

"I think he's gone mad. I've always found him good and devoted and I admit that I can't explain his conduct today."

Jean had followed unperturbed the advice of Father Roquelaure. When the cart arrived near the river, he began to rub the wheels with oak moss, and the bridge was formed at once to let the carriage pass over, to the great astonishment of the Princess Emilienne.

"Who is this fellow," she thought, "who has such a sorcerer in his service?" She said: "Your Jean frightens me. If you love me as you say, promise me to imprison him for the rest of his days upon our arrival."

The prince was so surprised at Jean's conduct and so captivated with the princess that he promised her anything she wished.

The very next day they arrived at the king's capital. What astonishment to see him come back with this princess of such rare beauty! His disappearance had afflicted the whole populace; they thought him dead and they were in mourning for him. But they got a lovely revenge on the occasion of his marriage. Never anywhere was there such enjoyment! There was a slaughter of beef, of pork, of mutton. They emptied all the wine barrels and they danced night and day for a week.

Meanwhile the king didn't forget the promise that he had made concerning Jean, and he spoke to him in a severe tone:

"Jean, the moment has come to explain your conduct during our trip. You killed several men against my wishes and the queen's. I hope that you will justify yourself and that you will also tell me by what means you were able to throw a bridge across the river which permitted us to cross over."

"Your Excellency, I have nothing to say. I gave my all to obey you, to satisfy you, to obtain the result that you desired. You're happy and I am happy. That's all I have to say."

"Your words, Jean, are not sufficient to justify you. In the name of the good services that you have rendered me, in the name of the devotion that you have often shown me, tell me why you acted in a way so contrary to your custom, like a murderer and a madman."

"Prince, I have nothing further to say."

"Well, then, since you defy me you will be punished. Not only do I withdraw my confidence, but tomorrow you will be thrown into a dungeon."

The unhappy Jean didn't know what to do. Must he keep silence? This meant to incur the disgrace and the punishment that his master was preparing for him. Speak? But he still had in his ears the threat of Father Roquelaure. His affection for the prince, fear of displeas-

Father Roquelaure

ing him, made him decide to tell what he had heard in the forest; he revealed all, even the last words of Father Roquelaure. The prince, moved to tears, ran forward to embrace his faithful servant, but he saw nothing in front of him save a marble statue.

He cursed his curiosity, his defiance, his ingratitude. I think that he would never have been consoled save for the love that his wife showered upon him. Before the end of the year they had a baby, a boy, whom the king wanted to name Jean in memory of his good servant. The day of the baptism he held a great festival and invited all the princes of the area, all the noblemen of his court, and at the moment of sitting down to table they noticed in the corner of the room an old woman covered with rags who was hiding behind the furniture.

"Who are you, and what have you come to do here?" the prince asked her.

"I haven't come to do ill," replied the old woman. "Don't chase me away. Don't mistreat me and you will not be sorry."

"At the occasion of my son's baptism I don't want anyone here to be unhappy. Let this woman be served food and drink. She is one more guest."

"Sire, what would you say if I gave you the means of having still another—the absent one about whom you are thinking at this moment?"

"Jean?" murmured the king.

"Yes. If you want, you may see him take the place here to which he has so much right."

"It is to him that I owe my happiness. I should give everything, anything in the world, to restore his life."

"Well, if you are speaking sincerely, kill your son and rub his blood on the feet of the marble statue. At once Jean will be restored to you."

The prince turned pale as death. Kill his son! And yet to whom did he owe this child if not to this servant, so unjustly punished? He ran to the baby's cradle, plunged his dagger in its breast as he turned his eyes aside; then, gathering the blood in his open hand, he went and rubbed the feet of the statue. At that very instant Jean dashed into his arms, while the old woman arrived near them carrying the poor massacred child.

"Sire, you have acted in all justice. May you be rewarded. Here is your son."

And taking a wand from beneath her poor gown, she touched the child with it, and it opened its eyes once more smiling, while *she* was transformed into a beautiful lady dressed in silk, resplendent with gold and diamonds. The queen, who had been present without understanding anything that had transpired and who was as if paralyzed at these scenes, recognized the fairy who had guided her into the castle, and she threw herself at her feet.

"Forgive me for having fled, you who were always so good to me!"

The fairy raised her up and kissed her. "What has happened had to happen. Now be happy."

And so they were.

10

THE LOST CHILDREN

Long ago there were in the village of Gargeac a married man and woman whose names were Jacques and Toinon. Both of them were very miserly, especially the woman; she was so very miserly that she would shave an egg.

They had two children, a boy and a girl, who suffered a great deal because of the avarice of their parents; but they were so good and loved one another so much that no one ever heard them complain. The boy was twelve; his name was Jean, and the little girl, a bit younger than he, was called Jeannette.

Jacques and Toinon found that their children caused them a good deal of expense and they resolved to lose them in the forest.

The mother said to her husband: "I'll take them into the middle of the wood and order them to gather dead branches; when they are very busy, I'll leave them alone, and we'll be rid of them, for the wolves will eat them when night comes."

The next day at dawn the woman told Jean and Jeannette to get up; she took them into the forest and told them to gather dry branches, and when she saw that they were busy she ran away. When Jean and Jeannette noticed that they were alone, they began to call their mother, but when she didn't answer they began to cry, and then they tried to find their way, but they couldn't succeed in getting out of the forest.

Jeannette said to her brother:

"Jean, climb high up in a tree and perhaps you'll see a house."

Jean climbed into a tree, and when he had got halfway up his sister shouted:

"Can't you see anything, little brother?"

"No, sister, I see nothing but the branches of the forest."

"Go up higher and perhaps you'll see a house."

And Jean climbed up a few branches higher.

"Can't you see anything?"

"No, little sister, I see only the green branches of the forest."

"Go up higher and probably you'll see a house."

Jean went up still higher and he stopped on the top branch.

"Can't you see anything?"

"Yes, sister; I see two houses far away, one white and the other red. Which one shall we go to?"

"To the red house," replied Jeannette, "because it's prettier."

Jean came down from the tree, and the two children went toward the red house. They knocked at the door, and a big woman as strong as a man came and opened to them.

"Who are you?" she said to them.

"Little children lost in the forest, and we are afraid of the wolves."

"Come in," she said to them. "I'll put you to bed, but be sure not to make any noise, because my husband is mean and he will eat you."

She hid them as best she could, but the Devil, who was the woman's husband, smelled the odor of Christians, and he found them and beat his wife because she had not told him that she had taken in two children. He took Jean in his hand and, seeing that he was a bit thin, he de-

The Lost Children

cided that they would fatten him up and kill him when he had put on enough weight.

He shut him up in a little barn, and his sister, who had become the little servant of the household, brought her brother food to eat. The Devil was too fat to get into the barn where Jean was shut up; at the end of a few days he ordered Jeannette to cut the end off of Jean's little finger and to bring it to him to see if he was fat enough to be eaten. Jeannette caught a rat, cut off its tail, and brought

the end of it to the Devil, telling him that it was her brother's finger.

"Ah," said the Devil, "he's still too thin."

Some time afterward he ordered another piece of Jean's finger cut off to find out if he was fat enough or not. Jeannette presented him with another piece from the rat's tail and this time he found it still too thin. A third time the Devil asked for a piece of Jean's finger; Jeannette brought him still another piece from the rat's tail, but the Devil noticed that he was being deceived, and he put his hand in the barn and pulled Jean out and found him fat enough to be eaten. He made a sawhorse to lay him on in order to bleed him, and then he went to take a walk, after telling his wife to watch over Jean and especially over Jeannette, whom he mistrusted. The Devil's wife got drunk and started to get sleepy; Jeannette went to open the door of the barn for the little pigs. She had Jean come out and pretended not to understand how he was to be put on the sawhorse.

"Are you stupid!" said the Devil's wife. "Here's how you do it." And she got on the sawhorse. Jean tied her on it and cut her throat. Then they took the Devil's gold and silver and fled with his horse and carriage.

When the Devil came back he found his wife tied to the sawhorse, her head cut off beside her. He went to the little pigs' barn and found neither Jean nor Jeannette, nor his horse or carriage, and he set out in search of the two children.

On the way, after a while, he met a laborer, to whom he said:

"Did you see Jean and Jeannette depart
Riding in my cart,
With my bay horse and my white,
Spangled silver-bright?"

"What did you say, sir? That I'm not doing my work right?"

"No, stupid ass.

Did you see Jean and Jeannette depart
Riding in my cart,
With my bay horse and my white,
Spangled silver-bright?"

"No, sir."

A bit farther on, the Devil met a shepherd who was taking care of his sheep.

The Lost Children

> *"Did you see Jean and Jeannette depart*
> *Riding in my cart,*
> *With my bay horse and my white,*
> *Spangled silver-bright?"*

"You say that my dog doesn't bark? Well, bark, Labri, bark!"

The dog began to bark at the Devil as if he were going to bite him.

"Stupid animal!" said the Devil. "I'm not talking about your dog.

> *Did you see Jean and Jeannette depart*
> *Riding in my cart,*
> *With my bay horse and my white,*
> *Spangled silver-bright?"*

"No, sir."

The Devil came to a village at the moment when the beadle had just rung the Angelus:

> *"Did you see Jean and Jeannette depart*
> *Riding in my cart,*
> *With my bay horse and my white,*
> *Spangled silver-bright?"*

"What'd you say, sir? That I haven't rung the bells right?"

The beadle went back into the church and began to ring the bells as loud as he could.

"Imbecile!" said the Devil. "Who said anything about your bells?

> *Did you see Jean and Jeannette depart*
> *Riding in my cart,*
> *With my bay horse and my white,*
> *Spangled silver-bright?"*

"No, sir."

The Devil went still farther and arrived at the edge of a river where women were doing their laundry.

"Did you see Jean and Jeannette depart
Riding in my cart,
With my bay horse and my white,
Spangled silver-bright?"

"What'd you say?" asked one of the laundry women. "That I'm not washing my clothes as I should?"

And she began to wash the clothes on the stone with all her might.

"No, stupid washerwoman! I asked you:

Did you see Jean and Jeannette depart
Riding in my cart,
With my bay horse and my white,
Spangled silver-bright?"

"Yes, sir," said the woman. "We did see a handsome man and a beautiful girl with a lovely carriage and two horses."

"Which direction?"

"Over the river."

But there wasn't a bridge, and the Devil was miserable not to be able to cross it.

One of the laundry women said to the others: "We're dealing with the Devil. We must play a good trick on him."

She proposed to him that he let her cut his hair to make a bridge with it to cross the river. The Devil let her do it, and the hair was stretched out to form a bridge, but when he was in the middle of the river they let the hair fall and the Devil went splash! into the water and drowned.

The laundry women went to tell Jean and Jeannette, who had gone back to their parents, that the Devil had drowned. Jean and Jeannette made their parents rich, and everybody was happy. One must be good to one's parents even when they are evil.

Night came, the cocks sang, and so the story ends.

11

THE GODCHILD OF THE FAIRY IN THE TOWER

There was once a woman who found that she was with child. She had a desire to eat cabbage, but she couldn't find any save in the garden of a fairy, whom she didn't dare ask to give her some. She went and took some during the night. The next day the fairy saw that some cabbage heads were lacking. She grew angry and said that if she could catch the people who had stolen her cabbages she would make them pay dearly. The woman didn't go back the next night, and the day after, when the fairy went into her garden to visit her cabbages, she saw that no more heads had disappeared. But as the woman had by then finished eating those she had already stolen, she went back on the third night. The fairy thought nothing more of the cabbages, but in the morning when she was taking her walk she saw that a great many more heads were lacking and she got so angry that she said she wanted to catch the thieves at any cost.

She had bells tied to all of the cabbage heads. When the woman went back a third time, at the first head that she cut, the fairy heard the ringing of the bell, then at the second, and then at the third. The woman was in the act of cutting the third head when the fairy arrived in a furor.

"What! You're the one who is stealing my cabbages every night! You'll pay dearly for them!"

The woman began to cry and begged her pardon; she said that she was with child, that she had been overcome with a desire to eat cabbage, and that she had taken the liberty to go into the fairy's garden to cut them. The fairy told her that she would have done better to ask for them. The woman replied that she didn't dare, that she deserved her pardon, and that she wouldn't do it any more.

"I pardon you," the fairy told her, "but on condition that you will make me godmother of the child that you are carrying, and you may come and get cabbages as much as you please."

The woman quickly promised. When she went home she told her husband what had happened. Soon she gave birth to a daughter. At once the father went to notify the fairy, who came to act as godmother. When everybody was seated at the table, the fairy declared before beginning to eat:

"I want to make my godchild a gift. I wish that she may have golden hair and that she may be the most beautiful girl in the world."

But she added that as soon as her godchild had grown up she would take her into her household to have her educated; and as soon as the girl was old enough, she came to get her. The father and the mother were very much tormented to see their daughter depart, but there was nothing they could say. She was taken away into the fairy castle and told that she would be very happy if she behaved as she should. The godchild promised that she would be obedient. The fairy showed her the work that she would have to do in the castle, during the absence of her godmother, and gave her a little bitch dog to keep her company.

"Tomorrow I shall leave," she said. "Close all the doors tight. When I return I will call you thus: 'Godchild, give

The Godchild of the Fairy in the Tower

me your golden hair,' and with your hair you will pull me up through the window."

The girl promised to obey and the first days passed as they should.

The godmother came back from her trip; from far off she cried: "Godchild, give me your golden hair."

The daughter came to her window and let down her hair to pull her up.

"Have you been good?" said the fairy.

"Oh, yes, godmother. See how I have waxed all the floors and cleaned all the furniture."

"That's good, godchild. Tomorrow I shall go on a trip once more and I shall be absent for some time."

The godmother departed, but this time the trip lasted for two weeks and the daughter became bored. She spent hours at the window watching for the arrival of her godmother, and when a carriage came she thought that it was her godmother, and the passers-by admired the beautiful girl with the golden hair.

A prince chanced to pass by and saw her. He was charmed, stopped his horses to see her better, but didn't dare to speak to her. Meanwhile the godmother arrived.

"Godchild, give me your golden hair."

"At once, godmother."

The fairy asked her, as usual, if she had been good, and departed for several days once more. The prince, who had seen how she got into the castle, came back the next day, saw the beauty with the golden hair at her window, talked with her a little. He departed promising to return. She found the rest of the day and the night quite long while she waited for her prince. He came back early, and she pulled him up into her chamber through the window with her golden hair.

The godmother didn't stay away on her journey as long as before, and she arrived just as the prince was departing.

As soon as she was inside the castle the little bitch dog began to say: "Your godchild made love with the prince."

"What is that little dog saying?" asked the fairy.

"Godmother, she says that I have worked well and that I have cleaned the rooms carefully."

"Good, godchild. That's all."

The next day the fairy departed once more, but for only two days. As soon as she had come back the little dog said to her:

"Godmother, your godchild spoke for a long time to the prince."

"What's that little dog telling me now?"

"Godmother," she said, "she says that I have worked well and that I have set everything in order."

"Good, godchild. Tomorrow I'm leaving again and I don't know when I shall be back."

She left and immediately the prince arrived, but the

The Godchild of the Fairy in the Tower

fairy was suspicious. She came back the same day and the prince was still there when she called:

"Godchild, godchild, give me your golden hair!"

The godchild was much upset. She had the prince hide behind the bed, and as soon as the fairy had come inside, the little dog told her:

"Godmother, the prince is behind the bed."

"What is that little dog saying?"

"She says that I waxed the floors carefully under the beds."

The godmother didn't let on that she had understood. She went immediately into another room, and the prince left at once. The fairy didn't depart again until the next day, and the prince came back immediately and took the girl of the golden hair away.

When the fairy arrived, in vain she cried: "Godchild, give me your golden hair."

Nobody came, but the little dog called to her:

"Godmother, your godchild has departed with the prince."

Then the fairy got in her carriage and set out in pursuit of the fugitives. When she perceived the prince's carriage she began to shout:

"Godchild, may you turn into a frog and may your prince have a pig's snout."

The wish was no sooner expressed than the beauty with the golden hair turned into a frog, which jumped from the carriage, and the prince grew a pig's snout.

12

PETIT JEAN AND THE FROG

THERE WAS ONCE a king and a queen who were getting old and who had no children, which disturbed them a great deal for they feared that their crown might fall to a stranger. Finally, because they had gone on a pilgrimage, their wishes were rewarded and they had a pretty little girl. The king would have preferred a boy to be his successor, but he had to be content with a daughter.

On the day of baptism, to give more splendor to the ceremony, the king and the queen invited the fairies of the vicinity. They came, seven in number, two of them serving as godmother and godfather.

After the baptism the king offered the fairies a great banquet, for which he had made seven golden plates, one for each of them. But a very old fairy appeared, one whom they had forgotten to invite. They could give her only a silver plate, and this didn't please her.

The moment for wishes having come, each of the fairies that had been invited approached the cradle to give the young princess a gift.

The first said: "I wish that she may be the loveliest queen of all."

The second: "I wish that she may be the best singer that has ever been heard."

The third: "I wish that she may be the best dancer that has ever been seen."

Petit Jean and the Frog

The fourth: "I wish that she may have a great deal of wit."

The fifth: "I wish that she may live to a ripe old age."

The sixth: "I wish that she may always be goodhearted."

The seventh: "I wish that she may enjoy good health throughout life."

The only one left was the old fairy who had arrived last. The others begged her to make a wish too. She approached, shaking her head.

"Well, I wish that she may turn into a frog and jump into the cesspool."

At once the little princess was transformed into a frog and she jumped into the cesspool and began to paddle about, going: "Croak, croak, croak, croak!"

The king and queen and all of the fairies begged the old fairy to change the gift she had wished upon the poor little princess.

"Well," she said, "I wish that she may jump into the most beautiful of all ponds and that she be wedded to the most handsome of princes."

At once the frog disappeared, to the great sorrow of the group, and the king and the queen and the fairies took leave of each other, all of them greatly saddened over the loss of the princess.

In a neighboring kingdom there was a king and a queen who were very old and who had three sons. The oldest was called Petit Jean. One day when he was walking in the fields with his father he passed a group of men who were mowing near a pond, and he heard something going "Croak, croak, croak" in the water.

"Tell me, my good men," he asked the mowers, "what is it that I hear in that pond?"

"Oh, Your Excellency, it's a frog."

"Well," he said, turning toward the pond:

*"Frog of Froggyland,
Jump upon my back
And you shall be my wife."*

Immediately the frog jumped on the prince's back and he took her away to his chamber. He put her beside the fire in a basin full of water and he was careful to change the water each day. And, looking at his frog, he would say:

"I have chosen a beautiful woman who will not make me envious and whom no one will search to take from me."

The king, his father, was growing old, and he was thinking of ceding the crown to one of his sons; not wishing to show preference for any one of them, he summoned them one day and said to them:

"My children, I'm getting old and I don't know to which one of you I should give the crown, for I love you equally. Hence I have decided that the one who will bring me a piece of fabric long enough to be stretched seven times around my castle will receive the crown. Take recourse to your own devices and begin your quest."

Each of the princes set out in a different direction. Petit Jean, who was not ambitious, went back home saying to himself: "I don't even want to take the trouble to look. Let my brothers have the crown. It makes no difference to me."

Meanwhile, seated near the hearth with his head in his hands, he thought the whole thing over and decided that he was all the same the eldest and that he ought to succeed his father.

All of a sudden his frog, who was watching him dream, raised her head and said: "What's wrong, Petit Jean, my friend? What's the matter with you?"

Petit Jean straightened up, much surprised to hear his frog talk.

Petit Jean and the Frog

"Well," he said, "I didn't know frogs could talk. I'm delighted over it. This will be one more source of entertainment."

And the frog kept saying: "What's wrong, Petit Jean, my friend? What's wrong?"

"I will tell you anyway, even though you can do nothing about it."

"That depends, Petit Jean, my friend. That depends."

"Well, know that my father wants to give his crown to the one of the three of us who brings back a piece of fabric that will stretch seven times around his castle."

"Well, Petit Jean, my friend, we're going to try it. Wait for me; I'll come back in a moment."

The frog jumped from its basin and went hopping away, plop, plop, plop, plop.

Petit Jean, watching her, said: "Where in the deuce is she going? She'll get herself crushed for sure. So what? It will be a small loss. Yet I should have liked to keep her because she was good company."

Meanwhile the frog arrived at her godmother's, who lived not far from the prince's house. On entering she said in a very soft voice: "Hello, godmother."

"Hello, my godchild. What brings you here?"

"Well, godmother, I'll tell you. Imagine! My husband's father has promised his crown to the one of his children who brings back a piece of fabric that will reach seven times around his castle."

"Well, godchild, I will give you a silver box and you tell your husband to take it to his father and beg him to open it."

"Thank you, godmother. I'll hurry to carry this box to my husband."

The frog came back to her husband and told him:

"Here, Petit Jean, my friend, take this box. Give it to your father and beg him to open it."

"What do you want my father to do with a silver box? He's got thousands of them just like it."

"It doesn't make any difference, Petit Jean, my friend. It doesn't make any difference. Take it to him anyway and don't despair."

"Ha," said Petit Jean. "Since I care so little for the crown, I'll take it to him anyhow."

When Petit Jean arrived at his father's he found his two brothers, who had returned ahead of him. They were awaiting him to measure the fabrics.

On seeing him enter, his father said: "Well, Petit Jean, we were waiting for you. But where is your piece of cloth?"

"Oh, Father, I've got it in my pocket."

They all thought that he was joking, and they thought that he had left it in the courtyard. His brothers went down there with their fabric.

"All right," said the king. "We're going to begin with you, Petit Jean, since you're the eldest."

"Pardon me, Father, I prefer that my brothers be first."

So the youngest began by unrolling a beautiful piece. They measured it and its length equaled only twice around the castle, and that is as it should be. They measured the second. It reached three times around.

Then the father came back to Petit Jean. "But I don't see your fabric."

"I told you, Father, that it was in my pocket," said Petit Jean, presenting him his silver box. The king looked at it with astonishment.

"What do you want me to do with that box? You know that there is no lack of similar ones here."

"No matter, Father. Open it anyway."

"Well," said the king, "let's see what's inside."

He lifted the lid and found an egg, and he opened the egg and found a walnut; he opened the walnut and found

Petit Jean and the Frog

a little roll of cloth; and he seized it and pulled the cloth, which, as it came out, enlarged and lengthened, and he unrolled a piece more beautiful than any previously seen in the world. They measured it, and after it had reached seven times around the castle they could have still stretched it seven more.

So the king went back to his sons and told them: "You see, my children, it is Petit Jean who has won. But I have another test: the one who brings me back the most beautiful bird shall have the crown."

The three boys set out, but Petit Jean didn't need to go beyond his own house.

"I thought I was through," he said, "but I see that it's not so. A curse upon me if I bother myself! I don't care about the crown."

Having arrived back home, he sat thoughtfully before the fire, for at bottom he wanted to be king more than he was willing to admit.

The frog asked him: "What's the matter, Petit Jean, my friend? What's the matter?"

"What's the matter? It's that I thought I had won the crown, and it isn't so. Father promises it now to the one who will bring back the most beautiful bird."

"Well, Petit Jean, my friend, we're going to try. Wait for me."

And the frog departed, jumping, plop, plop, plop, plop. And she came to her godmother's house.

"Hello, godmother."

"Hello, my godchild. What brings you here?"

"Well, godmother, my husband's father has now promised the crown to the one of his sons who brings him back the loveliest bird."

"Take this, godchild," said the godmother, offering her a box. "Your husband will tell his father that he has nothing to give him but silver boxes. But his father must take the trouble to open this one, and he will see."

The frog took the box and thanked her godmother. "I shall tell my husband." And, plop, plop, plop, the frog came back home.

She said to her husband: "Take this little silver box, Petit Jean, my friend, and carry it to your father. Give it to him, and tell him that's all you have to offer, but that he should take the trouble to open it, and he will see."

Petit Jean took the box and went back to the castle, where he found his brothers.

After examining the birds of his two brothers, which were very beautiful, the king turned toward Petit Jean. "Now, where is your bird?"

"Father," said Petit Jean, giving him the box, "all I have to offer you are silver boxes, but take the trouble to open this one and you shall see."

Petit Jean and the Frog

The king opened the box and found therein an egg, and he opened the egg and found therein a walnut, and he opened the walnut and he found therein a hazelnut, and he opened the hazelnut and a little bird stepped out of it, ornamented with a thousand colors, and it began at once to fly about the room, and then went and rested on the king's shoulder, where it gave forth the loveliest warbling.

Then the king turned toward his sons and told them: "My dear sons, up to now it is still Petit Jean who has won. But I have one more test. This time he who brings back the loveliest wife shall have my crown. Go and choose carefully."

"Ah," said Petit Jean, "I can bring back a frog! How the king will like that! At the very moment I thought I was king, I am the farthest from it." And Petit Jean went back home very downhearted.

The frog asked him again. "What's wrong, Petit Jean, my friend? What's wrong?"

The prince replied in a harsh voice:

"Be quiet, frog. I ought to crush you under my foot."

"You'd be crushing your happiness, Petit Jean, my friend. You'd be crushing your happiness. At least tell me your sorrow."

"Well," said Petit Jean, "now my father has promised the crown to the one who brings back the most beautiful wife. I can bring him back a frog, but I'm sure I won't win, and besides they'll make fun of me."

"No matter, Petit Jean, my friend. Wait for me a moment and we'll go together."

And the frog went out in the garden. She picked a squash, hollowed it out and made a carriage of it, and she took six mice from their holes and harnessed them like horses to the squash, and she caught a big rat and put him on the coachman's seat, and she seized a lizard to serve as a footman, and finally she captured six bees to convert them into ladies-in-waiting. And when she had installed her personnel in the squash, the frog took her place inside and the carriage set out.

Passing in front of the house, she called to her husband: "Let's go, Petit Jean, my friend. Follow me. We're going to see your father."

Petit Jean was at his window when he saw his frog's carriage come out of the garden and he was overcome with such laughter that he had to hold his sides.

"My frog is very determined," he said, "but I'll certainly not follow her just to be laughed at!"

After a moment he changed his mind. He got on his horse and set out, following her at a distance.

Meanwhile the frog had got a long way ahead. She arrived before her godmother's door and was obliged to go through a big cesspool, but when the squash had arrived in the center she stopped and could neither advance nor withdraw. Then the mice squeaked, the big rat complained, the lizard hissed, the bees hummed, and the frog went "Croak, croak, croak." Hearing all this hubbub the godmother came out, and when she saw the sad condition of her godchild in the midst of the mire, she went quickly to find the old fairy and told her:

"Oh, my good sister, come and see what condition my poor godchild is in! Change her unhappy lot, I beg you!"

The old fairy arrived, still shaking her head, and when she saw this strange train mired down in the cesspool, she began to laugh, and she laughed so hard that she forgot her rancor and said:

"Well, I wish that the squash may become the loveliest carriage, the mice the most beautiful horses in the world, the lizard and the bees a footman and ladies-in-waiting more beautiful than have ever been seen, and I wish that the frog may become the most beautiful princess that has ever existed."

At once all were changed according to the old fairy's wishes, and the team and carriage set out at a gallop.

Petit Jean and the Frog

On a little hill the horses slowed down and the former frog, having become a beautiful princess, put her head outside the door from time to time to see if she couldn't find Petit Jean.

Far in the distance she saw him and she cried: "Come on, Petit Jean, my friend! Let's go faster. Can't you see I'm waiting for you?"

Petit Jean, seeing this lovely princess, said: "Ah, if I had such a woman instead of a frog how happy I should be!"

And still the lovely princess said: "Come on, Petit Jean, my friend! Come on! Can't you see I'm waiting for you?"

And Petit Jean said: "Well, too bad for the frog! I'm leaving her to accompany this lovely person."

And then he spurred his horse on, set off at a gallop, and caught up to the carriage.

The lovely princess said to him: "Tie your horse behind the carriage and come and sit beside me."

And that's what Petit Jean did without hesitating. And, at an order of the princess, the carriage set out full speed and shortly arrived at the king's court.

Seeing this lovely carriage arrive, all sparkling with gold and diamonds, everybody wondered who it was, while Petit Jean jumped from the carriage and took the princess's hand, and he conducted her to his father, to whom he presented her as his wife.

The king said to his other sons, who had also arrived with very lovely wives: "Well, my children, you see that it's Petit Jean that has won the crown."

His brothers recognized Petit Jean as their king, and the marriage ceremony was fixed for the next day; and the princess then said:

"Well, Petit Jean, my friend, you see that if you had crushed your frog you would have crushed your happiness."

"Is it true? Is it possible," said Petit Jean, "that you, so beautiful, were the frog?"

"Yes, it is I who as a little girl was changed into a frog. But a prediction had been made that I should marry a prince."

The king organized great festivities in the whole kingdom. At the moment of the marriage they saw a magnificent carriage of fire pulled by six sheep stop in the courtyard. It was the fairy godmother, who was bringing the princess's father and mother, whose identity had been revealed to her. They all embraced, and the ceremony was completed in the greatest pomp, and they all lived happy for a long time. And if they haven't died they are still alive.

13

THE GILDED FOX

There was once a man who had three sons. At his death he left them as their only inheritance a rooster, a cat, and a cherry tree. There was no need for a lawyer to divide the estate. It was accomplished without friction, and as soon as each had received his share, he tried to extract therefrom the best possible advantage. The eldest, who got the cock, set out with him in search of his fortune. He went far, much farther than I can tell you, and he arrived at a house where he asked for shelter for the night, but scarcely had he gone to bed when he heard people say that they had to get up the following day long before sunrise.

"Why," he asked them, "do you have to get up so early?"

"It's because we have to go to the seashore to bring back the day in our wagons."

"You won't need to do that tomorrow," he told them. "I have a little feathered animal. Where we live he's called a cock, and as soon as he sings, day will arrive."

The people of this country wanted to know if it was true, and for fear of failing to hear the cock sing they weren't able to sleep that night.

In the morning the cock began to crow. At once all the people in the household came to the window and saw day arrive, and they hastened to go and tell the lord of the country about it, and he had the boy come and asked to buy the animal that had brought the day.

"I'm willing to sell him," said the boy, "but only in exchange for a horse laden with gold."

"A horse laden with gold it shall be," replied the lord.

And the boy was very happy to have become rich, thanks to his rooster.

The one who inherited the cat also set out and went far, far away, farther than I can tell you. He arrived at an island and knocked at the door of a house and asked for a bed.

"Gladly," replied the host, "but I must warn you that as soon as it is night, little animals come who eat everything up and who don't let anyone sleep."

"I have with me," said the boy, "a little animal. He's called a cat in my country, and he knows how to conduct warfare against rats and mice."

Night came. The rats and the mice hastened from all directions. Immediately the boy set his cat free, and it killed so many rats and mice that you couldn't take a step in the house without walking on their bodies.

The lord of the country, having learned that a stranger possessed such a marvelous animal, had the boy brought to his castle. There were so many rats and mice there that when the lord was seated at the table the mice ran on the plates and rats put their feet in the soup.

The boy arrived at the castle. His cat killed more than a hundred mice and as many rats in no time at all. And the lord asked him if he could buy the cat.

"I'm willing," he replied, "but only on condition that you give me two beautiful mules laden with gold."

"Gladly," said the lord, "but you must go get this animal's family so that the whole country may be peopled by its species."

The boy left his cat in the castle and went back to his own country where he bought a neighbor's female cat at a reasonable price, and he brought her back to the lord.

The Gilded Fox

"She's nice," the lord told him, "but you must stay with me until she has had kittens."

The young man stayed in the castle, and at the end of two months there were some pretty kittens and on the occasion they had great celebrations throughout the island, and the lord gave the boy two beautiful mules laden with gold.

The cherry tree gave forth fruit in all seasons and the one who inherited it ate as much as he wanted and he easily sold the rest because the fruit was of excellent quality. His neighbors called him Prince Jabot.[1]

One day he had climbed into his cherry tree when Mr. Fox came by and said to him:

"What are you doing in that tree, Prince Jabot?"

"I'm picking cherries. Do you want some, Brother Fox?"

"Please, thank you."

The boy gave him some of the very loveliest cherries,

---

[1] *Jabot:* Craw, or maw. (TRANSLATOR.)

and Brother Fox ate a few and took the remainder to the king.

"Sire," he said, "here are some cherries that Prince Jabot sends you."

"The prince is very rich to have cherries that are so lovely. What do you want for your trouble, Brother Fox?"

"I should like you to color the tip of my tail gold."

The gilder came to gild the fox's tail, and he went away with his tail shining in the sun. And as he was coming back he met some partridges on the road.

"Brother Fox," they said to him, "how beautiful you are! The end of your tail is like gold."

"If you want to come with me you will be just as beautiful and as gilded as I am," he replied.

The partridges followed him, and Brother Fox took them to the king and said:

"Sire, here are some partridges that Prince Jabot sends you."

"He is indeed rich, this Prince Jabot," said the king. "What do you want for your trouble, Brother Fox?"

"I should like to have you gild my four paws."

The gilder came and decorated the four paws of Brother Fox, and he was even more beautiful than before. As he was going home he passed near a field where there was a band of hares.

"Ah, Brother Fox," they shouted, "how beautiful you are! Your tail and paws look like gold."

"If you wish, come with me and you shall be as beautiful and as gilded as I am."

And the hares followed him, and on the road they met and told other hares about it, and they joined them to get gilded. Brother Fox arrived at the court with a regiment of hares, and he said to the king:

"Sire, here are some hares that Prince Jabot sends you."

"He is indeed rich, this Prince Jabot!" replied the king.

The Gilded Fox

"What do you want for your trouble, Brother Fox? There's nothing that I can refuse you."

"Sire," he replied, "I should like you to gild the remainder of my body."

The gilder came and finished ornamenting Brother Fox, who now was all yellow and brilliant like the sun.

He went to find Prince Jabot and told him that the king wanted to talk to him. The boy followed him, and when they approached the court Brother Fox told him to take off his clothes. When he was quite naked the fox began to shout:

"Help! Help!"

The king's men arrived and the fox told them:

"As His Excellency, the Prince here, was arriving in his carriage, a band of brigands came and attacked him, stole his possessions, and left him as naked as your hand."

The king's men went and got clothes from their master, which they brought to Brother Fox, who said to them:

"Those that were stolen from us were more beautiful, but no matter. These at least will prevent His Excellency the Prince from catching cold."

Prince Jabot and Brother Fox came to the court. The king received them as best he could and he said that he would like to see the prince's castle. The boy replied that he would be delighted, for he had confidence in Brother Fox's skill and knew that Brother Fox would take care of him.

They set out and Brother Fox, all gilded, walked before them. They arrived in a field where washerwomen were putting out some beautiful linen to dry.

"Can't you see the king coming?" he asked them.

"We can't see him."

"He's going to pass in his carriage. If you don't say that all of this laundry belongs to Prince Jabot, he will come and kill you."

When the king arrived in the field, he said to the washerwomen: "Whom does this lovely field belong to, and this beautiful laundry?"

"To Prince Jabot."

"Ah," said the king, "that's a nice piece of property."

"Oh, it's nothing," said the prince.

Brother Fox, going on ahead, arrived in a field where there was a crowd mowing grain.

"Can't you see the king coming?"

"No," they replied. "We can't see him."

"He will pass shortly in his carriage, and if you don't say that all this wheat belongs to Prince Jabot, he will come and kill you."

When the king arrived in the field, he said to the mowers: "Whose grain is this?"

"It belongs to Prince Jabot."

"Ah," said the king, "you have a fine harvest."

"Ah, sire, it's nothing."

Brother Fox came into a field where some cattle were grazing and he said to the herdsmen:

"Can't you see the king coming?"

"No," they replied, "we can't see him."

"He's going to pass shortly in his carriage. If you don't say that all these cattle belong to Prince Jabot he will kill you."

And when the king arrived at the place where the cattle were grazing, he said to the herdsmen: "Whose cattle are these?"

"They belong to Prince Jabot."

"Ah," said the king, "what handsome cattle!"

"Oh, sire, it's nothing."

Brother Fox arrived at a monastery that was as fine as the king's palace, and he said to the monks:

"Can't you see the king coming?"

"No," they replied, "we can't see him."

"Well, he's going to pass in his carriage, and he's com-

The Gilded Fox

ing to kill you because he hates monks. If you don't want him to find you, you must hide in the midst of that heap of straw and not move. He won't think of looking for you there."

The monks crawled under the pile of straw; Brother Fox went into the monastery and said to the servants:

"The king is coming shortly; if you don't say that all of this belongs to Prince Jabot he will kill you."

The king came to the monastery, where he was served as well as in his own castle, and after the meal he took a walk, and as he was passing near the heap of straw Brother Fox said:

"There are some beautiful rats in that straw that consume everything."

"How can we get rid of them?" asked the king.

"We must set fire to it."

A fire was set in the straw; the monks were roasted except two or three who escaped, and Prince Jabot remained master of the monastery with Brother Fox, who was gilded all over and who shone like the sun.

14
THE LOVE OF THREE ORANGES

A KING AND A QUEEN have a son who is exceeding agile in body and learned in all things.

One day when the prince is playing ball an old woman passes by with a pot of oil in her hand. The young man throws his ball, which strikes the old woman's pot and breaks it, and he steps forward to offer his apologies, but the old woman says to him in anger:

"Prince, you will not be happy until you have found the Love of Three Oranges."

Then the prince becomes sad. He speaks no more and he eats no more. For days and days he dreams only of the means of going in search of the Love of Three Oranges. His parents don't want to let him go, but when they see he is falling ill they end by giving in.

The prince sets out with two faithful servants and goes first toward the Midi. The three men walk for months and years, and they arrive in a desolate country where they suffer hunger, thirst, and all sorts of privations. At last they find a poor cabin and approach it to ask for shelter. They knock for a long while on the door and finally an old woman opens to them and asks them what they want.

"Hospitality, if you please. We are searching for the Love of Three Oranges."

"Poor souls," the old woman answers, "if my son the South Wind sees you, you are done for."

The Love of Three Oranges

Then the old woman has them enter and hides them under an enormous kettle. They hear a great noise. It's the South Wind arriving. He pushes before him a cloud of dust and dries out everything as he passes by, and he opens the door and enters with a breath of hot air.

"Mother," he says, "I can smell fresh meat."

"Yes," replies the old woman, "it's a sheep that I have roasted for your supper."

"Bring it to me," he says, and he begins to devour it.

When he is finished she asks him: "Have you eaten well, son? Is your hunger satisfied?"

"Oh, yes, Mother. I have eaten well."

"Well," says the old woman, "there are three travelers here who are looking for the Love of Three Oranges."

"Oh, the wretches! Have them come here."

The old woman has the three men come out from their hiding-place, and the prince tells his story.

"Foolhardy men!" says the South Wind. "You don't know what you're exposing yourselves to. But—I'm going to give you some advice. Supply yourselves with oil and grease."

"Why?" asks the prince.

"You'll know later." And the South Wind goes to bed.

The next day, well rested, the three travelers take their leave and go to the east, and they walk for months and years, and get lost in the woods. Overcome with fatigue, they search for shelter and discover a poor cabin. They knock at the door and an old woman comes to open for them.

"What do you want?" she asks them.

"Hospitality. We're very tired."

"What are you looking for around here?"

"The Love of Three Oranges."

"Foolhardy," says the old woman. "If my son the East Wind finds you, you are lost, because he will devour you."

The prince begs her to let them come in, and the old woman gives in and hides them in the oven.

They hear a great noise; it's the East Wind arriving in the midst of a whirlwind, which breaks everything, overturns everything, as it passes by. He opens the door and enters with a gust of wind that sweeps the cinders from the fireplace.

"Mother," he says, "I smell fresh meat."

"Yes, son. It's the veal that I prepared for your supper."

"Bring it to me," he says, "for I'm very hungry."

Then he devours the veal, and when he has finished, his mother says to him:

"Are you still hungry, son?"

"No," he says, "I've dined well."

"Well, there are three very tired strangers here who are looking for the Love of Three Oranges."

"Oh, wretches!" he says; "bring them before me."

The woman has them come out of the oven, and the prince tells his story.

Then the East Wind says to him: "Supply yourselves with bread and acorns."

"What for?" asks the prince.

"You'll know later."

And the East Wind goes to bed.

The prince and his companions, well rested, set out the next morning and go toward the north, and they walk months and years and get lost in the snow; they are walking in it up to their waists, very tired, dying with cold, and at last they discover a little cabin and knock.

A woman still older than the other two comes to open up to them. "What do you want?" she says.

"We want hospitality."

"And what have you come to do here?"

"We're looking for the Love of Three Oranges."

"Poor souls! If my son the North Wind finds you, you are lost. He will devour you."

The Love of Three Oranges

"We're too tired to go farther. Hide us where you can."

At last the old woman gives in and hides them in a cellar. They hear a great noise. It's the North Wind arriving in the midst of a gust of snow and freezing everything as he passes by. He opens the door and enters with a whirlwind of snow, and the windowpanes of the cabin are immediately covered with a heavy coating of frost.

"Mother," he says, "I smell fresh meat."

"Yes, my son. It's the beef that I have put on the spit for your supper."

"Bring it to me, for I am very hungry."

Then he devours the beef. When he is finished, his mother asks him: "Are you still hungry, son?"

"No," he says, "I've dined well."

"Well, there are three strangers who are very tired who are looking for the Love of Three Oranges."

"Oh, the wretches! They are going to a certain death. Bring them to me."

And the woman has them come out of the cellar. The prince comes and tells his story, and the North Wind says to him: "Then supply yourself with ropes and brooms, and especially don't forget combs."

"Why?" asks the prince.

"You'll know soon."

And the North Wind goes to bed.

The next day the prince and his two servants, well rested, set out and go toward the west, and they walk for months and years, and one evening, not able to go any farther, they lie down and ask for death. But they see in the distance an old castle all resplendent with light.

"When day comes," says the prince, "we'll try to reach the castle. We are perhaps at the end of our troubles."

The next morning they set out, and after much backtracking and many detours they finally arrive in front of an old fortified castle. They walk around it and find only one door, but a door so old and so rusted that they can't open it. Then the prince remembers what the South Wind has told him. He begins to oil the lock and to grease the hinges, and after several hours of work the door opens by itself.

They enter the courtyard of the castle, and there some enormous dogs dash upon them to devour them. The three men throw them bread, and the dogs dash upon it. Farther on, hogs as fat as oxen advance upon them to eat them, and the three men throw them the acorns. The hogs hurl themselves upon this food, which is new to them. And they enter another court and encounter giant women drawing water by using their hair. The women want to throw the three men in the well, but they give them ropes and go on their way, while the women resume their work pulling the buckets up with the ropes.

Farther on they see women pulling coals out of an oven with their hands. The women want to throw the three

The Love of Three Oranges

men in the oven, but they give them brooms and the women continue to clean the oven using the brooms.

Next they reach an old stairway, a stairway so dirty, so covered with dust, that they can no longer see the steps. They begin to sweep it, and they climb when it is clean. At the top they open a door and find an old woman whose white hair reaches the ground and is all covered with vermin. They take their combs out and they begin to comb it and to clean her hair. The old woman, who hasn't slept for years, is relieved and goes to sleep.

Then the prince looks all around and finds three magnificent oranges lying on a trunk. Immediately he steals them and escapes, followed by his two servants.

But the old woman, who was only half asleep, begins to shout: "Stairway, stairway, throw them to the ground!"

But the stairway answers her: "You never swept me. They did. Let them go down."

And the old woman continues to shout: "Women cleaning the oven with your hands, throw them in!"

"You never gave us a broom, and they did. Let them pass."

"Women drawing water with your hair, throw them in the well!"

"You never gave us a rope, and they did. Let them pass!"

"Hogs, tear them to pieces!"

"You never gave us acorns, but they did. Let them pass!"

"Dogs, devour them!"

"You never gave us bread, but they did. Let them pass."

"Door, close upon them!"

"You never greased me or oiled me, but they did. Let them pass."

And so the prince and his two servants leave the castle and set out for their home. After walking a long time the

French Folk Tales

prince, who doesn't know what oranges are, decides to open one. Immediately a woman of great beauty comes out. Never had the prince seen such beauty.

"Love, love, quench my thirst!" she says.

"Love, love, I have no water," replies the prince.

"Love, love, I'm dying," says the princess. And she falls dead at his feet.

Then the prince, very sad, kisses her many times, and then he buries her and goes on his way, and after walking a long time, he feels an urge to open the second orange, but as the first woman had asked him for drink he thinks perhaps that this one will ask him for food, and he prepares what he will need. He opens the orange and there appears a woman still more beautiful than the first.

"Love, love, give me to drink," she says.

"Love, love, I haven't any water."

"Love, love, I die!" And she falls dead at his feet also.

Then the prince, despairing, kisses her many times and still many times more. Then he buries her and goes on his way. But he decides not to open the third orange until he arrives at the edge of a fountain. He finds one, he fills his hat with water, and opens the third orange.

Immediately there appears a woman still more beautiful than the other two.

"Love, love, give me to drink," she says.

"Love, love, here is water."

"Love, love, take me away."

The prince, at the height of joy, has her mount behind him and goes on his way. He travels months; he crosses seas; and he comes into a country whose king was a friend of his father. He goes to find him and tells him his story.

But this king has a daughter and he has dreamed for a long time of having this prince marry her. He hides his daughter, and he declares to the prince that it is not proper to bring into his country his future wife in such a state of poverty. The prince must first go home and bring back

The Love of Three Oranges

jewels and clothing worthy of her. And during this time the king will concern himself with the Love of the Three Oranges. And the prince decides to leave alone, but he does so regretfully.

Then the king puts his daughter beside the Love of Three Oranges and tells her to observe carefully what she does in order to take her place when the proper day comes.

One day the daughter of the king is combing the beautiful hair of her companion and she thrusts a long needle into her head, saying: "Love, love, change into a dove."

Immediately the Love of Three Oranges is transformed into a dove and takes flight, and when the prince comes back, the daughter of the king pretends to be the beautiful woman he had left behind. But she has reddish-brown hair, and her skin is sprinkled with freckles. The prince can't explain to himself such a transformation.

"It's the sun, the wind, and the rain, and the traveling that have transformed me," the king's daughter tells him. "But immediately after our marriage I shall be as lovely as before."

The prince takes her away to his estates, but his father and his friends are astonished that he has spent so many years and undergone so many tests only to bring back such an ugly woman. The day of the marriage is fixed and they begin preparations when one night the cook hears a voice saying to her three or four times:

> "Cook, turn the spit on the fire,
> For if you burn the meat
> The king won't want to eat."

The cook, looking up the chimney, sees a dove talking. He tells the king, who orders the bird to be captured, but the bird can't be caught. Then the king stands at his window, and the dove comes of herself and alights on his arm. The king caresses her, passing his hand over her head, and he feels a little bump that he wants to scratch, and he notices that it is the head of a pin and hastens to withdraw it. Then the dove becomes once more the most beautiful woman ever seen, and the prince recognizes in her his Love of the Three Oranges. She tells him her story, and then the father of the prince, greatly angered, has the pretended fiancée condemned to death, and she is burned alive the very day of his son's marriage.

But the condemned woman's father declares war on the prince's father, and a war ensues that lasts more than a hundred years, and will continue to last, between the kings of France and the kings of Normandy.

15

THE DOCTOR AND HIS PUPIL

There was once a poor man who had a twelve-year-old son. He sent him to find work.

The boy departed wearing a jacket that was red in front and white behind. He passed in front of a castle; it was the residence of a doctor, who happened to be standing at the window. As he needed a servant, the master of the castle called the boy.

"What are you looking for in these parts?"

"Since I'd like to make a living, I'm looking for work."

"Do you know how to read?"

"Yes, for I've been to school for six months."

"Then you won't do."

The boy went away; but in a few days he came back with his jacket on backwards and passed once more in front of the castle. Again the master was at his window.

"What are you looking for in these parts?"

"I'd like to make a living; I'm looking for work."

"Do you know how to read?"

"No, for I've never been to school."

"Well, then, come in; I'll hire you. I'll give you one hundred francs a year and board."

The boy entered and his master gave him something to eat. Then he showed him his book of secrets and gave him a duster.

"You will dust my book carefully every day, and that's all you'll have to do."

Then the doctor left on a trip and was gone a whole year. The boy took advantage of this absence to read his master's book and get acquainted with the doctor's skills.

The physician returned. He was very happy with his servant and departed for another year. During this second absence, the boy learned half of the book by heart.

The doctor returned and was so happy with his servant that he doubled his wages and departed for another year. During this third absence the young man learned the remainder of the book by heart. When his master returned he left the doctor's employ to return to his parents, who were as poor as ever.

On the eve of the village fair the young man said to his father: "Tomorrow go into the stable; you will find a beautiful horse that you must take to the fair. Sell him, but above all be sure to keep the halter."

The next day the father entered the stable and found a magnificent horse. He took it to the fair and buyers hastened around to admire the handsome animal. The father sold it for a good price, but he kept the halter and put it in his pocket. Then he set out on the road to his village and shortly he heard footsteps behind him: it was his son who, having transformed himself into a horse and then retransformed himself into his natural shape while the buyer of the horse was celebrating in the tavern, was hastening to catch up with his father. And both were delighted with the fine deal they had made.

After a time there was no more money left in the house.

"Don't worry about it," said the boy to his father. "I'll see that you get more. Go in the stable tomorrow; you will find a steer that you can take to the fair. But when you sell it be sure to keep the rope that you are leading it with."

All took place at the fair as before, and the boy caught up with his father, whose appetite had been whetted by this money which was so easily earned, and who now

The Doctor and His Pupil

proposed to take his son again to the next fair in the form of a horse.

But the doctor, by consulting his book, had become aware of what his former servant was doing. He went to the fair, recognized the horse, and bought it. He took the father to the inn to conclude the bargain and made him drink a great deal so that he forgot to keep the halter.

The doctor took the horse quickly away to a blacksmith. "Give him a good shoeing," he advised.

The horse was tied to the door. The children came out of school and a group of them came to hang around the blacksmith shop. The horse extended its muzzle toward a child and whispered to him:

"Untie me!"

The child was afraid and withdrew a bit; but the horse repeated: "Child, untie me!"

The schoolboy approached and untied him. Immediately the horse transformed itself into a hare and ran away. The doctor saw it and turned six boys into hunting dogs. The hare came to the edge of a reservoir, jumped in, and turned into a carp. The doctor arrived, bought all the fish in the reservoir, and had it fished clean. He recognized the carp and was about to grab it when it turned into a lark. He turned into an eagle and pursued the lark, which flew over a castle and fell down the chimney, where it turned into a grain of wheat, which rolled under the table in the bedroom of the girl of the castle.

The day passed. In the evening when the girl had gone to bed, the young man said:

"Mademoiselle, if you wish—"

The girl, hearing his voice, cried out to her parents, who came at once.

"What's the matter?"

"There's someone talking in here!"

But the young man turned back into a grain of wheat and rolled under the table. The parents turned on the lights, looked everywhere, and, finding nothing, departed.

The young man took his own shape and made more advances. The girl cried and her parents returned.

"There's been more talking in the room."

"Have you gone mad?" said the father.

"Well! Go to bed here if you want to hear it."

The father stayed a moment, then went away. The young man reappeared and the girl ended by acceding to him.

"Nights I shall sleep with you and days you may wear me as an engagement ring on your finger."

But the doctor found out all that was going on by consulting his books. He caused the father to become ill and came as a doctor to cure him.

"Heal me and I will pay you well," said the father.

"All I want is the ring on your daughter's finger."

The father promised. But the young man was aware of what was going on.

The Doctor and His Pupil

"The doctor is going to ask you for your ring," he said to the girl. "Don't give it to him; let it fall on the floor."

When the father was cured he called his daughter and told her to give the ring to the doctor. She took it off and let it fall; the ring turned into grains of wheat, which scattered out on the floor. The doctor turned into a rooster to pick them up. The young man turned into a fox and ate the rooster.

16

LITTLE JOHNNY SHEEP–DUNG

THERE WAS ONCE a young man who was no good, a real good-for-nothing! From his childhood all he knew how to do was beg and he didn't want to find a job. He ate what was given him, and as he had nothing with which to buy clothes and underwear, he went one time to prowl around the butcher shops and asked for a sheepskin that was all filthy, and he wrapped himself in it. From that moment on they called him Little Johnny Sheep-Dung.

One day he met a big bourgeois on a horse.

"Where are you going, Little Johnny Sheep-Dung?"

"I don't know. I'm looking for work, but I'm praying God not to find me any, for—I don't conceal it from you—I'm a good-for-nothing, such a good-for-nothing that other good-for-nothings are jealous of me."

"Do you want to come with me? You won't have much work."

"You'll feed me, at least?"

"Yes, you may depend on that. Let's go. Get on behind me."

It was the Devil, but Little Johnny didn't know it. When they arrived at his house, which was far, far away, the Devil served Johnny a fine meal.

"Eat all you want, my boy. Tomorrow you will work at your leisure."

The next day the Devil took Little Johnny to his stable.

Little Johnny Sheep-Dung

He showed him a horse whose name was Beautiful Body. It was a prince that he met once when he was hunting in the forest, whom he transformed into a horse and brought back to his home. He explained to Johnny that this horse must be groomed each morning by giving him a good bludgeoning:

"And don't forget, beat him first with one arm and then with the other."

So Little Johnny began his service. But he didn't beat the animal very much for fear of tiring himself out. At the end of a few days the horse said to him:

"Little Johnny Sheep-Dung, if you but knew where you are!"

"I am with a good master."

"You are at the Devil's. If you trust me, let's get away from here as fast as we can."

"But I have no desire to do so at all. I am fed, I work scarcely at all, I am happy."

"Watch out for the Devil. Let's both leave and I will make your fortune."

"How?"

"Untie me, get on me, and we'll go to my father's house. He is a king."

Johnny hesitated a few days, but he stopped beating the horse. He ended by agreeing, and one day when the Devil had gone to the fair, he and the horse decided to leave.

"First get ten sacks of one thousand francs each from the Devil's treasure," said the horse.

Little Johnny went to get the money, climbed on Beautiful Body, and they departed. First they had to cross an ocean, whose waters separated before them to form a road. When they were already far away the horse said:

"Little Johnny Sheep-Dung, look behind you. Can't you see anything coming?"

"I can see some dust coming very rapidly, very rapidly indeed!"

"Let it approach a little more."

"Here it is, coming upon us."

"Throw a sack of money to the ground."

The dust stopped and disappeared: it was the Devil, who had picked up his money and was taking it back.

A little farther the dust approached once more. Again, the horse told Johnny to throw down a sack of money. And in this way he threw down his ten sacks, one after another. But the last one they dropped just at the right moment: they were arriving on the other side of the ocean, which immediately closed over the Devil and swallowed him up.

Soon they were near the king's city. He believed that his son, who had been lost while hunting in the forest, had been devoured by wild animals. Moreover, he had three daughters.

The horse said to his companion: "Little Johnny Sheep-Dung, go to my father and ask for work as a gardener."

"Ah, so I'm going to have to work! I certainly was wrong to listen to you!"

"Go there without any fear. If they give you strawberries to clean and cultivate, cut them at the roots and lie down beside them. And this evening you must return here, where I'll be waiting for you."

Johnny departed with his filthy sheepskin and went to ask for work as a gardener of the king. They gave him a pick and told him to cultivate and clean the strawberries. With a few blows of the pick Little Johnny had cut all the strawberries, and then he lay down beside them.

The princesses, who had seen this individual arrive with his sheepskin, wanted to see him closer, but only the youngest dared to approach and she found him asleep. He didn't have his sheepskin on him any more, but was wearing a beautiful costume, which he was unaware of, and he had a handsome face; the princess looked at him for a long time in astonishment.

Little Johnny Sheep-Dung

He woke up and found himself in his filthy sheepskin. The cut strawberry plants had all sprung up again and the strawberries were already ripe. When Little Johnny went back to the horse to tell him about his day, he found that it had a man's head.

They spent the night together. The next day the horse with a man's head said to his companion:

"Little Johnny Sheep-Dung, go back to the palace garden. If they put you in the arbors or on the espaliers, cut them at the roots and lie down beside them."

Little Johnny went back and asked for work as a gardener of the king, and they put him to work trimming the arbors and espaliers. Little Johnny took his ax and cut the trees off at their roots; then he lay down beside them and went to sleep. The youngest of the princesses came back again, saw the arbors and espaliers cut, and looked for a long time at the handsome young man who was sleeping.

When he awakened, the trees had fruit already ripe, and Little Johnny went back to the horse and found that it was a man down to its waist. He told the horse what had hap-

(143)

pened, but he didn't know that the princess had come to see him during his sleep.

The next day the horse, now a man down to its waist, said to its companion:

"Little Johnny Sheep-Dung, go back to the palace garden. If they give you a plot of land to spade, plant your spade in the midst and lie down beside it."

Little Johnny went back to the castle and asked for work as a gardener, and they gave him a big plot of ground to spade. Little Johnny planted his spade in the midst of the plot; then he lay down beside it and went to sleep. The princess came to see him again; she found him so handsome that she was overcome with a desire to marry him.

When Little Johnny awakened, he found that his whole plot had been spaded, and that evening when he went back, the horse had turned wholly into a man.

Meanwhile the king had been thinking of marrying his three daughters. The two eldest were already promised to two princes, but the youngest had always opposed matches that her father had proposed. She went to find him.

"I want to marry Little Johnny Sheep-Dung," she told him.

"You're mad!" her father said.

But as he loved his daughter a great deal and did all that she asked, he ended by giving in, and when Little Johnny came back to work, the king promised him the princess. Then he called his three future sons-in-law together.

"I will give my crown," he said, "to the one who beats the other two in combat."

The three pretenders made a rendezvous for the next day outside the city. They gave Little Johnny a lame horse and he left first. The other two passed on fractious horses and scoffed at him: "Hurry, Little Johnny Sheep-Dung."

Little Johnny Sheep-Dung

But as soon as they had gone by, Little Johnny found that he was in a handsome costume on a beautiful horse. He started on again, passed them, and arrived first on the field. When the others arrived, they were astonished to find this handsome knight.

"I have come," he said, "to take Little Johnny's place."

The three knights fought without injuring each other, and then they separated, deciding to meet again the next day. The handsome stranger departed and the two princes shortly found Little Johnny in the mud with his old horse and his filthy sheepskin.

"Well, Little Johnny Sheep-Dung, you're still here, eh? Don't go any farther. A handsome knight came in your stead. We'll see you tomorrow."

And they left him. The king asked them the outcome of the combat.

"Little Johnny wasn't able to come. Someone came in his stead, but we didn't fight."

The next day they gave Little Johnny a horse that was both blind and lame, and everything happened as on the previous day, and again they put the combat off until the next day. The third day was to be decisive. They gave Little Johnny a horse that was blind and lame and as round as a clipped hedge.

Again he bogged down in the mud and again a handsome knight was the first to arrive on the field. He wounded one of the princes, and then the other slightly. The three combatants embraced and went away, but this time Little Johnny stayed with the two others, arrived at court in his brilliant costume, and revealed his identity. The princess was the only one who was not surprised, for she had known what he was like since the moment she had first seen him sleeping.

The king said to him: "You are the winner; you shall have the crown."

"No, sire. It belongs to your son."

"I no longer have a son. The one I had was lost hunting and must have been eaten by wild animals."

"He isn't dead; I'll get him for you."

Little Johnny went to get his companion, and everybody was happy. The three marriages were performed. The son received the crown, and Little Johnny stayed with him and became his most beloved friend.

17

THE THREE DOGS AND THE DRAGON

A YOUNG SHEPHERD was herding a skinny goat along the roadside. An old fairy came by, followed by three hardy dogs.

"Won't you give her to me?" she suggested. "In exchange I will give you these three companions."

"Certainly not," replied the young man. "She's not fat, I admit, but at least she supplies milk for me and my family, whereas your dogs—what use would they be to me?"

The next day the fairy reappeared. "Have you thought it over, my boy?" she asked.

"Of course I have," shouted the shepherd. "You keep your animals and I'll keep mine."

With a perseverance that indicated a great desire to gain her ends, the fairy was back the next day.

"Come on now," she said. "Agree and you won't regret it."

The boy thought: "After all, perhaps this good woman wants to do me a good turn and I won't lose much in the exchange. My goat isn't worth the rope she's tied with."

And he agreed to the bargain.

In addition to the three dogs, the fairy gave him a silver whistle. "Accept it," she said. "It will be useful to you. If danger should befall you, whistle, and at the same instant the dogs will be there to defend you."

But the shepherd's mother did not look at the situation with the same credulity. In learning of the singular bargain, which deprived her of her only resource, she was seized with anger and she raised her club over her son, but she didn't have time to strike. Already one of the dogs, who answered to the name of Break-iron, was on the club and with one bite broke it like glass.

Then her irritation was boundless. "Since that is how it is," she exclaimed, "and since you have such a fine understanding with your animals, go! Leave with them! They will keep you alive. As for me, I can no longer feed you."

"As you wish, Mother," replied the young man, who, accompanied by his dogs, went into the neighboring forest. No forests in the world were more filled with game. Animals of all species wandered about in innumerable bands and no one had ever bothered them. In a few days it was empty of its inhabitants. One of the dogs, whose name was Hunter, could run so fast and strike so viciously that not one animal escaped him, neither hare nor rabbit nor wolf.

Now at about that time there was talk of a wood in the outskirts of Paris where, it was claimed, there was more game than there were trees, but where no man dared to go, for no one ever came out alive.

"Suppose I try it," said the young man to himself. "The four of us make a team capable of defending ourselves. What matter if misfortune should befall me? At least I shall be informed concerning the mystery of that forest."

He took his sister in case he should decide to establish a home in that place, for a woman would be necessary to devote herself to the cares of the household.

As he was arriving at the edge of the wood he stopped, surprised. Before him there was a barrier of trees so thick, with foliage so leafy, that the light of the sun could

The Three Dogs and the Dragon

not penetrate. It was as dark there as in an oven, and it seemed to him that a voice was murmuring in his ear:

"Stop! Your life is in danger here."

"Bah!" he replied. "We shall see with whom we are to chat."

He discovered in a clearing an abandoned house, installed his sister there, and left to go hunting. He had not been deceived. He found an animal at each step, but never a human face; it was not the same for his sister. He had agreed with her that at the stroke of noon she should ring the bell to call him to lunch. Well, noon passed and the bell hadn't rung.

"Could something harmful have happened?" he asked. "Let's go back."

The girl had had unexpected visitors of a kind that are scarcely ever encountered. She had seen coming suddenly out of a trap door twenty-four giants so tall that a man of goodly stature would have appeared as a dwarf beside them, and so strong that they could have lifted a bull as one lifts a child's toy.

"Who are you, and why are you here? You're very daring, young woman!" they shouted in a gruff voice.

"Spare me, my lords!" replied the poor trembling girl. "It was my brother who brought us here."

"He shall be punished, this brother of yours. We shall gladly spare you for you seem to be too sweet to die: only on condition, however, that you help us get rid of him."

In her fright she promised all that they asked. Then they poured a poisonous drug into the soup and quickly went back into their hiding-place.

The trap door was scarcely closed when the hunter arrived. He asked why she had not rung.

"There is so much work to be done here," declared the treacherous girl, "that I didn't have time to finish it. You will be rewarded, for the soup is delicious."

She didn't have the satisfaction of serving it to him. The dog Break-iron, who was at the threshold, had guessed that something unusual was going on. He had smelled the poison and, seizing the caldron with his teeth, he upset it.

The next day the twenty-four giants were back. Their first question was:

"Your brother? Is he dead?"

"He is more hardy than ever," declared the girl. "His dog Break-iron upset the soup and the poison."

"This only means a delay," they said. "There is an armchair in this hall which has the property of freezing anyone who sits in it. Offer it to your brother while you are preparing his food. He will lose his appetite forever."

Again the evil calculations of these wretches were in vain. When the young man came home with his dogs, the first thing that attracted the attention of Break-iron was the fatal seat. The good animal dashed upon it and tore it to pieces.

Then in their anger the giants conceived a diabolical stratagem and got the young woman's co-operation therein, having promised her the loveliest rewards. On their advice she pretended to be gravely ill.

"Run and get me a doctor," she said to her brother. "Otherwise I shall die."

The young man left at full speed in search of the nearest doctor. It was the giants' doctor and they had bought him over.

"I know only one remedy for this woman's sickness," he said. "She must have goat's milk."

"Goat's milk? She shall have it in an instant."

The hunter went directly to the fairy with whom he had struck his bargain.

"Take back your dogs, good mother," he said. "Give me my goat. My sister will die if she doesn't have some of its milk."

The Three Dogs and the Dragon

The fairy cast a glance upon him that was at the same time worried and sad.

"Let it be done as you desire," she replied. "I hope that you don't have reason to regret the impulses of your good heart."

A terrible surprise awaited him, as a matter of fact, upon his return. The twenty-four giants were at the door. They received him with great bursts of laughter.

"So, proud hunter!" they exclaimed. "For a long time we have been searching for you. We have some accounts to settle with you."

And with no more explanations they seized him, threw him into a dungeon that was filled with the bones of their victims, and they stopped up the opening with an enormous stone, which removed all hope of salvation.

At first he thought that his fate had been settled. How

imprudent he had been to abandon his dogs! And the memory of his devoted companions recalled to him something else: his whistle.

"Saved!" he murmured.

With his instrument he gave forth a strident and prolonged note, which was answered by happy barking. The good animals came to his rescue. In the flash of an eye the stone of his sepulcher was shattered under Break-iron's efforts, and he was hurled outside of his cell by the dog that answered to the name of Quick-as-the-Wind.

He set out in search of his sister. How great was his stupor and his indignation when he found her among the giants joyously celebrating her engagement to one of them!

"Ah, wretched sister!" he shouted. "Your treachery will scarcely profit you!" And he ordered his dogs to assail the band. It didn't take long. The evil-doing creatures were not able to defend themselves against the fangs of the terrible animals and they were all strangled.

He stayed awhile longer in his castle and his forest, but in the end he grew tired of hunting and returned to Paris. He couldn't restrain an emotion of surprise when he entered the city: all the inhabitants seemed to be in mourning and their faces were profoundly sad.

"You're a stranger, no doubt," they told him, "and that's why you don't know of our misfortune. The story is worth the telling. A long time ago one of our queens who was of a capricious character had the whim to ask one day to be served fruit from the garden of the fairies. Her desire was satisfied; an old fairy brought her the fruit, but she asked a promise before giving it to her: that the princess should give her one of her daughters to be reared in the palace of the fairies and to become later a powerful fairy herself. She promised what they wanted. But when the time came to let her daughter go, the king opposed it.

"The vengeance of the fairies was terrible. They hurled

The Three Dogs and the Dragon

four monsters upon the kingdom, which sowed horror and devastation in the cities and countrysides. The king had to ask for mercy and he promised to take his daughter personally to the fairies. Still the fairies were not satisfied. They agreed to withdraw three of the dragons, but they left the fourth with the admonition that a girl should be furnished once a year to be eaten by it.

"The cursed beast is on the mountain, and just the sight of him with his seven heads and seven horns freezes you with terror. In vain the bravest knights of the country have tried to kill it. Not one of them has come back from the conflict. Already the most beautiful girls of the capital have been devoured without the fairies having given their forgiveness. Today it's the king's daughter, the daughter of our good master, who is to be sacrificed."

The young man had listened to the story with a great deal of interest. Immediately he made up his mind.

"This is turning out just right!" he shouted. "I was looking for a task of some importance for me and my companions. We will find out if this dragon is worthy of his reputation."

He ignored prayers and exhortations and went toward the hill. In the distance they heard the terrible howling of the beast awaiting his prey. When the boy was midway up the slope, he saw the princess seated against a tree at the entrance to a wood and murmuring, frozen from terror:

"I shan't go farther! I'll be eaten right here if the beast desires."

"You shall not be eaten, by the faith of a Breton! I promise you!" said the young man.

The princess turned around, astonished.

"Stranger," she said, "why are you here? Haven't there been enough victims?"

"I don't know what the people in the city think," he replied, "but in my region of Brittany we don't customarily let a woman perish so long as there exists a man to defend her. Before having you the monster will first have to defeat me."

The horrible beast lay at the entrance of his cavern, watching them, moving his heads and his horns.

"The honor is all yours, hunter!" he scoffed.

The brave dog dashed forward. He sank his fangs in the dragon's back, while it uttered wails and hurled flames from its mouth.

Quick-as-the-Wind dashed forward in his turn, fighting at the heads, at the ears, at the long tail, which was covered with scales, harassing the foe without respite and forcing him to beg for mercy.

Break-iron and the young man completed the job. With a few gnashes of the teeth the dog tore out the horns and crushed the heads, and with his sword the young man pierced its heart. A stream of blackish blood flooded the ground. The terrible dragon was dead.

The princess had witnessed the combat from a distance, immobile and terrified. Her gratitude was limitless.

"How can I repay you for such a service, stranger?" she said. "Accept this kerchief embroidered with my initial. By displaying it, the savior of the king's daughter will be recognized. Accept, too, this vial of water which I have always kept. It comes from the fountain of youth and restores the dead to life. As for my father, he will know how to pay his debt to you."

The young man thanked the princess and wished her good luck, and after taking the precaution to cut out the monster's seven tongues, he returned to his castle.

Ever since he had killed his own sister out of anger his soul had been torn with remorse.

"Perhaps," he said, "with this water I might bring her back to life."

And, as a matter of fact, a few drops sprinkled on her

The Three Dogs and the Dragon

face were sufficient to awaken her and to restore her to full health.

He was filled with a spirit of generosity and so he did the same thing for the twenty-four giants, who, no sooner than they had awakened, asked for food and drink.

"Indeed, young man," they shouted, "you are good-hearted and you know how to avenge yourself with nobility. We will repay you for your generosity."

A year later news reached the castle in the forest: it was announced that the king's daughter was going to marry the knight who had saved her. On learning this the young man's heart came into his throat. He left at once for Paris with his dogs and the twenty-four giants. He had not been deceived. Another person was stealing his rights, and here is how he had gone about it:

From a distance he had watched the combat with the dragon, and when everyone had departed he had cut off its seven heads, and by terrible threats he had extracted from the girl a promise that she would declare that he was the one to whom she owed her life.

The king, full of gratitude, had decided that they should be married.

Now, the day that was fixed for the wedding the Breton arrived. He was full of anger at the sight of the preparations. On his orders the giants seized the guards, and the dogs upset the tables for the banquet.

"What's going on?" shouted the king, indignant.

"Well, this is what's going on," the young man replied, showing the king the kerchief with the princess's initial on it, along with the dragon's tongues. "Who do you think your daughter's savior is? He who has the dragon's tongues or he who has their heads?"

"No doubt he who has their tongues."

The deceit of the treacherous knight was unveiled. He was taken in hand at once and they hanged him on the scaffold, and it was the young Breton who led the princess to the altar.

After his father-in-law's death he became king in his turn, and he governed France with wisdom, with no ministers save his giants, and with no guards save his dogs. Thanks to the water of the fountain of youth he prevailed over death for a long time, and if one day he did depart for the other world, it was because he chose to do so.

18

THE SELF-PROPELLED CARRIAGE [1]

Once upon a time long, long ago—it was in the time of the feudal lords—a poor woman whose name was Marguerite lived at Monteil-au-Vicomte. She had three sons; the two oldest were big, strong, strapping youngsters, but this was not so of the youngest. Not that he was less intelligent than the others, nor that he was sickly. But when he walked he always looked down at the ground or at one side or the other, and he was so timid that he wouldn't even have dared crush an ant.

In those times the king announced that he would give his daughter in marriage to the one who could build a carriage that would go by itself.

The eldest, when he heard of it, said to his mother: "Tomorrow you will prepare me a basket. I will go to the forest of Garenne to try to make that carriage."

He got up very early in the morning and departed. As he passed by the fountain of *Collation* [2] he found a little old woman who was soaking a very dry crust of bread in the water in order to be able to eat it.

"Well, hello, my good old woman," he said. "What are you doing here so early in the morning?"

---

[1] Dr. Queyrat, collector of this tale, observes that it would deserve as a subtitle: "The Invention of the Automobile."

[2] *"Collation"* as a common noun means any food taken between the regular meals.

"Ah, young man, I am soaking my crust of bread in the fountain. It will go down better. And where are you going?"

"I am going to the Garenne forest to make some forks and rakes."

"Forks it shall be, rakes it shall be!"

When he was in the wood the strokes that his knife made carved out either a fork or a rake. In the evening when he came back he was loaded with them, but no carriage.

The second son said: "I'm going to go in my turn."

And the next day he took his basket and departed for the forest of Garenne. He also met the little old woman who was soaking her bread in the fountain, and she asked him where he was going. He replied that he was going to the forest of Garenne to make goads and clubs.

And the old woman said: "Goads and clubs it shall be!"

And all the strokes of his knife made nothing but goads or clubs, and in the evening he came back loaded with them; but there was still no carriage.

When the youngest saw this he said: "Both of you have gone; I want to go in my turn; perhaps I shall have more luck."

Marguerite and her two other sons replied: "Where do you intend to go? You're certainly too stupid. You couldn't even cut a club."

And he answered: "Prepare me a basket; it won't put you to much trouble. I want to try."

The next morning he departed early as the others had done. And he also saw the old woman who was soaking her crust of bread in the water. As soon as he saw her he said to her:

"Oh, my good lady, why don't you take my white bread and my cheese? Also, please take my little bottle of wine to warm your stomach. I am young; I can eat your dry bread."

The Self-Propelled Carriage

"Thank you, my good boy," she replied. "You are very good to poor people. Where are you going?"

"Good woman, the king's trumpeters have announced that he will give his daughter in marriage to the one who will make a self-propelled carriage; my two brothers have tried but they didn't succeed; I am going to try in my turn."

"Well, a carriage it shall be, my good boy. May you make a carriage that will go all by itself!"

When he was in the woods all the ax blows that he gave produced parts of the carriage, and in the evening it was finished: when he climbed back up the slope, it traveled like mad. He met the old woman again, and she said to him:

"Well, my fine young man, so you have succeeded! You shall marry the king's daughter. But to do that you will have to hire all those whom you meet on your road as you take the carriage to the king, and you must set out at once without going back home."

So he set out immediately with his self-propelled carriage; and he had already gone a considerable distance when he met a poor devil who was licking the door of an old oven where bread had not been cooked for a hundred years at least.

"Well, my friend, what are doing there?" he asked.

"Oh, I am licking the doors to this oven. I like bread so much that it makes me feel as if I were eating some."

"Well, come with me and you shall eat bread at your leisure. Do you want to be hired?"

"I ask for nothing better."

"What wages do you want?"

"A hundred francs a year."

"A hundred francs? All right. Get in my carriage."

A little farther he met another man who was licking a barrel stave, and he hired him for another hundred francs. Farther on he saw a man running with big stones tied to his feet; he asked him why he put them on his feet, and the man answered:

"Those are millstones; when I run I go so fast that if I having nothing tied to my feet and I want to catch rabbits I pass right over them."

He was hired for a hundred francs too.

Farther on he found another man who was hurling stones in the air, and he said to him: "What are you doing, throwing stones in the air like that? Aren't you afraid of putting someone's eyes out?"

The man replied: "Don't be afraid. I throw them so far that I have already killed half a dozen partridges on the other side of the Red Sea."

And he got in the carriage, having been hired for a hundred francs.

The carriage kept going, and farther on our young man saw another man who was bent half over toward the earth and seemed to be listening to something.

"What are you listening to?" he asked.

"I can hear wool being spun in the center of the earth," came the answer.

For another hundred francs he got in the carriage.

After having passed Orléans he saw another great big fellow who had his legs spread apart, his feet on two little mountains, and his body bent double with his behind in the air. He said to him: "What are you doing in this fine posture?"

The other straightened up and replied: "Can't you see that with the wind from my behind I make thirty-six windmills turn in that little valley, and I could make that many more turn if I wanted to!"

After bargaining, he hired him for a hundred francs, and he got in the carriage, and finally they came to Paris.

The king, who had been advised that the carriage that went by itself was arriving, was in the midst of his court on the balcony of his palace, and when he saw all of these

The Self-Propelled Carriage

friends dressed in trousers and coats full of holes, he didn't like it and he was sorry for his bargain.

He said: "You do have the self-propelled carriage, it's true, but to win my daughter more is required. Among your associates is there one capable of eating a hundred bread rolls at one sitting?"

Marguerite's son turned toward the man who had licked the doors of the oven and said to him: "You like bread so much, can you do that?"

And the man replied: "Just bring them; I'll eat twice as many if necessary!"

And, as a matter of fact, the hundred rolls were eaten as if it were nothing at all.

The king watched him eat, quite astonished, and said: "You do have a companion who has a fine appetite. It will cost a lot of money to feed him. But do you have one who could drink a hundred barrels of wine?"

Then the boy turned toward the man who had licked the barrel stave. "Could you do it?" he said.

And the other replied: "To drink a hundred barrels of wine is nothing; afterwards I am still thirsty."

The hundred barrels disappeared just like the hundred rolls.

The king, more and more astonished, said: "As for eating and drinking, you have satisfied me. But have you got one who could go from Paris to Bordeaux and back as fast as the mail coach?"

"You, young man," the boy said to the man whom he had found with millstones tied to his feet, "can certainly do that!"

"Of course I can; even if I remove only one millstone, still I shall get back ahead of time."

And the man let the mail coach leave, then he took one of the millstones off his feet, and he departed as if the devil were carrying him. And he had soon caught up with and passed the mail coach and arrived in Bordeaux far ahead of it.

As he was ahead of time he said: "I have plenty of time before I must leave once more. I'm thirsty and hungry. I'm going to go break crust and have a drink."

He ate, but instead of having one drink he had two, then three, and he drank so much that he fell asleep at the table. The mail coach had arrived and departed once more, and the man was still sleeping. It was only five leagues from Paris when Marguerite's son, worried, said to the man who could hear wool being spun:

"Can you tell me what my employee is doing, if he is ahead of the mail coach, or if he is still behind it?"

The man listened a moment and replied:

"Our companion is snoring in an inn in Bordeaux, and the mail coach is no more than five leagues from Paris."

"Never will he arrive!" said the boy. "But you who throw stones so well, can't you wake him up!"

"Of course I can," said the other.

And he took a flat stone from his pocket, wound up, and threw it. The stone passed through a windowpane of the inn where the runner was sleeping, fell on his shoul-

The Self-Propelled Carriage

der, and he woke up, rubbed his eyes, looked at the time, and said:

"I certainly am late! Yet there's still nothing lost. But I must remove the other millstone."

When he had removed it, he departed at such a fast clip that he arrived fifteen minutes ahead of the mail coach.

The king remained calm, and his daughter, who was beside the carriage, laughed behind his back. The boy, who was afraid the king might make further demands, took her in his arms, put her in the carriage, and departed with all his associates. The king, in anger, had cannon aimed at the carriage, and the artillerymen were going to set the weapons off, when the man who caused windmills to turn bent over and let go with such a gust that the cannons and the cannoneers were hurled into the air so high that they still haven't fallen back to the earth. They may have been blown all the way to the moon.

The king was obliged to give his daughter in marriage to Marguerite's son, and that was the first time that the self-propelled carriage was used at a marriage.

19

THE OLD WOMAN IN THE WELL

There was once a widow woman who had a daughter, and she married a widower who also had a daughter from his first marriage. The woman could not tolerate her husband's child; she was jealous of her, and she noticed that she was as sweet and good as her own child was bitter and mean. She kept her out of the house as much as she could.

One evening she said to her: "You ugly girl! Why don't you spend the evening somewhere else?"

The little girl took her distaff and spindle and went out, disconsolate, for she didn't know where to go. Passing near the well, she leaned over the side and was much surprised to see in the bottom a big clear area and some girls, and her surprise was so great that she dropped her spindle and it fell in the well.

"May God help me," she said, "I am going to follow you."

And she jumped over the edge and was all of a sudden among the young ladies, one of whom said:

"Mother, Mother, here's a little girl who has come to spend the evening with us. What are we going to give her?"

"What do you want her to do for you?" replied the mother, who was a beautiful lady.

The Old Woman in the Well

"That she delouse me."

And the little girl good-naturedly began to search through the girl's hair.

"What do you find, my friend?" asked the mother.

"*Neither nits nor lice,
Your hair is nice.*"

"And may you have neither nits nor lice, young lady!"

At the close of the evening, when the girl was going to leave the well, the young woman said to her mother:

"What do you wish for her?"

"I wish that at each word she utters a gold coin may come out of her mouth."

The little girl went home, and her stepmother shouted at her in ill humor:

"Where'd you spend the night, you ugly girl?"

"In the well."

And at each word a coin fell from her lips.

"Ah!" said the stepmother, delighted. "You won't go back there, but my daughter will, tomorrow night."

And the next evening she took the mean girl to the

French Folk Tales

edge of the well and she saw the clear area in its depths, and she threw her spindle in, saying: "The devil help me, I am going to follow you."

"Mamma," cried the young woman in the well, "here is a girl who has come to spend the evening. What shall we give her?"

"What do you want her to do for you?" said the mother.

"That she delouse me."

But it was begrudgingly that she set about it, touching the young lady's hair with the tips of her fingers.

"What do you find, my friend?" said the lady.

"Both lice and mange, madame."

"May lice and mange befall thee, my friend."

And at once her head was covered with vermin.

At the close of the evening the young woman said:

"What do you wish for her, Mother?"

"I wish that at each word she utters she pass wind."

When the girl returned to the house, her mother asked for news of the evening, but as the wish was fulfilled, she got so angry that she died of it, and her daughter didn't delay in doing the same thing out of rage and shame, so that the others lived peacefully until the end of their days.

THE LITTLE GIRL'S SIEVE

There was once a widower who married a widow. The man had a lovely daughter who was pleasant and good, and the woman had one who was haughty and vain. The stepmother mistreated her husband's child. To go to the spring she gave her own daughter a jug; to the other she gave a sieve, and then she scolded her because she didn't bring back any water.

One day the child lay down beside the spring and dropped the sieve in the running water. So as not to be beaten, she followed the stream and found some shepherds with flocks of sheep.

"Shepherds, little shepherds," she said, "haven't you seen my sieve?"

"No, little girl, we haven't seen your sieve."

And, still following the stream, she met some women doing their laundry.

"Washerwomen," she said, "haven't you seen my sieve?"

"No, little girl," they said very sweetly, "we haven't seen a sieve pass by."

These washerwomen were fairies. They had her help them wash while she waited for the sieve, and the girl, who was timid, took nothing but towels and rags to wash, never any fine linen. She had been told not to wash the big pieces.

In the evening they took her into a room that was well supplied with linen and they had her change clothes. She took only those that were of the least value. For supper in the kitchen she chose the leftovers, though they passed her all the most delicate morsels.

Finally, one day the washerwomen fairies said to her: "Today in the room we have given you, when you hear the donkey bray you must lower your head, but when the bell rings, raise it."

The donkey came to bray and the little girl lowered her head, and the bell rang and immediately she raised her head, and at once a drop of gold burst upon her forehead and made her sparkle like one of God's little stars. Happy, she thanked the good fairies and went back to her family.

Ah, poor soul! When the stepmother saw her arrive so shiny, she had her tell all, and she sent her own daughter to the spring with a sieve and told her to let it float away in the current. She did so and then walked along the stream until she came to the washerwomen, and when she found them:

"Filthy old washerwomen," she said impudently, "haven't you seen my sieve?"

The Little Girl's Sieve

"No, hussy," said they, "we haven't seen your blasted sieve."

She wanted to wash nothing but the fine linen, and when it came to changing clothes in the evening, not a single dress pleased her. In the kitchen none of the food was to her taste.

The fairies decided to give her her due. They had her go into the enchanted room, saying to her:

"When you hear the donkey bray, raise your head; lower it when you hear the bell."

And when the donkey came to bray, our impudent girl raised her head; the donkey immediately raised its tail and let its soft dung fall on her forehead; immediately the haughty girl became a common, dirty ass. She wanted to cry, but she could do nothing but bray.

And so she came home humiliated. Oh, when her mother saw her as an ass, what curses, great God! And the other poor little girl, in order not to be torn to pieces, went back to the fairies, who kept her as if she were a daughter.

21

FATHER
BIG–NOSE

There were once two kings who were neighbors and so jealous of each other that they declared war. Several battles had already turned out disadvantageous to one of them because he could not direct his army as he chose, having been frustrated in his maneuvers by the windings of a wide river that had no bridge. To observe the movements of the enemy, one of his officers one day climbed to the top of an oak tree that dominated a large forest. As he looked in all directions, he saw quite close to him a group of children who were playing around a fire that was lighted in a clearing, and almost immediately he saw come among them a man who had a very long nose, so long that it had no end.

"Ah," cried the children, interrupting their play, "here is Father Big-Nose."

And they hastened toward him.

"Hello, Father Big-Nose."

"Hello, my children."

"What news do you bring us, Father Big-Nose?"

"Oh, children, I do have some news for you."

"Tell it, Father Big-Nose."

"I'll tell it, but don't talk about it. There are two kings who are making war on each other. One of them will always be beaten because he can't cross the river, for there's no bridge. And yet in this forest not far from us is found the Red Tree. One would merely have to cut a

Father Big-Nose

branch and place it on the water of the river to see a lovely bridge formed at once. But you mustn't tell.

> *Crick, crack!*
> *He who lets this truth be known*
> *Shall forthwith be turned to stone."*

The officer had heard enough: he came down from his observation post and set out in search of the Red Tree, which he discovered without any trouble. He cut off a branch and carried it away to go find the king.

"Sire, tomorrow night I will build a bridge on the river. Let your army be ready to cross. Don't ask me anything more."

"If you do what you say," replied the king, "you shall have a good reward."

All the officer had to do was to place the branch on the water. It expanded and lengthened in the shape of a bridge and the army passed, surprised the enemies, and executed its first victory. But the others didn't consider themselves beaten and they regained the advantage within a few days.

The officer had the idea of going back to his oak tree, and as soon as he was on the highest branch he looked toward the clearing and saw the children assembled around the fire; almost at once the man with the big nose arrived.

"Here's Father Big-Nose," shouted the children. "Hello, Father Big-Nose!"

"Hello, my children."

"What news do you bring us, Father Big-Nose?"

"I do have some news."

"Tell it, Father Big-Nose."

"I'll tell it, but don't talk about it. The king found a way of building a bridge across the river, but his army will be beaten anyhow. And yet in the forest not far from here is found the Hollow Tree. A small portion of the dust contained within it thrown in the eyes of the enemy would be sufficient to blind and smother them. But you mustn't tell it.

> *Crick, crack!*
> *He who lets this truth be known*
> *Shall forthwith be turned to stone."*

The officer, happy to know such a secret, left his oak tree and went in search of the Hollow Tree. He ended by finding it and filled his pockets with the powder it contained. Then he went and spoke to the king:

"Sire, do not fear the attack of the enemy. Offer battle tomorrow and put me in the first rank. See that the wind is favorable, and I will be responsible for the day."

"May it be done as you desire," said the king. "If you succeed you shall have a good reward."

The next day they were engaged in combat, and as the officer threw dust from the Hollow Tree in the wind, big clouds of smoke were formed, which asphyxiated the enemy soldiers. Many of them fell as if struck by lightning. The others took flight, pressed closely by the officer and his men. Not one in a thousand remained, so that their king was obliged to capitulate, and a peace treaty was signed.

The officer who was the hero of the day was directed to come before the king and was complimented by him.

"I promised you a good reward," he said. "I can't do better than give you my daughter in marriage."

As beautiful as the day, that king's daughter! And the officer was already in love with her.

Awaiting the day fixed for the marriage, he spent all his time in the palace, taking walks and attending entertainments with his fiancée.

One time she said to him: "How did you go about it to build a bridge across the river? And what is that powder that you used so well in battle?"

Father Big-Nose

"Ah, princess, I will tell you all. To observe the enemy I had climbed up into the highest tree of the forest when my gaze fell on a fire that was burning in a near-by clearing, and around the fire a group of children were playing. A moment later I saw come to them a man who had a long nose, and I overhead their conversation."

"And what did they say?"
"This, princess . . ."

And the officer revealed the secrets that he had learned. But scarcely had he ended his story than he was changed into stone. The princess, horrified, called for help, and all the people of the palace dashed forward, including the officer's uncle.

"Ah," he cried, "what has happened to my nephew?"

The princess told what she had just heard and seen. Immediately she too was transformed into a statue of stone.

Sorrow was great in the court. The king ordered the two victims put in the church on each side of the main altar, and all the kingdom went into mourning.

French Folk Tales

Meanwhile the officer's uncle couldn't stop thinking of the strange story the princess had told. He was overcome with a desire to see this mysterious Big-Nose. Not being able to resist any longer, he went into the forest, arrived at the foot of the tall oak tree, climbed from branch to branch, and found that the princess had spoken nothing but truth, for the fire was burning in the clearing, the children were playing around it, and the man with the long nose did not delay in making his appearance.

"Hello, Father Big-Nose," cried the children.

"Hello, my children."

"What news today, Father Big-Nose?"

"I have some, my children."

"Well, tell us."

"I will, but you mustn't repeat it. When I told you about the king who couldn't build a bridge across the river nor win a victory, one of his officers climbed a tree near here. He heard my words and he took advantage of them to build a bridge and to beat the enemy by means of the powder from the Hollow Tree. And the king to reward him promised him his daughter in marriage. But he was not able to keep my secrets. He revealed everything to the princess and he was changed into stone. And the princess, having repeated his words, came to the same end. The whole kingdom is in mourning. And yet in the midst of the forest there exists a spring covered with ice. One merely has to raise up the ice to take a bit of water from the spring and pour it on the stone fiancés in order for them to be restored to their natural life. But it mustn't be told.

> *Crick, crack!*
> *He who lets this truth be known*
> *Shall forthwith be turned to stone."*

The officer's uncle didn't stay in the tree long; he hastened to go in search of the spring, which he discovered

Father Big-Nose

within a few hours. Before the end of the day he was entering the church with the precious water, and eager to try it out. No sooner had he poured a few drops on his nephew than the officer flew into his arms thanking him, and the princess did the same a few moments later.

Joy was universal and they resumed the preparations for the marriage.

Several times the king had interrogated the officer's uncle concerning the means that he had used with so much success to restore his daughter to life, but he refused to reveal a secret that might have such terrible consequences. Questioned every day, however, he feared that the secret might escape him.

"If I were to return to the big oak," he thought, "I might perhaps come into possession of some other secret that I could use to my advantage."

So one day he climbed again into the tree and turned his eyes toward the clearing. Just at this moment the children, assembled around the fire, were greeting the arrival of the man with the big nose.

"Hello, Father Big-Nose."

"Hello, my children."

"What's new?"

"I have something new, my children. I'm going to tell you, but you mustn't talk about it. You know that the officer and the king's daughter had been transformed into stone. The officer's uncle, hidden in the tree, heard what I told you concerning this matter and he took advantage of it to go and get water from the spring, so that his nephew and the princess are today alive in flesh and bone as before. But the uncle, pressed to tell how he did it, can't keep the secret. He's going to let it escape and will be changed into stone. And yet on the edge of the river I know an Orange Tree. One would merely have to pick an orange, eat it, and thereafter make a hole in the trunk and whisper into it what he heard me say. His words would follow the trunk, go down into the roots, and be lost in the river. Then he could repeat them aloud without fear of being changed into stone. But this mustn't be told either.

Crick, crack!
He who lets this truth be known
Shall forthwith be turned to stone."

The uncle strained his ears to listen: nothing was more urgent than to run toward the river. He found the Orange Tree and followed Big-Nose's instructions carefully. And after that he came to the palace and advised the king about what had happened without any bad results. The marriage was performed the next week. If I had to tell you all of the enjoyments which took place on that occasion, it would take me until tomorrow. What I can tell you is that the bride and groom were happy and that peace and abundance reigned for a long time in the country.

22

THE SERPENT AND THE GRAPE-GROWER'S DAUGHTER

A MAN WAS CULTIVATING his vineyard. As he was picking up stones he saw a large one and began to pick it up also. What was his surprise to discover a hole out of which a big serpent came! He was greatly afraid.

The serpent spoke to him: "Who gave you permission to remove the door to my house?"

The man excused himself by saying that he would never have taken that stone to be the door of a house.

Then the serpent answered him: "I know that you have three marriageable daughters. If you don't give me one of the three I'll come at night to crush you. Begone, and give me your reply shortly."

As he went home the man was sad, so very sad that his daughters asked him what the cause of his sorrow was, and he explained to them that, while he was working in the vineyard, moving a big stone, a serpent came out of a hole that it covered and said to him: "Who gave you permission to remove the door to my house?" And he had excused himself by saying that he would never have taken that stone to be the door to a house, and that the serpent had answered: "I know that you have three marriageable daughters, and if you don't give me one of the three I'll come in the night to crush you. Begone, and give me your response shortly."

Then the eldest of his daughters cried that she would never be the wife of a serpent, and the next one made the same answer. The youngest alone consoled her father by telling him not to worry, and she assured him that she would make this sacrifice. So the father took the youngest of his daughters by the hand and went with her into the vineyard.

The serpent was waiting for them there at the entrance to his hole. From the threshold he invited them to come down underground, and he led them, crawling on his stomach, and the father and daughter followed him. Soon they arrived in a marvelous castle whose doors opened on magnificent apartments, with walls that were upholstered in diamonds, furnished with beautiful furniture, lighted by resplendent chandeliers. The father and the daughter were surprised to see such beautiful things, and the girl was so astounded that she turned toward her father to tell him that she would be happy to become the serpent's wife.

At once they came to an understanding concerning the marriage. The serpent offered to his fiancée the white wedding dress and a dress to wear thereafter. The marriage took place. People of the highest society attended. They went to the church ceremony, and the bride was dressed in her white dress, which had a long train, and the serpent crawled beside her. After the marriage the guests went to the castle where there was a great banquet at which delicious and rare morsels were served, such as pheasants cooked on the skewer over a wood fire. Footmen in livery served.

That evening when all of the guests had withdrawn, the girl followed her husband into her bedroom, but she was horrified to find herself without relatives, without friends, and a serpent beside her. He, seeing her fright, reassured her by explaining to her that he could become a man

The Serpent and the Grape-Grower's Daughter

when he chose, either day or night. Immediately he asked her to say when she desired that he become a man. His wife replied that she preferred him to be a man at night, for thus she would be less terrified; by day she would have less fear than by night to have a beast near her. So the serpent took off his skin immediately, hung it on a nail near his bed, and appeared to her as a beautiful prince who had been bewitched by an evil fairy. The fairy had

cast this fate upon him, hoping that he would never succeed in getting married. The next morning he put his snakeskin back on, and so every night he was a prince and every morning a serpent.

A few days later the bride went to visit her parents. Her sisters were jealous of her, seeing her clothed so sumptuously with lovely dresses covered with diamonds. And they suggested that they come to visit her in her castle. And they went and spent a few days with her. She showed them all her beautiful wardrobe and her fine diamonds.

They asked her if she wasn't afraid at having a big serpent beside her. Her husband had told her that if one day she invited her sisters, she should be careful not to touch the skin while he was sleeping, that otherwise a great misfortune would befall the two of them. When the young married woman brought her sisters into their bedroom to answer their worried curiosity and to show them that her husband was a handsome prince, she warned them about what her husband had told her: that if she invited them one day, they should at least be careful not to touch his skin while he was sleeping, that otherwise a great misfortune would befall the two of them.

Nevertheless the eldest sister, seeing such a handsome prince, was filled with desire and jealousy; to see him closer she had taken a torch in her hand and she approached the serpent's skin out of sheer spite. It was consumed in flames. The prince woke up with a start and said quickly to his wife that she should have remembered the advice he had given her. Immediately to punish her sisters he touched both of them with a magic wand: the two sisters then found themselves outside the castle in the countryside, from which they returned to their home.

The prince said to his wife: "You did not heed my advice, I must punish you too; take seven empty bottles and seven pairs of iron shoes. When you have filled these seven bottles with your tears and when you have worn out the seven pairs of shoes, you may come back to me."

Then he touched her with his magic wand and she was in the open countryside alone and lost. She cried night and day and walked unceasingly; she was all the more afflicted and her wandering was all the more painful in that she was with child.

At the end of several months she gave birth to a beautiful son. She fed herself on what she encountered on her way; she ate grass and fruit, and she succeeded thus in staying alive and in suckling her baby. She walked un-

The Serpent and the Grape-Grower's Daughter

ceasingly for seven years and filled one bottle with her tears each year, and used up in the same amount of time one of the pairs of iron shoes; she was all in rags.

At the end of seven years of wandering she saw a village and heard the bells that were ringing as loud as they could. She asked the first person that she met what the big festival was and the reply came:

"It's a prince who's getting married but who lost his wife seven years ago. He is remarrying today."

Then the serpent's wife took her baby by the hand and went and stood at the door of the church. Her husband, who recognized her, was overjoyed, stopped on the threshold, and said to all of those in attendance:

"I had a pretty key, I lost it seven years ago. Today I have recovered it. What must I do? Keep the old one or have a new one made?"

And all of them replied: "If you were satisfied with the old one, why should you have a new one made?"

And they shouted: "Keep the old one!"

Then the prince said: "Here is my wife, whom I have found after seven years; I am taking her back."

And he took her into his beautiful castle, where they lived happily and where they had many children.

THE THREE STAGS

There was once a widower who had four little children, three boys and a girl. Poverty had struck him to such a point that one day he said:

"I've done everything I can; rather than to see my little ones suffer from hunger I'll take them into the woods and leave them there."

The little girl had overheard. Very miserable, she went to complain to her stepmother, who gave her a hard piece of cheese:

"When your father takes you to the wood, take care to crumble your cheese as you walk along and in this way you will find your way back."

The next day the father said to the children: "We are going to the woods to gather sticks for kindling."

The little girl understood but she didn't let anyone notice it, confident in the device that her stepmother had told her of.

Arriving in the woods, the father took his pruning hook. "I'm going to make my bundle of kindling here; you children go a little farther. I'll call you when I have finished."

They waited a long time. The father had gone back home when they returned to the place where he had left them, and so they tried to find their way back guided by the little girl. But, alas, not a single crumb of cheese remained! A dog had eaten them. . . . So they were lost.

While walking through the woods a burning thirst

The Three Stags

overcame them. They met shepherds, whom they asked to direct them to a spring.

"There is the Stag's Spring, but all who drink of it are changed into stags."

"Let's go there," said the three boys.

"No, no," replied their sister, "let's look for another one."

They found some more shepherds and again asked about a spring.

"There is the Serpent's Spring, but no one ever drinks from it because he would be transformed into a serpent."

"Let's go farther on."

The fear they felt at the possibility of becoming serpents made them forget the thirst that was overpowering them. They reached a field of stubble where shepherds were herding their sheep.

"Could you direct us to a spring?"

"There, right close, you'll find the Toad Spring, but don't drink of it. You would be changed into toads."

"What shall we do?" said the children. "Go back to the first spring? It's better to be changed into stags than to die of thirst."

So now we see the three boys, out of breath, lying down to drink at the Stag's Spring.

"Don't drink!" cried the little girl. "Don't! Don't!"

But they were parched with thirst, and so they drank, and now it's three young stags we see accompanying the little girl. But she resisted; she didn't drink.

The stags found it easy to live; their sister ate a few roots and wild fruit. One day she sat down crying at the edge of the wood when the sergeant of the guard at the castle came by.

"What are you doing there?" he asked her, surprised to see this little girl who was already growing up and whom he did not know.

"I'm a poor wretched little girl," and she told her story.

"Come with me," the guard said to her. "I have in my house two boys whom I found just as I have found you. You will complete my household."

"Oh, thank you, but I can't leave my three brothers."

"They can come with you, and they will be happy in the castle park."

And that's how it was arranged. They all arrived at the castle with the guard, who said to the two boys:

"I have brought you a little girl, whom you must treat as your sister."

They promised, but they weren't happy to see this newcomer watching over them. As soon as the guard had left they mistreated her. And she threatened to tell the master all that they had done. Then they decided to throw her in the well to make sure that she didn't tell on them.

When the guard came back he asked them where the little girl was.

"She has gone," they replied. "She said that she wouldn't come back; she was too bored."

That day the brothers of the guard came to see him.

"Why are these three stags surrounding the well?" they asked their brother. "And why don't you kill them?"

The Three Stags

"Those three stags aren't doing anybody any harm."

As soon as their sister had been thrown into the well, they had dashed up to it and stayed there.

"Let's see," said one of the brothers of the guard. "I'm going to take my gun and shoot them."

And as he approached the well he heard a voice that seemed to come out of it and that sang sadly:

> "Oh, brothers, handsome brothers!
> What sad misfortune to us befalls
> Since coming within these castle walls!"

And the stags replied:

> "Oh, sister, pretty sister!
> What sad misfortunes do we bring
> From drinking water at the spring!"

The man came away promptly, frightened.

"Leave the stags alone; if only you could hear their voices!"

One of the bad boys said:

"Give me a gun. I'm not afraid!"

He arrived near the well, and he came back to the house running, all atremble.

"What's going on?" the sergeant then said to the guards. "I'm going to go myself."

And he heard the mournful voices, the one in the well:

> "Oh, brothers, handsome brothers!
> What sad misfortune to us befalls
> Since coming within these castle walls!"

And those of the stags:

> "Oh, sister, pretty sister!
> What sad misfortunes do we bring
> From drinking water at the spring!"

"Quick, quick, bring what is necessary so that I can go down into the well!" cried the guard.

And soon the little girl had been hauled back up.
"How did you fall in the well?"
"It's the two boys who threw me in."
They were punished as they deserved, and the day when the girl married one of the brothers of the guard, her brothers, the stags, were transformed back into human beings.

24

THE MILLER'S THREE SONS

There was once a couple who operated a mill that had very little business. One day there wasn't much left to eat in the house. The miller's wife said to her husband:

"Go fish in the millstream and bring us back some fish for dinner."

"How do you expect me to catch any fish? You know that there's neither fish nor devil nor anything else in the whole river!"

"You make me angry! We've got to have some fish for dinner."

"Well, I'll go anyway."

The miller plied his net in the millstream and brought in a little tiny fish. It was the king of the fish, and it said to him:

"Miller, let me go and you will catch as many fish as you want."

The miller, much surprised, threw the fish back in the water, and then he plied his net again and brought it in full. He continued and he brought it in full each time. He had so many fish that he kept some in reserve in a backwater and brought home only the three biggest ones. The miller's wife was indeed surprised.

"You must have stolen these fish," she said.

"Oh, no. I caught them in the millstream."

She got angry. "How could you catch any fish there? You know that there are neither fish nor devil nor anything else in the whole river."

"Well, I'll explain it to you."

And the miller told his wife what happened to him with the king of the fish.

"That's the little fish that I should like to have had," said the wife. "Next time you'll bring him back to me."

The miller sold all the fish from the backwater in the cities and they brought him a lot of money. Then he came to fish at the same place, and at the first haul once more he brought in the king of the fish, who said to him:

"Miller, let me go once more and you will catch all the fish that you want."

"I can't. My wife wants to see you."

"Ah, women have the devil in their heads! You mustn't listen to her."

The miller threw the fish in the water once more, and afterward he caught as many fish as before, kept three to bring home to his wife, and saved the rest.

His wife was again surprised. "You must have stolen these fish."

"No, I caught them in the millstream."

She got angry. "It's not true. You know that there is neither fish nor devil nor anything else in that river."

Then he told her that once more he had caught the king of the fish and thrown him back in order to have good fishing.

"Imbecile! You don't pay any attention to your wife," she said to him in anger. "That's the little fish that I wanted and none other."

"Don't get angry. Next time you'll have it."

The miller sold all the fish in the markets and they brought him a great deal of money as before. Then he went back to fish in the same place and at the first

The Miller's Three Sons

haul he brought in the king of the fish, who said to him:

"Miller, let me go and again you will catch all the fish you want. You'll earn your fortune."

"This time I can't. My wife wants to eat you."

"Ah, women have the devil in their heads! Well, as yours wants to eat me, listen to me and do as I say: you and your wife will eat my body and your wife will give birth to three boys marked with suns on their foreheads. You will divide up my bones between your mare and your bitch dog; your mare will have three colts marked with moons, and your bitch will have three pups marked with stars. You will put my head in a cupboard and three Damascus blades will appear there which will cut at ten leagues' distance. You will plant my tail in your garden, and a rosebush will grow there with three roses; if one of your boys gets sick, his rose will wither, and if he dies his rose will fall."

The miller did as the king of the fish had told him, and at the end of a certain time his wife had triplets marked with suns and resembling each other so closely that you couldn't tell them apart; his mare had three colts marked with moons, and his bitch three ferocious pups marked with stars, and in his cupboard he found three Damascus blades, which cut at ten leagues' distance, and in his garden a rosebush appeared with three lovely roses.

When the children were of age, they went to school, and they worked well and became very learned.

When they were fifteen or sixteen the eldest of the three said: "I want to go see the world."

"Why do you want to leave," replied the father, "since here you have all that you want for entertainment?"

"That doesn't matter. I want to leave."

"Well, take a horse, a dog, and a Damascus blade, which cuts at ten leagues, some gold and silver, and go to the city of Batafia, where they kill flies with their fists."

The young man set out and walked a long while. He arrived in a city where everybody was in mourning.

He stopped at the inn of the Golden Ball and asked: "Why is everybody sad and dressed in black?"

"In the wood there is a beast with seven heads and every year at this season we must give it a virgin to eat, and this year it's the king's daughter's turn."

"At what time is she to be devoured?"

"At eight o'clock she must be in the forest where the beast will come to take her."

The next morning the youth led his horse and his dog and took his sword that cut at ten leagues' distance. He arrived early at the entrance to the forest and awaited the princess. Soon he saw her coming, alone and dressed in black.

"Hello, mademoiselle!"

"How do you do, sir?"

"You seem sad."

"Alas, I am going to be eaten in a little while by the beast with seven heads."

"Well, I am going to try to save you."

"Oh, sir, it's useless; you would be lost."

"Don't worry, my dog will help me."

He placed the princess on the horse and tied her behind him with a belt, and they went farther into the wood. Soon they heard howlings and the cracking of trees; the beast was coming.

"Worm of the earth! Dirt of my hands! Shadow of my mustaches! What do you want?" said the beast to the young man.

"I want to prevent you from eating the princess."

"All right, then, instead of one person I shall eat two. I'm going to have an excellent meal."

"You'd better look out."

The battle began. Each blow of the Damascus blade wounded a head. At the end of four hours the young man

The Miller's Three Sons

had cut off four heads. The beast begged for quarter until the next morning at eight o'clock.

"Mademoiselle, you see that we shall be victors," said the young man to the princess, and he took out of the saddlebag a girl's wearing apparel and gave it to her.

"Take these to go back to the inn."

Both of them went back and ordered a dinner, and no one recognized them.

The next day they set out once more for the forest. The princess put her black dress back on and got on the horse; the furious beast arrived, and the battle was resumed. At the end of five hours the other three heads had been cut off and the beast was dead.

The princess began to laugh, thanked the young man, and said to him: "And now marry me if you wish."

"I accept your hand, but I must continue my journey and I can't marry you for a year and a day."

Then the king's daughter gave him a ring and a kerchief, both of them marked with her name. The young man put the ring on his finger; then he cut out the seven tongues from the seven heads, wrapped them in the kerchief, and put it all in his pocket.

The two young people separated and the princess started back to the city. Before leaving the wood she met three coal miners.

"Where are you coming from, lovely girl?"

"I am the king's daughter who was supposed to be devoured by the beast with seven heads, but a handsome knight has delivered me and I am going back to my father."

"How did he manage to save you?"

"He fought with the beast and cut off its seven heads and it died."

"Take us to the body of the animal."

The princess took the miners there and they picked up the seven heads and put them in a coal sack.

(191)

"And now," said the oldest of them, "take us to your father and tell him that we are the ones who delivered you; otherwise we're going to kill you."

The princess took the three of them to the palace, and the king was much surprised and very happy to regain his daughter, and she showed him the miners.

"There," she said, "are the three men who saved me."

And the coal miners displayed the seven heads of the beast. The king received these three men very well, had them bathed and dressed fittingly.

"My daughter," said the king, "you must marry one of the three."

"I am willing," said the daughter, "but I think I am too young. I will wait for a year and a day."

The coal miners were installed in the king's palace, well lodged, and they lived well and were very happy.

At the end of a year the king said: "The moment has come; we're going to prepare for the marriage."

But the young man came back to the city of Batafia at the end of a year and a day, and stopped once more at the inn of the Golden Ball and found that everybody was joyously preparing for a festival.

"Why all the festivities?" he asked.

"It's because a year and a day ago three coal miners killed the beast with seven heads and saved the king's daughter; one of them is going to marry her, and everybody is preparing for the festival and the wedding."

The next day the young man said to his dog: "Dog, go into the king's chamber and bring me the three most beautiful wedding presents that are on the table."

The dog went there as quick as the wind; no one could stop him in front of the king's palace. He went in, took the three most beautiful presents, and brought them back to his master. The soldiers on guard set out in pursuit and reached the hotel.

The Miller's Three Sons

"Isn't there here," they asked, "a gentleman who has a dog marked with a star?"

"Yes."

"Well, have him come down at once."

The soldiers' message was taken to the young man.

"I'm not coming down," he said. "Let them come up if they want to see me."

The soldiers went up to his room, but the dog took each as he entered and hurled him through the window.

"Dog," his master said to him, "leave the last one, so that he may tell his master where the others are."

When the king learned this, he ordered cavalry and artillery to attack the inn of the Golden Ball and demolish it with cannon fire. But the dog stopped them. He parried the balls and bullets with his body; then he hurled himself upon the soldiers and left only one to tell the king about the battle.

The princess said to her father: "You see that this dog is more dangerous than the beast with seven heads. It would be better for you to come to terms with its master."

"It's very hard for a king to submit."

"Father, you must go."

The king and his daughter went to the hotel in a carriage and they asked to speak to the owner of the dog. They went up to the young man's room and the princess immediately recognized her savior, but didn't say a word about it. The king invited his vanquisher to come to court, and they went there together, the young man following the carriage on horseback and accompanied by his dog.

A big banquet was given, to which the coal miners were invited, along with the generals and all of the great personages of the court. When the meal was at an end, each told his story. When it was the coal miners' turn, they told how much trouble they had had killing the beast with seven heads.

Then the young man, who had not yet said anything, made fun of them: "But how did you arrange to kill it with a miner's tools?"

Then the miners, annoyed, said that they really did kill the beast, the proof being that they had brought back its seven heads and preserved them in a sack.

"Well, go get them, then," said the young man.

And when they had been brought: "But these seven heads ought to have seven tongues. What has become of them?"

The miners were embarrassed. Then the young man pulled out of his pocket the kerchief marked with the princess's name, spread it out, and displayed the seven tongues. Then he showed the ring he was wearing on his finger.

"Princess," he said, "haven't you anything to say?"

"Father," said the princess, "he is my savior."

And she told all that had happened. Then the coal miners wanted to leave, but they were arrested. A great fire was lighted in the courtyard, and they were thrown into it.

The king recognized the young man as a prince. He sent to get the miller's and the miller's wife's consent to the marriage. The parents and the two brothers of the young man were very happy and the marriage took place.

Some time afterward the young couple went into one of the king's castles in the outskirts of Batafia. The first evening, when they were taking the air on the balcony at the close of day, the young husband showed his wife a beautiful castle that was all illuminated which stood in the midst of a great forest.

"What is that castle?" he said.

"It's a castle inhabited by fairies; those who go there never come back."

He said nothing. But as soon as his wife had gone to

The Miller's Three Sons

bed he got up silently, took his Damascus blade, slipped outside, and departed with his horse and dog. He went toward the castle, and at the entrance he found an old woman serving as doorkeeper.

"Good evening, madame."
"Good evening, sir."

"May I go into the castle?"
"Yes, but first tie your dog with one of my hairs."

This hair was as thin as other hairs, but as strong as an iron chain. Once the dog was tied, the old fairy doorkeeper invited the young man to enter; as he was crossing a drawbridge he fell into a moat and lost his life.

The next morning when the miller and his wife came to the garden, they saw that a rose had fallen to the ground at the foot of the rosebush.

The older of the two remaining sons said: "I must go in search of my brother, be he dead or be he alive."

He took his Damascus blade and some gold and silver,

and departed with his horse and his dog. He walked quickly and went toward Batafia, where he knew that his brother had got married. For several days they had already been looking for the prince who had disappeared in the night and they had promised a reward to the one who found him. The miller's son arrived in the outskirts of the city and met an old man.

"Hello, prince," the old man said.

"Hello, sir."

"I don't think I'm mistaken; you are the son of the miller who married the king's daughter. I recognize you by the sun marked upon your forehead."

"Yes," replied the young man, who had become aware that he had been taken for his brother.

"Then you left your wife alone in the castle?"

"Yes, I went hunting and got lost."

"Well, I am now looking for you, and many others like me, for all of us want to earn the promised reward."

"Then take me to the court."

The king thought that he was seeing his son-in-law and embraced him. "Ah, my son," he said, "how could you have left your wife thus?"

"I went out to look for game and I got lost."

"Hurry and find her in the castle."

The princess took him for her husband and hurled herself into his arms. He didn't tell her anything, but tried to find out where his brother had gone. Evening came and they took a walk together on the balcony.

"What's that illuminated castle which shines in the forest?" he asked.

"I told you the other day," replied the princess. "It's a castle inhabited by fairies. Those who go there never come back; I was afraid that you had gone there."

"That's where my brother is," said the young man to himself.

He went to bed, but in the night he got up silently, took

The Miller's Three Sons

his Damascus blade, and departed with his horse and dog. And he went to the castle where the old woman doorkeeper was at the entrance.

"Good evening, madame."

"Good evening, sir."

"May I go into the castle?"

"Yes, but first tie your dog with one of my hairs."

Once the dog was tied, the young man started to cross the drawbridge, and he fell into the moat as had his brother.

The next morning when the miller and his wife went out to the garden, they saw that another rose was on the ground.

"Our second child is dead!" they said.

"I want to go in search of my brother," said the youngest son. "I will bring him back, dead or alive."

"Then we shall have no child at all!" said the parents.

And they wanted to prevent him from leaving, but the boy persisted. He took his Damascus blade, gold and silver, and departed with his horse and dog, going toward Batafia.

When he arrived near the city, he met an old woman.

"Good evening, prince."

"Good evening, madame."

"This makes twice now that we have been out looking for you, and there will be a good reward for whoever brings you back. If you wish, I shall earn it."

He saw that he was being taken for his eldest brother and he let himself be conducted to the court. When he arrived the king threw his arms around him:

"Oh, my son, are you discontented with your wife, to have left her for the second time?"

"I went out to look for game and got lost."

"You don't know the forest well enough; another time have hunters and beaters accompany you."

"But where is my wife?"

"She's over there in the castle waiting for you, and very worried. Hurry to rejoin her."

They took the miller's son to the castle, and the princess threw herself into his arms, all in tears.

"My husband! Aren't you satisfied with me, to have left me for the second time?"

"I love hunting a great deal; I went hunting and I got lost."

That evening they took a walk on the balcony.

"What's that illuminated castle shining in the forest?"

"Oh, my husband! This is the third time you have asked me! It's a castle inhabited by fairies, and those who go there never come back. I was afraid you had gone there."

"That's where my brothers are," thought the young man.

In the night he got up silently, took his Damascus blade, and departed with his horse and dog. Before arriving at the castle he met an old woman. It was a fairy who was angry with the other fairies at the castle.

"Good evening, madame."

"Good evening, sir. Where are you going?"

"I don't know; I'm looking for my two brothers, who have disappeared."

"Your two brothers are dead; the rose blossoms informed you of that. They are in this castle inhabited by the fairies. The door is guarded by an old woman doorkeeper. Ask to enter. She will want you to tie your dog with one of her hairs. Don't do as your brothers did; don't listen to her. Take your sword and force her to go over the bridge in front of you. But don't go first, as your brothers did; it's a drawbridge and you would be annihilated as they were. Then have her take you to the victims. Here is a vial of ointment and a feather. Dip the feather in the ointment and rub it on your brothers' lips, and on the lips of all who are there, men and women, horses and dogs."

The Miller's Three Sons

The young man arrived at the castle and saw the old woman doorkeeper.

"Hello, madame."

"Hello, sir."

"May I visit the castle?"

"Yes, but first tie your dog with one of my hairs."

"No, evil woman, I don't want to do that. You have found your master, and you can go ahead of me and take me to my brothers."

And he struck her with his sword, and she was forced to go over the drawbridge first, and she led him into an underground cavern where all the fairies' victims were: his brothers, princes, generals, princesses, horses, and dogs. The young man dipped his feather in the jar of ointment and brushed it over the lips of all, and all of them were restored to life. Then he went into the fairies' chamber and forced them to sign a document in which they promised to cease living in the castle. Then everybody went away.

The three brothers arrived at the castle of the princess, where they entered, one behind another.

The princess first saw the youngest, marked with a sun.

"There's my husband," she said, and she wanted to kiss him, but he replied:

"Princess, I am not your husband."

She saw the second brother, marked also with a sun.

"Then this is my husband!"

"No, princess, I am not your husband."

Finally she saw the eldest, marked with a sun, and she embraced him. This time it was her husband.

"Yes, it is I, your husband, and here are my two brothers, who came after my departure, and this is the one who delivered the two of us from the enchantment of the fairy castle."

And he explained to her what had taken place. Then all of them rejoiced greatly.

French Folk Tales

The next morning the miller and the miller's wife went into their garden and saw the three roses shining on the rosebush. They received a letter inviting them to come to Batafia, where everybody was assembled at court. The king was told all and was much surprised not to recognize his son-in-law among the three brothers. Great festivities took place in the city, and all kinds of food were served, even pigs roasted with mustard under their tails.

THE MARRIAGE OF MOTHER CRUMB

There lived a long, long time ago near the forest of Ahun an old woman whose name was Crumb. She was a widow and lived with her niece in a poor tavern at the edge of the wood.

She was so miserly that she picked up dung for a penny, and as she had her snood full of crowns she spent half of the day sitting behind the wall of her garden counting them and re-counting them on her knees, and striking them against each other to hear them ring.

One day she was busy at this work when a young man passed by and heard the noise. He stopped, opened the garden gate, looked at the crowns, and then he said to the old woman:

"If you will give me your crowns we'll get married."

The old woman hesitated an instant, but the boy was handsome, and then there were frequent occasions when the presence of a man was necessary to that poor woman; she made up her mind suddenly and replied:

"I am willing."

The young man picked up the crowns and then he said:

"Hold yourself ready; I will come to get you on a foggy night."

And thereafter every night Mother Crumb had her niece get up to see what the weather was like. As it was a year of especially fine weather, the girl would say:

"Oh, aunt, it's always lovely weather; there's such pretty moonlight that you could find a needle on the ground."

And the old woman would reply: "Good weather for thee, my little one, good weather for thee; bad weather for me!"

This went on a long time and poor Mother Crumb began to despair, when one night her niece said:

"Oh, aunt, what wretched weather! Tonight it's as black as it is inside an oven. There's so much fog that you can't see beyond the tip of your nose."

"Bad weather for thee, my little one; good weather for me, good weather for me!"

Then the old woman jumped quickly out of her bed, put on her pretty red skirt, washed herself with a clean washcloth, put on her white hose, her painted wooden shoes, her hat with ribbons, her loveliest dress, her silken apron, and then she opened the door.

It was as black as ink, but she saw before her door something that looked like four lanterns shining.

Mother Crumb, who always kept her instinct for miserliness, said: "Oh, my fine man, it isn't necessary to light four lanterns. It costs too much. One is quite enough; my poor dead husband never lighted any more than that."

And she went out, but scarcely had she crossed the threshold of the door when she was dragged away at a gallop through the woods, and she was bruised first on one side and then on the other, pulled to the right, then to the left.

All disheveled, she cried in vain: "Ah, my poor boy, you're dragging me too far. Let's not go so fast. Let me catch my breath for an instant. I no longer have my twenty-year-old legs!"

And the more she spoke, the more their flight was hastened. Mother Crumb hadn't seen that she was dealing with two big wolves and that what she had taken for four

The Marriage of Mother Crumb

lanterns were their four large eyes. Finally she fell. At once the wolves hurled themselves upon her and ate her.

The next day the young man to whom Mother Crumb had given her money came to get her. He had got lost the evening before and instead of coming at night as he had said he would, he came by day. But he didn't find the old woman, he found only her niece, who was pretty as an angel of paradise. Both of them went looking for Mother Crumb, following her footsteps. Soon they found the place where the wolves had eaten her; there was nothing left but blood and the wretched tatters of her clothes. They went back to the house together, and all along the road they looked at one another and found each other nice, so that in the end they got married and lived happy ever after.

They had a great many Masses said for poor Mother Crumb, and they certainly owed her that!

FATHER LOUISON AND THE MOTHER OF THE WIND

There was once a man called Louison and a woman called Marioulic who were husband and wife. They were old and without children, and poor it goes without saying. All that they possessed beyond their cottage was a little garden in front of their door, and in this garden a few lovely trees which gave them fruits in season and which brought them a little money on which to live very humbly.

On a dark, rainy evening a hard gust of wind came such as never had been seen before. It broke and uprooted the trees of these poor people without sparing a single one of them, so that when Louison saw the disaster the next morning, he was greatly saddened; and he said to Marioulic:

"Now we are ruined! I must go find the Mother of the Wind; perhaps she will give us something to repair this damage for us."

And he took a big piece of bread on the end of his stick and departed without loss of time. He walked and walked right straight ahead; and by dint of walking he arrived at the place where the Mother of the Wind lived.

"Hello, Mother of the Wind."

"Hello, Father Louison. What brings you here?"

"Mother of the Wind, I must complain about your son; during the night he uprooted and broke all the trees of my garden, which were laden with fruit; he hasn't left me a

Father Louison and the Mother of the Wind

single one! And that's all I had to subsist on. Now I am reduced to beggary and I have come to find you to see if you can't give me something to repair this damage for me."

"Since it is so, my friend," said the Mother of the Wind, "you are right to have come. All I can give you is a napkin, but no weaver can make one like it, for it will make it unnecessary for you to work for the rest of your life. May you only keep it."

Then the old woman went to her chest, took a napkin from it, and gave it to Louison, saying:

"When you want to eat or drink, all you'll have to do is stretch it out in front of you, no matter where you are, pronouncing these words: 'By the virtue of this napkin, may nothing be lacking on my table,' and you will be served at the very instant."

Louison took the napkin, thanked the Mother of the Wind a great deal, and departed as happy as a king.

He walked and walked, and when he was halfway, as he was beginning to be hungry and thirsty, he unfolded his napkin, stretched it out before him on the ground, and said:

"By the virtue of this napkin, may nothing be lacking on my table."

And that very instant the napkin was covered with bread, wine, and other items of food sufficient to satisfy ten people.

"Good!" thought Louison. "The Mother of the Wind hasn't deceived you. Henceforth I think we are going to be able to leave dry bread to others and to feast at no cost whatever."

And he sat down there on the grass and ate to his heart's content. He ate enough for two, drank enough for four, and when he was fully satiated he folded his napkin and set out once more on his way, singing as loud as he could.

When he arrived in a village, the people of the inn were on the doorstep. They called him from a distance and asked him:

"Won't you come in awhile, Father Louison? Well, are you happy over your trip? What did the Mother of the Wind give you?"

"Well," he said, "she gave me a napkin."

"So much as that!" said the mistress of the inn, bursting out laughing.

"Yes, so much as that," said the good man, entering. "And you would be all too happy to have one like it: for the remainder of your life you would no longer have to buy either bread, wine, or any other thing to entertain your clients."

"Bah," said the woman, "show it to me; show it to me, Father Louison."

Louison, very proud, took his napkin from his pocket, placed it on the table, and said:

"By the virtue of this napkin, may nothing be lacking on my table."

And at once there was bread, wine, various dishes, enough to satisfy ten people.

The innkeeper and his wife were amazed; they couldn't get over their surprise. Louison invited them generously to share all that was on his table, and he himself began to eat and drink. But by dint of drinking while they were conversing he ended, fatigue helping somewhat, by going to sleep with his head on the table. What did the mistress of the inn do? She took his napkin, ran and hid it in the back of a cupboard, and laid one out exactly like it in the same place, so that when Louison awoke a moment later, he took this napkin, put it in his pocket, and went away whistling without suspecting anything. Finally he arrived home.

"There you are, poor man," said Marioulic. "It's time

Father Louison and the Mother of the Wind

you were back! Did you find the Mother of the Wind? Did she give you anything?"

"Ah, woman," replied Louison, "now we are rich! Henceforth I think we shall eat our bread with gravy. We shall no longer have to toil and sweat so much to earn our living. Look!"

And, so saying, he stretched out the napkin before him on the table and said:

"By the virtue of this napkin, may nothing be lacking on my table."

But the napkin remained bare and Louison was quite confused. And Marioulic burst out laughing.

"Well, that's certainly some trouble," she said, "spending three whole days walking the highways to bring back a rag that isn't worth twenty sous in good cash! You really must be stupid, poor man!"

Louison was not happy. He scratched his head, which was scarcely itching, and didn't know how to answer. And he thought that there was nothing better or quicker to do than go back to the Mother of the Wind. And at daybreak the next day he took his napkin and departed anew by the same road. And he kept going straight ahead, and by dint of walking he arrived at his goal.

"What!" said the old woman when he entered. "You're back, Father Louison?"

"As you see, Mother of the Wind, I have returned here so that you can give me something in place of this napkin."

"What do you want me to do with it?"

"Its power failed just as soon as I got home!"

"If you believe me," replied the old woman, "there is more than you have said. But, after all, this time I won't go into the problem too carefully. Now I am going to give you a duck such as you have not often seen. You shall merely have to say: 'Duck, lay silver,' or 'Duck, lay gold,' and she will furnish you each time as much as you want of each. Only take great care not to let it get stolen. Remember what I am telling you, and don't come back any more."

Then the Mother of the Wind went to her coop and came back with a duck that she gave to Louison. He thanked her, took leave, and departed once more quite happy.

When he was halfway home he was curious to see if his duck would obey him; he put it on the ground, put his beret under its tail, and said:

"Duck, lay silver."

And the duck laid him a big heap of silver coins.

"Duck, lay gold."

And the duck laid him a big heap of gold coins.

"Good," thought Louison, rubbing his hands. "Now my fortune's made for sure. I'm through with buying bread by the pound."

And he filled his pockets with the gold and silver, took his duck, and went on his way.

When he arrived in the village, the innkeeper and his wife were on the threshold and they didn't fail to call him from a distance as before and to induce him to enter, asking him what the Mother of the Wind had given him.

"Oh," he said, "it's still better; she gave me a duck that lays gold and silver, as much as I want. All I have to do is command."

"Bah!" they said, "you're joking, no doubt? Let's see."

Louison didn't have to be asked twice; the man, heaven knows, would gladly take a drink, nor was he annoyed to show off what he could do with his duck. So he went in, put the duck on the table, and said aloud: "Duck, lay silver."

And at once silver coins began to roll in all directions on the table.

"Duck, lay gold."

Father Louison and the Mother of the Wind

And gold coins came from the same source.

The innkeeper and his wife opened their eyes wide and gaped like pretty jay birds without knowing what to say. Louison, proud like a man, picked up all of his gold and silver, sat down on the stool, and ordered a pint, and after the first one, another, and after that one, still another, so that in the end he grew drowsy and went to sleep on the edge of the table, as he had done before.

That's exactly what the mistress was waiting for: immediately she laid hold of this duck, hid it with the napkin, and brought another one exactly like it and put it in the same place. As for Louison, when he had slept enough,

he awoke, took the duck that was in front of him, and went away humming, and when he was at home:

"There you are, poor man," said Marioulic, "and what fine thing are you bringing back? The Mother of the Wind this time probably gave you something worth two francs?"

And Louison answered, making his pockets ring and pulling out handfuls of crowns and golden louis:

"Look here a minute and see if all this is worth two francs."

"Good heavens! Where'd you get all that?" asked the woman, astounded.

"Now I shall have as much as I want without much trouble," said Louison, puffing up with pride. "It's this duck who gives it to me; all I have to do is command."

And he put the duck in the middle of the table and said: "Duck, lay silver." Not a thing. The duck didn't even seem to hear.

"Duck, lay gold." And this time the duck laid a plateful of filth for him.

And Marioulic began to laugh and scoff at him more than ever.

"Yes, honestly, she really serves you up money! What a good joke! Can't you see that you're losing your mind, poor man?"

Louison, shameful, lowered his head without having anything to answer. What was there to say? He thought to himself: "The Mother of the Wind really jokes at the expense of poor people! Anyway, you'll have to go back to her again; all it will cost you is your trip!"

So the next day at daybreak he got ready once more, took the duck under his arm, and set out again, and he walked and walked until he arrived. And when she saw him there, the Mother of the Wind began to get angry:

"You again, Father Louison? What have you come to ask for? Didn't I tell you not to come back to me?"

"I know, Mother of the Wind, but what could I do? The duck was worth exactly the same as the napkin. She preserved her ability only until I reached my threshold. What you give me serves only to make people laugh at me. I'm getting tired of it!"

"Listen, my boy," said the Mother of the Wind, "you

Father Louison and the Mother of the Wind

like to drink a bit too much; there's the whole trouble. You haven't said anything to me about an inn where you have gone to sleep at the table each time you have come back. Well, the napkin and the duck that I gave you were changed on you there. Now, here is a walking-stick; it's the last thing that you'll get. It's not much, if you wish, but you won't find one like it every day. It knows how to work well, as you shall see."

Then the Mother of the Wind took a walking-stick that was in a corner of the closet and she said:

"Walking-stick, go through your act."

And the walking-stick hurled itself upon Louison and began to strike and thrust at his back, his shoulders, everywhere, so much and so hard that he could see nothing but fog, and he cried like a man on fire:

"Enough, enough, you're going to kill me! Call this club off!"

The Mother of the Wind tried to conceal her laughter, but didn't reply. After a moment, seeing that the club had sufficiently worked him over, she cried: "Walking-stick, come here."

And the walking-stick went over beside her.

"Take it," said the old woman, offering it to Louison. "Now you can lose it and it may still be useful to you. You deserve punishment for having got a swelled head."

Louison grumbled; he was not at all happy and didn't hasten to take that cursed walking-stick which treated people so. But, having thought it over a little, he reconsidered. He said that he would accept it, and even thanked the Mother of the Wind, and he went away at once, rubbing his back.

When he was at the place where he had stopped on the other occasions, he was overcome with a desire to witness the walking-stick's know-how, and he said:

"Stick, go through your act."

And at once the stick hastened through the trees, striking, thrusting right and left in a fury; the tips of branches flew into the air in all directions!

"Good!" thought Louison. "The Mother of the Wind was right. I do think that this will be useful to me, and shortly too."

And he had the walking-stick come back to him and set out without losing time. When he arrived in the village, the people of the inn, who were on the lookout for him, called him from as far as they could see him to find out what present the Mother of the Wind had given him this time.

"Ah," he replied, "she gave me this old stick. I don't know what she wants me to do with it! Yes, it is true it will serve me to punish evil people and thieves if any come my way, for it can strike by itself alone; all I have to do is command. And so, if you'd like to see— Walking-stick, go through your act," he said.

And the walking-stick jumped upon the shoulders of the innkeepers, striking and thrusting like a deaf person, and whim! wham! on one and then on the other without mercy; their backs were smoking as they shouted and asked for pardon and forgiveness. Louison wouldn't listen. The blows kept falling. At the end of a moment when the club was well entertained at their expense, and seeing them almost at the end of their strength:

"Wretches!" he said, "my napkin and my duck are here; you stole them from me. Give them to me quickly or I shall have you beaten to death on the spot."

"We'll give you back everything," they cried, half-dead. "Deliver us."

"Walking-stick, come here," said Louison.

And when they had returned everything to him, which was done without any delay, he turned his back on them without thanking them and set out for home.

"Well, poor man, aren't you tired of running around?"

Father Louison and the Mother of the Wind

asked Marioulic as soon as he appeared on the threshold. "What are you bringing back this time? It must surely be the most curious of all."

"That may be. Look!" said Louison, showing her the walking-stick.

"This stump of a club?" said the woman, bursting out in laughter.

"Listen, Marioulic, it's not much, it's true, but it might be useful all the same, more often than you think. Do you want to see a bit? Walking-stick, go into your act."

And the club, dancing, struck and thrust on Marioulic's back, up and down, so much and so well that the old woman ran about crying like a madwoman.

"Well, what do you say?" Louison asked her in a moment, calling off the stick.

Marioulic, astounded and black with anger, began to heap curses upon him, but without answering her, he took the napkin from his pocket and spread it out on the table, saying: "By the virtue of this napkin may nothing be lacking on my table."

And there was bread, wine, various dishes, more than enough to satisfy ten people.

And who was astonished? It was Marioulic. She softened up on the spot and didn't have to be asked twice to sit down to the table with Louison; never in her life had she been present at such a feast. When both had eaten and drunk to their full, Louison got up, went to get his duck, and put it on the napkin, saying: "Duck, lay silver. . . . Duck, lay gold."

And there was silver and gold; never had Marioulic seen so much of it at one time.

"By heaven, my man," she said, "I must admit after all that you're no more stupid than anyone else. Now, thanks to you, our bread has been earned. We can let the rain fall and scoff at the ill-clothed."

And she took the duck and the napkin and went to

shut them up behind double locks in the cupboard, and as for the walking-stick, Louison kept it for himself alone to make use of as needed.

And then by dint of extracting gold and silver from their duck, Louison and Marioulic became very rich, very rich indeed, in a very short time, and they had a castle built that was so big and so beautiful that none like it had ever been seen. As they had previously been known to be very poor, people were much astonished and jealous ones were not lacking to gossip and disseminate all sorts of evil rumors about them, so that one fine day the judge and constables fell upon them all of a sudden, without saying hello, and ordered them to explain at the very instant whence the money had come that was necessary to build such a castle.

"If that's all there is to it, I'll satisfy you without difficulty," said Louison.

And, knowing precisely how those birds go about things, he invited them to dine with him, promising to tell them thereafter what they wanted to know since they were so insistent. When they were ready to sit down to table, the judge and the constables smelled no odor of cooking and saw nothing served or ready anywhere. And they thought that they were being made fun of, and they began to pout and to look at each other askance. But then Louison came forward, unfolded his napkin, and stretched it out before them, saying:

"By virtue of this napkin may nothing be lacking on my table."

And at once there were bread, wine, and dishes enough to satisfy ten people, all of the very best. Those men were beside themselves, opening eyes as wide as your fist, which didn't prevent them from sitting down at once to eat and drink, nor from taking their good share of all that was there.

When they were well satisfied, Louison got up, went to

the cupboard to get his duck, and put it on the tablecloth, saying:

"Duck, lay silver. . . . Duck, lay gold."

And coins of gold and silver rang all over the table.

"Now," said Louison, "you know as much as I do; there's where I got what I needed to build this castle. It didn't cost me much trouble, as you see."

What could the judge say? Nothing, and he didn't say anything. All of them praised the duck and began to drink again in order to keep even with Louison. Soon, by dint of pouring and drinking, the good fellow ended by getting drowsy and going to sleep on the end of the table, as he usually did.

Seeing that, the judge and the constables said in a whisper: "Our man's asleep. We'll take away his duck and his napkin."

But when they were getting ready to leave, after having hidden everything under their coats, Louison awoke. He understood at a glance all that had happened; he said to the judge, without any pretense:

"Mr. Judge, you haven't seen everything; wait, so that I can show you what is most curious."

"Hurry, then," he said, "we've been at table long enough; we must leave."

"It won't take long," said Louison. . . . "Walking-stick, go through your act."

And he went to the door and shut them in, and the stick set to it, striking here and beating there on each in turn without respite; blows were unleashed upon their hides and they cried for help and brayed like donkeys!

"Father Louison, Father Louison," cried the judge, "here's your duck and your napkin. Deliver us!"

When he saw finally that the good-for-nothings had received their due, Louison opened the door, took back his duck and his napkin; and then he said: "Walking-stick, strike harder."

And while they were fleeing as fast as they could, the stick ran after them and worked them over all the more, striking like a deaf man, and making their hats fly in the air on either side. It was a pleasure to behold!

And the judge and the constables went home, shameful, their heads hanging, swearing that never again would they feel like coming to give Father Louison any trouble.

*I set my foot in a rock chuck's lair,
And so came back to Labouheyre.*

27

GRAIN-OF-MILLET

There was once a married couple who were getting old and they still had no children, which gave them a great deal of pain indeed. The wife continued to pray God to give them one out of mercy. One day, while praying God, she said:

"What happiness for me if I had a child! Even though he was no bigger than a grain of millet, I should still be quite happy."

Then the Good Lord spoke to that woman:

"You shall have a child since you desire it so much; but he shall be born as you have requested, and he won't get any bigger."

And a little while afterward that woman discovered that she was with child, and when her time had come she brought a child into the world, but he was so very, very little that he would have been taken for a grain of millet. They were none the less happy, she and her husband, and both of them took the best possible care of him, and because he was so small they named him Grain-of-Millet.

Grain-of-Millet didn't get any bigger than he was at birth, but he was so gay and so happy to be alive that he was a pleasure to see. And he was, moreover, very skillful and knew so well how to go about things that he accomplished all that his parents asked him to do. One day when his mother had a lot of work in the household, she sent him all alone to take the cattle to the field, and she told him:

"Be careful to see that they stay on the grass and don't go into the garden. If it should rain, you can take shelter under a cabbage leaf. Come back early and don't stay out after dark."

So Grain-of-Millet left for the pasture, following the cattle as brave as a man. When he arrived, a great downpour suddenly came up so he ran and took shelter under a cabbage leaf in the garden, as his mother had told him. But the rain didn't stop. He waited so long that he finally went to sleep, so that while the oxen were grazing, one of them approached and ate the cabbage leaf and swallowed the child at the same time.

When evening came, the cattle went back home but Grain-of-Millet didn't reappear, and his mother was all in tears. She set out at once to go and search for him in the field, calling as loud as she could all along the way:

"Halloo! Grain-of-Millet! Halloo! Grain-of-Millet!"

But there was no answer, either from the field or from elsewhere. The woman became more and more worried, and she came back toward the house, not ceasing to call:

"Halloo! Grain-of-Millet! Halloo! Grain-of-Millet!"

And as she arrived, Grain-of-Millet cried: "Mother! I'm in here, in Baldy's stomach!"

The poor woman, hearing that, thought she would fall in a faint. She began to cry and wail and ran to tell her husband what had happened.

"Oh, misfortune, misfortune! Baldy has swallowed our Grain-of-Millet! He's in Baldy's stomach! He answered me!"

"Is it possible!" said the man. "My heavens, what are we going to do?"

"Let's kill the ox," said the woman, "and we'll find him."

So they killed the ox and they cut it open on the straw that had been laid out at the barn door. Then they examined the entrails. They searched and searched with great care, always calling: "Grain-of-Millet!" but he didn't answer. It was in vain that they strained their eyes; they re-

Grain-of-Millet

moved the flesh without being able to find the child, and they left the entrails there on the manure pile, throwing the lungs there because they were a bit spoiled.

What had become of Grain-of-Millet? He was in the lungs. From the ox's mouth he had fallen there, but his father and mother, unheeding, had struck him such a blow as they removed the entrails that the poor boy remained half-dead and speechless.

He remained in a faint there in the lungs until twilight, when an old woman passed by and, seeing the lungs, said:

"Oh, what lovely lungs! They didn't want them; I might just as well take them."

And she picked up the lungs, put them in a basket, and carried them away on her arm.

Farther along beside the road the old woman reached an oven. They had just taken bread out of it. The door was still warm; and as it was very cold she put her basket on the ground and approached to warm her hands. Thereupon Grain-of-Millet came back to his senses and, seeing that old woman there all bent over toward the door of the oven, he began to say to himself:

"Cover yourself up, old woman; I can see you."

And the old woman turned around, much surprised, opening wide her eyes; she couldn't see anyone! Gripped with fear, she picked up her basket and escaped as fast as she could along the road without looking behind her!

At the end of a moment Grain-of-Millet said: "Trot, trot, trot, old woman; night's catching up with you."

"God forgive me!" exclaimed the old woman. "Aren't these lungs talking?"

And she ran with all her strength, puffing like a badger!

A little farther on, Grain-of-Millet repeated: "Trot, trot, trot, old woman; night's catching up with you."

"Lungs, I'm throwing you away!" said the old woman.

"Trot, trot, trot, old woman; night's catching up with you."

"Witch of a lung, go to the devil," said the old woman. And she took it from the basket and threw it as far as she could.

And Grain-of-Millet shouted: "Old woman, pick me up; old woman, pick me up! Ha, ha, ha!"

The old woman took off her wooden shoes and fled like mad toward her home, more dead than alive, so much was she frightened.

Night had fallen. Grain-of-Millet could no longer think of returning home, but he was not sorrowful for so little. He fixed himself up in his lungs as best he could to await day; but as he was about to go to sleep, a wolf passed by, smelled the lungs, and swallowed them in one gulp, and there is Grain-of-Millet shut up in the wolf's stomach.

The wolf went on his way, and the next day he found a flock of sheep.

"Happy day!" he said. "I'm going to put a lamb with the lungs."

He ran toward the flock, but Grain-of-Millet cried from inside his stomach:

"Beware, shepherd, beware, the wolf is after your lambs!"

And the shepherd arrived, shouting at the wolf, and the wolf ran off quickly in the direction whence he had come, much surprised, his ears dragging.

He went and went and he found a flock of goats. "It makes no difference," he said, "the goats will make up for the lambs." And he dashed upon them.

But Grain-of-Millet cried: "Beware, goatherd, beware, the wolf is after your goats!"

And the goatherd hastened up; he set a big dog on the wolf so that all he could do was look in the direction whence he had come, and take off at full speed, without saying anything.

Grain-of-Millet

He went and went until he met the fox, who asked him what had happened, why he was so sad.

"I am bewitched," said the wolf. "I don't know what's got into my stomach; I can no longer approach a flock without its shouting and kicking up a fuss to warn the herdsmen. I don't know what to do!"

"Of course," said the fox, "it's some little chap that you have swallowed alive without noticing. Get rid of him or you will die of hunger."

The wolf set to work; he strained and coughed but to no avail, and he set out furious, swearing that he would satisfy his hunger whether it cried and made a fuss or not. In the end he came upon a herd of cows.

"I'll have a cow," he said, "surely I shall strangle one."

"Beware, cowherd, beware! The wolf is after your cows!"

And the cowherd arrived, but the wolf, famished, advanced anyway. The cows had arranged themselves in a circle, hind quarters pressing against one another, and they received him with great thrusts of their horns. He thought he would be disemboweled, and withdrew once more, growling like a hungry dog.

Then he said: "Who are you, demon? Night has come, and I am still empty. Must I die of hunger?"

"You shall have peace," said Grain-of-Millet. "I will even tell you a place where you can eat and feast at your pleasure, but promise me to release me as soon as we have arrived."

"I promise you," said the wolf.

"Go back where you found the lungs; right close there is a sheepfold [1] on a strip of pasture. The sheep are inside; to enter you will dig a hole underneath the door; but deliver me first on the pile of straw before you touch the lambs."

The wolf set out full speed toward the sheepfold. When he arrived, he dug underneath the door until he had made a hole, and as soon as he had entered, he jumped at the throat of a lamb.

"What about me?" cried Grain-of-Millet. "Free me, or I shall stir up another fuss."

"Be patient," said the wolf, and he strained so well this time that with great difficulty he finally succeeded.

"Here I am," said Grain-of-Millet, and the wolf threw himself upon the lambs, killing some of them, and taking away what he could, and I've never had news of him since.

As for Grain-of-Millet, he reached one of the corners of the sheepfold and made himself as comfortable as he could in the straw to spend the night. As he was about to go to sleep, he heard the door open and saw two men come into the sheepfold and approach the lambs.

One of the men said:

"Oho! There's been some carnage! The wolf has been here!"

"That's luck," said the other. "All we need do is take away two of the dead ones."

It was two men of the neighborhood who were to cut their grain the next day; but they didn't have money to buy a lamb and they had come there at night together to

---

[1] *Borde:* a sheepfold with a roof of heather or straw; the word *parc* is reserved for sheepfolds covered with tiles.

Grain-of-Millet

steal one for each of them. As they bent over toward the dead lambs, touching them along their backs, each in turn, to choose the fattest:

"Good!" said one. "I've got one here who will certainly have fat on his kidneys."

"I've got one that isn't bad, either," said the second man.

"Bah," cried Grain-of-Millet. "I'll bet that I've got the best one of all."

"Who's there?" asked the two men, much surprised.

No one answered, so that they were overcome with fear and fled as if the devil were on their heels, leaving the lambs where they were.

After this, Grain-of-Millet went to sleep and nothing else befell him during the night. He was so tired that he didn't wake until morning, when the shepherd came to the sheepfold to take out his flock. Seeing the carnage, the poor man began to wail and create a hubbub, heaping curses on this evil wolf, swearing and flying into a rage.

"You're bursting my head," said Grain-of-Millet in his corner. "You shouldn't wail like this; if I hadn't been here during the night, even the carcasses wouldn't be here."

The shepherd opened his eyes wide. "It must be the devil," he thought, and having driven his lambs out, he dragged the dead ones outside hastily, trembling with fear, and went away to skin them at some distance from the sheepfold.

Grain-of-Millet, meanwhile, was tired of so many adventures. He really would have liked to go back home. While he was thinking about it two women came to the sheepfold to lay out straw. He thought that they might possibly get him out of his difficulty, but a great misfortune almost befell him again: one of these women went to put her first rakeful of brush at the very spot where he was located, and, before the little fellow, quite terrified, was able to take cognizance of the situation or say anything, with the back of her rake she struck a spot so near him that he was really terrified and uttered a great cry:

"Ieee, yieee! You almost killed me! Watch where you're beating."

And the women took off very quickly, terrified, leaving their rakes behind.

"Don't be afraid," he cried to them. "I won't harm you. Rather, come back and get me out of here."

"Who's there?" they called, coming back. "We can't see anybody."

"Here, under the brush. I can't get untangled."

Both of them began to remove the brush, searching and rummaging in the spot whence they heard the voice come, so that at last they saw him.

"Who are you, little crumb?" they asked him, quite surprised.

Grain-of-Millet said: "I am the son of so-and-so at such-and-such a place. I got lost yesterday evening coming back from the pastures, and I spent the night in this sheepfold. I don't know where I am; you will render me a great service if you will be so kind as to show me the way."

"With pleasure," said the women.

And they took him and carried him to the road, without forgetting to tell him where he should turn in order to take the shortest route. Grain-of-Millet thanked them and set out, quite bold. He walked and walked, and he moved his limbs so much that he became tired, and he stretched out near a patch of heather at the roadside to rest for a moment.

Scarcely was he there when three thieves arrived and stopped just at the edge of this patch of heather to divide a sum of money they had just stolen in the neighborhood. They began to count the money, and when all was counted, one of them said to the others:

"You have so much there, and you so much, and so much remains for me."

Grain-of-Millet

"And what about my share?" said Grain-of-Millet from the bottom of the hole where he had hidden.

And the thieves got up quickly, all three of them, and looked about. Not seeing anybody, fear overcame them to the extent that they escaped each in a different direction, leaving all of their money on the spot.

Grain-of-Millet picked up that money and set out joyfully. Finally he got home.

And when his father and mother, who thought he was dead and who had cried so much for him, saw him, they almost fainted from surprise and joy.

"Where have you been?" they said. "We've looked for you everywhere."

Grain-of-Millet told from beginning to end what had happened to him, and how he had got out of everything, and he ended by jingling his money in his pocket. These poor people couldn't get over it.

As for him, he began to work without delay just as before, not saving himself in order to relieve his parents, so that they ended by having very little to do, and they grew very, very old and lived very happy with their Grain-of-Millet.

I set my foot in a rock chuck's lair,
And so came back to Labouheyre.

THE LITTLE SARDINE

There was once a man and a woman who were very poor. One day the woman said to her husband:

"My poor man, we have neither bread nor stew. What shall we do? I have an idea: suppose you went fishing. We would sell what you caught and then we would have some bread."

So the man went down to the river, but in vain he cast his line and spent the whole day fishing; he caught nothing. Finally he ended by catching a lovely little sardine.

The little sardine then said to him: "My good man, if you will spare me I will give you anything you want."

"All right, my little sardine," replied the man. "We are very wretched; if you want to help me, I should like to have bread and stew for my good wife and myself."

"You must merely go home," said the sardine, "and you will find a table that is well served."

He threw the sardine back in the water and it hid in a hole. The man thanked it and went home, where he found the table all covered with fine wines and good things.

The good man told his wife what had happened and how it was the sardine who was offering them this feast, and then they sat down to the table. And when they had eaten and drunk well these good people went to bed very happy.

The Little Sardine

Then the next morning the good woman said to her husband:

"We are very happy to have had such a good stew, but there is something lacking; you must go back to the river and ask the sardine for a better house than the one we have."

So the man went back to the river, and he shouted on arriving: "Little sardine, where are you?"

"In my hole. What do you want?" said the sardine, appearing.

Then the good man continued: "My wife sends me to tell you that we are very happy but that our house is not suitable, that we need a more beautiful one."

"Go home," replied the sardine, "and you will find the house rebuilt." Then it disappeared.

Arriving home, the good man found a beautiful house and his wife installed in it and very happy over such a lovely dwelling.

So these people were very happy for some days; but

soon something else was lacking, and the woman said to her husband:

"You're going back to see your sardine and ask it for some fine furniture to put in the house, for ours is too old."

The man went back to the river and said: "Little sardine, where are you?"

"In my hole. What do you want?"

And when the sardine appeared the good man asked for the furniture that his wife wanted.

"It is in place," said the sardine, disappearing, and the good man went back home.

For some time the woman was pleased to see her fine shiny new furniture, but soon she found that her linen was not in harmony with her lovely cupboards, and her husband had to return to the river again.

He said upon arriving: "Little sardine, where are you?"

"In my hole. What do you want?"

"My wife would like to have some fine linen to fill her cupboards."

"Go back home," the sardine said, diving. "Your wife already has what she asked for."

And when the good man reached home, he found his wife admiring her cupboards, which were stuffed full of fine linens. And this happiness lasted for some days; then the woman said to him:

"My poor husband, we're beginning to get old; soon we shall no longer be able to walk. We will need a carriage."

The man went back to the river and said: "Little sardine, where are you?"

"In my hole. What do you want?"

"Oh, my poor sardine, my wife is tired of walking and would like to have a carriage."

"Go back home," said the sardine; "there will be a carriage at your door." And it dived.

The man left and, arriving at his door, he saw the hand-

The Little Sardine

some carriage that was sparkling with gold, two horses, coachman, and lackeys.

So here we have our fine couple, driving about the countryside in their handsome carriage and living as happy as kings. And everybody in the neighborhood envied their happiness and asked whence this wealth could have come to them.

One day when they were out driving, they met a beggar woman who was very old, leaning on her stick. She asked the good people if they wouldn't let her get in the carriage with them, because she was tired and couldn't walk any farther. But the woman, who was very proud of her lovely carriage, turned up her nose at the beggar woman's rags and refused to let her get in. Then the beggar woman addressed the man, but he didn't want to contradict his wife and he told the coachman to whip up the horses.

Then the old beggar woman stood up straight and touched the carriage with her stick and it turned into a squash, and the two horses became, one of them, a big flea, and the other a big louse.

The old woman—it was the sardine fairy—crushed these two hideous animals, and the couple died in wretchedness as a punishment for their selfishness.

29

THE STORY OF GRANDMOTHER

THERE WAS ONCE a woman who had some bread, and she said to her daughter: "You are going to carry a hot loaf [1] and a bottle of milk to your grandmother."

The little girl departed. At the crossroads she met the *bzou*,[2] who said to her:

"Where are you going?"

"I'm taking a hot loaf and a bottle of milk to my grandmother."

"What road are you taking," said the *bzou*, "the Needles Road or the Pins Road?"

"The Needles Road," said the little girl.

"Well, I shall take the Pins Road."

The little girl enjoyed herself picking up needles. Meanwhile the *bzou* arrived at her grandmother's, killed her, put some of her flesh in the pantry and a bottle of her blood on the shelf. The little girl arrived and knocked at the door.

"Push the door," said the *bzou*, "it's closed with a wet straw."

"Hello, Grandmother; I'm bringing you a hot loaf and a bottle of milk."

---

[1] *Époigne. Épigne*, a small loaf of bread, usually made for children, which has slashes on it made with a knife prior to cooking. From Vulgar Latin, *poigneia, pugneia, poignée;* from the Latin *pugnus*.

[2] I asked the storyteller: "What is a *bzou*?" He replied: "It's like the *brou, or garou* [werewolf; the modern French form is *loup-garou*]; but in this story I have never heard anything said except *bzou*." A. Millien.

(230)

The Story of Grandmother

"Put them in the pantry. You eat the meat that's in it and drink a bottle of wine that is on the shelf."

As she ate there was a little cat that said: "A slut is she who eats the flesh and drinks the blood of her grandmother!"

"Undress, my child," said the *bzou*, "and come and sleep beside me."

"Where should I put my apron?"

"Throw it in the fire, my child; you don't need it any more."

And she asked where to put all the other garments, the bodice, the dress, the skirt, and the hose, and the wolf replied:

"Throw them in the fire, my child; you will need them no more."[3]

"Oh, Grandmother, how hairy you are!"

---

[3] For each item of clothing the teller repeats the question of the girl and the reply of the wolf.

"It's to keep me warmer, my child."
"Oh, Grandmother, those long nails you have!"
"It's to scratch me better, my child!"
"Oh, Grandmother, those big shoulders that you have!"
"All the better to carry kindling from the woods, my child."
"Oh, Grandmother, those big ears that you have!"
"All the better to hear with, my child."
"Oh, Grandmother, that big mouth you have!"
"All the better to eat you with, my child!"
"Oh, Grandmother, I need to go outside to relieve myself."
"Do it in the bed, my child."
"No, Grandmother, I want to go outside."
"All right, but don't stay long."

The *bzou* tied a woolen thread to her foot and let her go out, and when the little girl was outside she tied the end of the string to a big plum tree in the yard. The *bzou* got impatient and said:

"Are you making cables?"

When he became aware that no one answered him, he jumped out of bed and saw that the little girl had escaped. He followed her, but he arrived at her house just at the moment she was safely inside.

30

THE SHARPSHOOTER

There was once a man and a woman who had three children. One evening they were sitting around the fire, and the man said to his wife:

"When one of us dies, the other must go to Rome to have a Mass said."

"Yes, I am willing. But why have you come to this decision?" said his wife.

The man died in a short time, and his wife no longer thought of the Mass. At the end of a year she heard a pounding noise in the attic. She sent her eldest son to see what it was, and he saw a big black dog and ran away.

Then she sent the second son, and he saw a big black cat, was filled with fear, and ran away also.

The third son said: "I'm not afraid; I'll go."

But he was his mother's favorite and she didn't want to let him go. But he went anyway and saw a man all in white whom he recognized as his father, and he went to kiss him:

"It's you, Daddy?"

"Yes, it is I."

"Come and eat soup with me, Father."

"No, I have come to remind your mother that she promised to have a Mass said for me in Rome."

The boy took the message to his mother, and all four of them decided to leave the next day for Rome. The youngest, who set out hunting, said:

"I'm going to kill some game to feed us on the way."

And so they departed, and the youngest went hunting in the woods with his gun, and he brought back food. When he had gone a little deeper into the forest he climbed a tree to find the road once more. He saw two giants, and he shot one of them in the ear, which caused the giant to say: "A fly has bitten me."

He did the same with the other, who said: "Me, too."

They saw him in the tree.

"So you are the sharpshooter, eh? Well, come with us to our castle, which is not far from here. We will need you."

"I can't. I'm too tired."

Then one of the giants took him on his back, and as the woods were very thick, the other one walked in front to separate the trees with his arms to make a path, and they came to the castle.

"In this castle," said the giants, "there are three girls who are asleep. They are guarded by a dragon. Won't you kill it, being the sharpshooter that you are?"

"Yes," replied the young man.

In front of the castle garden there was a big wall. The giants threw the hunter over it. He seized the dragon, which was going to hurl itself upon him, and killed it at the first shot of his gun.

As the giants couldn't climb over the wall, the young man shouted to them:

"Dig a hole. We'll get back together."

When the hole was made, the first giant put his head under and the young man cut it off. He did the same with the second, and threw the two heads in the middle of the garden besided the body of the dragon. Then he went through the castle. He came to a chamber where he found a girl sleeping. He spent the night with her, and took her two gloves before leaving.

The next day he entered another chamber and found another sleeping girl, and he kissed her and took her ring.

The Sharpshooter

The next day he entered a third room and found the loveliest of the girls, and he took her earrings.

Then he went away to find his mother and his brothers. But where were they? He walked a long time, asked everywhere if they had been seen, but they had got ahead of him; they had had time to go to Rome and to return.

Finally one day he was told: "They have entered an inn over yonder." He went there and found them.

"Where have you been?" asked his mother. "You must have killed some game."

"Oh, I didn't waste my time; I have killed two giants."

And they all departed to go home.

After the departure of the hunter the three girls had awakened without knowing who had drawn them from their sleep and had stolen the gloves, the ring, and the earrings, and they had a beautiful house built on the edge of the highway, arranged it as a beautiful inn, with an inscription: "Come in. No payment required."

And they inquired of everybody who came their way.

Finally the mother and her three sons saw this inn.

"Mother, let's go in since it's free."
"No doubt you pay on leaving."
"Certainly not; let's go in and see."
And they went in and were served. Then they asked to pay: "How much is it?"
"Nothing. But we want to ask you what you have seen on your journey."
The mother told what she had done, and the two elder sons said the same thing.
"And you?" asked the girl of the third boy.
"Ah, I have seen many things."
The mother wanted to stop him from talking, but the girls asked her to be quiet, and he continued:
"I have cut the heads off two giants and I have killed a dragon, and I saw three girls sleeping in a castle."
"Would you recognize them if you saw them sleeping?"
"Certainly."
"Well, come with us."
They went back to the castle with him. They went to sleep and he went into their rooms, and he recognized the first girl and gave her her gloves, and he recognized the second and gave her her ring, but when he arrived at the third girl's he said:
"This one I don't recognize."
But she got up and said: "Here are my earrings in your hand; they are mine."
The three girls said to him: "You have delivered us; choose one of us to be your wife."
"It is you, the youngest, that I will take," he said.
And he married the two others to his brothers, and their mother stayed with them, and they lived happily in the castle.

GEORGIC AND MERLIN

In a mysterious wood near the castle of a rich lord a bird was singing delightfully. Its voice went straight to the heart, as did its caressing music. It would have made the most melodious nightingale jealous.

The lord used to say: "There is a nice neighbor that I should like to have even closer to me. I would give a great deal to the person who would help me put my hand upon it."

A soldier was returning from service in the king's army and he fulfilled the lord's desire; he succeeded in capturing the bird.

They made a lovely cage with golden latticework, they put a variety of food in it, fresh water in a saucer that had the splendor of crystal. Vain precautions! The bird scarcely took a beakful, and it ceased to sing. Its music was lost with its freedom. Its body was imprisoned but its soul had remained in the depths of the mysterious wood.

The lord still had a longing for his prisoner; for no money in the world would he have let it go.

"Woe to him who lets it go!" he frequently said. "Death will be the punishment."

This lord was a hard man and no one in the world would have prevented him from executing his sentence, even were it against his eldest son.

He did have a son by the name of Georgic, a child of

ten who had no equal on the earth for his qualities of mind and of heart. One day when the lord was traveling and the boy and the bird were alone together, the bird began to speak:

"Georgic, Georgic, open the door of my cage, and I will sing you a beautiful song."

"All right," replied the child, who, without thinking, freed the prisoner. Wild with joy, it flew away.

"Thank you, friend," it cried. "You have rendered me great services. Know that you have not done it for one who will be ungrateful." And detaching a feather from its wing, it said: "Take this; when you need my services move it about and say these words: 'Merlin, Merlin, come quickly to my aid,' and on the instant I shall be with you."

Already the little bird had flown away toward the wood, singing the most melodious of its refrains.

Then the child understood the seriousness of his error; he understood it still better when he saw his mother cry out her soul.

"My son, my son," the poor woman wailed, "what have you done? Have you forgotten your father's threats? Will you then have to die?"

A salt-vendor who chanced to be in the country passed by selling salt and he heard this crying.

"To condemn a child to die for such an act of forgetfulness," he cried, "would be an abominable crime. If you wish I will get you out of your difficulty. Give him to me. In a few days I will be far from here and never will your husband hear of it."

The proposition was accepted as a favor from heaven. Georgic was confided to the merchant with a sack of a hundred crowns for the two of them to live on, and they set out looking for adventure in new lands.

Meanwhile the salt-vendor, going along the road, thought to himself: "I doubt that I was very well advised

Georgic and Merlin

to take this brat under my wing. At the first opportunity I'll abandon him and take his money away with me."

The occasion shortly presented itself. They had arrived before an old castle whose towers were reflected in the waters of a pool on the edge of a forest. Leaving his little companion at the door, the man went in.

"Don't you need a shepherd?" he asked.

"Yes, we do," he was told, "provided he is strong."

"Why strong?"

"Because our fields are infested with wolves and he will no doubt have to fight for his life against them."

"He is quick-witted and good. Take him anyway."

It is thus that the child, without knowing it, was engaged as a shepherd at this lost castle. Already the salt-vendor was going away without any more concern for him.

"And my money," said Georgic, "aren't you going to leave it here with me?"

A threatening gesture was the only answer.

"Merlin, Merlin, to my help," cried the little boy, waving his feather.

There was a rustling of wings, the bird of the forest appeared, and a hard club brandished by an invisible hand fell upon the back of the thief, striking with vigor. The salt-vendor had to submit and return the hundred crowns.

The next day the little shepherd took his sheep to the pasture. "Beware," he was told, "otherwise the wolves will eat you."

"We shall see," he replied. And again he called: "Merlin, Merlin, help!"

The bird came.

"I want," said the boy, "a whistle to call the wolves and muzzles to prevent them from biting."

You can imagine the surprise of the servants who at

noon came to bring him his lunch. He was playing near his sheep, which were grazing peacefully in the midst of the field, and around them a pack of wolves who, seated on their behinds, each with a muzzle on its nose, seemed to be watching over them.

"Why don't these ferocious beasts devour the flock?"

"Because," replied the child, "I haven't permitted them to."

Now, in those times in the depths of the forest there lived a serpent that was the terror of the countryside. He was a hideous monster with seven heads, and each year to avoid the results of his anger the inhabitants were obliged to give him a young woman to devour. This had been going on for a long time, and for a long time Georgic had been filling his function to the great satisfaction of his master, when the master's daughter's turn came. And she's precisely the one who that day at noon brought the lunch to the shepherd in the field.

The poor girl cried more and more as the fatal day approached, and the shepherd didn't stop comforting her.

"Pray! Pray!" he said. "You will see that God will help you."

Finally the assigned day came and the victim had to resign herself to go. She went sadly toward the dragon's cavern, having no more hope, when suddenly she heard the gallop of a horse running at full speed. It was Georgic. The brave boy had asked his bird for what he needed: a horse, a black cloak, and a steel sword. And now he was ready to confront the most formidable dangers.

"Get on behind me," he told the girl. "We shall see if the serpent will attack an armed man as willingly as he does a feeble woman."

The hideous beast was waiting on the threshold of his lair.

"Come," Georgic cried to him. "Come, cruel dragon, to get your prey."

Georgic and Merlin

But no doubt it did not expect to see its victim appear in such company, and it pulled back.

"No," said the beast, "I don't want her until tomorrow. Today I have no appetite."

Georgic sank his spurs into the flanks of his horse and departed. An instant after, he put the girl down on the edge of the wood and disappeared. The poor girl was so disturbed that she hadn't recognized him in his disguise. Yet she had had enough presence of mind to cut a piece off his black cloak and to bring it back to her father.

At noon, as on previous days, she brought Georgic his lunch and she told him of her singular adventure.

"Didn't I tell you so?" he declared. "Prayer is fruitful; so pray."

The next day at dawn the girl began once more her sad pilgrimage. She heard the terrible dragon's howls of anger, and she trembled throughout her whole body, but she was no sooner in the midst of the forest than the knight, a gray cloak over his shoulders, joined her and invited her to get on behind him.

The monster, who seemed to be pricked with hunger, didn't dare to come out of his cavern in spite of it.

"I prefer to wait until tomorrow," he said.

Georgic had to go back. He took his companion to the same place and went away. The girl, who once more had failed to recognize him, had again taken the precaution to cut a piece out of his gray cloak.

The third day came, and the victim had to take the route to the forest. For the third time she met her savior, clothed in a superb purple cloak.

As they were passing near a house where a man was busy heating his oven, having in his hand a long iron fork, the knight stopped.

"Will you lend me your fork an instant?" he asked. "I have to get rid of an evildoer."

"Yes, yes, gladly," consented the man. "As long as it is a question of a good deed, I'm your servant; take it."

The serpent had taken refuge in the depths of its cavern, for, on hearing the gallop of the horse, he had been frightened.

"Here I am back, cruel beast," cried Georgic at the entrance. "I am bringing back your prey; if you want her come and take her."

"I'm in no hurry," replied the monster. "Another day, perhaps, I shall feel more like it."

Georgic felt his soul filled with a violent anger. "Do you think then, accursed one, that I shall permit you to make fun of us any longer?" And seizing the fork, he thrust it into one of the dragon's throats and dragged it outside. The steel sword did the rest. In seven blows the seven heads fell.

The victor pushed the dead beast back disdainfully with his foot, cut out the seven tongues, which he put in a kerchief, and suddenly took leave of the girl. As before, she had cut off a piece of his purple cloak without his knowing it.

Georgic and Merlin

It had been announced everywhere by order of the master of the castle that he who would get rid of the cruel dragon would have the hand of his daughter. All he had to do was to bring back as proof the seven heads.

A coal miner whose hovel of branches stood in the wood, and who had watched the fight in hiding, thought he had found a good thing. He picked up the seven heads and went with them to the castle, affirming that he was the victor.

"The victor?" exclaimed the girl. "That cannot be. He who killed the beast took away its tongues and not its heads."

"I have eaten the tongues," replied the imposter. "All I have left are the heads."

To bring the affair out into the open, the lord ordered a great banquet, to which he invited gentlemen and peasants of the region. There was a chance that the knight with the black cloak might also attend. Georgic went, as a matter of fact, but so well disguised that it was impossible to make out his features, but the girl nevertheless had no difficulty in recognizing the black cloak.

"That's he," she cried. "I'm not mistaken."

The piece of cloth fitted the cloak exactly. Who was that man? They didn't have time to find out. Georgic had disappeared. Some time thereafter the lord gave a second banquet. The people came to it in as great numbers as before, and among the crowd there was a brilliant knight wearing a gray cloak, which the girl recognized at once.

"That must be he," she murmured in her father's ear. And a cut made in his cloak fitted the fabric that she had detached.

"Are you the one who saved my daughter?" asked the father.

"Perhaps," replied the knight, who withdrew instantly. And seeing him go away, the girl remained silent.

"I don't know if I am mistaken," she said, "but it seems to me that it's Georgic."

A third festival took place, at which as many people appeared as before. The coal miner was there too, but one could feel that he wasn't going to grow fat in a corner, for the outcome was approaching. A personage of distinction, his shoulders draped in a rich purple cloak, attracted particular attention.

"I'm sure that it's he," joyfully exclaimed the girl. And the cloak had a cut in it which corresponded exactly with the piece of fabric she held in her hand. Seeing that he was discovered, the mysterious stranger wanted to flee once more. But there were guards all about. One of them at the moment when he was going through the door hurled a lance between his legs, and they had no trouble in stopping him. It was indeed Georgic, and he was her savior, and the best proof was the serpent's seven tongues, which he had in his kerchief. As for the impostor, he had withdrawn silently.

Now the girl belonged rightfully to the valiant boy.

Several days after the marriage had been celebrated, the couple was living happily together when suddenly the master of the castle fell gravely ill. The skill of the doctors was of no avail.

They called an old wizard, who advised: "Three things are necessary to heal him: a piece of orange from the orange tree of the Armenian Sea, water from the Fountain of Life, a piece of bread from the Yellow Queen with a bit of her wine. The Fountain of Life, moreover, is not far from the palace of that queen."

The lord had two other sons-in-law who were very jealous of Georgic and who claimed the honor of going to get these cures. They departed and for months they didn't come back. The first had got lost in a country that was dry and cold, and he was found half-dead at the foot

Georgic and Merlin

of a mountain. The second embarked upon the ocean and was hurled by a tempest on a deserted shore.

Georgic went in his turn at the prayers of his wife. He had a horse called Giletic, who was as fast as the wind. As he was going through a forest he met a hermit.

"I know the object of your mission," the holy man told him, "and I want to help you in your designs. Take first the road to the sea. Here is a wand that will always guide you. Follow it; it will lead you to the orange tree. You must pick an orange, and cut it in four parts, and bring back one part. Going straight ahead of you, you will arrive at the Fountain of Life. It's not easy to approach it, for it is guarded by a gigantic lion, whose body covers seven leagues of countryside, just barely leaving a path to reach the water. Before trying to get water out of it, go first to the palace of the Yellow Queen. You must find her lance near the hearth and bring it back, and you must cut a piece of her bread, and fill a bottle with her wine, saying: 'Yellow Queen, Yellow Queen, it's for my father-in-law's health.'

"When you are outside, you will see a stag tied near the house. Get on his back after taking care to leave your horse on the road in order not to frighten the stag, and go back to the fountain. The lion will be asleep. If he awakens, you must hide behind a hawthorn bush and attack suddenly. With your lance it will be easy for you to overpower him. Once he is dead, take care to cut his body in four equal parts and make three cuts in his tail. Then nothing will prevent you from getting water at the Fountain of Life."

Everything happened as the hermit had predicted. Georgic arrived without too much difficulty at the orange tree of the Armenian Sea and at the palace of the Yellow Queen. He took the lance, the bread, the wine, the princess's stag, and went toward the fountain, and found the lion sleeping. "A fine business," he said. And on tiptoe he approached the water. Unhappily, while he was dipping water, there was a gurgling sound. The wild beast awakened with a roar, and scarcely did he have time to hide behind the hawthorn.

Five minutes after, the lion was sleeping again. "This is the moment." A blow of the lance full in the heart and he was dead. Georgic quartered its body as he had been told, and left to find his horse.

He had left it grazing in the tall grass in the field, but during his absence a hungry wolf had devoured the poor Giletic. There was only one way of escape: to take the wolf in place of his mount.

He blew his whistle, the wolf came forward, and he climbed on the wolf's back and galloped along the road back.

The first man that they approached was one of the brothers-in-law. The poor chap was almost done in. The water of the Fountain of Life with the bread and wine of the Yellow Queen restored his health. He couldn't retain a cry of contentment and admiration, which was mixed with envy:

"Give me your remedies, Georgic. I'll pay you the price they are worth."

Georgic had a grudge against this brother-in-law, who out of jealousy up to this day had never ceased to humiliate him.

"I will gladly give you a bit of my water, but on heavy conditions. I require your wedding ring and the tip of your ear."

The other uttered a deep sigh and accepted.

A little way from there the travelers met the second brother-in-law, who was also in a bad way. Thanks to the precious remedy, he was soon on his feet, and in his turn he asked:

Georgic and Merlin

"What do you want in exchange for your water, your bread, and your wine?"

This brother-in-law hadn't been any better toward Georgic than the first one.

"The price I require for a bit of bread and a few drops of wine?" he replied. "I must have one of your toes."

After a moment of hesitation the bargain was accepted.

Content at having humiliated these two proud individuals, Georgic let them heal the father-in-law and brag at leisure of having gone themselves to get the marvelous remedy. But he was reserving for them still another disagreeable surprise.

"I warn you," the hermit had told him, "that you have rights to this water, this bread, and this wine only for one month. At the end of that time if you haven't returned them, the Yellow Queen will come to get them, and beware of her anger!"

As is only just, the brothers-in-law, who weren't aware of any of these things, hadn't given any back at the end of a month, so the Yellow Queen arrived at their houses full of anger, a whip in hand. Georgic wasn't there. Suspecting what was going to happen, he had gone to work in the field with his wolf.

"My water, my bread, my wine!" cried the queen.

The first brother-in-law brought his few drops, the second his bit of wine and his crumbs of bread.

"Is that all that I gave you?" replied the queen. "I don't tolerate being made fun of."

And her whip came down violently on the shoulders of these two unhappy men. In vain they wailed: "Georgic has the rest! Georgic has the rest!" The whip continued to strike with violence. They had to run to the field where their brother-in-law was working.

"Georgic, I beg you," they cried, "give back the Yellow Queen's water, wine, and bread."

"Gladly," replied Georgic, "and I give you back over and above the bargain the ear, the wedding ring, and the toe. The first lesson that you have deserved for your disdain and your pride was not sufficient to heal you. May the second be more profitable to you: it is to no good that you blow yourselves up at the expense of others."

32
THE LITTLE BLACKSMITH

THERE WAS ONCE a little boy who was working as an apprentice in a blacksmith shop.

One day he said to his boss: "By heaven, sir, you haven't got very much work. I feel like leaving you to go on a trip."

"Well," replied the blacksmith, "since you want to gad about the world, I'll give you a saber and a helmet."

So the little blacksmith departed. He went very, very far without either eating or drinking, and he was very hungry when he saw a house. He hastened his step to arrive at it, and when he was at the door he asked if they didn't need a servant.

"Yes," replied the people of the house, "we should like one, but it isn't a very desirable place. We have had several servants and all of them have been killed while they were in the fields, without our knowing how it happened."

"I'm not afraid," said the little blacksmith. "But before beginning my service I should like to eat, for I've been traveling for three days without having found even a piece of bread."

They served him enough to satisfy him and when he had eaten his fill, they showed him where the pasture was. He noticed that all the fences that were used to form an enclosure had been cut, and he began to repair them. As he was finishing his work, a giant arrived riding a big horse, and he said in a terrible voice:

"What are you doing there, youngster?"

"It's no business of yours, giant. I'm doing what I'm supposed to do."

"Well, for what you are doing I am going to kill you."

"We shall see," replied the little blacksmith, unmoved.

He took his sword, put himself on guard, and cut the giant's head off and his horse's as well. And then he kicked them with his foot, saying:

"Look, you've still got feet to dance on!"

When he was back at the house, they asked him if he had seen anything.

"Yes," he replied, "I saw someone, but I have laid him low and he will no longer bother anybody."

The next day when he went back to the pasture he found the fences cut as before, and he began to repair them, and at the moment that he was finishing mending them, he saw another giant, who came and cried to him:

"What are you doing there, little earthworm?"

"It's none of your business, big man; I'm doing what I'm supposed to."

"I'm going to kill you for what you're doing."

"We shall see," said the little blacksmith, and he took his sword out and cut the giant's head off.

He went back to the farm, and everyone asked him: "Did you see anything?"

"Yes," he replied, "I saw someone, but I treated him just as I did the person who came yesterday, and so he won't bother us any more."

Going back to the pasture the following day, he found the fences cut for the third time. He repaired them as before, and at the moment that he was finishing he saw a giant, who said to him:

"What are you doing there, little earthworm, dust of my hands, shadow of my mustaches?"

"It's no business of yours, giant; I'm doing what I'm supposed to."

The Little Blacksmith

"Well, that's why I'm going to kill you."

"We shall see," replied the little blacksmith, who, with a stroke of his sword, cut off the giant's head.

Then he took the road whence the giants had come, and he arrived at their castle and entered, and saw their mother crying hot tears.

"My good woman," he said, "what's the matter that you are so sad?"

"I had three sons," she said, "and I don't know what's happened to them."

"Well, I know where they are, and I'll show them to you if you're willing to give me all the keys to your castle."

The good woman gave him the keys, and he said to her:

"Here, climb up to the window and look."

And when the good little woman, who was no higher than a jug, had climbed up to the window, the little blacksmith took her by the legs and threw her into the yard, where she died, and he remained master of the castle and of its treasures.

33

LA RAMÉE AND THE PHANTOM

There was once a soldier whose name was La Ramée. After having served for seven years he had re-enlisted twice in the hope of becoming a corporal. At the end of this third leave he went to see his captain.

"Captain, my time is up. Will you promote me to corporal?"

"Not yet, La Ramée. You shall have it if you enlist another time."

"The devil with enlisting! I'm leaving. I'd prefer to serve the devil for seven years than to stay a year longer with you."

And so he left as a simple soldier, and not happy at all. And as he left the city he took a road that led him into the midst of a big forest of saplings, and he walked a long, long time along roads that were winding and full of quagmires. And then he got lost in the underbrush and scratched up his legs. He was already longing for his regiment when at last he came out of the forest.

Then he saw a city on the plain which stood out on the horizon with great black flags raised as a sign of mourning, and he entered an inn, dying of hunger, and ordered a meal.

"I see over there," he said to the innkeeper, "a city with great black flags. What's it all about?"

"It's a very sad affair," replied the innkeeper. "The

La Ramée and the Phantom

king had a daughter, the most beautiful on the earth. He lost her some time ago, and since that moment there comes every night into an old church a kind of phantom that's very dangerous. At eleven forty-five it raises up a paving stone of the church, comes out of a crypt, and goes back into it at the stroke of midnight. Each night the king posts a soldier to guard the church, and the next morning he is found smothered. It is said that a man who could spend only three nights in the church would be able to chase the phantom away and free the city thereof, but no one has succeeded and everybody is desolate."

"Is that all?" asked the veteran. "I'm willing to try, but put in my bag a bottle of good wine."

La Ramée went toward the city and presented himself to the king.

"Your Majesty, I am a veteran and afraid of nothing; I have come to ask your permission to spend the night in the church."

"My friend, do you know what you are risking?"

"Yes, I know, but have no fear, I shall free you of the phantom."

"If you succeed you will be well rewarded."

La Ramée waited until night came and went to the church, said a short prayer, and then went and lay down behind the altar. At fifteen minutes before midnight he heard the noise of the paving stone that was being raised up, and the phantom appeared, searching in every corner, now approaching, now withdrawing; and finally it went toward the altar and it perceived La Ramée and dashed upon him. But midnight rang and it disappeared.

The next day the whole city was much surprised and very happy to see the soldier still alive. As for him, he had been so afraid and yet so brave that he was already worried about the next night.

When evening came, he went to sleep at the pulpit, but this time the phantom had a half-hour, for at eleven thirty it came out of its vault. It went first behind the altar, where it had seen the soldier the night before, and rummaged around a great deal there. Then it followed a wall and went down toward the main doors. It came back following the other wall, arrived at the foot of the pulpit, and put its foot on the steps at the moment when the first stroke of midnight sounded. Once more La Ramée was saved.

He came out of the church at the break of day and acted brave before the people who were awaiting him for the festival:

"Oh, your phantom, I was scarcely afraid of it. I took it by the shoulders and I said: 'You run along back into your hole.'"

But the third night remained, the most terrible of all for the phantom came two hours early, and the soldier was trembling in advance. His heart was beating very heavily in his chest when he saw that he was shut up in the church. He climbed to the bell tower and waited. At ten o'clock he heard the phantom beginning its search and seeming to be in a great anger. It explored all the corners of the church, creating a big fuss, and had completed its search when eleven o'clock sounded. Then fear overcame La Ramée. He scampered down from the bell tower and ran away on a road that was supposed to take him back to his own country; but he hadn't taken a hundred steps when he met some knife-grinders who had a carriage. A woman walking behind the carriage spoke to him:

"Aha, you were afraid, just like the others."

"I don't know what you mean," replied La Ramée, much disturbed inside.

"I'm saying what I know; I know you well. You just left the church, didn't you?"

"Yes, that's true."

"Go back quickly, for there is still time and I'm going

La Ramée and the Phantom

to help you. Take this pair of scissors. With them you have nothing to fear. When the phantom wants to smother you, don't defend yourself, but bend over and cut the nails from its feet and hands."

La Ramée thanked the woman and went back into the church. As soon as he had closed the door he felt arms

closing around him, but without losing his head he began to cut the phantom's nails, first those of the feet and then those of the hands, and it was easier than he had thought. At once the phantom turned into a beautiful girl and threw herself into his arms.

"Here is my liberator," she said. "I am the daughter of the king and they thought that I was dead, but I had been bewitched and shut up in a crypt in this church."

La Ramée took the princess to her father, who was beside himself with joy.

"My friend, what do you want as a reward?" asked the king.

"Sire, the only reward I desire is the hand of your daughter."

The princess had already asked her father if she could marry La Ramée, and so the marriage was agreed upon. The soldier first went back to his own country to settle his business, and then he came back to the princess. They were married a week later, and the wedding lasted for two weeks. When the king was old he gave the crown to his son-in-law, and La Ramée reigned a long time in peace and wisdom.

34

THE WOMAN WITH THREE CHILDREN

There was once a man and a woman who had three children. The man died leaving his wife alone with the children. The eldest was fourteen, the second twelve, and the third seven. One morning the eldest went to his mother.

"Mother," he said, "bring me a cake; I want to go to work for wages."

"Where will you go, my poor boy? You're still too young."

"It doesn't matter. I'll earn my living as best I can. Make me a cake, please."

The mother prepared a cake and the child departed. When he was far away he came to a fountain, and he sat down and began to eat his meal.

All of a sudden an old man appeared. "Where are you going, poor boy?" the man said to him.

"I'm going to find work."

The man asked him: "Will you give me some cake?"

The boy replied: "Certainly not."

The man asked: "Which do you prefer, a sack of gold louis or the sky?"

"A sack of gold louis."

The man replied: "Then go home and you will find a sack full of gold louis."

The child went back home and found the sack there, and he told his brothers how he had gone about making his fortune. Then he went off to the forest with his gold louis.

A few days after, the second son went to his mother.

"Mother," he said, "make me a cake; I want to go find work; I'll bring you back money."

His mother made him a cake and the child departed. Like his brother, he found the fountain and stopped there, and the same man asked him where he was going.

"I'm going for work."

The man replied: "Will you give me a piece of cake?"

The boy replied: "You're joking."

"Which do you prefer, a sack of gold louis or the sky?"

"A sack of gold louis."

"Well, you'll find a sack of gold louis back home."

The child hurried back, found the sack of gold louis, and departed without saying anything to his mother or his brother; and the poor woman was dying of poverty.

"Well," said the youngest child, "listen to me; there's no reason for your sorrowing so. Make me a cake, please, and I'll go find work."

"Where are you going? You're too young; no one will want to hire you."

"I don't care. I want to go!"

The mother made his cake and he departed. It took him a long time to arrive at the fountain, and when he arrived there, he was exhausted. He sat down and was eating his little cake when the old man appeared.

"Where are you going, poor little boy?"

"I'm going to find work."

"You're pretty young."

"It doesn't matter. My mother's all alone; I must earn money to feed her."

"Well, are you going to eat lunch?"

"Oh, yes, I'm very hungry."

"Would you give me a bit of that cake?"

"Yes. Take this, grandfather; take all of it if you wish."

The Woman with Three Children

"Which would you prefer, a sack of gold louis or the grace of God."

"The grace of God, which would save Father and Mother."

Then the man struck a stone with his wand, and a little donkey came out of it.

"Heavens," said the child, "how will I be able to get on it?"

"Don't be afraid," replied the old man, helping him climb on.

"Now," said the man, "continue along this road and you will find a heap of things, each prettier than the others. Don't stop to look at them; stop when the donkey stops."

"Yes, master."

"Then," said the man, "when you have arrived call the mistress and tell her that you were sent by me; tell her what you have seen on the way, and she will tell you what you must do."

"Yes, master."

The child departed and when he was a little farther on he found a fountain with blood flowing in it.

"Good heavens," said the child, "how pretty! But the master told me to go on my way. Keep going, donkey."

And when he was a little farther, he found a fountain from which milk was flowing.

"Heavens, how pretty! I should like to stop and taste it, but the master told me to keep going. Get up, donkey."

A little way farther he found a fountain that flowed as clear as crystal.

"Heavens, how pretty! I would refresh myself, but the master told me not to stop. Get up, donkey."

A little farther he saw a bull and a cow fighting. It astonished him and he would have stayed to watch them, but the master had told him not to stop.

"Get up, donkey."

A little farther he found two sheep that were fighting, and he was quite astonished at this. He would have liked to stop but the master had told him to keep going.

"Get up, donkey."

Finally, after trotting a long way, the donkey entered a yard and stopped.

"Master," cried the child, "here I am."

The mistress came out.

"I have been sent by the master and I want to tell you about the pretty things I have seen on the way."

"Good. Are you tired?"

"Yes."

"Let's go eat. Then you will go to bed and you will tell me of your trip."

The child ate, went to bed, and fell asleep, and he slept for seven years. Finally the mistress went and awakened him.

"Don't you want to get up, poor boy?"

"What time is it?"

"It's noon."

The Woman with Three Children

The child stretched, rubbed his eyes, and got up.

"Well," he said, as he wanted to pull his trousers on, "they only reach to my knees. How can this be?"

"Don't you know, poor boy," the mistress told him, "that when you came here you were seven years old, that you have slept seven years, so that now you are fourteen?"

The child's mouth flew open from surprise. It seemed to him that he had slept for only one night. The mistress served him a good meal and asked him what he had seen on the way.

"Oh," said the child, "I saw lots of pretty things. First I saw a fountain flowing with blood, then another one flowing with milk, and a little farther on another one flowing with water as clear as crystal."

"You don't know what it was?" said the mistress.

"No."

"Well, the blood that was flowing from the first fountain was that shed by Our Lord on Calvary; the milk at the second was that which Our Lord drank from the breast of Our Lady; the water of the third was the sweat that Our Lord gave forth as he climbed to Calvary. Didn't you see anything else?"

"Yes, farther on I saw a cow and a bull fighting."

"You don't know what those beasts were?"

"No."

"Well," replied the mistress, "it was your father and mother in purgatory, who have got out because instead of bringing home a sack of gold louis you preferred the grace of God to save your parents. Didn't you see anything else?"

"Yes, farther on I saw two sheep that were fighting."

"Don't you know what it was?"

"No."

"Well, it was your brothers who are damned. They preferred the gold louis; they were unwilling to give alms; they will burn for all eternity."

"Poor me. What will become of me in all this trouble?"

"Don't be afraid. You, poor boy, wanted to go to heaven. Do you see this ladder? Well, climb it."

And the child began to climb.

When he was near the top: "Mistress, there are still steps. What shall I do?"

"Keep climbing and you will arrive."

Finally he arrived at the gates of heaven. It wasn't very far. He knocked and Saint Peter came to open to him. The child was in the midst of the saints of paradise.

And I, climbing up behind him, wanted to go in too, but Saint Peter closed the door in my face and I came back to tell you:

Trick, track,
My tale is done.

35

THE KID

Once there was a man who had invited all his relatives to a great celebration. "Nothing will be lacking," he had promised.

But this man had a wife and a servant who were very bitter; at the last moment they refused to prepare anything, or even set the table.

The husband said to them: "You are unwilling to prepare anything and set the table? Good! That doesn't bother me."

He went to the barn to get his kid, and, having put him in the middle of the room, he ordered: "Kid, please set the table."

To the great astonishment of the two women, the kid set the table.

When he had finished, the man ordered him: "Kid, please take your skin off and thread yourself on the spit."

The kid slipped out of his skin and threaded himself on the spit, and from time to time his master told him:

"Kid, please turn yourself so as to roast on all sides."

The relatives arrived, and when the moment to eat came, the man said:

"Kid, please climb on the table and carve yourself."

The kid climbed on the table and carved himself, to the great astonishment of all. Finally each ate, and a long while after the meal the guests were still content, stuffed and filled enough to last them for several days.

Then the man said to his kid: "Kid, please assemble your bones and become as you were."

The kid assembled his little bones and became as he was before.

"Kid, please go back to the barn."

And the man went to bed, for the next day he was to depart well before dawn, to go to the fair. The next day his wife got up at noon and said to the servant:

"Now that we are alone, go tell the curé that I want to have him for tea."

The curé didn't have to be asked twice, and he followed the servant at once.

"But I see nothing ready," he said to the woman.

"Sit down, *Monsieur le Curé,* and you're going to see something that you've never seen before."

Then the woman told the servant to go get the kid. On reaching the stable, the servant tried to catch the kid, but the animal refused to be touched, and the girl began to cry: "Filthy kid, filthy kid!" (Which is not very nice to say, even to a goat!)

She opened the door and showed him the open fields of tall grass but the kid didn't want to go out. The serving girl went back to her mistress and told her that the kid refused to listen to her.

"Take this iron rod and strike it on the back."

The girl took the rod, returned to the barn, and there began to strike the kid on the back.

"Bang, bang, you filthy kid. So you refuse to obey? Take that—and that—and that."

But suddenly the rod remained stuck to the animal's back and the servant's hand stuck to the rod without her being able to let go! At the end of a moment the priest, who found time dragging, wondered whether or not they were making fun of him, and he said to the woman:

"You should go see what's going on. I haven't got much time to lose."

The wife went to the barn and, seeing the goat, the rod

(264)

The Kid

and the servant stuck together, she exclaimed: "What are you doing, instead of coming back to the house?"

"I can't let go; something prevents me. Help me pull."

Then the mistress caught her by the skirts and pulled with all her might, but her hands couldn't let go of the servant's skirts, and the goat pulled on the rod, which pulled on the servant, who pulled on the mistress, and all of them began to run about the barn without being able to stop.

More and more impatient, the priest went in turn, and, seeing the condition of the two women, he seized the mistress by the shoulders and pulled to detach her from the servant, but he felt his hands paralyzed on the woman's dress, and he was obliged to run behind her.

All day they ran thus. In the evening the master, returning from the fair, found the house empty; he went to look for his wife and the servant and he wasn't long in finding them.

He said to the kid: "Kid, please keep them well until tomorrow morning."

And as he was tired he went up to bed, and he slept all he wanted while the others exhausted themselves running behind the goat. In the morning he went to the barn.

"It's time for Mass," he said. "Please, kid, take them to the church."

And they went to the church, all of them, running. On the threshold people of the village laughed heartily and followed them, making fun of them.

They went into the church, and the man said to the kid: "Kid, please let them loose and come back to me."

The goat let them loose and came back to his master's side, and the priest said his Mass with his head bent, while they made fun of him and the two women.

HOW KIOT–JEAN MARRIED JACQUELINE

Kiot-Jean was in love with Jacqueline, the daughter of a farmer in a neighboring village. So Kiot-Jean was very happy, you were about to say? Well, no, he was not happy, and here is why: Jacqueline was rich and Kiot-Jean was poor.

One day, however, Kiot-Jean took his courage in both hands, put on his best clothes, and went to the village of his lady fair to ask the farmer for his daughter's hand. As he might have expected if he had thought it over a little more before going, Kiot-Jean saw his request rejected; the farmer didn't think twice but took him by the shoulders, made him turn on his heels and walk down the steps quicker than he had climbed them.

Imagine the consternation of the poor lovers! It must be admitted that he was greatly to be pitied: to be loved by the prettiest girl of the canton and to see himself put out of the house by a father who wasn't worth his daughter's little finger isn't amusing! And, above all, what were the young people of the village going to say when they learned in what a ridiculous way the unhappy Kiot-Jean had been thrown out! What would the girls who were jealous of Jacqueline say! Surely he wouldn't dare to present himself in the future at the smallest festival, dance, square dance, or cotillon.[1]

Kiot-Jean kept telling himself all of this as he went

---

[1] A folk dance of old Picardy.

back, sad and embarrassed. Pretty soon he couldn't contain himself any longer. He began to cry like a calf! "Aye-e-e, yie-e-e, yie-e-e," he went all along the road. . . .

I said that he cried like a calf and I repeat it, for if he had cried otherwise the shepherd who was two hundred yards from there certainly wouldn't have been able to hear him. Yet, though he was snoring peacefully in his little cabin in the fields, he was awakened with a start and got up to see what the trouble was; he saw Kiot-Jean.

"Well, well, what's happened to Kiot-Jean? I've never seen him so sad. He's a brave boy. I'm going to try to console him and be helpful to him."

And the shepherd approached Kiot-Jean and tapped him on the shoulder.

"Well, what's making you cry like this?"

"Aye-e-e, yie-e-e-e, yie-e-e-e! . . ."

"Enough of this 'Aye-e-e, yie-e-e, yie-e-e-e!' . . . Why are you crying so?"

"Aye-e-e-e, yie-e-e-e, yie-e-e-e. I went to ask for Farmer Thomas's daughter in marriage, but, woe—aye-e-e-e, yie-e-e-e, yie-e-e! . . ."

"You were refused, I see, because you're poor."

"Aye-e-e-e, yie-e-e-e, yie-e-e-e! . . . Yes."

"All right, my boy; you mustn't cry so. Take your courage in hand. Here's something to vanquish the resistance of your future father-in-law. Take this little package of red powder and use it as I tell you."

The shepherd gave the little bag of powder to Kiot-Jean and instructed him in its use.

Kiot-Jean went back to the village, stuffed his pipe, and entered Farmer Thomas's house. Jacqueline was alone in the kitchen.

"I have come to light my pipe; may I, Jacqueline?"

"I should say so! Why not? How are you going to fix it so that we can get married, Kiot-Jean?"

"I'm scarcely worried about that! And don't you worry

How Kiot-Jean Married Jacqueline

either. Shortly, Jacqueline, I shall have your family's consent."

"How?"

"It makes no difference. You'll find out later. I'm lighting my pipe and leaving."

Kiot-Jean approach the hearth, lighted his pipe, threw

a pinch of powder in the fire, and left Jacqueline. She went to the garden for a moment and then came back to find the fire three-fourths out. She wanted to light it again, blowing on the coals, and she began to do it, puff, puff, puff . . . continuing for a long time, but in vain. Quite astonished, she went to get her mother.

"Mother, Mother—puff, puff, puff—I can't—puff, puff—how I have—puff, puff, puff—but—puff—for some time—puff, puff—and I don't succeed—puff, puff!"

The farmer's wife, astonished, had her daughter tell as best she could what had happened.

"It's certainly not the fire that makes you puff—puff—puff thus. It must be something else. You'll find out that such a thing as this couldn't have happened just because of blowing in the fire."

The mother came to the hearth and, beginning to speak, saw that she went puff—puff like her daughter. You may imagine that she was disturbed; so not daring to tell her misfortune to her husband, she made a gesture to him when he came back from the fields to relight the fire, which was almost out. But the same thing befell him as had befallen his wife and daughter, and none of them was able to speak any more without going puff—puff—puff unceasingly.

"You must believe—puff, puff," said Thomas, "that—puff, puff, puff—the devil—puff—has come—puff, puff—to dwell—puff—in our fireplace. I am going at once—puff, puff—to find the—puff, puff—curé to—puff, puff, puff—beg him to come here—puff, puff—to chase away the demon."

And here the farmer, out of breath at having thus spoken, gave forth fifteen or twenty puffs in succession.

He went to find the curé, who wasn't too eager to go and dislodge the devil from a fireplace he had chosen to dwell in. He came grudgingly with a choir boy carrying the sprinkler of holy water, and they arrived at the farmer's house and, after drinking a good round of cider, the priest set about saying the required prayers, and all went very well for a moment until the priest started to blow in the fireplace, telling the demon to withdraw, and, the powder operating, he said:

"*Do*—puff, puff, puff, puff—*minus*—puff, puff, puff—*us, us*—puff, puff—*vobis*—puff, puff, puff—*vobis—vobiscum*—puff, puff . . ."

"*Et cum*—puff, puff—*spiritu*—puff, puff, puff—*spirtu*—puff—*tuo*—puff, puff, puff!" added Thomas, his wife, and Jacqueline.

The curé, seeing that there was no way to break the charm, took leave of the farmer, not without having

How Kiot-Jean Married Jacqueline

drunk several more glasses of cider, to stop his puff, puffs, no doubt. The curé started back to the village. On the way he met a shepherd.

"Good day, *Monsieur le Curé;* you seem very sad today, if I am not mistaken."

"Don't talk about it—puff, puff, puff. For an hour—puff, puff, puff—I have been in the devil's claws, and —puff, puff, puff—he's making me say puff, puff, puff—every second."

"Let's see, *Monsieur le Curé,* there might be a way of curing you. I know the cause of all this, and I know that Farmer Thomas, his wife, and his daughter Jacqueline are afflicted with the same ailment. I alone can be useful to you, and with the help of Kiot-Jean from your village I will do my best to cause you and the Thomas family to be free of the affliction that you have."

"Oh! Then, what must I do? Puff, puff, puff—I am ready to do anything; my life—puff, puff, puff—is no longer worth living; it would be impossible—puff, puff, puff—for me to say—puff, puff—the slightest sermon."

"We shall ask you for very little, merely that Kiot-Jean marry Jacqueline, and we shall heal you."

"If that's all there is to it—puff, puff, puff—I give you my word—puff, puff—I'm going back to make Thomas change his—puff, puff, puff—mind—puff, puff. . . ."

The priest did as he had said and he made Thomas give his daughter in marriage to Kiot-Jean. And from that moment on, the old shepherd broke the spell and all of them were cured. A week later Kiot-Jean married his dear Jacqueline, and the priest and the shepherd attended the marriage. . . . But I can't finish my tale. . . . The cock is crowing; it is dawn.

37

HALF–MAN

THERE WAS ONCE a man and a woman who were very poor. They had three boys but the third was only a half-man; that is to say, he had one arm, one leg, one half of everything.

One day the mother sent the three boys into the forest to get wood. The two oldest, who went much faster, left their brother behind. In the road they met an old woman at a point where there was a stream to cross.

"Carry me across," she asked them.

"We don't have time," they replied, and they went on their way.

Their brother Half-Man arrived.

"Carry me across," asked the woman.

"I am much less strong than my two brothers," he replied, "but I will do my best."

And with a great deal of difficulty he succeeded in carrying her to the other side. The old woman gave him a wand and said to him:

"With this wand you will be able to do anything you want to."

Half-Man wanted to make use of it at once.

"By the virtue of my wand," he said, "may there appear beside our house a heap of wood as big as the house, and me beside it."

And it was done. When the two brothers came back with their loads of wood, their mother told them that Half-Man alone had brought in as much as the two of them. And then, without anyone seeing it, by virtue of his wand, Half-Man converted himself into a big bourgeois, and he went to find his father, who was in the vineyard, and said to him:

"Is it true that you are very poor?"

And the father, without knowing whom he was talking to, replied: "I couldn't be poorer."

The bourgeois said to him:

"You no doubt have a batch of children?"

"No," he replied, "I only have two and a half."

"What! A half?"

"Yes, like a man who is cut in two, with one arm, one leg, and one-half of everything."

"And that one, if he were to die you wouldn't be angry, I suppose?"

"On the contrary, I like him better than the others."

And Half-Man went back home, converting himself back to his normal form. And he had appear in their pantry, by virtue of his wand, all of the dishes that are the tastiest to eat, and thereafter he told his mother to call his father to dinner. And she replied that that morning she had grated all the crusts in the pantry for their meal.

"No matter, Mother. Call him anyway, and have my brothers come."

And she went out to get them, and when they had all come back they were much surprised to see a table so well supplied, and Half-Man told them all to eat, that they should want for nothing.

And when the meal was ended, he converted himself back into a bourgeois and went to take a walk, and on his way he saw the daughter of the king, and said:

"By the virtue of my wand, may she become pregnant, and give birth to a boy child who will walk and speak at once and say that I am his father."

And when the king's daughter fell ill, they had a doctor come, and he said the sickness wasn't dangerous, that it was a nine months' illness, and the king said that it wasn't possible, that his daughter had never seen a boy, and he had the doctor put in a cell. Then he had a second doctor come, who said the same thing and was subjected to the same fate. A third invented a sickness as a guarantee for himself, and they accepted him as a good doctor, but at the end of nine months the princess gave birth to a boy who could walk and talk. He said that he could recognize his father. Then the king had all the men of the realm pass before the child. Half-Man passed last, and as soon as he saw him the child said:

"There is my papa."

When the king saw that it was Half-Man that was the father of his grandson, he was so angry that he gave his daughter a little reed cradle and a roll and he made all three of them depart.

As soon as Half-Man saw a suitable place, he used his wand to cause a lovely castle to rise up, with a great many rooms furnished with all that was necessary, and he said to his wife that he was well looked upon in this castle,

Half-Man

that they were going to go into it, and that he was going to go on ahead of them to announce their arrival. He left her, then he came back toward her as a bourgeois and wanted to kiss her, but she repelled him, saying that God had given her Half-Man and that she didn't want to deceive him. Then he made himself known and instead of having half a man, she had the most handsome of men in the most beautiful of castles.

At the end of some time Half-Man organized a great banquet, to which he invited three kings, his father-in-law among them. The kings were much astonished to see a castle more lovely than their own. During the meal the child played with three golden apples, and at the end of the meal Half-Man said:

"By the virtue of my wand, may one of my son's apples be placed in his grandfather's pocket."

And all of a sudden the little boy cried for one of his apples that he couldn't find.

"My son," said Half-Man, "we'll find it. It must be in the room."

And when they had searched everywhere without being able to find it, Half-Man said to his guests:

"I don't care to treat you as thieves, but one of you must have taken my son's apple."

All three of them said: "I haven't got it."

Half-Man searched them and found the apple in his father-in-law's pocket.

"I'm very much astonished," said the king, "that the apple was in my pocket."

Then his son-in-law said to him: "Father, that apple was in your pocket when your daughter became pregnant."

And at the same moment his daughter, who had been hiding, appeared and was recognized. And the king, who had thought his daughter was married to a half-man, recognized that she was with a man more powerful than he.

THE THREE BLUE STONES

There was once a poor widow who spun for the king. She had a big boy of eighteen who was very impatient at the fact that he had no work.

"I want to go look for work and earn my living," he said to his mother. "Give me a few pennies for travel money."

But the mother refused to let him leave. Then the boy, during an absence of the mother, opened the cupboard, took the pennies that he needed, and went away. Following the road, he arrived at a field where he saw three laborers who were chasing a female serpent. As the beast came toward him he prepared to stop it. The laborers cried to him:

"Let her alone. We need her."

But he took his knife out, seized the serpent, and cut her head off, and he found three blue stones in the beast's neck. He took them and put them in his pocket and went away.

Farther on he met the Holy Virgin.

"Where are you going, my boy?" she said to him.

"I'm looking for work, Good Lady."

"Don't you have three blue stones from the neck of a serpent?"

"Yes, Good Lady."

"Well, keep them carefully, for with them you may get anything you want, but if you lose them, all that they

The Three Blue Stones

have given you will be taken away. Do you want to become rich? Go to the corner of the field of Saint-Julien and say, 'By the virtue of my three little stones, may I have three horse-drawn carts loaded with gold and silver!'"

The boy went to the corner of the field, pronounced the words that the Holy Virgin had told him, and the three carts loaded with gold and silver arrived at once. He took them home to his mother.

"Bad boy," she said to him, "where did you steal this treasure?"

"I didn't steal it," he said. "I earned it."

And he told her about his encounters.

He had a beautiful house built, with big stables, and he had rich carriages and lots of horses with gold and silver harnesses.

One day his mother found him all dreamy.

"Are you bored?" she said.

"No, but I want to ask a favor of you. Next time you carry thread to the king's palace, ask him for his daughter's hand in marriage for me."

"What are you thinking of, my poor child?"

"Ask and let him decide."

The woman went at once to the king to give him his thread.

"Sire, I'm bringing you your thread."

"Good day, weaver. Come in, and I will pay you."

But when he had paid her she didn't dare to speak. Finally she made up her mind.

"Your Majesty, I have something to say to you; my son would like to marry your daughter."

The king was a good fellow and didn't want to hurt her.

"Why not? Let him come and we shall see."

The weaver returned quickly to her house.

"My son," she said, "you may make your request."

"Mother, come with me."

Then the boy took his stones and said: "By virtue of my three little stones, may my mother be still more beautiful than the queen."

Then he left with his mother in a fine carriage that was pulled by a richly harnessed team. The king, seeing them in such a fine carriage, didn't recognize them.

"Your Majesty," said the mother, "here is my son, who wants to ask for your daughter's hand."

"What? You are the weaver? And whose is that lovely carriage?"

"It belongs to my son."

The king had them enter. He called his daughter and she consented to marry the young man. The marriage soon took place. By the virtue of his blue stones, the young husband built a castle roofed with gold and silver, with a yard paved in six-franc coins, and he had it guarded by soldiers furnished by the king.

One day he departed on a hunting trip, but as he put on his lovely hunting clothes, he left the blue stones at home in his jacket. At the first gunshot he was suddenly dressed once more as a humble peasant. Then he became aware of his forgetfulness, and went back quickly to the castle, but his guards wouldn't let him come in. Then he said that he had a message for the princess. She came and didn't recognize him.

"Your husband," he said, "requests that you give him a little package that is in his coat pocket."

His wife went to get it.

As soon as he had it, he hid and said: "By virtue of my blue stones, may I become once more as I was."

And he was once more in a beautiful hunting costume.

As he had to go hunting again the next day, he put his blue stones in his hunting boots ahead of time, but at the moment of departure he hurried to put his shoes on, and without paying any attention he failed to put on the boots in which he had hidden the blue stones. At the first gun-

The Three Blue Stones

shot he was once more in rags. He hurried back to the castle and did as he had done the day before in order to get the stones and to become once more what he had been.

The following day he had to go hunting again, and he tied his stones in a fold of his undershirt and slept with them. But that morning he changed underwear and departed again without his stones. At the first shot he was

again in rags and became aware of his forgetfulness. He hastened home, but this time he no longer saw his castle. In its place there was nothing but an old hut full of chicken dung.

The undershirt had been put in the dirty clothes, and the devil, who had been watching for this opportunity for a long time, had turned himself into a washerwoman in order to get possession of the three blue stones. And he immediately transported both the princess and the castle far across the sea.

The king arrived at the place where the castle had been and, furious, said to his son-in-law: "If in forty-eight hours my daughter is not here in her castle, you will be shot."

The young man was disconsolate, but his dog was there, and the dog said to him:

"Be of good courage, master. I know where the devil has taken the three blue stones. Give me a loaf of bread and I will go get them."

The cat, who heard, said to the dog: "I'll go with you."

And so the two departed, but the dog didn't want to lose time, whereas the cat always sought opportunities for delay.

After a moment the cat said: "Let's stop awhile to eat."

"We haven't time," replied the dog, as he threw him a piece of bread. "We must eat while we're running."

At the end of a certain time they had no more bread.

"It doesn't matter," said the dog. "Let's keep going."

The cat caught larks and wanted to stop to pick them.

"No," said the dog. "Eat them feathers and all.

*Feathers and wool
Make a belly full.*"

They arrived at the edge of the sea and found a plank, which they climbed upon.

"I'm going to make it go," said the cat.

"No," said the dog. "Your paws aren't large enough."

They arrived on the shores of an island and were very hungry. They passed in front of a house and smelled the odor of cooking.

"I'll go in first," said the dog. "I'll distract the people and you steal the roast."

And they went in and the cat took away the roast, and farther on he wanted to stop and eat.

"No," said the dog. "Let's eat while we run."

Finally they arrived at the devil's door. They scratched and the door opened. The king's daughter recognized the dog, who said to her:

The Three Blue Stones

"I have come to search for my master's blue stones; if he doesn't have them soon, he will be shot."

The mistress gave them to him and the dog departed running, without listening to the cat, who would have liked to rest. They arrived at the seashore and took the plank, which the dog propelled as fast as he could.

When they were in the midst of the sea, the cat said: "Give me the blue stones; it's my turn to carry them."

"No," said the dog, "I don't trust you. I'll keep them."

But the cat tormented him so much that the dog ended by letting him carry them. The cat began to play with the stones and dropped them in the ocean. The dog, angry, reproached the cat, but they saw a fish, and as he was very hungry, he jumped on it to eat it.

"I don't want the head," said the cat.

"Well, I'll eat it," said the dog.

And the dog found the three blue stones in the fish's head. He kept them in his mouth and set out as fast as he could on the plank. When they were a few yards from shore the dog began to swim to arrive quicker, while the cat wanted to keep his feet dry on the plank. The dog arrived just at the moment when his master was going to be shot. He gave him the stones and the young man said at once:

"By the virtue of my little blue stones, may my castle appear once more where it was with my wife in it."

And it was all accomplished as before.

Part II
ANIMAL TALES

I

THE JOURNEY TO TOULOUSE OF THE ANIMALS THAT HAD COLDS

There was once a chicken that had had a cold since the beginning of winter. She was advised to go get herself healed at Toulouse, so she set out, and when she was on her way she met a goose.

"Hello, Sister Goose."

"Hello, Sister Chicken. Where are you going at that pace?"

"I'm going to Toulouse to cure my cold."

"I need to go there too. I have a bad cold."

"Well, come with me."

The goose accepted and here they are on their way together. After a while they met a dog.

"Hello, Brother Dog."

"Hello, Sisters Goose and Chicken. Where are you going?"

"To Toulouse to get rid of our colds."

"Well, I have a cold too. I hunted foxes all night long in the dew, and I can't stop coughing."

"Come with us."

"All right."

So they all set out. A little farther on they met a sheep on the edge of the road. He was coughing like a smoked fox.

"Hello, Brother Sheep."

"Hello, Brother Dog and Sisters Goose and Chicken. Where are you going?"

"To Toulouse to get rid of our colds. It would be a good idea for you to come with us, for you have a bad cough."

"By heaven, I won't refuse. I slept out last night in the rain and I have a bad cold, and I can't stop coughing. Let's go."

The four travelers walked all day. At sunset they started looking for a shelter. They approached a cabin they saw in a near-by field, but the door was closed and they had to go farther on. At nightfall they found another. The chicken scratched at the door, the goose beat on it with its beak, and the dog put his paw on the latch, but the house stayed closed.

"Get in line," said the sheep. He hurled himself forward, and with a blow of his head he shattered the door into the interior of the cabin. It fell upon wolves that had taken refuge there, and they took off without putting up any resistance.

"We shall be comfortable here," said the chicken. "I'm going to perch on the mantel."

"And I," said the goose, "shall get under the table."

The Journey to Toulouse

"And I, under the kneading-trough," said the sheep.

"And I," said the dog, "near the door."

An hour later the wolves sent one of their number back to find out whether or not the intruders were still in the cabin. The wolf went in without difficulty and went straight toward the hearth. But the chicken dropped something on his head; he withdrew as far as the table, and there the goose caressed his muzzle with her wing. Terrified, he went toward the kneading-trough; with a bound the sheep pinned him to the wall.

He just had time to dash toward the door to escape; but the dog nipped his flank and let go only after retaining a piece of it. The wolf arrived among his companions all bloody.

"Well, what did you see?"

"What did I see? Ah, it's certainly nice in that cabin! A whole band is there! Beside the chimney I found a mason who threw a trowel of mortar in my face. Under the table there was a laundrywoman who struck my face with a washboard. Under the kneading-trough a woodman gave me a blow in the stomach with his ax. And near the door a locksmith nipped my flank with his big pincers. I had a terrible time escaping. Look what they've done to me."

"The devil! What a fine place!" said the wolves, who, terrified by this tale, slept in the open, while the four sick travelers spent a peaceful night in the house.

2

THE LION THAT LEARNED TO SWING

THE FOX THAT LEARNED HOW TO PICK CHERRIES

THE WOLF THAT LEARNED HOW TO SPLIT WOOD

A YOUNG MAN wanted to marry the daughter of a king. He went to see him but the king, to get rid of him, as he had already done with other pretenders, told him:

"I am willing, but first you must sleep for a night with my lion."

The daughter, who had noticed the young man and who had found him to her taste, went to him. "Here," she said, "is a jar of honey and some comfits. Put them in your pocket and give them to the lion so that he won't eat you. . . . And before dawn I will go and open the door to you and we shall leave together."

The young man went into the lion's chamber.

"I'm going to eat you," said the lion.

"Not now! Wait. I've brought you something much better."

And the young man smeared the walls with honey. Then the lion began to lick the walls, and when he had finished he said: "Now I'm going to eat you."

(288)

The Animals That Learned Tricks

"Not right away! Wait. I've something else that's very good."

And the young man scattered the comfits about the room, and the lion picked them up and ate them, and then when he had finished:

"This time I'm going to eat you," he said.

"Not yet," said the young man. "I'm going to show you a very amusing game; I'm going to teach you to swing."

The young man put a peg in the ceiling and tied a rope to it, made a loop at the other end, put his foot in the loop, and swung back and forth, pretending to have a great time.

"I want to swing too," said the lion.

"Wait till I fix your feet for you."

He inserted the lion's paws very tightly into the loop, and then pulled him by the tail to swing him. The lion, who couldn't get loose, began to howl furiously. The king's daughter came quickly, opened the door to the young man, and they left together.

At dawn the king's men arrived and found the lion hanging by his paws.

"Who did that to you?"

"It was the young man that they gave me to eat."

And they untied him.

"Go fast to avenge yourself."

The young man and the king's daughter met a fox who, standing beneath a cherry tree, was ogling the cherries while he licked his jowls with his tongue.

"Do you like cherries?" asked the young man.

"Oh, indeed I do. I should like to go up in the tree to pick some."

"Well, turn your behind. I'll teach you to climb."

The young man pulled out a stake, sharpened it at both ends, and planted it in the earth. Then he seized the fox and seated him on this picket.

"And now, pick cherries."

And he left the fox impaled.

Farther on, the young man and the king's daughter met a wolf who was piling wood.

"What are you doing, Brother Wolf?"

"I'm preparing my wood for winter."

"Your logs are very big," said the young man. "I'll teach you to split them."

He took a big log and split it halfway with an ax.

"Put your paws in the crack," he said to the wolf.

Then he withdrew the ax, and the wolf remained captured.

"And now go right on splitting wood by yourself," said the young man, and he went away.

The lion came into the forest and saw the fox on his picket.

"What are you doing there?" he asked.

The Animals That Learned Tricks

"The young man who just left put me here."

The lion got the fox down.

"Come with me. We're going to catch him and avenge ourselves."

Both of them came upon the wolf who had his paws caught in the log.

"Who did that?" said the lion.

"It's the young man who just left in that direction."

The lion and the fox released the wolf.

"Come with us. We're going to catch him and avenge ourselves."

When the king's daughter saw the three animals approaching she said: "We are lost!"

The wolf was in the lead, the fox next, and the lion behind. The young man took his ax and split a log, looking the wolf squarely in the eyes. Then the wolf turned around and escaped as fast as his legs could carry him.

Now the fox was in the lead. The young man began to sharpen a picket, looking squarely at the fox; so he escaped, crying as loud as he could.

The young man next took a rope with a slipknot in it and swung it back and forth while he looked fixedly at the lion; the lion ran away, roaring with all his might.

And the young man and the king's daughter were able to go on their way peaceably.

3

THE SOW
AND
THE WOLF

Some women were doing their washing at Font-Badant. Their washing clubs were pounding; their tongues as well.

"Tell me, what are you others going to kill for Mardi gras?" said one.

"I'm going to kill my cock."

"And I my gander."

"We're going to kill our sow," said another.

The gander, who was swimming near by, went to warn the cock and the sow. And all three of them were very sad. At last they decided to go away into the forest of Montagan, and they left together. But the cock, soon tired, was the first to have to stop and build his house. A little farther on, the gander became exhausted and left the little sow to go on her way alone. She was the last to stop and she built herself a beautiful house of stone.

A short while after, the wolf came by. Intrigued by the cock's house, he sniffed it, and he ended by crushing it with his big paw and he ate the cock. The poor gander was subjected to the same fate.

At last the wolf came to the little sow's house. He wanted to eat her too.

"Knock, knock, open up to me, piglet!"

"Oh, no, wolf, I shan't open to you; you would eat me and my little ones!"

"Of course not, sow! Come on and open to me! It's so

The Sow and the Wolf

cold. If you don't, I'll crush your house, as I have the cock's and the gander's."

But he knocked in vain, he pounded, and he shouted. The house stood up under all his attacks.

"Say, sow, if you only knew what lovely apples there are at such-and-such a place!"

"Is that so?"

"If you wanted, we could go to get some. Just meet me at such-and-such an hour and place; we'll go together. Ah, what lovely red apples!"

So the next day the sow got up early, very early, went to the apple trees, ate as many as she could, and even brought a load back home with her. Meanwhile, after having waited a long time for her in vain, the wolf came to her house.

"Well, by the way, sow, how is it that you failed to meet me?"

"I failed to meet you! You're the one, good-for-nothing! Look! Are there apple peelings in front of my door or not? We have certainly feasted, my children and I!"

"Oh! My poor sow . . ."

"But, listen" (he really wanted to catch her, didn't he?), "I know a vineyard where there are grapes, but the most beautiful, juicy, sweet, ripe grapes that you have ever seen! If you wish, we could go there together. But this time you'll wait for me, eh?"

"Just be ready at such-and-such a time and place and we'll go together."

"Agreed!"

Again the next day the sow got up early, very early, went to the vineyard, ate her fill, and brought back as many as she could. A good while afterward the wolf knocked once more at her door.

"Knock, knock! Say, sow, you've played a fine trick on me. Were you really at our meeting-place at the appointed time?"

"I wasn't there! Rather it was you! Look here, all these grape stems along the road! I waited for you a long time. Then, not seeing you, I decided to go alone. You're a fine one to keep promises!"

"All right! All right, my dear! But I am reminded, won't you go with me to the fair at Jarnac?"

"I'm not that stupid, wolf! You would eat me."

"Surely you know that I wouldn't eat you, don't you?"

"Well, if you promise not to eat me, I will go with you. But we'll have to leave early, for I have a lot of things to buy. I especially need a tub to do the washing."

"Well, wait for me; I'll come for you at such-and-such a time."

"You promise not to eat me?"

The next day, very, very early, the sow got ready and left without waiting for the wolf, and not without having warned her little ones not to open to him when he came. A few moments after her departure the wolf arrived. He came on the run, planning to eat her before setting out for the fair. Knock! Knock!

The Sow and the Wolf

Through the window the little pigs told him that their mother had gone an hour before. The wolf grumbled: "So! You've escaped me! But never mind! I'll catch you!"

He ran in vain; he didn't catch her. After taking a turn about the fair he hurried back to the sow's house. But on the road the sow had seen the wolf coming toward her; quickly she hid under the tub. The wolf came, walked around the tub sniffing, and finally—raised his paw, then departed.

The sow, who wanted to get home as fast as she could, took a short cut. Once home, she lighted a good fire, filled her tub, and put water on to heat on a trivet in the fireplace.

Brother Wolf arrived! He was very warm! He heard the sow grunting and said to her: "What did you say?"

"Nothing! Just that my pot is boiling well."

"Boil, pot, boil to scald this wolf," the sow was muttering through her teeth.

The wolf was licking his chops and looking at the little pigs.

"Hum!
*Come rain, come hail,
I'll eat this sow
From head to tail.*"

The little pigs, hearing that, said to their mother:

"Oh, Mamma, do you hear what Brother Wolf is saying?"

"No! What is Brother Wolf saying anyway?"

"He says:
'*Come rain, come hail,
I'll eat this sow
From head to tail.*'"

"Is that true, Brother Wolf?"

"Oh, no, sow! I said your pot was boiling well."

And the sow, stirring her fire, kept saying: "Boil, pot, boil, to scald this wolf!"

All of a sudden she went toward the window, looked out fixedly, and shouted:

"Well, Mr. Wolf, you must have really done something stupid; there are some policemen following you. You've surely done something bad!"

"Is it true, my poor sow? If only you could hide me!"

"There is a kneading-pan here. I could hide you in it, but you must promise not to eat me."

"Of course! I won't eat you."

She lifted the lid of the kneading-pan, let the wolf enter, telling him to stay real quiet. Then, as her water was boiling, she poured it over the wolf, who bounded away at a gallop crying:

"Ah, hussy, you have killed me!"

4

THE THREE PULLETS

There were three pullets in a wood, one white, one gray, and one black. They decided to build a little house with pieces of wood.

Then the little white pullet said: "I'll go in and see if it's comfortable and then open the door to you."

She was so comfortable inside, this little white pullet, that she wouldn't let the others in.

Then her two sisters cried: "Open the door, open the door! We are afraid!"

"No, no!"

She didn't open the door, so the other two decided to build a house of their own. The gray pullet went into it, and she was so very, very comfortable there that she refused to open up to the black pullet.

"Open the door, open the door! I'm all alone, I'm afraid!"

"No, no! I shan't open the door!"

It was raining very hard. So the little black pullet began to cry. All of a sudden a man arrived. He was a mason and he asked why she was crying.

"It's my little sisters, who each have a house and who won't let me in."

"Well, if you will lay me a dozen eggs I'll come back and build you a house."

When the mason came back, the little black pullet had laid the dozen eggs, and so he built her a lovely solid house, and the little pullet was happy. And the very next day the wolf came by and knocked at the white pullet's door. Knock, knock, knock!

"Who is there?"

"It's the big wolf, who wants to talk to you. Open the door."

"No, no, no! I don't want to open up."

"I'm going to demolish your house and eat you." And so saying, he upset the house and ate the little white pullet.

Then he went to the house of the little gray pullet. Knock, knock, knock!

"Who is there?"

"It's the big wolf; I want to talk to you. Open the door."

"No, no, no! I don't want to!"

"I'm going to demolish the house and eat you." And he upset the house and ate the little gray pullet.

Then the wolf went to the house of the little black pullet. Knock, knock, knock!

"Who is there?"

The Three Pullets

"It's the big wolf come to talk to you. Open the door."

"No, no, no! I don't want to open!"

"I'm going to demolish the house and eat you!"

"Well, come down the chimney if you want: I can't open the door."

Meanwhile the little pullet was making a great fire. The wolf, who had no fears about going down the chimney, fell in the fire and was roasted.

5

THE GOAT AND HER KIDS

One day Sister Goat fell in a well while she was drawing water to make soup for her kids. She broke her leg. As you may imagine, she wasn't going to spend her life with a game leg, so she decided to go see a doctor. Calling her children, she said to them: "My kids,

> I am going to Saint-Leg Saint-Jacques,
> To splint here,
> To splint there,
> My broken leg,
> My wooden peg."

She departed, and on the way she met Brother Wolf.
"Where are you going in that condition, Sister Goat?" asked Brother Wolf.
"Ah! Brother Wolf,

> I am going to Saint-Leg Saint-Jacques,
> To splint here,
> To splint there,
> My broken leg,
> My wooden peg."

"This is convenient!" said Brother Wolf to himself as he ran to the goat's house to eat the kids. He knocked at the door.
"Who is there?"

The Goat and Her Kids

"Open the door, kids," said Brother Wolf with altered voice.

> *"I come from Saint-Leg Saint-Jacques,*
> *From splinting here,*
> *From splinting there,*
> *My broken leg,*
> *My wooden peg."*

"Oh, it's not our mamma," said the kids. "The voice is too rough."

And they refused to open the door. Brother Wolf left and met some cowherds who were making whistles. He asked them to file his tongue to make his voice sweeter. And they did it. Brother Wolf went back to the kids' house to eat them.

"Open the door, my kiddies,

> *I come from Saint-Leg Saint-Jacques,*
> *From splinting here,*
> *From splinting there,*
> *My broken leg,*
> *My wooden peg."*

"Oh, it's not our mamma," said the kids. "The voice is too sharp."

Brother Wolf went back to find the cowherds.

"Cowherds, cowherds, can't you give me back a bit more tongue?"

And the cowherds put back a bit of his tongue. Then Brother Wolf came back a third time to eat the kids.

"Open the door, kiddies,

> *I come from Saint-Leg Saint-Jacques,*
> *From splinting here,*
> *From splinting there,*
> *My broken leg,*
> *My wooden peg."*

"That's our mother," said the kids. And they opened the door wide.

Brother Wolf went in, pulled the littlest one from under the bed, and ate it. He wanted to take the second, which had hidden in a bottle, but was only able to eat its tail. And to the third he was able to do nothing because it had hidden in a wooden shoe.

Then Brother Wolf went into the attic, ate the jars of butter that he found there, and stretched out on the straw to take a nap. But the goat soon came back from the doctor's and learned from the kid that was in the wooden shoe that the kid that had been under the bed had been eaten, and that the one in the bottle was missing a tail.

"Good," said Sister Goat. "We shall see."

She set about making a good fire on the hearth, filled the kettle with oil, and hung it on the pothook. While throwing kindling and logs on the fire, she kept saying between her teeth:

> *"Good, good, good,*
> *My pot, my kettle,*
> *To throw upon the wolf's head."*

Then she said louder:

The Goat and Her Kids

*"Good, good, good,
My pot, my kettle,
To throw upon the wolf's head."*

In this way she awakened Brother Wolf, who called from the attic: "What's wrong, Sister Goat? Why do you talk like that?"

"It's nothing," replied the goat. "It's a prayer that I'm teaching my children."

And she continued while stirring the fire:

*"Good, good, good,
My pot, my kettle,
To throw upon the wolf's head,"*

until the oil was boiling. Then she cried to him:

"Oh, Wolf! Here are the dogs from Orléans coming to eat you."

"Hide me, Sister Goat," the wolf asked her.

"Get in my kneading-pan," said the goat, "and the dogs won't find you."

The wolf got in the kneading-pan, which had a hole in it. And through the hole she began to pour the oil.

"You're burning me, you're burning me, Sister Goat!" howled the wolf.

"You'll have to endure it!" replied the goat, as she kept on pouring the burning oil in. "Give me back my kid and my kid's tail and I'll stop."

"Stop, stop, Sister Goat. I'll give them back!"

Sister Goat raised the lid of the kneading-bowl and lifted out the scalded wolf, who ejected the tail in the room and the kid near the door. Then he went shamefully away.

And this time the kettle boiled for the supper of the mother goat and her three little goats.

6

BROTHER MAZARAUD

Brother Mazaraud made charcoal in the winter in the forest of Moulzonne. One December evening when it froze very hard, he lay down on a bed of dry ferns, wrapped in a sheepskin, and there, very warm, he watched the trunks of the beech trees that were burning on the stones of the hearth.

"What pretty wood embers!" he thought. "What a pretty pudding one could cook on them!"

And while he looked at the flames and his head nodded, his mind very softly flitted away. But he heard a scratching at the lattice that served as a door, the light scratching of tiny feet.

"What's that?"

He went and opened and saw the hare trembling from cold, the hairs of his mustache stiff as needles.

"Oh, Coalman, let me warm myself at your fire. I know a field of carrots, turnips, and cabbage; I'll go get you some tomorrow and we'll have a feast."

"Well, come on in and sit down before the coals."

A moment afterward they heard another scratching at the lattice. Brother Mazaraud got up and opened to the fox, who arrived like a wet cat with her long bushy tail dragging on the ground.

"What cold weather, poor people! My ears are frozen. Coalman, if you'll let me warm myself before your fire, I know of a chicken coop, and I assure you that tomorrow, Sunday, you will be able to roast a pullet for dinner."

"Well," said the coalman, "lie down near the hare."

Brother Mazaraud

And they were just beginning to snore when they heard a knocking on the frame of the lattice and a gruff voice cried from outside:

"Coal master, I am frozen from head to tail. Let me in and tomorrow for a feast you will have a tender lamb."

"And you will eat me, won't you?"

"No, by my faith, I won't touch you. I swear it. Let me get warm."

Brother Mazaraud opened the door and the wolf came in. One would have said that he was carrying all the frost of the wood in his hair. The others snuggled up together to leave room for him.

The stumps of oak and pine flamed on the hearth, and the warmth put everybody to sleep, man and beast, in a happy beatitude, when a great blow at the door of the cabin made them all tremble. Who could it be now? And through the shattered lattice they saw pass the big head of a bear.

"Oh, Coalman," he cried, "let me come in. It's colder

than I have ever seen. The frost has stiffened my hair so much that when I shake myself I tinkle like a bell."

"Do you want me to let you come in, and then with your paws you will smother us all, me and those who are getting warm with me?"

"Don't ever think so, good Coalman. I promise you that I won't touch the hair of anybody's head. I'll get warm very peacefully, and tomorrow we'll feast on a lovely calf that I'll go get at the Marou farm."

"Well, come in, then, but I don't know if all four of you will fit around the fire."

The bear came in and the other beasts made a bigger circle in order to make room for him.

And when all of them were warm: "Well, now," said the fox, "we must go marauding; let's see who comes back first with what we need."

All of them went, and Brother Mazaraud, alone, thought:

"What am I going to do to get rid of all these animals, who are going to kill me for sure?"

The first that came back was the hare, and he came with a load of cabbage, carrots, and lettuce as tender as water.

"Who has come, Coalman?"

"Nobody, my friend. You are the most valiant. Put it there on the table and come and get warm, for you must be frozen."

The hare approached the fire and, as he was tired, he went to sleep at once. Then the coalman took a spray of heather, put it on the fire, and, when it was well lighted, passed it under the hare's stomach, and he got up like a spring and fled outside crying.

The man arranged the vegetables in a little room and then went to bed again on his ferns.

In a moment the fox arrived; she had broken the neck of a very pretty pullet.

Brother Mazaraud

"You are the first, fox. May you live long for being the most agile. Put the pullet under the table and come and get warm, for you deserve it."

The fox lay down in front of the fire and was asleep almost immediately. Brother Mazaraud then took the ax, and with a single blow he cut the poor animal's tail off, and it fled wailing.

This done, the coalman again sat down in a corner and began to nod.

But he got up a short time afterward to open the door to the wolf, who was carrying a very tender lamb and put it in the middle of the cabin.

"Who has come?"

"Nobody, my friend. You're the best hunter by far. Come and get warm, poor thing. You must be frozen."

The wolf lay down near the fire and soon began to snore. The coalman took the fire shovel, heated the handle in the coals, then, raising the wolf's tail, he sank it in his behind. Wails of pain resounded in the wood. The poor beast fled with fire in his insides.

Finally the bear arrived, out of breath. He was carrying a pretty calf that weighed at least two hundred pounds. The coalman laughed with pleasure, for he would have food for a long time.

"Have the others arrived?"

"No, you are the first, and you are carrying a lovely bit of food. Get warm, my friend. You must have traveled a long way during this icy night."

The bear lay down before the fire, and his snoring was soon shaking the cabin. Then Brother Mazaraud took a big sledge hammer which he used to drive the wedges into the wood, and, bang! a great blow on the head of the bear. Martin emitted a growl and fled in the night. The coalman began to laugh.

"Now I am rid of them," he thought, "but I'd like to know if these nasty animals have gone a long way."

He wrapped himself in a cape and, an ax in one hand and a flaming brand in the other, he walked all around the area. In the distance he heard the wailings and crying of the animals.

"I got a big fist blow square in the head, which makes me dizzy," the gruff voice of the bear was saying.

And the hare wailed: "As for me, he set my breast on fire so that it won't grow any more."

"And I am dishonored, for all undressed, where is my bushy tail?" sobbed the sharp voice of the fox.

And the hoarse voice of the wolf stammered: "He shoved the shovel in my behind, which is burning hot, burning hot."

"Fire of heaven," yelled the coalman, "are you evil beasts still there?"

And with his flaming brand, which he shook, you would have taken him for a devil of hell. The animals escaped as fast as they could, and Brother Mazaraud never saw them again.

7

A LOVELY DREAM AND A FATEFUL JOURNEY

A WOLF WAS SLEEPING at Routel;[1] he had made a beautiful dream, which was all full of something or other. Upon awaking he set out and, crossing the road of Rouelle, he found a ham which he tasted.

"Oh," he said, "it's too salty. I'll certainly find something better."

He went on his way and, crossing the road of Villers, he found a beautiful strip of bacon and tasted it.

"Oh," he said, "it's too rancid; I'll certainly find something better than that."

A little farther on he arrived at Les Pendus and he met a mare with her colt.

"You must give me your colt," he said.

"You may have it if you wish," the mare said, "but I have a thorn in my foot; withdraw it for me."

So our wolf approached. The mare raised her foot and unleashed a kick in his muzzle, reducing his jaw to marmalade. And she vanished with her colt. Then the wolf began to grieve.

"That ham wasn't too salty," he reflected. "I could have eaten it as it was. That bacon wasn't too rancid. I could have eaten it too. And am I a blacksmith to pull thorns out of the feet of mares? I might have taken her colt too."

---

[1] Le Routel and, farther on, Rouelle, Villers, Les Pendus, Les Fausses-Eaux, Le Nid de la Suque, Saint-Laurent, are place names of the region.

After that he went away to Les Fausses-Eaux and he met a sow with her little pigs.

"There's just the thing," he said to the sow. "You must give me one of your pigs."

"They're too dirty," the sow said to him. "You wouldn't like them like that; wait a bit and I'll go wash them."

The sow jumped into the mill canal with her pigs, swam them to the other side, and they all went into the barn.

By heaven, there was no way of getting them now!

"Oh," said the wolf, "how stupid I am! That ham wasn't salty, the bacon wasn't rancid, I might have eaten it too. Am I a blacksmith, I, to pull thorns from the feet of mares? I might have taken her colt. And these little pigs; they weren't too dirty. I might have caught them too."

And from there he went to the Nid de la Suque. The shepherd was there with his flock and there were two rams fighting beside him.

"By Jove," our wolf said to them, "I must have one of you two!"

A Lovely Dream and a Fateful Journey

"Get between us," they said to him, "and you may choose."

Well, our big numbskull of a wolf got between them, the two rams backed up, then dashed upon him, each giving him a butt in his middle so powerful that he turned somersaults, and then they ran away with the flock. It was unpleasing to have made such a lovely dream and so fateful a trip.

He went to the wood of Saint-Laurent, near the cabin of the coalman, and he began to think over all his misfortunes:

"That ham wasn't too salty and that bacon wasn't too rancid; I might have eaten both of them. And am I a blacksmith to pull thorns out of the feet of mares? I might have eaten the colt, and those little pigs weren't too dirty; I might have eaten them too. And I didn't have to choose between those two rams; otherwise I would have got one of them. I am so angry that I wish the coalman were in his cabin so that he could cut my tail off even with my backside." (I hadn't thought to tell you that he was seated by the door, which wasn't too well closed, and that his tail was passing underneath it.)

Just at that moment the coalman was in his cabin and he took his ax and struck the wolf's tail.

"Aye, yiee," cried the wolf. "I was just joking when I said that."

"Ah," said the coalman, "you shouldn't joke about such matters."

And when you see a wolf with his tail cut off, he's the one that made such a beautiful dream and such a fateful journey.

8

HALF-CHICK

I AM GOING to tell you—or else; it goes:

A little tale,
A little pup,
Kiss the spot
Where the tail stands up.

There were once two ladies who had a rooster. One wanted to divide it. The rooster was split in two, and the one who asked that it be divided ate her half, and the other kept hers.

Half-Chick began to jump and scratch and search for his food around the house. One morning he uncovered a bushel of money.

The miller passed by. "What have you found, Half-Chick?"

"A bushel of money."

"If you wish I will give you three heads of wheat for your money."

Half-Chick accepted; he ate the heads of grain and the miller took the money away.

Going back to the house, Half-Chick cried: "Ah, mistress, I had a good lunch this morning!"

"What did you eat, Half-Chick?"

"I ate three heads of grain."

"Who gave them to you?"

"It was the miller."

"Why?"

Half-Chick

"Because I found a bushel of money and traded it to the miller for the three heads of grain."

"Oh, evil beast!" cried the good woman, taking her broom. "Get out of here and don't come back until you've got a bushel of money."

And so Half-Chick departed, hopping toward the miller's house. On the way he met Brother Fox.

"Where are you going, Half-Chick?"

> "Come with me o'er hill and vale."
> "I cannot, my legs would fail."
> "Then crawl inside, under my tail."

The fox accepted, and farther on Half-Chick met Brother Wolf.

"Where are you going, Half-Chick?"

> "Come with me o'er hill and vale."
> "I cannot, my legs would fail."
> "Then crawl inside, under my tail."

And the wolf followed the fox, and then Half-Chick came upon a colony of ants, which, after the same remarks, followed the wolf and the fox, and finally Brother River, who also accepted Half-Chick's offer. Thus laden, Half-Chick arrived at the miller's.

"I want my bushel of money; I want my bushel of money."

"How can we get rid of this Half-Chick?" said the miller to his wife.

"Let's put him to bed with the chickens; they will kill him and we won't be bothered by him any more."

When Half-Chick was attacked by the hens he cried:

*"Brother Fox, come out, I pray,
Or I'll die today."*

And the fox came out and strangled the chickens. The next morning the miller found all the chickens dead, and Half-Chick said to him:

"Give me back my bushel of money."

"We've simply got to get rid of this evil little beast."

"Let's put him in the sheepfold; the lambs will crush him."

Pressed by the lambs, Half-Chick cried:

*"Brother Wolf, come out, I pray,
Or I'll die today."*

And the wolf killed the lambs. The miller, seeing his flock destroyed, was much disturbed.

"This time I'm going to put him in the serving girls' bed and they will smother him."

As soon as he was in bed, Half-Chick felt ill at ease and cried:

*"Brother Ants, come out, I pray,
Or I'll die today."*

Half-Chick

The ants spread out in the bed and bit the girls, who got up crying and who in their fear awakened the whole household.

"Let's warm the oven," said the miller, "and put him in it, and then he won't escape."

As soon as he was in the oven Half-Chick shouted:

"Brother River, come out, I pray,
Or I'll die today."

And the river began to flow and flooded the oven and the house.

Then the miller came and said: "Here, take your bushel of money, and get the devil out of here, and may we never see you again."

And Half-Chick brought back his money to the good woman, and they have lived happy, both of them, ever since.

Part III
HUMOROUS TALES

I

TURLENDU

Turlendu's only fortune was a louse. He went to a house and asked them if they wouldn't keep the louse for him, and he was told: "Leave it on the table."

He came back in a few days to get it.

"My dear," he was told, "the chicken has eaten it."

"I shall cry and I shall shout," he said, "until I have that chicken."

"Don't cry and don't shout; take the chicken and get out."

He took the chicken and he went to another house.

"Hello, Turlendu. Come and get warm."

"I'm not cold; I have come to ask if you will keep this chicken."

"Certainly. Put her in the chicken coop."

And he came back after a few days to get her.

"My dear," he was told, "the other day she fell in the hog pen and the hogs ate her."

"I shall cry and I shall shout until I have that hog."

"Don't cry and don't shout; take the hog and get out."

And he took the hog and went to another house.

"Hello, Turlendu. Come and get warm."

"I'm not cold; I have come to ask if you will keep my hog."

"Certainly. Put him in the barn with the others."

And he came back in a few days to get it.

"My dear," he was told, "the other day he approached the mule, and the mule killed him with a kick."

"I shall cry and I shall shout until I have that mule."

"Don't cry and don't shout, but take the mule and get out."

And he took the mule and went to another house.

"Hello, Turlendu. Come and get warm."

"I'm not cold; I have come to ask if you will keep my mule."

"Certainly. Leave it over there."

And he came back in a few days to get it.

"My dear," he was told, "the other day the chambermaid was leading it to drink and she let it fall in the well."

"I shall cry and I shall shout until I have that chambermaid."

"Don't cry and don't shout, but take the chambermaid and get out."

And he took the chambermaid and he put her in a bag and he went to another house.

"Hello, Turlendu. Come and get warm."

Turlendu

"I'm not cold; I have come to ask you if you will keep this bag."

"Certainly. Leave it there behind the door."

And Turlendu went away. Scarcely was he outside when they took the girl out of the bag and put a big dog in her place.

He came back to get his sack, and after having carried it a moment: "Walk a little," he said. "I'm tired of carrying you."

But, on opening the bag, the dog jumped at his face and bit off his nose.

And he said: "From a little louse to a little chicken—from a little chicken to a little hog—from a little hog to a little mule—from a mule to a girl—and from a girl to a big dog—which has bitten off my nose."

2

THE FANTASTIC ADVENTURES OF CADIOU THE TAILOR

(A Tale of Lower Brittany)

Cadiou was, by your leave, a tailor by trade living in a little village at about one mile from the village of Plouaret. Each morning he went to sew at farms and manors of the countryside, and as he was not married, he lived easily by his needle.

One day it took his fancy to go to the September fair on the mountain of Bré, one of the prettiest fairs of the country. So he put on his Sunday clothes and set gaily out.

After having visited the fair, seen the ox markets, the horse markets, the cow markets, the hog markets, and after having made his prayer to His Grace Saint-Hervé in his chapel on the summit of the mountain, he also wanted to act the young man a bit, though he was already more than forty; in the bottom of his heart he loved to dance.

He noticed at a dance a beautiful girl with cheeks as red as an apple, with black hair and lively eyes.

"That's what I'm looking for," he said to himself. "I'm going to ask her if she won't please take a walk with me in the fair and dance with me at the ball."

The girl asked for nothing better.

After they had gone all through the fair and danced

Cadiou the Tailor

several rounds and *passe-pieds* [1] Cadiou said to his dancing partner:

"I want to buy you a present, my sweet friend, to thank you for you friendship."

Cadiou bought her a penny's worth of almonds.

The girl, disappointed by her escort's meager generosity, thought: "All right, my boy, as you give, so shall you receive."

They took another stroll or two around the tower of the chapel, holding on to each other's little fingers as lovers do, after which Cadiou said:

"The sun's going down and it's a long way home."

"Come and let me offer you your fair gift," the girl said to him.

And she took him to the shop of an ambulant mercer.

"Choose what you want," she added, "provided that it costs no more than a penny."

Cadiou took a big needle; then, saluting the girl:

"Now I say good-by, my sweet friend, for the sun is going to go down and I live a long way from here."

"So do I: I'm going back home," she replied, "and as you are of Plouaret and I of Louargat, we shall follow the same route for a time, and you will even pass by my father's threshold at the foot of the mountain."

So they went down the mountain of Bré together. The girl, having arrived near her father's house, which was an old dilapidated manor, said to her companion:

"Here is our house; come in a bit to light your pipe and taste our cider."

After a few protests Cadiou went into the house. He saw a big old man seated in an armchair near the fire with his legs stretched out in front of it, and these legs were so long that they reached the other side of the hearth, though it was an immense one.

---

[1] A folk dance of Brittany.

Cadiou first remained immobile, seized with astonishment; never had he seen anything like it.

"So, there you are back, my dear daughter," said the old man when he heard the door open.

"Yes, Father. I'm not coming back late, am I?"

"And, according to your custom, you aren't coming back alone, good daughter that you are. We shall dine well this evening it seems to me."

"No, dear Father, we won't eat him this evening, but tomorrow morning for breakfast."

"All right, it will be tomorrow morning, since you desire it, my daughter. But go get my scythe so that I can cut him down at once for fear he might escape during the night."

"I'll get it for you, Father."

Cadiou, hearing this conversation, remained motionless, like a stone pillar. But when the daughter opened the door, the tailor dashed out and ran and ran. . . .

"Unleash the dogs," cried the old man. And the daughter unleashed the dogs, enormous bulldogs that began to bark like unleashed demons.

Happily, Cadiou was a long way ahead of them, and he ran across fields toward the Séguer River, saying to himself that he would be safe if he could put the river between him and the dogs. At the moment when he was going into the water, one of the bulldogs snipped out the seat of his trousers.

Cadiou was saved, for the rights of the old man with the big legs didn't extend across the river.

The tailor was exhausted from fatigue and fright. So as soon as he got out of the water he stretched out on the grass and went to sleep. When he awoke, it was pitch-dark; noticing piles of hay around him, he crawled into one of them to protect himself from the cold and awaited morning.

Cadiou the Tailor

A little while afterward he was much surprised to hear the following words pronounced near the pile of hay where he was:

"Here's the best heap; let's take it."

It was some hay-thieves, and they had begun to tear the heap apart with pitchforks, to put it on a wagon and take it away. Poor Cadiou was much disturbed.

"If I remain here," he said, "they're going to wound me with their forks. And if I try to flee they'll catch me quickly and kill me, no doubt, so that I won't denounce them. Oh, lord, what should I do?"

He felt the cold tine of a fork rub his right hip; then he came out of his hiding-place and ran.

But, alas, he was caught.

"Well, well," cried the thieves, "it's Cadiou, the tailor! What shall we do with him?"

"We must kill him at once so that he won't denounce us," said one of them.

"No," said another, "we could easily get rid of him without burdening our conscience with so great a crime."

"What do you mean?"

"Well, it's like this. Let's lay him out on his back, pin each of his four limbs with wooden crampons to the earth, and abandon him to the wolves. You may be sure that they won't delay in arriving and will devour him quickly."

"That's true. Let's do it," said the others.

Poor Cadiou cried and begged in vain, swearing by the honor of a Breton never to reveal what he had seen that night. But they didn't listen to him. The thieves nailed him to the ground as they had said, and then they went away with the hay.

A little afterward a she-wolf arrived in the field. She approached Cadiou, sniffed him, and then sat down on his chest and began to howl to call her little ones.

"My lord, I'm done for," thought Cadiou.

Then he felt the wolf's tail in his face, and he bit it. The wolf gave a cry and wanted to flee, but Cadiou was holding on to her tail with all his might and wouldn't let go, so that the animal, lashing about, ended by pulling out the crampons which held the tailor to the earth. Then he let go of the wolf's tail and she escaped without injuring him.

Cadiou hurried to leave that unfortunate field and he arrived without delay at a little thatched adobe house. He knocked at the door, and as no one replied he went inside. He saw in the house a little old bearded woman with long black teeth who was busy making pancakes.

"Good evening, grandmother," he said.

"What are you looking for, my boy?" replied the old woman.

"If you are willing, shelter until dawn."

"Here, my boy, we never receive Christians: I have three sons who are giants. They'll come home soon, famished, and if they should see you they would surely devour you."

"You frighten me, grandmother; and yet where am I to go to await the dawn? If you knew what had happened to me since sunset . . ." And he told his adventures.

"Ah, I pity you, my child. Stay. I'll be able to arrange it so that my sons don't injure you; I shall tell them that you are my nephew and their cousin, my brother's son. Eat some pancakes while you wait."

Cadiou began to eat pancakes, but soon he heard a great noise in the hearth like the crying of owls: "Whooooo, whooooo, whooooo . . ."

"What is it, grandmother?" he asked, trembling with fear.

"It's my son January, who's coming for his supper."

And at once an old man with a long white beard arrived through the chimney, blowing on his fingers and crying:

Cadiou the Tailor

"Whoooo, whoooo, whoooo . . . I'm dying of hunger, Mother. Give me something to eat quick, quick, quick."

"Yes, my son. Here are some nice pancakes; eat as many as you want."

And he began to eat. Pieces of pancake disappeared in his mouth as in a chasm. When his hunger was a bit

calmed he raised his head: "Hummmm . . . I smell Christian flesh. . . . I'd like to eat some."

And he got up and began to look the house over from top to bottom. Cadiou, who had hidden under the table, wished he were a hundred leagues from there.

"All right, sit down near the fire, son, and be good. A cousin, the son of my brother, came to see me and I don't think you'll make him afraid just talking about eating him. He has hidden under the table and doesn't dare move, hearing you act like an uncivilized person. I'm going to show him to you; but don't hurt him, for I repeat it, he's my nephew and your cousin."

And then the old woman took Cadiou by the hand and had him come out from his hiding-place, saying to him:

"Come, my child, come and let me present you to your

cousin January; and don't be afraid of him because he is not as mean as he seems."

"Since he's my cousin," said January, "I certainly won't hurt him; so why didn't you tell me right away?"

And so Cadiou and January became friends, being cousins. A little while afterward the other sons of the old woman arrived, February and March, both as hungry as January, and as desirous as January to devour Cadiou. Their mother calmed them and deceived them with the same story. And now we see them great friends, all four, talking peacefully before a fire and awaiting the dawn.

Meanwhile Cadiou was not without worries in the presence of such cousins, and he looked for an occasion to leave them there and go away.

"If you wish, cousins," he said to them, "let's play some game or other to kill time."

"Yes, cousin, let's play a game to kill time."

"Do you want me to teach you the past and the future?"

"Yes, cousin, teach us the past and the future."

Cadiou took two clubs, formed a cross with them on the floor of the house, and said:

"Look, cousins, let each of you sit on the end of one of these clubs, and my aunt will also sit on an end, for it takes four to play this game."

The mother and the three sons sat down on the clubs.

"Good," said Cadiou; "now I'm going to go out a bit to look at the stars, and when I come back I will tell you the past and the future, but don't move; stay exactly as you are now."

Cadiou went outside, and then he ran toward Plouaret.

The old woman and her sons, not seeing him come back in, ended by getting tired of their position.

"January, you go tell him to hurry," said the mother to her eldest son, "for I don't want to stay like this any longer."

Cadiou the Tailor

January got up and went out, but he looked in vain and called aloud in all directions: no cousin Cadiou.

"We've been duped," he said, coming back in. "The funny fellow has run away, but let's go after him, and if we catch him we'll teach him to make fun of us."

And the three brothers left like three enraged demons, howling, breaking the trees, and upsetting houses as they passed by.

Cadiou heard them coming and said to himself, horrified: "Here they come. Where shall I hide?"

In a garden he noticed some beehives, one of which was bigger than the others, empty and upside down. He stood it upright and hid in it.

But the sons of the old woman, who loved honey, shouted as they arrived: "Oh, the lovely beehives! Let's take them away!" And, ceasing their pursuit, each one took a beehive. March had the one in which Cadiou was hiding.

"I've got one that's really heavy," he said to his brothers. "What a lot of good honey it must contain!"

Meanwhile Cadiou took from its case the big needle that the giant's daughter had offered him at the fair, and he pricked March in the back.

"Ouch!" he shouted. "What bad stings these bees have!"

Cadiou still plied his needle so well that March, not being able to endure it any more, threw the hive in a pond along whose bank he was walking.

Cadiou almost choked in the mud where he fell head-down. He managed, however, to get free. But he was in such a state that he had to take off all his clothing to wash it. Then he stretched it out on a bush to dry and got in the water to take a badly needed bath.

The owner of a neighboring mill, who had got up early

to release the water for his mill, passed by at this moment and, seeing clothing that seemed abandoned, took it away.

When Cadiou had finished bathing, he came out of the water and went toward the bush and was much surprised not to find his clothing there, and not able to guess who had taken it away. He was quite disturbed to be naked thus, as day was soon going to dawn. He began to run, hoping to be able to reach his house before people began to circulate on the roads to go to work. He had to cross the village square. An old woman opened her door as he was crossing it, so Cadiou threw himself quickly into the yard of Yves Thépaut, the cabinetmaker, and hid among the lumber which was in a corner.

They needed a new Saint Crépin in the church of Plouaret; the old one was all rotten and falling into dust and it had to be replaced. Yves Thépaut had gone the evening before to a neighboring village, to Kerminihi, accompanied by the rector, to get a Saint Isidore which had been there in an attic of the chapel that had fallen into ruins.

This poor saint had lost his nose and a few fingers only, and Yves Thépaut had been asked by the rector to replace them so that when the old Saint Isidore, thus restored, had been painted anew, it would make a magnificent Saint Crépin.

The cabinetmaker got up early that day and went to get wood in his yard to repair the damaged saint. It was to his great surprise that he found a naked man in the wood. He was afraid at first. Then, reassuring himself, he asked:

"Who are you? What are you doing there?"

No reply. Cadiou didn't move any more than a wooden statue.

"Christ!" said the cabinetmaker, who was fairly simple-minded. "It must be a Saint Crépin here by the will of God to take the place of the old one."

Cadiou the Tailor

And he went to the rector and told him: "What a miracle, Mr. Rector! God has sent us a new Saint Crépin. Come and see him quickly."

The rector followed the cabinetmaker. He greeted the saint and asked him who had sent him. No reply. He touched him with his hand. He was cold like a wooden saint.

"There's no doubt about it," he said, "it's certainly a miracle. The bells must be rung so that the parishioners may come and the new saint be carried solemnly to the church."

They rang the bells madly and the parishioners came from all sides. Cadiou was carried triumphantly to the church and placed in the niche of Saint Crépin. Report of it spread throughout the parish, and the parishioners came in crowds to see the new saint.

"Oh, the lovely saint!" everybody cried. "How clear his eyes are; you'd think he was alive!"

One good woman came with a lighted candle and, as there was no candlestick, she put her candle between the saint's toes, and when the candle was almost burned, Cadiou, feeling his foot burn, jumped out of the niche, to the great astonishment of those in attendance, and fled, running out of the church. He crossed the village as quick as a flash of lightning, disappeared, and no one knew what became of him.

"He has gone back to heaven," said some.

"It's a devil and not a saint," said others.

He had simply gone back home without meeting anybody on the road, and gone to bed.

All this is true, for my grandmother knew Cadiou the tailor, and it was from her that I learned this story.

3

THE MIRACULOUS DOCTOR

THERE WAS ONCE a king, a widower with an only daughter. He loved that child more than himself, and as she was old enough to marry, he often invited the princes of neighboring kingdoms to feasts and festivities. One of these great dinners was remarkable, especially for the fish that was served at it. There were carp and pike, salmon such as have never been seen. Everyone ate a great deal, including the princess. Unfortunately a big fishbone stuck in her throat, and the meal, which had begun in joy, ended before dessert in sorrow, for despite every effort and every means employed, they couldn't dislodge the bone.

The princess suffered agonies. The doctors of the court sent for their most learned colleagues: one even came from England, but not one of them was able to heal the sick girl, and their general opinion was that a dangerous and delicate operation must be attempted without delay. Report spread throughout the country that they were going to operate on the princess's throat. As she was universally loved, there was great desolation, even in the back country. In one of the villages that was most isolated there lived a poor old woman who, hearing talk of the sad plight of the king's daughter, was very moved by it, and she decided in her simplicity to go see her. . . . She set out, with a stick and a half loaf of bread in her beggar's wallet, arrived with difficulty at the king's castle, and asked for

The Miraculous Doctor

the honor of being admitted to the presence of the princess. At first the guards turned her away, but the king, who was good to humble people, insisted on letting her enter the chamber.

She asked if it was true that the doctors were going to cut open the sick girl's throat.

"Alas, yes," said the king, "it's too true, unfortunately!"

"Well, your doctors aren't as good as ours. We have some that are more dependable, who heal by secret means. To heal they don't even need to touch the sick person, and if they were here the princess would be well again."

The king didn't give much weight to what the old woman said. When she had left, however, her words kept coming back to the king's memory, and, not knowing whom to trust, he decided to have one of these village doctors whom she had spoken of come, and so he gave the order to two of his men to mount and go bring one back from the old woman's hamlet.

Now, in this hamlet lived a couple who caused a lot of scandal. The man, already old, had married a very young woman. She was flirtatious, he was miserly, so that peace did not last long between them, and the poor woman was beaten more than she deserved.

The envoys of the king, coming into the village, saw this woman wiping her eyes at her doorstep, sad and suffering; her husband had just given her a beating before going to work in his vineyard.

"You seem ill," said one of the horsemen, approaching the young woman.

"I am sicker than I appear, gentlemen."

"And what doctor is treating you?"

"Who's treating me? . . . Look over there; there he is, going into the vineyard."

"Is he a good doctor? We have come to get one for the king, and perhaps he will do the job for us."

"He's a doctor, uh—an excellent doctor, sirs . . ." said

the woman, after a moment of reflection. She had a thought that made her smile. "Excellent," she continued, "but very whimsical too: he won't do anything unless he is beaten, and beaten again and again."

"That's nice to know, thank you; we shall act accordingly."

"That's the doctor we need," said one of the horsemen to the other. And both of them took the road to the vineyard, where the man was already at his work in his shirt sleeves.

"Doctor!" they cried on arriving. "Doctor, we come on behalf of the king, to ask you to come to his daughter, who is very ill."

"Well, sirs, what do you expect me to do? . . . You're mistaken. I'm not a doctor."

"Let's not trifle; time is pressing. Here's a horse for you. Mount and let's go."

"But I tell you I'm not a doctor!"

"All right," said one of the horsemen, "that woman was right. He must be beaten. You do it."

The other fell upon him with might and main until, showered with blows, he ended by crying: "Leave me alone, leave me alone. . . . I'll be a doctor if you please. I'll do all that I can."

A moment later he left with them to go to the palace. The king was waiting for them impatiently. He saw them coming from afar and went to meet the doctor.

"Ah, sir," he said, "get quickly off your horse and follow me. My daughter is very ill."

"I'm not a doctor, king," cried the countryman, "I don't know what's going on."

"Sire," said one of the men, "he only admits he's a doctor when he is beaten; we've been forewarned concerning his whimsicality."

"Well, beat him, since it must be done."

At once the poor devil found himself between the two

The Miraculous Doctor

men as between the anvil and the hammer; blows came down like hail.

"Stop! Stop! I'll be a doctor! Yes, I'll be a doctor; I'll do all that I can."

"All these people are raving maniacs," he said, following the king into the bedroom of the princess, who was suffering and crying a great deal. "There's only one way out and that's to displease the sick girl at once so that she will have me sent away."

So he asked to stay alone with her and he began to dance with his big wooden shoes and his cotton bonnet. He turned cartwheels, stood on his head, turned somersaults.

And the princess, seeing the villager, ugly as an ape, disport himself thus, execute grimaces and contortions, far from getting angry, gave way despite her suffering to such sudden and convulsive laughter that the fishbone was ejected violently from her throat. Feeling herself suddenly cured, she began to clap her hands and redoubled her laughter, so that the king from a neighboring room heard this happy noise and dashed in.

"Ah, how happy I am!" cried the princess. "This doctor has saved me without even touching me."

"My friend, your fortune is made," said the king. "Come and stay here as long as you want and I shall deny you nothing."

Throughout the kingdom it was soon known how the princess had been healed. From all directions sick people and invalids came into the capital to see the miraculous doctor. One day they assembled in the royal palace, requesting healing with trumpets and shouts; the king had to promise to come the next morning with the great man for whom they were waiting. Before sunrise they were there, more than eight hundred of both sexes and all ages.

"My friend," said the king to the grape grower, "here are sick people who are asking for your help. With your knowledge it will be easy for you to cure them."

"Sire, what do you want me to do? I am not a doctor."

"Decidedly," said the king, "you won't do a thing without being beaten." And turning toward his guards: "Come and beat him by turns."

The poor villager didn't delay in begging for mercy.

"Enough . . . enough . . . I'll be a doctor as long as you wish."

An idea had come to him.

"Sire, give the order to bring a hundred fagots here, and as much straw."

The king gave the order and it was promptly executed.

"Good. Now, let them heap the fagots and straw up in the shape of a pyre and set fire to it."

When the flame began to crackle, the miraculous doctor had all the sick people lined up around the fire and, approaching a young man who was moaning in the front rank, he said:

"You seem very ill, my friend?"

"Yes, doctor, I have a great headache; I'm suffering probably more than any of those others who are here."

"Very well. To heal all the others," he said, raising his voice, "I must throw the sickest of you into the

The Miraculous Doctor

fire. Approach, therefore, my friend, since you are the one . . ."

The young man was already running away like a madman and crying: "I'm no longer ill. . . . I feel better."

"It must be someone else, then."

And in a glance the band scattered and fled as fast as their legs could carry them. The spectators, who hadn't heard the villager's words, seeing all the sick people become suddenly alert and nimble, made an ovation to this miraculous doctor. He returned triumphantly to the palace, where the king promised him such new rewards as he might ask for.

However, the pretended doctor said to himself: "I extricated myself this time, but tomorrow it will all have to be done over again and it will never cease. A curse upon the reward that the king promises me; I prefer to save my skin and return home."

That very evening he slipped away. He arrived at the village at midmorning. His wife was taking the air on the threshold. She was as happy as ever and was congratulating herself on the craftiness by which she had been able to get rid of her husband.

"If only," she thought, "he doesn't come back."

All of a sudden she saw him at the corner of the street running straight toward her.

"Ah," she sighed, "I am lost."

At the same moment her man seized her and kissed her, telling her: "Here I am back. Oh, my poor wife, if you but knew how I have been beaten!"

The good woman couldn't refrain from smiling as she turned her head aside.

"What, my husband, you have been beaten?"

"Yes, I have been. And I know how painful it is. . . . So I promise never to beat you again."

He kept his promise: the couple lived from that time on in perfect peace and harmony.

4

THE MOLE OF JARNAGES [1]

At Jarnages there are good fairs: lots of people go there with handsome cattle. It has a fairground that is very flat, well leveled, planted with beautiful linden trees, where it's a pleasure to take an animal and lead him about.

But a rascal of a mole had the idea of going and establishing herself there and whim, wham, she began to upset the earth in every direction, making mole runs and molehills out of sheer spite.

At the next fair people got angry.

"It's no use," they said, "to bring animals into fairgrounds that are so unsuitable, all molehills!"

A man who had been drinking fell down, landed in a mole hole, and threw his shoulder out of joint; a hog sank into one of the holes with his front foot and broke it. Everybody was unhappy.

When he saw this, the mayor had the game warden come, a man called Labuse, and he said to him:

"Labuse, you've got to catch that she-ass of a mole; otherwise our fairs are done for!"

The game warden, who was as sure of it as were all the other inhabitants of Jarnages, replied: "Mr. Mayor, I promise you that I will get this hussy of a mole for you and without delay!"

---

[1] In each province there is a locality—sometimes several—which is made the butt of the jokes of other people, and all sorts of asinine acts are attributed to its inhabitants. In Creuse and in the neighboring department of Corrèze it is at Jarnages that all these stories are localized, and its inhabitants, no more stupid than those of the other regions, are the first to laugh.

The Mole of Jarnages

And he went out to watch for her with an old pistol. Morning and evening you could hear him on the fairgrounds: bang! bang! It was Father Labuse shooting at the mole. But never did he succeed in killing her and she didn't cease to dig. After a week he gave up the pistol and took a club. At the spots where the mole was piling up the earth, wham! he would give her a good blow with the club.

"I'll end by hitting this she-devil!" he said.

But the mole continued to dig as if it were no trouble at all.

"Decidedly," said the warden, "it's not so easy as you think to catch a mole, even at Jarnages! But, after all, all you have to do is to get her to come out of the earth. Well I'm going to try with my mattock."

And when the mole raised the earth, he drove his mattock in the ground behind her. Then he pulled it out of the ground, but never did he succeed in bringing the mole out, because he didn't know that to catch a mole you have to place the blow exactly six inches behind the point where she raises up the earth.

Not succeeding, the poor Labuse was greatly humiliated, when a young man from Deaftown, who had hired out as a servant at Jarnages, said to him:

"But where I live it's not difficult to catch moles; you look for their passages, then you put in a trap made of wood and having a little door that closes by itself, and in this way you catch the mole alive."

"Ah, my friend," said the warden, "if you could catch her for me, I promise you we would drink a good stein together!"

The servant went back home; then he returned with the mole trap, after having rubbed it with wild camomile so that the mole wouldn't be suspicious, and the next day the animal was caught in it.

That day was a Sunday and there was a meeting of the municipal council. The warden brought the mole in the mole cage.

"She gave me some trouble," he said, "but you don't come from Jarnages for nothing, and I have finally caught her!"

And all the councilmen, the deputy, and the mayor got up to see this cursed animal, and some of them put their fingers through the little door to touch it. After a moment the mayor had everybody sit down, and he said to the warden:

"Labuse, the community owes you a debt of gratitude! Moreover, I thank you in the name of all of the domestic animals, without forgetting the members of the council. As for this filthy beast of a mole, now that she has been captured, it is for the council to decide what must be done with her."

"She must be killed! She must be killed!"

"Ah, it's agreed," continued the mayor, "but it seems to me that she has done us so much ill, that she has annoyed

The Mole of Jarnages

us so much, that she has brought us so great prejudice with respect to our fairs, that she deserves a great punishment indeed, and so I think we should kill her by causing her to suffer as much as we can, in order to dissuade other moles and prevent them from coming to dig in our fairground. So let's try to find a way of killing her that is especially cruel."

And all of them began to search: one of them wanted to throw her in boiling water, and another wanted to kill her with a gun (but they found that too mild), others wanted to stick a red-hot iron in her stomach, or else press her between two planks and saw her through the middle of the body, or else hang her by the nose, using a fishhook on the end of a line, or let her die of hunger hanging from a tree.

When they had all spoken, the mayor got up and said:

"My friends, I have often thought of the significance of dying and of the different ways to do it. But it seems to me that I would find the saddest end being buried alive, so I propose burying this evil beast alive in the fairground that she has ruined. It is via the earth that she has sinned; it is via the earth that she will be punished!"

And everybody shouted: "That's it! That's it! Let's go bury her alive. Our mayor is a man of wit. Long live our mayor!"

And they departed, the mayor in the lead, for the fairground. The warden was still carrying the mole in the mole trap. A councilor went to get a pick and a spade; he made a deep hole, then they threw the mole in alive and on top earth that they tamped down carefully, and the mayor said:

"Now perish, cursed beast! You, my friends, may go home. I think that the execution we have just performed will increase, if possible, the renown of the inhabitants of Jarnages!"

... And in the very bottom of her hole the mole was

already beginning to dig a gallery as she laughed and said to herself:

"The mayor has called me a she-ass; 'she,' that's possible, but as for the 'ass,' I think that the inhabitants of Jarnages are bigger asses than I am."

5

THE SHEPHERD WHO GOT THE KING'S DAUGHTER

THERE WAS ONCE a king who was supposed to have never lied, but he continually heard the people of his court saying to one another: "It isn't true! . . . You're a liar! . . ."

This displeased him a great deal, so that one day he said:

"You make me angry; if a stranger heard you speaking in this way he would think that you are all liars and I would pass as a king of liars. I no longer wish to hear such talk in my palace. I shall set the example. If anybody hears me say: 'You're a liar,' I will give him the hand of my daughter."

A young shepherd who had overheard said to himself: "Good; we shall see."

The old king liked to hear the old songs sung and hear old tales of the supernatural told. Often after supper he came to the kitchen and took a great deal of pleasure listening to the songs and stories of the valets. Each one sang or told something in his turn.

"And you, young shepherd, don't you know anything?" the king asked him one evening.

"Oh, yes, I do, king," replied the shepherd.

"Let's see, what is it, then?"

And the shepherd spoke thus:

"One day when I was passing through a wood I saw an enormous hare coming toward me. I had a ball of pitch

(343)

in my hand. I threw it at the rabbit and struck it right in the middle of the forehead, where it stuck fast. And the rabbit began to run faster with the ball of pitch on its forehead, and it ran into another rabbit coming from the opposite direction, and their foreheads stuck together so that I was able to take both of them. What do you think of that, sire?"

"It's pretty strong," replied the king, "but go on."

"Before coming as a shepherd to your court, sire, I was an apprentice miller in my father's mill, and I went to carry the flour to the clients on an ass. One day I had loaded my ass so heavily that, by heaven, his spine broke and he was cut in two."

"The poor animal," said the king.

"So I went to a hedge near there, and with my knife I cut a club from a hazelnut tree. I joined the two pieces of the ass and stuck the club in the body of my donkey from the rear to front to hold it together. The animal started walking again and carried his burden to the destination as if nothing had happened to him. What do you say to that, sire?"

"It's strong," said the king. "And after that?"

"The next morning I was much surprised (for this took place in December) to see that branches had grown, and leaves, even hazelnuts, on the hazelnut stick, and when my donkey came out of the stable the branches continued to grow and climbed so very, very high that they reached the sky."

"This is very strong," said the king. "But go on."

"Seeing this, I began to climb from branch to branch on the hazelnut tree, so that pretty soon I arrived at the moon."

"That's pretty strong, pretty strong, but go on."

"There I saw some old women who were winnowing oats, stripped from their beards, and I stopped to look at them, but I quickly grew tired of looking at these old

The Shepherd Who Got the King's Daughter

women and I wanted to go down to the earth. But my ass had gone off with the hazelnut tree on which I had climbed. What was I to do? I began to tie oat beards end to end in order to make a rope to go back down."

"That's very strong," said the king. "But go on."

"Unfortunately my rope wasn't long enough. I lacked thirty or forty feet, so that I fell on a cliff head first and with such impact that my head was driven into the stone up to my shoulders."

"That's very, very strong. But go on."

"I wiggled so much that my body got detached from my head, which remained buried in the stone. I quickly ran to the miller to get an iron bar to get my head out of the stone."

"Stronger and stronger," said the king. "But go on."

"When I came back an enormous wolf also wanted to get my head out of the rock in order to eat it. I gave him a blow on the back with my iron bar, such a blow that a letter was forced out of his behind!"

"Well, you can't make it any stronger than that!" cried the king. "But what did the letter say?"

"The letter said, by your leave, sire, that your father was formerly a miller's apprentice at my grandfather's house."

"You're a liar, young joker!" cried the king, and he got up in anger.

"Well, sire, I have won," peacefully said the shepherd.

"What do you mean, you have won?"

"Didn't you say, king, that you would gladly give the hand of the princess, your daughter, to the first man that would make you say: 'You're a liar'?"

"That's true," replied the king, calming himself, "and I have said it. A king must keep his word, so your engagement to my only daughter will be celebrated tomorrow and the wedding will be in a week!"

And that's how the shepherd got the king's daughter.

6

SIMPLE-MINDED JEANNE

There was once a man and a woman who had a daughter: she wanted to get married, but she was quite simple-minded. One Sunday when her suitor was to go to the High Mass to ask her parents for her hand, her mother told her:

"Jeanne, since your boy friend is supposed to come to dinner here, you must make him some good soup. Here is a piece of bacon: put it in the pot with a bit of this and that and garnish it with cabbage."

The girl stayed alone at the house, where she had a little dog whose name was "This-and-That"; she took him and put him in the kettle. When her mother came back she asked her if she had made some good soup.

"Yes," replied the girl, "I put This-and-That in, as you told me too."

The good woman raised the lid to taste the soup.

"What!" she said. "My poor Jeanne, you put the dog in the kettle?"

"Didn't you tell me to put This-and-That in it?"

"Are you stupid! If your boy friend knew that you are so stupid, surely he wouldn't come for you. But leave the pot alone and put the stew on the fire while I go get water. You can separate the meat from the broth in the basin, and see that you bind the broth well."

The girl stirred in vain; the broth would not bind as she wanted it to, so to bind it better she put in a roll of binding twine.

"Does your broth bind?" her mother asked.

"Of course it does. Just look and see."

When the good woman saw the binding twine in the basin she raised her arms, crying: "Heavenly days, how stupid you are, you poor Jeanne! But Mass will be over soon and they will come any moment. Put some bread and butter on the table."

When the good man came back from Mass with the suitor and his parents, the woman told them:

"We didn't have time to prepare a big stew; my daughter has been busy all morning with her cow, which was bothered with flies: another time we shall do better. Jeanne," she added, "go to the cellar and draw a pitcher of cider."

The girl put the pitcher beneath the spigot, opened it; then she began to think:

"I'm going to get married, but that's not all. If I have children what will I name them? Imagine all the names that are already taken!"

In vain she racked her brain; she couldn't find a name that didn't already belong to someone else, and she stayed in the cellar seated on one heel, while the cider filled the pitcher and ran all over the floor.

The mother, worried at not seeing her come back, went down into the cellar.

"What are you doing there, my poor simpleton, seated peacefully while the cider is running everywhere."

"Oh, Mother, getting married's not all. If I have children what names will I give them? All the names have been taken!"

The good woman was as confused as her daughter, and she began to think and the cider continued to flow.

The man came to the cellar in turn and, seeing the two women, who seemed to be meditating, he said to them:

"What are you doing there, my poor simpletons? Can't you see that the cider's overflowing everywhere?"

"You're right," replied the woman, "marrying our daughter isn't all there is to it. If she has children what names are to be given them? All the names have been taken!"

The man began to think too, without even waiting to close the spigot, and the cider continued to flow.

When the boy saw after some time that nobody was coming back from the cellar, he went to see what had happened, and there he found the man, the woman, and the girl all busy thinking.

"What are you doing?" he cried. "While you stand there with your mouths under your noses all your cider's running out on the ground."

"You're right, boy," replied the father, "but if you get married what names are you going to give your children? All the names have been taken!"

"By Jove," said the boy, "when I have found three people as stupid as you I will come back."

He set out, and after having traveled a long time he met some people who were harvesting. They would cut a blade of grain, carry it to their house, and then come back and cut a second, and they kept on doing it in this way.

"What sort of a game is this?" he asked them.

"It's not a game," they said. "We're cutting our grain and it's a lot of trouble."

The boy, who had found a sickle, cut a whole sheath, and then gave them the sickle and said:

"Here's something to cut your grain with. And if you know how to go about it, it won't take long."

"What's that strange thing?" said one of the reapers. He took it in his hand, but instead of holding it by the handle he seized it by the blade and cut himself.

"Ah, evil beast," he cried. "She bit me!" He threw it to the earth and began to strike it.

"By heaven," said the boy, "if I find two more people like you I'll go back to Jeanne."

Farther on he met a good woman who wanted to take a wheelbarrow full of sunshine home; as soon as the wheelbarrow went into the shade, the light disappeared and she would start over again.

"What are you doing there, good woman?" he asked.

"I'd like to take some sunshine home, a whole wheelbarrowful, but it's difficult for as soon as I get in the shade it vanishes."

"What do you want a wheelbarrowful of sunshine for?"

"It's to warm my little boy who is at home half dead from cold."

"You would do better, good woman, to take him in your wheelbarrow and bring him to the sunshine."

"That's true," she replied. "I hadn't thought of it."

"That makes two," said the boy, "and if I can find another one as stupid as she, I shall go back to Jeanne."

He set out and, arriving in front of a beautiful castle, he saw three men trying to raise it up with a crowbar.

Simple-Minded Jeanne

"What are you striving like this for?" he asked.

"It's to move the castle to another location," replied the men. "A wolf came and did his business beside it and the king is annoyed at the odor."

"It would be easier, my good men, to take the wolf dung and carry it away from the castle."

"By Jove, that's true," they replied. "You're quicker than we are; we hadn't thought of it."

And they put the dung in a basket and carried it ten leagues away.

"Now," said the boy, "I have found three people more stupid than my bride-to-be, her father, and her mother. So I'm going back to Jeanne."

When Jeanne saw her suitor coming she cried:

"I knew that he wouldn't stay away forever!"

7

JEAN–BAPTISTE'S SWAPS

There was once a man and a woman, Jean-Baptiste and Marguerite.

"Jean-Baptiste," Marguerite said to him one day, "why don't you do like your neighbor? He keeps trading and he earns a lot of money."

"But," said Jean-Baptiste, "if I were to lose would you get angry with me?"

"Of course not," replied Marguerite, "I know you can't always win. We have a cow. Why don't you go sell her?"

So Jean-Baptiste left with the cow. On the way he met a man who was leading a goat.

"Where are you going, Jean-Baptiste?"

"I'm going to sell my cow to buy a nanny."

"Don't go any farther. Here's one."

Jean-Baptiste traded his cow for the goat and went on his way. Not far from there he met another man who had a goose in his basket.

"Where are you going, Jean-Baptiste?"

"Oh, I'm going to sell my goat to buy a goose."

"Well, don't go any farther. Here's one."

They traded animals and Jean-Baptiste went on his way, and he met another man who had a rooster.

"Where are you going, Jean-Baptiste?"

"I'm going to sell my goose to buy a cock."

"There's no need to go any farther. Here's one."

And Jean-Baptiste gave him the goose and took the cock.

Jean-Baptiste's Swaps

Coming into the city, he saw a woman who was sweeping up filth in the street.

"My good woman," he said, "do you earn a great deal at this work?"

"Why, yes, quite a bit," she said.

"Will you trade me a piece of dung for my rooster?"

"Gladly," said the woman.

Jean-Baptiste gave her the rooster, took his dung, and went at once to the fair, and there he met his neighbor.

"Well, Jean-Baptiste, are you doing any business?"

"Oh, I didn't plan to do much business today. I traded my cow for a nanny."

"How stupid you are! What will Marguerite say?"

"Oh, she won't say anything. That's nothing. I traded my nanny for a goose."

"Oh, what will Marguerite say?"

"Marguerite won't say anything. That's not the end of it. I traded my goose for a cock, and the cock I traded for a piece of dung."

(353)

"What a stupid bargain you have made! Marguerite's going to beat you."

"Marguerite won't say anything."

"Let's bet two hundred francs. If she quarrels with you, you will pay the two hundred francs; otherwise, I will pay."

Jean-Baptiste accepted and they went back to their village together.

"Well, Jean-Baptiste," said Marguerite, "did you do any business?"

"Oh, I didn't do much," he said. "I traded the cow for a nanny."

"Well, fine. We haven't enough forage to nourish a cow; we shall have enough for a goat and we shall still have milk."

"That's not all. I traded my goat for a goose."

"Well, that's good, too; we'll have feathers to make a bed."

"That's not all. I traded the goose for a cock."

"Well, that's very good; we'll still have feathers."

"That's not all yet. I traded the rooster for a piece of dung."

"That's still better. We'll put the dung in the best spot in our garden and flowers will grow there to make a nice bouquet."

The neighbor, who had heard everything, was obliged to pay the two hundred francs.

8

CIRCULAR TALE

Three brigands were seated on a stone. The youngest said to the oldest:

"Tell us a story, Edward."

And Edward began:

"Four brigands were seated on a stone. The youngest said to the oldest: 'Tell us a story, Edward.' And Edward began: 'Five brigands were seated on a stone. . . .'"[1]

---

[1] Some storytellers always keep the number three instead of adding one each time to the number of brigands.

Sources and Commentary

PART I

Tales of the Supernatural

1. THE THREE MAY PEACHES. (T. 570)[1] [*p. 3*]
This is a version which the teller, Louis Briffault, a farmer at Montigny-aux-Amognes, Nièvre, where he was born in 1854, wrote down himself in a notebook. The ending, which has been added, is owed to Marie Boukau, whose married name is Millot, born at Balleroy, who assured Paul Delarue that certain storytellers of her region in Amognes closed all their stories with this formula. Achille Millien and Paul Delarue: Contes du Nivernais et du Morvan (Paris, 1953), p. 30. "Contes merveilleux des provinces de France" (Éditions Érasme).

This tale, of which I have noted thirty French versions, is known throughout Europe, western Asia as far as India, and North Africa.

In certain French versions, instead of May peaches the fruit that will cure the king's daughter is Christmas peaches, miraculous figs, more often oranges. Sometimes the hero has tests imposed other than that of guarding the rabbits: to build a boat that will sail on land and on sea; to sort in a single day seeds of different varieties (and then he gets aid from the ants), a universal motif, found already in the ancient tale of Cupid and Psyche and encountered in modern versions of Cinderella.

2. JEAN, THE SOLDIER, AND EULALIE, THE DEVIL'S DAUGHTER. (T. 313) [*p. 10*]
Told by Marie Moreau, whose married name is Balet, called la Mère Balette, born at Prémery in 1817, a resident at Beaumont-la-Ferrière, Nièvre. Collected by Achille Millien and published in the newspaper Paris-Centre, *March 22, 1909.*

---

[1] Numbers following the titles are those of the Aarne-Thompson classification, or, when followed by the name of a country, of the appropriate national catalogues of folk tales.

(359)

This tale is represented in France by more than a hundred and twenty versions, and is found throughout the world in various forms. It is one of the most popular, one of the longest, one of the most complex, and one of the loveliest in international folklore.

It is extracted from the same folk sources as the myth of Jason and Medea; in the latter the hero is sent to a king who is a wizard, the tests are imposed, a number of which are found in modern versions: to put the yoke on two oxen which have hoofs of bronze and exhale flames from their nostrils; to plow a field, sow dragon's teeth, and reap the harvest before the end of the day; the magical aid brought by Medea, who gets the hero to take her away as his wife, the flight by sea, the pursuit by the father, whom Medea delays by throwing the fragments of her brother's body into the sea.

The Tempest of Shakespeare had as its point of departure a play, of which a manuscript of the end of the sixteenth century is known, *La Comédie de la belle Sidéa,* written by Jacob Ayrer, of Nuremberg (1540–1605), and that play has certain points of resemblance with Scotch versions of our tale. But Shakespeare transformed the original play according to his own genius and retained only a few of the elements of the tale.

3. THE GIANT GOULAFFRE. (T. 328)   [p. 20]

Told by Barba Tassel of Plouaret in 1869. Collected and translated by F. M. Luzel: Contes Bretons (*Quimperlé, 1870*), pp. 1–21.

This tale, of which I have noted fourteen French versions, has its loveliest form in Brittany and Canada. It belongs to the cycle of tales where an ogre is duped by a child, and its elements are often mixed with those of tales of the same cycle: "Hop-o'-My-Thumb" and "Hänsel and Gretel."

4. THE WHITE DOVE. (T. 312)   [p. 36]

Told by Mr. Sadourne of Puivert, Aude, in September 1950. Taken down by Gaston Maugard. In Gaston Maugard: Contes des Pyrénées (*Paris, 1955*), p. 50. "Contes merveilleux des provinces de France" (*Éditions Érasme*).

SOURCES AND COMMENTARY [*p. 36*]

A version of the famous tale of Bluebeard, immortalized by Perrault, is recognized in this tale. The tale in this form is peculiar to France, and many of the thirty-eight versions in the French language which I know (of which three are from Canada, one from Louisiana, and four from the French Antilles), have preserved ancient traits that have disappeared from Perrault's version or have been altered there.

In the version of Perrault the monster is a rich bourgeois such as existed at the time of Louis XIV, and his only abnormality is his blue beard; in the popular French versions the monster is often a bloodthirsty chatelain, an ogre, or the Devil.

In the version of Perrault it is by her request and in order to pray that the heroine goes to her chamber; in the oral versions it is at the order of the murderer to put on wedding clothes or her most lovely ones that the woman withdraws to her chamber, like a victim who is to prepare herself for sacrifice. And to delay the fatal instant, instead of having recourse to "one more minute . . . I'm coming . . . one more moment . . ." of the literary version, she enumerates the items of clothing that she is putting on.

In Perrault it isn't because the heroine has called her brothers that they come to deliver her; if she counts on them it is because, as she says, "They promised me that they would come to see me today." In the folk versions it is an animal messenger who goes to warn her brothers, a bird as in the version of this collection, or else, more often, a little bitch dog with a message tied to her neck; as often, instead of her sister, it is a talking animal who keeps watch from her window or from the rooftop to signal to the unfortunate woman the arrival of her bothers.

The stanzas that are sung or chanted are also more numerous in the oral versions, the formula that the cruel husband chants as he sharpens his knife between two calls, a rhythmical formula that the wife repeats as she puts on each garment or, in a few versions, at each step of the stairway as she descends.

Perrault found it necessary to prune, simplify, condense the folk tale to adapt it to the taste of his century, but he has maintained the dramatic dialogues between the husband and his wife, between her and her sister Anne; he has preserved certain formulas: the call that is as regular as an incantation: "*Anne, ma sœur Anne, ne vois-tu rien venir?*" And this rhythmical and assonanced reply:

"*Je ne vois que le soleil qui poudroie et l'herbe qui verdoie.*" And it is thanks to authentically folk details that it was possible for Perrault to make the humble oral tale a little masterpiece of literature, which will live as long as our old humanity itself.

Certain investigators have hoped to see the origin of the tale in the misdeeds of Marshal Gilles de Rais, who was the companion of Joan of Arc and served King Charles VII. It is known that upon retiring to his castle of Tiffauges in Vendée he put to death a great number of children in the course of his practice of magic, which was to bring him power and riches. But the story of this child-killer has nothing in common with that of the killer of women such as the tale presents us. The central motif—the woman who must die for having gone into a forbidden chamber—is an international motif and is found in the neighboring tale, "Three Sisters Rescued by Their Sister," and, moreover, the primitive details, the numerous formulas, the rhymed dialogues cited above give witness to the age of the tale.

5. The Devil and the Two Little Girls. (T. 312B

France) [p. 42]

Unpublished version from the manuscripts of A. Millien. Written in the hand of the teller and of his wife on sheets of paper about 1885, with no name attached. The version is from the valley of the Nièvre.

This tale is a Christianized and profoundly modified form of the tale of Bluebeard peculiar to central France (Nivernais, Berry), from which the motif of the forbidden chamber has disappeared.

6. The Story of John-of-the-Bear. (T. 301B) [p. 45]

Léon Vidal and J. Delmart: La Caserne, Mœurs militaires (*Paris, 1833*), *pp. 223–53. An edition appeared in Brussels the same year in octavo under the name of Delmart alone, pp. 142–62.*

This tale of John-of-the-Bear is extremely popular in France, where it is represented by a hundred versions, and earlier it followed our colonists to Canada, to Missouri, and to the Antilles. The soldiers' version given here is the oldest known under this

SOURCES AND COMMENTARY [*pp. 65, 70*]

form, and at the same time one of the finest and most complete. It is a unique form of a more general type of tale which has as a title: "The Three Princesses Delivered from the Underworld," already attested in Grimm, but where the hero is no longer the son of a bear and a woman: the three companions are three boys who go in search of three kidnapped princesses to win their hands.

7. THE STORY OF CRICKET. (T. 1536) [*p. 65*]
Vidal and Delmart, op. cit.

This tale, represented in France by thirty-five versions, rests on the similarity between the name of the animal shut up in the hand and that of the hero, who is called in other French versions *Grillot* or *Grigri*—names used to designate the cricket.

It is known that the tale is spread throughout the zone of the Indo-European tale and beyond it, from Ireland to the Philippines and Indonesia, and from the Scandinavian countries to southern Algeria, with the same play of words, founded at times on another animal's name: the crab, the rat, the frog, etc.

It is already noted in a collection of tales of India of the eleventh century, *Kathâ Sarit Sâgara* (*The Ocean of Story*), that the hero is called "Frog," the same as noted in our modern oral tale in a French collection published in 1641: *L'Élite des contes*, of d'Ouville.

8. KING FORTUNATUS'S GOLDEN WIG. (T. 531) [*p. 70*]
From Colonel A. Troude and G. Milin: Le Conteur breton ou Contes bretons (*Brest, 1870*), *pp. 64–131.*

This tale, represented in France by some forty versions, belongs to a theme that is called "The Clever Horse" in the international classification (the hero being generally advised by a marvelous horse), but which the French folklorists called rather *La Belle aux cheveux d'or,* from the name of the version immortalized by Mme d'Aulnoy, which is in many a version about a beautiful girl whom the hero must bring back to the king.

Instead of a wig of gold belonging to the father of the girl, it

(363)

[*p. 70*]

is, in versions more logical and seemingly in more conformity with the primitive theme, a golden hair of the girl herself, which falls into the king's hand, and he, in love with the far-away princess, sends the hero in quest of the girl, at the instigation of a jealous individual.

This initial motif is already encountered in the Egyptian story of "The Two Brothers," of the thirteenth century before Christ: as a young woman is walking under the parasol pines near her house the God of the Sea rolls his waves toward her to seize her, but she takes refuge in her house and he gets only a tress of hair, which the parasol pine gives him; the tide carries it into Egypt to the place where the Pharaoh's laundrymen are working; its odor is so agreeable that the hair is picked up to be given to the Pharaoh; he sends messengers to bring the girl back from the gods to whom she belongs (Gustave Lefebvre: *Romans et contes égyptiens,* Paris, 1949, p. 151).

Much closer to our tale is an episode from a German redaction of *Tristan and Iseult,* dating from the twelfth century. King Mark of Cornwall loves his nephew Tristan so much that he considers him as his son and wants to make him his heir. The lords of the kingdom, who are jealous of Tristan, ask King Mark to take a wife in order that he may have a son to succeed him. Two swallows enter through the window of the palace, fighting with their beaks, and letting fall a hair that was both "beautiful and long." The king declares to his lords that he will marry no one save the woman to whom this hair belongs, and Tristan must depart in search of the beautiful unknown woman.

The editor of the old poem must have used the traditional elements that had been transmitted for a long time already, since, about the year 500, a Buddhist monk translated into Chinese, to insert in the compilation of the *Tripitaka,* a folk tale of India which is an ancient form of our tale.

And the tale is encountered, as in our modern tradition, in a Hebrew manuscript of the twelfth century preserved in the Bodleian Library at Oxford and in a collection of the *Facetious Nights* of Straparole (*Piacevoli Notti,* Vol. I, 1550, Night III, Fable II).

SOURCES AND COMMENTARY [*pp. 86, 97*]

9. FATHER ROQUELAURE. (T. 516) [*p. 86*]
Told by François Valarché, born at Epiry, Nièvre, in 1883, residing at Vauclaix in Morvan. Published by Achille Millien in the Revue des traditions populaires, *Vol. XXIII (1908), pp. 27–34.*

I have noted five French versions of this tale, which has meanwhile spread throughout Europe and in western Asia, in Turkey, and from the Caucasus to India.

It is already noted in the *Kâtha Sarit Sâgara* (*The Ocean of Story*), and the final motif of the faithful friend transformed into stone and restored to life by sprinkling him with the blood of children of an obliging friend is already in the tale of *Amicus et Amilus*, famous in the Middle Ages as a poem, as a tale, and as a novel.

A very pretty version whose form is similar to that of modern folk versions was published in 1635 by Basile in the fourth day of his *Pentamerone,* and Gozzi draws from it a comedy *Lo Cuorvo* (*The Crow*) which played for the first time in Venice in 1761, and which has often since been presented on the stage.

10. THE LOST CHILDREN. (T. 327A) [*p. 97*]
Noted by Antoinette Bon in Cantal, Auvergne, published in the Revue des traditions populaires, *Vol. II (1887), p. 196.*

This version is attached to the tale-type represented by "Hansel and Gretel" in the Grimm collection, very close to the type of *Petit Poucet* of Perrault. In France these two types are generally intermixed and are represented by eighty-four versions.

In oral variants the episode of the pursuit of the children by the ogre is much more developed than in the version of Perrault. In most of the versions of the *Massif central* it takes place as in the variant of this collection, with the same rhymed formula to interrogate the persons who are met. In the rest of the basin of the Loire the ogre pursues the children while riding a sow, to the rhythm of whose walking he forms a couplet, and he interrogates different workmen, as in this tale: threshers, scythemen, bell-ringers, who also reply with a rhymed formula.

SOURCES AND COMMENTARY

11. THE GODCHILD OF THE FAIRY IN THE TOWER. (T. 310) [*p. 103*]

From a collection of manuscripts gathered by Achille Millien from 1885 to 1890. Transcribed, completed, and classified by Paul Delarue.

I have noted eighteen French versions of this tale, all from Paris.

A French version of this tale was given by Mlle de la Force in her collection: *Les Contes des contes,* which appeared in 1698 under the name of *Persinette.*

Instead of desiring cabbages, as in the version here published, the mother of the heroine has more often an invincible desire to eat parsley, and the names most frequently given to the girl are *Persinette, Persillette, Persillon-Persillette.* This is also the name given to her in Italy, where the oldest version is that of Basile: *Petrosellina* (Night I, tale 7). Moreover, it is in Italy that the greatest number of versions are found, including the most complete ones.

Whereas in France the tale ends badly, in Italy the end is generally as follows: the fairy pursues the prince and the girl, who escape; when the fairy sees that they are going to escape by magic, she gives the girl a dog's or a goat's head, but later she pardons her and gives her back her lovely face.

12. PETIT JEAN AND THE FROG. (T. 402) [*p. 108*]

Written in the hand of the narrator, Gobillot Philippe, of Beaumont-la-Ferrière, Charité Canton, Nièvre, who was born in 1835. Achille Millien and Paul Delarue: Contes du Nivernais et du Morvan *(Paris, 1953), pp. 101–14, from the collection* "Contes merveilleux des provinces de France" *(Éditions Érasme).*

A version published by Mme d'Aulnoy under the title of *"La Chatte blanche"* in 1698, in her *Contes nouveaux ou les Fées à la mode,* is the oldest one known and has influenced oral versions (some ten of the thirty French versions I have noted).

Instead of being a white cat, the married animal that is in reality an enchanted princess is more often a frog, sometimes a mouse.

In other countries, the directions that the three brothers take are

SOURCES AND COMMENTARY [p. 119]

sometimes indicated by three feathers that are hurled in the wind, as in the version of the Grimm brothers (no. 63 of the complete edition, "The Three Feathers"); but more often it is the very place where the fiancée is located, which, for the three brothers, is designated by the point where the projectile falls (the projectile usually being an arrow, a ball, or a bullet), the third falling near the enchanted animal. In the north and east of Europe the girl is generally freed when the hero has burned or destroyed her animal envelope when she has come out of it.

The second part of the tale of *Pari Banou* of the *Thousand and One Nights* collection is a pretty version of our tale; Galland, moreover, did not take it from a manuscript of the famous collection, but introduced into his translation an oral version that he got from a Maronite of Aleppo who was residing in Paris; and one finds similar versions in all of the Near East, from Albania to Turkey.

13. THE GILDED FOX. (T. 1650 and T. 545) [p. 119]
Told in 1880 by Joseph André, of Trébry, a tailor and chorister.
From Contes des Landes et des Grèves (*Rennes, 1900*), p. 104.

This tale fuses two themes:
1. The three lucky brothers, called most often in France *Le Coq, la Faucille et le Chat;*
2. Puss-in-Boots or The Helpful Fox, of which the most famous version is *Le Chat botté* of Perrault.

Tales pertaining to the first theme generally have the following form: Three brothers inherit from their father three objects or animals of little value; they go into countries where the objects or animals are unknown, sell them at a fine profit, and come back having made their fortunes.

The oldest known version is in the *Grand Parangon des nouvelles nouvelles,* composed by Nicolas de Troies in 1535, of which the manuscript is deposited in the Bibliothèque nationale, and which was published only partially in 1869 at Paris by E. Mabille in the collection of the *"Bibliothèque elzévirienne."* Story X develops the first theme under a title that is sufficiently descriptive of its content: *D'un bonhomme qui, en mourant, avait trois fils, mais*

[*p. 126*]

des biens de ce monde n'avait qu'un coq, un chat et une faucille, et comment cependant lesdits enfants devinrent riches.[1]

In the versions of this tale-type the brother who has the cat arrives in a land where mice wreak enormous damage and importune people, even eat on the king's table without anyone's being able to drive them away; he receives for this unknown animal an enormous quantity of gold. It is natural that in certain versions this episode should have been replaced by that of the cat which brings wealth to his master in another manner: by marrying him to a princess, following crafty behavior like that of the *Chat botté*. Thus contamination by the second theme was accomplished.

The theme of the *Chat botté* or of the *Renard secourable*[2] is spread from Ireland and France to the Philippines and Indonesia. But the helpful animal is a cat only in the Italian versions, in half of the French versions with which I am familiar, and in a few scattered versions, generally influenced by Perrault's version. More often it is a fox in the other European countries and in western Asia, a jackal in India, the Philippines, and North Africa, exceptionally an ape in the African versions, a gazelle in one version from Zanzibar.

The outcome of Perrault's version, with the cat that swallows the ogre who had been transformed into a mouse, is a contamination from another tale represented in our collection by No. 15, "The Doctor and His Pupil"; the outcome of the version of our collection is more common, even in versions from India: the master of the castle who covets the helpful animal is invited to hide in a stack of straw, hay, or flax, in an attic, in a heap of fagots, etc., and fire is set thereto. In the Philippines the ape tells him to take refuge at the bottom of a well, which the animal quickly fills with stones.

14. THE LOVE OF THREE ORANGES. (T. 408) [*p. 126*]

Told in 1886 by Nicolas Montassier, who asserts: "This story was told me by my grandmother. I am sixty-eight. My grandmother heard it from her grandmother, she assured me. My grandmother

---

[1] Of a man who, upon dying, had three sons, but of the goods of this world had only a rooster, a cat, and a sickle, and how nevertheless the aforementioned children became wealthy.

[2] The helpful fox.

SOURCES AND COMMENTARY [p. 135]

died of cholera in 1831, at the age of eighty-five. I might have been eight, nine, or ten years old when she told me this story."
Manuscript in the Millien-Delarue collection; text from the valley of the Yonne, region of Tannay, Nièvre.

I have encountered about ten French versions of this tale, one of which comes from the French Antilles (Guadeloupe).

It is a tale that is known especially in the Mediterranean basin (though very rare in North Africa), and the countries where one finds the most numerous versions are Turkey, Greece, Italy, and Spain. European colonists, especially Spaniards and Portuguese, have taken it to America; sparse versions are encountered in central Europe, in Russia, and one isolated version in Norway.

The oldest version known to us is that published by Basile in 1636 in his *Pentamerone* (Night V, Fable 9, *"Le tre Cetre"* ("The Three Lemons"). In the following century, in 1761, Carlo Gozzi, the Venetian, developed another version in a *comedia fiabesque* (that is, inspired from fable) for a local troupe of the *Comedia dell'arte,* under the title of "The Love of Three Oranges"; and the presentation met with great success.

This theatrical production of Gozzi, in turn, was transformed by the Russian musician Prokofiev into a comic opera, which was produced in New York in 1918–19 and has been given since both there and in several great cities of Europe.

One version of the tale was published under the title: *"Incarnat, Blanc et Noir,"* in an anonymous collection published in Paris in 1718: *Nouveau Recueil de contes de fées,* and printed in 1786 in the *Cabinet des Fées* (Vol. XXXI, p. 255).

A great specialist in the folk tale, Professor Walter Anderson of the University of Kiel, is preparing at the present time a monograph on the tale of the "Three Oranges" following the method of the Finnish school.

15. THE DOCTOR AND HIS PUPIL. (T. 325) [p. 135]
Manuscript in the Millien-Delarue collection. Told in 1887 by Émile Marache, farmer, born at Saint-Léger-de-Fourches, Côte-d'Or, in 1856.

[p. 140]

I have encountered twenty-eight French versions of this tale, which is noted throughout Europe, in western Asia and India, the Philippines, in North Africa, and in North America.

The struggle by a series of metamorphoses is already encountered in the most ancient works of the Near East, in Ovid (Legend of the Daughter of Erysichtion, in *Metamorphoses,* VIII, 847), in an Egyptian tale of the second century (*L'Histoire véridique de Satni-Khamoïs*), and, much later, in one of the oldest stories of the *Thousand and One Nights* (the second Calender recounting the struggle of the genie and of the wizard princess); but it is also encountered in one of the most ancient documents of Celtic literature, in the Gallic novel of *Taliesin.*

But it is the whole tale that is encountered in an old collection of Kalmuck tales, the *Sidhi-Kür* or "The Dried-out Corpse," adaptation of the original Indian *Les Vingt-cinq Récits du Vetala;* and a version published by Straparole three centuries ago in his *Piacevoli Notti* (Night VIII, Fable 5, "The Tailor's Apprentice Who Devours His Master") is very near to the modern folk version.

16. LITTLE JOHNNY SHEEP-DUNG. (T. 314)   [p. 140]

Manuscripts in the Millien-Delarue collection. Told in 1889 by Charles Ledoux, called Father Doux, of Pougues-les-Eaux, Nièvre, where he was born in 1818.

This version presents certain variants that are peculiar to it. Generally, before the departure from the Devil's house, the hero bathes his hair in a fountain that gilds it, either on the advice of the horse or because he has the curiosity to touch the water of this fountain in spite of the Devil's injunction; it is this episode that has caused certain German folklorists to give the tale the name of "The Golden Story" (*Das goldene Mächen*). When he enters the king's service, generally on the advice of the horse, the hero hides his golden hair under a pig's bladder, which gives him the appearance of a person with scurvy. That is why in many popular versions of all countries the tale is called "The Man with Scurvy."

Finally, in the version here published, the horse is gradually transformed into a man, like the heroine of a well-known French tale "The Girl with Fish Scales" (T 400). More often at the close

SOURCES AND COMMENTARY   [pp. 147, 157]

of the story the horse is decapitated by the young man and then he appears in the form of a prince, who is the brother of the princess whom the man with scurvy has married. In spite of these alterations I have chosen this version, hitherto unpublished, because of its originality.

If we are not familiar with versions older than that of Grimm, we have at least the proof that the tale existed in the Middle Ages in the utilization of the theme in compositions of the period. The story of *Robert le Diable* developed in a long poem in the twelfth century, told in the form of a legend or exemplum throughout the Middle Ages, taken up once more in the form of a novel in the fifteenth century, worked over and reprinted in the eighteenth and nineteenth centuries, in the literature of *colportage* in the *Bibliothèque bleue*, is, to a large extent, an arrangement of the tale in an edifying and chivalrous sense consistent with the Christian and warfaring ideal of the Middle Ages.

17. THE THREE DOGS AND THE DRAGON (T. 300)   [p. 147]

François Cadic: "La Paroisse bretonne," Revue Mensuelle, *March 1907. Told by Mathurin Guilleray, tailor at Noyal-Pontivy (Morbihan).*

This tale presents an association of themes which is frequent in France, that of the unfaithful sister and that of the dragon-killer, called more often in France "The Beast with Seven Heads," from the name of the monster that the hero generally has to fight. We shall find this second theme as a constituent part of another more developed tale, No. 24, "The Miller's Three Sons." Comparative studies have shown the relation of the episode of our tale, the combat between the dragon or the beast with seven heads, with the ancient legend of Andromeda saved by Perseus from the marine monster to whom she was to be delivered.

18. THE SELF-PROPELLED CARRIAGE. (T. 513)   [p. 157]

Dr. Louis Queyrat: Le Patois de la région de Chavannat. *Part I,* "Grammaire et Folklore" (*Guéret, 1927*), *pp. 183–90.*

[*p. 164*]

Instead of a carriage that goes by itself, in the greater portion of the thirty French versions I have encountered, as in foreign versions, it is a boat that sails on land and sea ("The Land and Water Ship") that the hero must bring to the king.

It has been considered possible to identify in the association of the two episodes that compose this story, "The Companions with Extraordinary Gifts" and "The Boat that Goes on Land and Sea," a survival of the ancient myth of the *Argonaut,* with the marvelous ship in which Jason and his companions departed with the supernatural gifts; Lynceus with the piercing vision, the sons of Boreas that were as speedy as the wind, Hercules with the superhuman strength, etc. Certainly the tale does not derive from the myth, but both of them may have been formed from elements of a common legendary and narrative source, a true plankton on which formerly fed ancient myth, the folk tale, and legend.

19. THE OLD WOMAN IN THE WELL. (T. 480) [*p. 164*]

Told by the Widow Sourdeau, at Rigny, a commune of Nolay, Nièvre. From Revue des traditions populaires, *Vol. I (1886), p. 24.*

Our tale belongs to the same type as *Les Fées* of the famous collection of Perrault published in 1697. It is known that in this tale two sisters, one beautiful and good, the other brutal and haughty, go successively to the fountain where they meet a fairy; the first, who shows herself to be amiable and agreeable with the fairy, receives from her the gift of scattering diamonds, precious stones, and flowers each time she speaks; and the second, who proves to be sullen, receives the disgrace of casting forth a serpent or a frog at each word.

It was thought for a long time that Perrault got this tale directly from oral tradition. In a communication made to the French Ethnographic Society in October 1954, and reproduced in the revue *Arts et Traditions Populaires*[1] I have indicated that the version of the Perrault collection came from a tale of Mlle Lhéritier, which she published in 1695 in her *Œuvres meslées* (pp. 163-228), where

---

[1] Second year (1954), No. 1 (January–March), pp. 1–22, and No. 3 (July–September), pp. 251–74.

SOURCES AND COMMENTARY   [p. 167]

she had drawn it out into a long story, "*Les Enchantements de l'éloquence ou les effets de la douceur.*"

On the other hand, a manuscript of the *Contes de ma mère l'Oye* signed by the son of Charles Perrault (P. P.—that is, Pierre Perrault), dated 1695 and dedicated to "Mademoiselle," as was also two years later the printed collection, presents this tale in a form which has preserved certain details and certain expressions of the version of Mlle Lhéritier [2] which have disappeared in the printed edition.

This tale is presented in France in several forms. After this form in *langue d'oïl*,[3] I give in the following version, with tale No. 20, a form especially disseminated in France in the region of *langue d'oc*.[4]

20. THE LITTLE GIRL'S SIEVE. (T. 408B *France*)   [p. 167]

Dardy: Anthologie populaire de l'Albret, *Agen, 1891, Vol. II, pp. 23–7.*

Same tale-type as the preceding one, under another form.

This is the most common form of the tale in the Midi, in Catalonia, in Italy. In the versions of the north and the center of France two little girls go in turn to the spring, as in the Perrault version, or else, while herding sheep, they let their spindle fall. It rolls and rolls and they follow it to the fairies' house; the pretty and good child, the ugly and evil child, receive gifts that recall those of the version of Perrault. In our versions from the Midi they follow a sieve which is carried away by the river and come to the

---

[2] The manuscript was purchased by the Pierpont Morgan Library of New York for a sum that the French Bibliothèque nationale was unable to match. I was authorized, however, to consult it and to note the variants before its departure for America. This manuscript comprises five tales only: "The Sleeping Beauty," "Little Red Riding Hood," "Bluebeard," "The Master Cat or Puss-in-Boots," "The Fairies." In *Arts et traditions populaires* I have presented in three parallel columns the versions of the tale of "The Fairies" of Mlle Lhéritier, of the manuscript of 1695, and of the collection printed in 1697. Following the communication, I have given the list of variants of the text presented by the manuscript compared with the printed collection.

[3] Medieval dialect of northern France, which is the basis for modern (classical) French.

[4] Dialect of the south of France, which persists only in rural areas.

[*p. 170*]

fairies, or else they go to the fairies' castle. The pretty girl receives one or three stars on the forehead, the ugly one, excrement or a donkey's tail. Quite often in versions of the north as in those of the south the fairies are replaced by the Holy Virgin.

The oldest known version is found in a curious Elizabethan play, *The Old Wive's Tale* of George Peele, printed in 1595, after having been played about 1589. Our tale is recognized in it, mixed with other folk themes, in the form encountered in Celtic versions of the Highlands of Scotland and of Ireland: the two girls go to the spring with their jars, and each time a head with a golden beard juts out and asks to be combed. The first girl, who was brutal, broke her jar on the head and went away; the second took the head on her knees, caressed it and combed it, causing a great quantity of gold and of grains of wheat to fall into her apron.

21. FATHER BIG-NOSE. (*Unclassified*) [*p. 170*]
Told to Achille Millien by François Briffault, born at Montigny-aux-Amognes, Nièvre. From Revue des traditions populaires, Vol. XI, pp. 148–51.

No other version is known of this folk tale.

Two motifs are found in it which are encountered in various forms in other tales: the secret discovered by listening to the conversation of animals, spirits, or fantastic beings, which must not be betrayed under pain of being changed into stone, a motif that is an organic part of the tale-type called "Faithful John" in the international classification of themes, represented by our tale No. 9, "Father Roquelaure."

A secret that one cannot get rid of save by confiding it, not to a tree, but to the earth is found in the mythological legend of Midas: the hairdresser who knows that the king has ass's ears and must not tell it under pain of death is freed from his desire to tell it by digging a hole in the earth and confiding his secret to the earth. But the reeds that grow on the shore in their turn repeat it to the wind that's passing: "Midas, King Midas, has ass's ears."

SOURCES AND COMMENTARY   [*p.177*]

22. THE SERPENT AND THE GRAPE-GROWER'S
    DAUGHTER. (T. 425)   [*p. 177*]
Story gathered by Déodat Roché at La Nouvelle, Aude, in *1893*,
from Mme Ferrié, sixty years of age, who, being uneducated, had
received it from oral tradition in langue d'oc. Translated and edited
by the collector in the Cahiers d'Études Cathares, No. *4* (*October
1945*), *pp. 49–52*, published by the Institut d'Études Occitanes de
Toulouse, *1* rue Lafaille, Toulouse.

 This tale belongs to the theme that has often been called by the name of its most famous version, *"L'Amour et Psyché"* ("Cupid and Psyche"), introduced by Apuleius in his work *The Golden Ass* or *Metamorphoses*, which he wrote toward the middle of the second century.

 The ancient tale is an arrangement of folk stories that the writer got either by the intermediary of a Greek author who inspired him, or from oral tradition; it is just that he presents it as an *anilis fabula*—that is, an old wives' tale—though he has bedecked it with literary graces and mythological ornaments.

 This version has not ceased to inspire for centuries the plastic arts, the theater, music, and literature; but it has had no influence on an oral tradition that was much anterior to it and has not ceased to be transmitted in forms independent of the printed ones noted throughout the civilized world; and many recent oral versions are more complete than the version of Apuleius and free from alterations that deform the second part: the woman abandoned to searching for the husband who has disappeared.

 A second form of this same theme of the "animal husband" almost as well known, "Beauty and the Beast," is another folk version developed at length by Mme de Villeneuve in *La Jeune Amériquaine et les Contes marins* (The Hague, 1740). The version of Mme de Villeneuve was to be picked up a bit later by Mme Leprince de Beaumont, who enlarged it, simplified it, gave it more unity by making it a common children's tale. It is this reworking which, thanks to numerous popular and juvenile reprints, is now alone known under the title of "Beauty and the Beast," and which had a renewal of its popularity following a film that Jean Cocteau extracted from it some ten years ago.

 The tale-type represented by "Cupid and Psyche" and by "Beauty and the Beast" is among the most well known in France, where I have found eighty versions.

23. THE THREE STAGS. (T. 450) [p. 182]

Manuscript in the Millien-Delarue collection. Told about 1885 by Marie Briffault, a farmer's wife at Montigny-aux-Amognes, Nièvre.

This pretty tale, very well known in eastern Europe, and whose most famous version is that of the Grimm brothers, "Little Brother and Big Sister," is not widely disseminated in western Europe. I give the prettiest of the ten French versions that I have noted.

24. THE MILLER'S THREE SONS. (T. 303) [p. 187]

Manuscripts in the Millien-Delarue collection. Told by Berthon Bonaventure, born at Arthel, Nièvre, in 1820.

I have indicated earlier the common parts of the tale-type to which this version belongs, and of the tale-type to which belongs tale No. 17 of this collection, both of them having as a central motif the delivery by the hero of a princess who is being given to a monster, an episode that is related to the ancient myth of Andromeda and Perseus.

Our second tale, No. 24, represented in France by more than sixty versions, is called there most commonly "The Beast with Seven Heads," but sometimes also "The King of the Fish," by reason of the initial motif.

All of the elements that compose it, pregnancy by the absorption of a fish, the life-token attached to the state of health or to the life of the hero (a tree in blossom, agitated water, a rusted blade, etc.), the weapons, the dogs, and the miraculous horse, the struggle against the dragon for the delivery of the girl, the tongues of the beast, which serve to confound the impostor, the sword that separates the brother lying near his brother's wife (a motif not present in our version), the hair of the sorceress which becomes a chain in motifs attested in remote antiquity, each of these motifs would deserve an examination, which I could not perform here.

SOURCES AND COMMENTARY [pp. 201, 204]

I refer the reader to the excellent monograph on this tale made by Professor Kurt Ranke, who gave to his study the name of the Grimm version: *"Die zwei Brüder"* (*Folklore Fellows Communications*, No. 114, Helsinki, 1934). After having assembled 1,138 versions and compared about one thousand of them, the author shows the relationships of the tale with the myth of Perseus; but he thinks that the tale, much more complex and more fully developed than the myth, may have been composed in western Europe toward the fifteenth century, seemingly in France, where the best versions are still found.

25. THE MARRIAGE OF MOTHER CRUMB. (T. 717 *France*) [*p. 201*]
Dr. *Louis Queyrat:* Le Patois de la région de Chavannat. *Part I,* "Grammaire et Folklore" (*Guéret, 1927*), *pp. 234–7.*

This pretty children's tale, where one finds expressed a malicious and poetic fantasy, is peculiar to the France of *langue d'oc*, where I have found four versions, all of them very lovely.

26. FATHER LOUISON AND THE MOTHER OF THE WIND.
(T. 563) [*p. 204*]
Told in 1880 by Baptiste Sounet, called Pit, a shepherd, of Commensacq, Landes, approximately seventy years old. Edited by Arnaudin: Contes populaires de la Grande-Lande (*Paris, 1887*), *pp. 39–55.*

This tale belongs to a cycle about magical gifts whose story, as well as it can be worked out by comparative studies, is very complex by reason of the reactions which each of the tale-types and the elements that have been added in various European countries to a prototype, probably of Asiatic origin, have had upon one another.[1]

In France the tale appears in different forms. In most versions of the West, as in that of this collection, the hero, whose harvest has been destroyed by the Wind, goes to find the Mother of the

---

[1] See the summary of this study in Stith Thompson: *The Folktale*, p. 72, and for more expanded information the communication published in *Le Journal de la Société Finno-ougrienne*, XXVII (Helsinki, 1911): *"Die Zaubergaben; eine Märchenuntersuchung,"* by Antti Aarne.

Wind to ask her for restitution; in a number of versions scattered throughout France the hero plants a broad bean, which climbs to the sky. He climbs it and goes and knocks at the door of Saint Peter, or even addresses himself to God, and this beginning is also that of another tale-type represented by No. 28 of this collection; finally, in a certain number of other versions, it is on the earth that the poor devil, who often "has as many children as there are holes in a sieve," meets the sacred personage who gives him the magical objects.

In another version that I have also collected, a very poor man plants a bean in a dungheap, and the stalk that comes out of it grows until it ends by touching the sky and serves him as a ladder to reach God, whom he asks for help to feed his children. God gives him successively a table that supplies him food and drink, a horse whose droppings are of gold, and a club that strikes at his command. The table, then the horse, having been stolen at an inn, he gets back by the help of a club, etc. (Note of Arnaudin, the collector.)

I have encountered eighty French versions of this tale.

27. GRAIN-OF-MILLET. (T. 700)   [p. 217]

Told in 1885 by Jeanne Dupart, of the Grande-Lande. Arnaudin: Contes populaires de la Grande-Lande (Paris, 1887), pp. 89–103.

Labouheyre is the region of the storyteller. This story is one of the most popular of the Grande-Lande, where there are few people of the illiterate class who cannot tell some episode of it. The variations in detail which I have gathered are numerous, and I have already indicated one of them; in another, Grain-of-Millet comes into the world while his mother is dunking her bread in the soup, and the little one cries out: "O! Jasus! mama, caou toupin de soupe!" ("Oh, Jesus, Mother, what a pot of soup!") In still another, Grain-of-Millet takes a lunch to his father who is at work in the field, and he is swallowed by one of the oxen during the siesta. (Note of Arnaudin, the collector.)

This tale, of which I have gathered seventy-five French versions, has long been popular among us under the name of *Poucet* or

SOURCES AND COMMENTARY [*p. 226*]

Pouçot, as attested to by allusions made in works of the sixteenth and seventeenth centuries.

It is as result of a contamination that the name of *Poucet* has become that of the famous hero of Perrault, *"Le Petit Poucet,"* ("Hop-o'-My-Thumb"), which is a very different tale and whose title in folk versions is often "The Lost Children."

Poucet, Pouçot, Poucelot, Petit Poucet are the most frequent names of the tiny personage in the northern half of France; in the southern half (region of *langue d'oc*), there is another name that evokes his minute size by comparison with a seed: *Grain de Mil, Grain de Millet, Grain de poivre* (pepper); or by a handful of dough: *Plainpougnet,* or similar names. His name is derived also at times from fantasy: *Jean-bout-d'Homme* (Alsace), etc. . . .

The circumstances of his birth vary. In a version of the region of Nice all the broad beans that are cooking in a caldron are transformed into tiny children by a witch to whom the mistress of the household has denied food; but the woman cuts off their heads, save for one that remains hidden in a mousehole and that she considers thereafter as her son. In a version of Picardy a woman who wants to have children sows peas, which she irrigates every day, and thousands of little babies' heads appear out of the ground, then boys running in every direction; a fairy has to intervene to change them all into elves, who fly away, save for one, whose name becomes *Jean-des-Pois-verts* (John-of-the-Green-Peas). Most frequently a woman wants a child, even though he might be of the size of her thumb, or of a grain of millet, or of a handful of dough; her wish is realized, and this explains the size and the name of the hero.

28. THE LITTLE SARDINE. (T. 555) [*p. 226*]

Told by Marie Morin, a seamstress at Nantes, April 8, 1897. Taken down by Mme E. Vougeois. Revue des traditions populaires, *Vol. XVIII (1903), pp. 13–15.*

This tale, of which I have collected thirty French versions, is known from the Atlantic to India.

The traditional development is as follows: a man, generally urged by his wife, requests gifts which go according to an increas-

(379)

[*p. 230*]

ing progression, but their final indulgence provokes his fall, or that of the husband and wife.

But in France, as in foreign countries, one finds certain peculiar developments.

In an old tale of the Indian *Panchatantra*, in Turkey, and in southeastern Europe, it is a genie dwelling in a tree who grants his gifts, as in the oldest known French version, which was put in verse by an anonymous poet of the thirteenth century: *"Du vilain qui devint riche et puis pauvre,"* also called the tale of Merlin. The voice of Merlin comes out of a bush and grants successively to a woodman, whose wretchedness inspires pity, a treasure, titles, a rich husband for his daughter; but the beneficiary of these goods becomes more and more arrogant as he rises, and in the end he speaks disdainfully to Merlin whom he calls Merlin-Merlot; the magician makes him return to his original misery.

This form was Christianized in the southwest of Europe (Italy, France); the wretched person climbs a tree trunk that rises to the sky, and receives the gifts from God or from Saint Peter until the day when, asking for divine power, he receives his punishment.

In another form, which is peculiar to the north of Europe and is encountered in France, it is a genie of the waters who accords the gifts, most often a miraculous fish, as in Pushkin's famous tale "The Golden Fish," as in the well-known tale of Grimm, "The Fisherman and His Wife," and as finally in the version of this collection.

It seems that the two forms of the tale, having come possibly from Asia by two European currents, were reunited in France.

In an ending that is quite frequent in France, instead of being restored to their original miserable condition, the husband and wife, and sometimes their children, are changed into night-birds: owls, barn owls, or screech owls, which, after their metamorphosis, hide by day out of shame, but which cry at night because they regret their past.

29. THE STORY OF GRANDMOTHER. (T. 333) [*p. 230*]

Manuscript in the collection of A. Millien. Told by Louis and François Briffault, at Montigny-aux-Amognes, Nièvre, about 1885.

SOURCES AND COMMENTARY [*p. 230*]

A.M. has given somewhat arranged extracts of this version in Mélusine, *Vol. III (1886–7), Col. 428–29.*

I have devoted to this tale a little monographic study published by the *Bulletin folklorique d'ile-de-France* [1] in the series of works that I have undertaken on *Les Contes merveilleux de Perrault et la tradition populaire* (Perrault's tales of the supernatural and folk tradition). Therein I analyze the content of thirty-five French versions that I have encountered and compare them with known foreign versions. I limit myself to summarizing here certain observations and certain conclusions.

The documents assembled by collectors are of three types: oral versions that owe nothing to printed texts (about twenty); published versions that owe everything to the version of Perrault, which returned to oral tradition, following an enormous diffusion by the literature of *colportage* and children's books (only two); mixed versions which contain in variable proportions published elements and independent elements, and a few fragmentary versions.

The independent or mixed versions are all localized in an east-west zone that corresponds approximately to the basin of the Loire, to the northern half of the Alps, to northern Italy, and to the Tyrol.

Outside this zone, in France as in foreign countries, versions are very altered or come from the tale of Perrault, directly or through the intermediary of the version of the Grimm brothers, for the Grimm version comes from that of Perrault, as is revealed by a careful comparison and as certain facts explain: it presents the same details, the same literary adjunctions more agreeably developed, the same lacunæ; the Grimm brothers got their version from a storyteller of French descent who mixed in her memory German and French traditions, and she and her sister furnished them for their first edition three other tales of Perrault and one of Mme d'Aulnoy, which were suppressed from subsequent editions. If "Little Red Ridinghood" was retained, it was no doubt because of the different outcome, which made it possible to presume an independent version; but this outcome is a contamination by the German form of the tale of "The Goat and the Kids." Moreover,

---

[1] Years 1951 (pp. 221–8, 251–60, 283–91) and 1953 (pp. 511–17).

[*p. 230*] SOURCES AND COMMENTARY

although for several generations almost all Germans have known from childhood the loveliest tales of the collection of the Grimm brothers, the tale of "Little Red Ridinghood" is not in German oral tradition (two oral versions only, both of them derived from the Grimm version, have been noted up to this time in all of Germany). One cannot insist too much on this origin of the Grimm brothers' tale for invariably theorists have considered it as more complete and more primitive than that of Perrault, and they have found all sorts of symbolic meanings in the episode of the little girl swallowed by the wolf and coming out alive from its body.

The independent oral versions present a remarkable identity from one extremity of the zone of extension of the tale to the other. They permit one to ascertain that the red headdress of the little girl is an accessory trait peculiar to the Perrault version, not a general trait on which one could base oneself to explain the tale; moreover, many other tales have also a particular version that is called "Red Bonnet," as other tales have titles which evoke a headdress, a piece of clothing, or colored footwear: "The White Bonnet," "The Green Hat," "The White Coat," "The Green Garter," "The Red Shoes"; and all these titles inspired by a detail of the heroine's clothing in a particular version have a character that is accessory and accidental in the story. And one discerns the error of those who have wished to find a symbolic sense in our tale, taking their departure from the name of the heroine with a red headdress in whom they perceive the dawn, the queen of May with her crown, and so on. Nor in most of the versions is the girl named; they begin simply: *"une petite fille," "une petite," "la piteta,"* etc. . . .

In Perrault's version the wolf, after having got information concerning the place where the little girl is going, tells her that he will go "by this road" and she "by that road"; in the folk versions the conversation is quite different. The wolf asks her: "What road are you taking? The Road of Pins or the Road of Needles?" The little girl takes one road and the wolf takes the other. There are some variations in the names of the roads; one also finds the Road of the Little Stones and the Road of the Little Thorns in *langue d'oc,* the Road of Roots and that of Stones in the Tyrol. But this question of the wolf on the choice of roads is so general that folk storytellers of the zone of extension of the tale have introduced it

SOURCES AND COMMENTARY [p. 230]

into versions which owe everything else to Perrault. These absurd roads, which have surprised adults and provoked scholars, delight children, who find their existence in fairyland quite natural.

The cruel and primitive motif of the flesh and blood that are laid aside and that the girl is invited to eat is encountered in all of the folk versions with variations in detail. For example, the teeth of the grandmother, which remain attached to the jaws and provoke the questions of the girl, are presented by the wolf as grains of rice in the Tyrol, as beans in the Abruzzi.

The dramatic dialogue and the tragic ending of the story of Perrault form an ending also for the greatest number of the folk variants.

But it will be noted that the version of this collection possesses a happy outcome: the girl, perceiving that she is with a monster, pretends that she has to take care of one of nature's needs, lets herself be tied to a string, from which she frees herself when she is outside, in order to escape. The same ending is encountered in other versions of Touraine, of the Alps, of Italy, and of the Tyrol. It is encountered in the Far East, in versions of a well-known tale in China, Korea, and Japan, "The Tiger and the Children," which, by the subject and number of motifs, seems to be related to the tales of "Little Red Ridinghood" and of "The Goat and the Kids."

When one examines the content of our French versions and of Italo-Tyrolean versions that owe their whole content to oral tradition, one notes that they have common traits which are absent from Perrault's version. It seems unlikely that elements that are so general should have escaped from the version with which he was familiar at a period when the folk tale was much more lively than it was at the moment of modern collections. But the common elements that are lacking in the literary story are precisely those which would have shocked the society of his period by their cruelness (the flesh and blood of the grandmother tasted by the children), their puerility (Road of Pins, Road of Needles), and their impropriety (question of the girl on the hairy body of the grandmother). And it seems plausible that Perrault eliminated them while he kept in the tale a folk flavor and freshness which make of it an imperishable masterpiece.

(383)

30. THE SHARPSHOOTER. (T. 304) [*p. 233*]

Manuscript in the A. Millien-Delarue collection. Told in 1887 by Jeanne Martin, whose married name was Bardet, from Glux, Morvan, where she was born in 1864.

I have gathered fourteen French versions of this tale (of which one is from Canada and two from Missouri) which present only variations in detail: the magical weapon is sometimes a bow, sometimes a gun; the animal that guards the castle may be a dog, a serpent, a dragon, often with a white spot that represents the vulnerable point, etc.

The tale, which is encountered sporadically in all of Europe and in Turkey, has, in the Near East, a particular form which is already attested in the manuscript collections of *The Hundred and One Nights* (see the translation of the *Cent et une Nuits* of Gaudefroy-Demombynes, No. 7, p. 98, "Histoire du roi et de ses trois fils").

31. GEORGIC AND MERLIN. (T. 502) [*p. 237*]

Told by Louis Gouillou, a tailor at Melrand, Morbihan. François Cadic: "La Paroisse bretonne," *Revue Mensuelle, June, 1903.*

The wild man who becomes captive of the civilized man is a motif as old as civilization itself, and one is reminded of an episode of the oldest epic, of the Babylonian poem of *Gilgamesh*, of which we have four fragments that are four thousand years old: Gilgamesh, taking Eukidou in hand by craftiness, the wild man who is prodigiously strong, with long hair, with a body covered with hair, who lives with the animals.

L'Histoire de Valentin et Orson, one of the popular books that from the closing years of the fifteenth century to the middle of the nineteenth century were most read in France, tells us how Valentin got possession of Orson, a man of the woods with a hairy body who inspired fright around about him.

But the theme of the child who delivers the wild man and thereafter enjoys his magic aid, as in the modern tale, first appears in a written document of the collection of Straparole (Night V, Fable 1).

SOURCES AND COMMENTARY   [*p. 249*]

Almost always, in France as abroad, the wild man helps the child who has delivered him to triumph over a dragon or a beast with seven heads (as in our tale No. 17), or furnishes him marvelous horses that permit him to accomplish exploits which are those of the hero of tale No. 24; and our tale of Georgic and Merlin has that peculiarity of making available to the hero at the same time the adventures of each of these tale-types. But there are two other peculiarities which deserve attention.

Whereas the personage is generally a wild man whose appearance can vary, a man of iron in a version of Lorraine, a man of the woods in Poitou, a sort of a monster in Lower Brittany, a *Tartaro*, monster of local mythology, in the Basque country, it is a marvelous bird having magic power in the version of this collection, as in several other versions of Upper Brittany.

And another curious trait is that the captured being, most frequently a wild man and rarely a bird, is called Merlin or a similar name in a certain number of versions from Brittany: *Merlin* in this version, or else *le Murlu, Merlik;* and he is called *Merlin* or *Morlin* in two as yet unpublished versions of Canada, no doubt versions derived from the west of France, and in these tales the fabulous being has magical and divinatory powers.

Could the enchanter Merlin, the famous hero of Arthurian literature, derive his name and some of his characteristics from the sylvan hero with magic power? Certain Celtic scholars have believed so, and I bring here a bundle of facts, among which certain ones are new, which might support that thesis. Has the name of the old enchanter passed into oral tradition? Or have tradition and literature reacted upon each other? These questions would deserve a study that can only be realized after a critical and minute examination of the documents of literature and of folklore.

32. THE LITTLE BLACKSMITH. (T. 317 *France*)   [*p. 249*]

Paul Sébillot: "Contes de Haute Bretagne," Revue de Bretagne, de Vendée et d'Anjou (*1892*). *Reprint Vannes (1892, 53 pp.), pp. 16–18. A story told in 1880 by Virginie Hervé of Evran, Ille et Vilaine.*

This tale is not in the Aarne-Thompson international classification of themes, though it is disseminated throughout Europe

[pp. 252, 257]

(twenty versions in France), and rarely in isolation, but with a more notable development of the supernatural it serves as an introduction to other tales.

Thanks to a magic weapon, the hero, who is most often a little shepherd, kills successively three giants at one-day intervals and each time occupies the castle of the one that he has killed; he thus takes possession of a copper or iron castle, a silver castle, and a gold castle, in each of which he finds a horse and marvelous trappings. Then he appears successively in his three outfits on his three horses as a mysterious knight; he is triumphant in a series of deeds of prowess, is recognized only at the end, and wins the hand of a princess. But the acts of prowess accomplished may be those of the tale of "The Beast with Seven Heads" (No. 17 and No. 24 of this collection), of "Little Johnny Sheep-Dung" (No. 16), and of the "Mountain of Glass" (a tale that is rare in France, and not represented in this collection).

33. LA RAMÉE AND THE PHANTOM. (T. 307) [p. 252]

Manuscripts in the Millien-Delarue collection. Told in 1885 by Marie Briffault, a farmer's wife at Montigny-aux-Amognes, Niévre, where she was born in 1850.

This tale of the supernatural, of which I am familiar with fourteen French versions, is spread throughout Europe, but it seems to find its favorite soil in Russia, where it is well known, and Gogol has extracted a *novela* from a popular version of it.

34. THE WOMAN WITH THREE CHILDREN. (T. 471) [p. 257]

Told in 1900 by an old woman of the Hospital of Foix, Ariège. Published in L'Almanach patois de l'Ariège *(1902), p. 64.*

I have found some thirty versions of this tale, fourteen from Brittany and five in Gascony and Languedoc, where the typical form of this story exists.

This story of traveling in the next world with symbolic meanings finally explained to the traveler makes a contrast with the usual repertoire of French storytellers. This tale is very well

SOURCES AND COMMENTARY [*p. 263*]

known in all of Europe and in North Africa, and must be very old.

A literary tale of Rutebœuf, a French troubadour of the thirteenth century, *Le Chemin de Paradis* (The Road to Paradise), reminds one slightly of this tale.

But an Egyptian tale, "The True Story of Satni-Khamoïs and of his son Senosiris," deciphered on a papyrus of the second century of our era, presents in certain of its passages a sure kinship with it.

The wife of the scribe Satni obtains by her prayers a son, Senosiris, who grows up rapidly and becomes so wise that he holds his own with the magicians of the Pharaohs. One day Satni, his father, seeing the pompous funeral procession of a rich man side by side with the wretched burial of a poor man, wishes for himself at death the lot of the rich man. His son wishes for him in the next world the lot of the poor man. When Satni shows astonishment at his son's words, the boy recites his black book and by the force of his magic has him pass with him into the seven halls of the next world, and explains to him the symbolic scenes that take place before his eyes; for example, people running and bustling about, and asses eating behind them: they are women who live at the expense of others. . . . And finally, he shows him Osiris and the other gods weighing the misdeeds and the virtues of the dead, the poor man honored and the rich man enduring a cruel punishment.

35. THE KID. (T. 571) [*p. 263*]

Told in 1945 by Mme Eclaucher, fifty-two years old, to her grandson, Albert Lespinasse, a schoolchild twelve years of age, at Saint-Martin-de-Curson, Dordogne. Claude Seignolle: Contes populaires de Guyenne *(Paris, 1946), Vol. II, p. 83.*

I have encountered twenty-two French versions of this tale, which is spread throughout Europe and is found in North America.

As in the Grimms' version, where it is a golden goose, or in the version of this collection, where it is a kid, it is sometimes a magical animal, generally given by a fairy, which causes people to get

(387)

[p. 267]

glued together, or a red goose in Poitou, a golden goose in Le Maine, a red turkey in Touraine, etc. Or else, one asks a man whom one wants to separate from his wife in order to deceive him the easier to supply some undefined object having a strange name, and the man receives from a fairy a wand that permits him to cause beings to stick together in postures that are sometimes improper, and he brings in the chain thus formed, which he calls by the name he has been told: a *mahi-maha* in an Upper Brittany version, a *micmac* in Aunis, a *capricorne* or else an *anus* in two versions of Nivernais, a game of *Trincmal* in Artois, etc.

Quite often the king has a daughter who never laughs, and he promises her to the man who will cause her to laugh; three brothers leave successively to try their luck; the first two make disrepectful answers to an old woman whom they meet on the road, the third alone replies to her with gentility and receives a wand, thanks to which, by saying: "Hold fast," he causes people and animals to stick together, and brings them back under the windows of the king's daughter and she laughs and the boy marries her.

Often these tales have an obscene character.

The oldest known version is an English poem of the fifteenth century, "The Tale of the basyn," reproduced in Hazlitt, *Remains of the Early Popular Poetry* (1866), IV, 42. As in numerous modern versions, a peasant who has been deceived by a priest receives a magic wand which permits him to cause to stick to the priest, at the moment when he is using a chamber pot in the night, all those who come to take it away from him—the peasant's wife, the maid, the sacristan, etc.

36. How Kiot-Jean Married Jacqueline. (t. 593)   [p. 267]
Told in March, 1881, by M. A. Bonnel, of Thièvres, Pas-de-Calais. Henry Carnoy: Littérature orale de las Picardie (*Paris, 1883*), pp. 202–8.

This tale is represented in France by only five versions; the one published here has toned down a detail that is ordinarily filthy: the product which the suitor puts in the ashes of the fireplace has the property of releasing sonorous winds in all who want to light the fire. The father, the mother, the daughter, and the priest

SOURCES AND COMMENTARY [p. 272]

whom they have called try in vain.... They think that it's the devil.... The boy offers to chase the devil away if they promise him the girl; he withdraws the product or the herb and marries the one he loves.

37. HALF-MAN. (T. 675) [p. 272]

Manuscripts in the Millien-Delarue collection. Told in 1885 by Louis Briffault, a farmer at Montigny-aux-Amognes, where he was born in 1850.

I have encountered fifteen French versions of this tale, which is disseminated throughout Europe, in Turkey, here and there in the rest of Asia as far as Vietnam, and in North America.

The hero is always a lazy or stupid person, or a disinherited one as his name commonly indicates: Half-Man in our version as in a Greek version, John the Dunce, or John the Stupid in Brittany, *Morvette* (that is, "Snotty-nose") in Canada, Dirty-Feet in a version of Missouri, etc.

The oldest version noted in a written document is that of the *Piacevoli Notti* of Straparole (Night III, Tale 1): a poor fisherman, Peter the Fool, catches a tuna one day which begs him to be thrown back into the water, promising him very good fishing as a reward. Peter frees it and brings back a great many fish. When the king's daughter makes fun of him he goes and asks the tuna for the princess to become pregnant.... Peter's paternity is recognized as in our version of "Half-Man." Peter, the princess, and the child are abandoned on the ocean in a closed barrel, but Peter calls the tuna, and tells him to obey the princess, who asks him for a happy landing, the gift of beauty or of wit for her husband, the construction of a rich palace. The king and the queen, parents of the princess, go on a trip, see this palace, stop there, and one of the three golden apples of a tree in the park, having disappeared, is found on the person of the king, and the tale ends as in our version.

The tale is also found in a quite different form in the *Pentamerone* of Basile (I, 3): Pervonto, ugly, stupid, and lazy, is sent by his mother to get sticks; on the road he meets three young men who are sleeping exposed to the heat of the burning sun. He builds

(389)

[p. 276]

for them a shelter of foliage. When they awaken, as they are the sons of a fairy, they grant Pervonto that his wishes be realized, and he wishes to be transported home on his bundle of sticks; he wants the princess who makes fun of him to become pregnant by him, etc. . . .

In most modern folk versions (and it is no doubt a primitive characteristic of the tale), the hero has merely to invoke the being to whom he has rendered service, a fish usually, in order for his wish to be accomplished. For example, in the first version of Upper Brittany, cited earlier, in which the hero has put a little eel back in the water, he says at the beginning of each wish: "By virtue of my little eel . . ."

The golden apple (in other versions or other tales a golden cup) found on the innocent guest is a frequent folk motif; it makes one think of the silver cup that Joseph had put in his brother Benjamin's sack and whose guilt he feigned to begin with (Genesis xliv).

38. THE THREE BLUE STONES. (T. 650) [p. 276]

Manuscripts in the Millien-Delarue collection. Told in 1887 by Vincent Valet, a resident of Pougues-les-Eaux, Nièvre, born in 1845 at Jouet-sur-l'Aubois, Cher.

I have encountered fourteen versions in the French language, nine in France, one in Canada, four in Missouri.

Following a monographic study, Antti Aarne established as follows the primitive form, which he localizes in India:

A boy buys a dog and a cat that some children want to kill. Then he frees a serpent which is the son of the king of serpents; he receives from it in reward a magical stone that permits him to realize what he desires. Thanks to this stone, and even though he is the son of a poor woman, he is able to marry the daughter of the king by accomplishing the prodigious things that are asked of him: to bring precious stones, a marvelous castle, etc. . . . But a thief steals the stone and transports the castle and the princess beyond the sea. Yet, thanks to the aid of the dog, he repossesses the stone and wishes for the return of the castle with his wife.

(390)

SOURCES AND COMMENTARY [*p. 285*]

It is seen that the version of our collection is fairly near to the primitive form. In a version of the *Pentamerone of Basile* (IV, 1) "*La Preta de lo gallo,*" ("The Cock's Stone") it's in the head of the cock that the magic stone is found, whereas in several French versions it is in the head of a serpent.

In numerous versions, particularly in the Near East, the stone is fixed to a ring, which has caused the name of "The Magic Ring" to be given to this tale-type. And precisely, the famous tale of the *Thousand and One Nights*, "Aladdin and the Magical Lamp," combines ingeniously two tale-types," "The Magic Ring," and that to which the international classification of themes gives the name of "The Spirit in the Blue Light," from the title of the Grimm version, which is represented also in the tales of Andersen by the well-known tale of "Briquet" ("Fire-Steel").

PART II

Animal Tales

1. THE JOURNEY TO TOULOUSE OF THE ANIMALS THAT HAD COLDS.
(T. 130)   [*p. 285*]

Told in 1885 by François Briffault of Montigny-aux-Amognes, Nièvre. Collected by Achille Millien, who gives a somewhat retouched version thereof in Étrennes nivernaises (*1895*), *pp. 51-4, without any indication as to origin. I have re-established the original text from the manuscripts of Achille Millien.*

I have found forty-five French versions of this tale which is scattered throughout the old continent under two forms:

1. A Western form, to which belongs, naturally, the version of this collection as well as the famous version of Grimm: "The Musicians of the City of Bremen"; in this form it is always domestic animals who leave their village and occupy the house of wild animals (of thieves in more recent versions);

2. An Oriental form, in which the group that is being chased out has certain misapprehensions about what happens, and one in

(391)

[p. 288]

which one or several inferior animals (insects, crustaceans, etc.) go into the house of an old woman, usually, and kill her when she comes back.

Here is a typical very brief summary of this Oriental form:

An egg, a scorpion, a needle, a piece of dung, and a mixing-bowl are traveling together. They get into the house of an old woman while she is absent and hide, the egg on the hearth, the scorpion in the water jug, the needle on the floor, the piece of dung on the threshold, and the mixing-bowl above the door. The old woman comes home and wants to light a fire in her fireplace, but the egg blows up and dirties her face; she goes to the water jar to get washed, but the scorpion stings her; overcome with fear, she wants to flee from the house, but the needle pricks her foot; near the door she slips on the dung and the mixing-bowl falls on her head and kills her.

This Oriental form, popular in Japan, China, Korea, Melanesia, Indonesia, has penetrated into Europe, is fairly well known in Russia, and becomes more and more rare as it goes toward the west; it is represented in the Grimms' collection by the pretty tale of *"Herr Korbes"* (No. 41), but is very rare in France, where I have encountered only two versions.

According to a monographic study of Antti Aarne (*Die Tiere auf der Wanderschaft, eine Märchenstudie* (Helsinki, 1913), Folklore Fellows Communication No. 11), the Western tale is derived from the Oriental tale, which penetrated Europe long ago. The origin of the Western form must be old in reality, for it is found in the old animal epic of *Ysengrimus*, written in Latin about 1280 by Master Nivardus, of Gent, seemingly based upon an old Flemish version of the north of France; from there it passed into the *Roman de Renart* (Branch No. 8), where it forms one of the most successful of that fresco of tales under the title *"Le Pélerinage Renart"* ("The Pilgrimage of Renard").

2. THE LION THAT LEARNED TO SWING—THE FOX THAT LEARNED HOW TO PICK CHERRIES—THE WOLF THAT LEARNED HOW TO SPLIT WOOD. (T. 151) [p. 288]

SOURCES AND COMMENTARY [*p. 292*]

Manuscripts in the Millien-Delarue collection. Told in 1889 to the Curé Sery, of Hubans, by the painter Cernoy, who got the story from Pierre Picard of Maulaix, Nièvre.

Outside of France only a few more or less altered versions of this tale-type are known. Alone, the twelve French versions that I am familiar with have a logical development which is generally that of this collection. In a few versions, however (Brittany, Normandy), instead of teaching a lion to swing, the hero takes turns with it in squeezing each other in a press, but the boy squeezes it tightly and then leaves it.

3. THE SOW AND THE WOLF. (T. 124) [*p. 292*]

Manuscript in the collection of Mari Leproux. Collected by Mme Hagland, teacher at Jarnac, told by her grandmother, Mme Ménard, born in 1830 at Mérignac, Charente.

This tale, which is particularly beloved in France where I have found about fifty versions, is little known in oral tradition beyond our frontiers, where one finds only occasional specimens. It is known somewhat more than elsewhere (except for France) in Italy and the Anglo-Saxon countries, where the best-known variant was published by J. O. Halliwel in 1843 in his *Nursery Tales* (No. 55, p. 16), "The Three Little Pigs," which children's books have not ceased to reproduce until it has even returned thence to oral tradition.

It is from this version that Walt Disney drew his famous film, spreading on a world-wide scene a taste for this tale of children and nurses.

In the French versions, as in the English tale, the animals who leave seeking adventure are sometimes three little pigs; but it may also be three little pullets, as in the following tale of this collection, three geese, three little ducks, three kids, or three little nanny-goats; but most frequently the animals are of different species, generally a pig (or sow), a goose, or a duck (or a cock).

In the case of the different animals, the animal that constructs the third house and resists the wolf is almost always the pig or the

[p. 297, 300]

sow, and this hero or that heroine has a bellicose name, *Ricochon* or *la Coichotte* in Morvan, *la Couchenotte* in Burgundy, *la Gorette* in a version of Angoumois; in Normandy it's a goose, *la Pirotte*, and in a version of Roussillon the hero, who has become a human being, is called *Parpansot*.

4. THE THREE PULLETS. (T. 124) [p. 297]

Manuscript in the collection of Ariane de Félice. Collected by her at Monsireigne, Vendée, in 1942, in the course of an inquiry organized by the Musée des Arts et Traditions Populaires. This tale is noted here exactly as it was taken down stenographically on listening to the peasant girl storyteller with her direct style, her development, which eliminates every word that is foreign to the action, and where it would be difficult to change a single word.

This is a particular form of the preceding animal tale.

5. THE GOAT AND HER KIDS. (T. 123) [p. 300]

Collected in 1944 by Jean Drouillet from his mother, Eugénie Drouillet, whose maiden name was Riffet, born at Neuvy-sur-Barangeon, Cher, in Sologne in 1879. She got the tale from her mother, Octavie Riffet, who was born at Theillay, Cher, in 1851.

This tale, of which I have assembled sixty French versions, has its zone of predilection in France, as do the two preceding tales, for if it is found in most of the countries of Europe, in the Caucasus, Turkey, North Africa, it is represented there only by an occasional version.

The theme in a rudimentary form has already been encountered in the collections of fables which, inspired by Æsop, Phædrus, and Avianus, were composed in Latin first under the most common name of *Romulus*, then in French under the name of *Isopets* (from the name of Æsop).

But there is a great difference between these artlessly composed fables and the versions of our folklore to which a long tradition has given numerous formulas and sometimes couplets that are sung.

SOURCES AND COMMENTARY [pp. 304, 309]

6. FATHER MAZARAUD. (T. 162 *France*) [p. 304]
Story told by Mme Raymonde Tricoiré among the villagers of Olmès, Aude, in the Pyrenees and published in Folklore du Pays de Monségur, *by Jean and Raymonde Tricoiré (Paris and Toulouse 1947), pp. 93-9, in the local dialect with a French translation.*

This tale, which is encountered only in France and Spanish Catalonia, is not in the Aarne-Thompson classification. The version of this collection is the most attractive of seven French versions I have found.

7. A LOVELY DREAM AND A FATEFUL JOURNEY. (T. 112D
France) [p. 309]
Collected by A. Jeanroy. "Quatre Contes meusiens de Mangienne, canton de Spincourt, Meuse," Revue des patois gallo-romans, *Vol. II (1888), p. 101.*

This tale, of which I have collected five French versions, has episodes that may exist as isolated tales: the horse that kicks the wolf in the jowls; the wolf that loses his booty by listening to the sow; the rams that strike him from both sides. . . .
But it is the whole sequence of our version that we find already in tales of the Middle Ages.
In a collection of seventeen Latin fables republished from another Latin collection, from a *Romulus* of the fifteenth century: *Æsopi extravagantes dictæ Fabulæ,* fable 10 resembles our modern tale a great deal.
Concerning the wolf that passed wind: A wolf who, one morning, passed wind decided that it was a lucky omen for the day. He set out, disdained a piece of bacon, then two hams, wanted to devour a colt but, invited by the mare to remove a thorn from one of her hind feet, received a terrible kick; he was half-crushed between two sheep whom he wanted to prevent from quarreling; he agreed to baptizing two piglets before eating them and, taken to the mill by the sow, fell under the wheel; he agreed that some goats sing hymns before dying, mixed his voice with theirs, was beaten by the shepherds who hastened to the noise; at the foot of an oak he recapitulated his misfortunes and wished that Jupiter would hurl a

[*p. 312*]

steel lance at him to punish him. A butcher who had climbed the tree and heard everything threw his ax and wounded his thigh: "How prompt the gods are to execute my wishes!" he said. And he escaped, limping.[1]

This fable, reproduced in several manuscripts and collections of the fifteenth century, was taken up by Hans Sachs in 1562 under the title: *Von dem stoltzen Wolff* (Of the Presumptuous Wolf).

The attitude of the wolf who disdains the first morsels presented to him and finally finds nothing to eat recalls that of the heron of La Fontaine in his famous fable *"Le Héron"* (VII, 4).

8. HALF-CHICK. (T. 715) [*p. 312*]

Collected about 1880 in Sologne by Armand Beauvais. Revue des traditions populaires, *Vol. XXXI (1916), pp. 44–6.*

"Half-Chick" is one of the most popular tales of France, where I have encountered eighty versions.

The tale, well known throughout Europe, in Turkey, and in the former French and Spanish colonies of America, is especially disseminated in France, and to a lesser degree in Spain.

It is mentioned in a play of Destouches: *La Fausse Agnès* (1759), where a simple girl says that she knows *"les contes de Peau d'Ane, de Moitié de Coq et de Marie-Cendron"* (that is, Cinderella). And a writer, Restif de La Bretonne, developed it to some extent in a version in *Le Nouvel Abélard* (1778).

Although the form of the tale is quite uniform, popular imagination has been exercised on the minute details which vary infinitely. The animal is most often a cock, or gander, with various names: *Moitié-de-Coq, Moitié-de-Poulet, le Poulet rouge, le Poussin pelé, Coquelet, la Poule à moitié coq, Quartille de Jau,*[2] *Compère Jaulet,* etc.; but it may also be a duck, male or female: *Bout de Canard, Moitié de Cane,* etc.

Instead of going to find loaned money or a purse that has been taken from him in certain versions, Half-Chick goes to Rome to get his tail gilded.

---

[1] Translated into French in Robert: *Fables inédites des XIIème, XIIIème et XIVème siècles* (Paris, 1825), Vol. I, p. xcviii.

[2] *"Quartille,"* piece of a fruit that is cut in four pieces; by extension: quarter of an object, or simply a piece. *"Jau,"* jars = gander.

SOURCES AND COMMENTARY [p. 319]

Half-Chick most often meets the Fox, the Wolf, and the River, which he causes to go into his behind when they are tired; but there are versions that have other meetings with objects or animals which the fowl introduces into its body: hornets that sting man when he wants to sit down on Half-Chick to smother him, a ladder that Half-Chick uses to get out of the well into which he is thrown.

In a few versions it is to the king that the animal has loaned his money, but he doesn't limit himself to recovering his crowns; he takes the king's place on the throne, to the great satisfaction of the subjects.

PART III

Humorous Tales

1. TURLENDU. (T. 1655) [p. 319]
Montel and Lambert, Revue des langues romanes, *Vol. III, p. 208. A version collected in Lozère.*

I have encountered thirty-five French versions of this tale, three in Canada.

The hero has diverse names, which are often picturesque: *Barlicloclet, Merlicoquet, Vadoyer, Merlificochet, Le Vieux Tripet, Charly-Berdin,* etc.

Or else he is called from the first thing he puts in trust, usually a grain, *l'Homme à la lentille, l'Homme à la fève, l'Homme au grain de blé* (the Man with the lentil, bean, grain of wheat), or the head of wheat, or with the chick pea.

The ending varies; most often the dog escapes before the eyes of the consternated boy, who shouts in vain. In a version of Velay, the man with the bean requires, instead of the hogs, which he gave in the end and which got mired down in the mud, the daughter of the house, who is very rich, and he marries her. In a version of Provence, the hero, Janoti, exchanges his oxen for the cadaver of an old woman, whom he puts on the edge of a ditch in the posture of a washerwoman; the girl of a near-by castle comes, touches

[p. 322] SOURCES AND COMMENTARY

the old woman, and causes her to fall in the water; Janoti swears that she has drowned the woman, and he marries the girl for damages.

The tale is encountered throughout Europe, in Asia as far as India and here and there beyond it, in North Africa, and occasionally in North America.

It also exists in the form of an animal tale in Estonia, Finland, and Russia. The fox and the cock are lodged in a house; the fox eats his companion and accuses a sheep that they give to him in compensation. At the next inn he eats the sheep and accuses a hog, and so on, and he gets bigger and bigger animals, or else in the end a girl, in whose place they substitute a bitch dog, as in our tale. (See, for example, Guterman and Jacobson: *Russian Fairy Tales*, p. 371, "Little Sister Fox and the Wolf.")

2. THE FANTASTIC ADVENTURES OF CADIOU THE TAILOR. (T. 1875A and T. 1875B *France, and* T. 1827 *Flanders*)   [p. 322]

Noted by F. M. Luzel, told by Barbe-Tassel, Plouaret, Côtes-du-Nord, in December 1868. From Revue des traditions populaires, Vol. II (*1887*), pp. 9–15. Luzel: "*My old storyteller localized her story, as frequently happens. Cadiou was really a tailor of Plouaret, and Yves Thépaut a cabinetmaker of the same village, and I did know them in my childhood.*" (*We have made a few very slight modifications in the text. P. D.*)

A complex tale. As often happens in this type of story, the teller refers to a known personage, as here, or else he tells, as if they had happened to him, adventures that are so many little independent tales belonging generally to the cycle of liars' tales.

If we exclude details that localize the tale and motifs that belong to the imagination of the man of Lower Brittany (the big old man who wants to "scythe" the limbs of the hero, the giants who personify the months), we distinguish, framed by these elements of linkage, three principal tale-types: the boy pulled by the wolf, the boy in the beehive, the saint replaced in its niche by a living person.

1. The boy on the wolf's tail.

In the most frequent form of the tale a boy whose wanderings

SOURCES AND COMMENTARY [*p. 322*]

have brought him among a group of thieves is shut up by them in an abandoned wine cask. A wolf arrives, the boy grabs him by the tail through the bung, and he is dragged by the horrified wolf until the barrel breaks.

I have encountered fifteen French versions of this tale. It has often passed into literature and has already been noted in old collections. One version is found in the *Nouvelles* of Franco Sacchetti, assembled in the fourteenth century (*Nouvelle* XVII), another in *Les Aventures du baron de Fœneste,* which the old French writer Agrippa d'Aubigné wrote in 1616 and 1617. The tale was adapted to the stage for the theatricals of the fair of Saint-Germain, at Paris, in 1713 (*Théâtre de la Foire,* tome I, 1721, pp. 3–9). And finally, the Provençal writer Frédéric Mistral tells the story as having happened to him personally in the prettiest and most alertly told of stories which make up his *Mémoires (Mémoires et Récits,* Paris, 1906, Chapter iv, pp. 106–33).

I have long studied elsewhere this episode and a related one: the boy pulled from the earth, where he is buried up to his neck, by a wolf, a fox, or a jackal—a story that takes us back to a *jataka* of ancient India. (See *Arts et traditions populaires,* No. 1, January–March, 1953, pp. 33–58, Paul Delarue, *"Le Conte de l'enfant à la queue du Loup.*)

2. The boy in the hive that thieves are taking away.

A tale-type not included in the Aarne-Thompson classification.

I have noted eight French versions of this tale, which is found almost everywhere in Europe and which exists in a related form in China.

It is found in the famous popular German book *Tyl Ulenspiegl,* whose earliest know edition is a German one of 1515, and which was translated into almost all European languages where it circulated as a popular book. In the French edition of 1532, which was among us at the basis of numerous editions of *colportage,* it forms Chapter ix: *"Comment Ulespiègle se cache dans une ruche et fait battre deux individus qui voulaient voler cette ruche"* (How Eulenspiegel hides in a beehive and has flogged two individuals who want to steal that hive).

3. The saint replaced in its niche by a living person.

Tale-type not classified in Aarne-Thompson.

I have encountered twenty French versions of this tale. It also

(399)

[p. 332, 338]   SOURCES AND COMMENTARY

figures in humorous works from the Middle Ages on under quite diverse forms: as a *fabliau* (*"Le Prêtre crucifié"* ("The Priest Crucified"), see Bédier: *Les Fabliaux*, p. 468), and as a tale (Sacchetti: *Nouvelle* 25; Morlini: *Nouvelle* 73; Straparole, Night VIII, Tale 3, etc.).

3. THE MIRACULOUS DOCTOR. (T. 1552 *Wallonia*)   [p. 332]

Told in 1887 by Marie Briffault, a farmer's wife at Montigny-aux-Amognes (Nivernais), where she was born in 1850. Published by Achille Millien in the Revue du Nivernais, *July 1900.*

This tale is already found in the same form in a fabliau of the Middle Ages, *"Le Vilain Mire"*; that is to say, *"The Peasant Doctor"* (see Bédier: *Les Fabliaux*, p. 476). It is the fabliau that gave birth to our version and to a few similar versions of Flanders and Italy.

But the two parts that make it up already existed in oral tradition independent of the fabliau, and by the tradition the fabliau was itself inspired.

The episode of the peasant whom his wife passes off for a doctor, who is beaten in order to force him to exercise his art and heal the princess, is found in the *Exempla* of Jacques de Vitry (thirteenth century) and inspired the famous play of Molière: *Le Médecin malgré lui* (*Doctor in Spite of Himself*).

And the final motif of the sick people whom the false doctor pretends to heal by first burning the sickest of them is already encountered in a German poem of the thirteenth century and forms a chapter of the story of *Tyl Ulenspiegl*, already mentioned concerning a previous tale.

4. THE MOLE OF JARNAGES. (T. 1310)   [p. 338]

Dr. Louis Queyrat: Le Patois de le région de Chavannat. *Part 1,* "Grammaire et Folklore" (*Guéret, 1927), pp. 177–82.*

This theme of the unsuccessful punishment, consisting in putting an animal back in his natural element with the hope of punishing

(400)

him, amuses primitive as well as civilized people, and one finds it everywhere in varied forms: an eel, a tortoise, or a shrimp condemned to be drowned in the river or in the sea; a rabbit to be thrown into the briers, a crow to be thrown from the top of a cliff; a mole or mole-cricket to be buried alive, etc. . . .

See the abundant bibliography given by Stith Thompson in his *Motif-Index* (K. 581).

In France the episode of the mole condemned to be buried is found among the stupidities attributed to the inhabitants of numerous villages considered by their neighbors as the *Bœotians* [1] of the region.

In a tale gathered in French Guinea in Creole French, the tortoise, taken by the tigers, chooses his type of death and asks to be drowned in a pond.

5. THE SHEPHERD WHO GOT THE KING'S DAUGHTER.

(T. 825) [*p. 343*]

From F. M. Luzel: Cinquième Rapport sur une mission en Basse Bretagne (*Plouaret, September 1, 1872*), *pp. 8-10. Published in* Archives des Missions scientifiques et littéraires (*2nd series*).

This tale is already attested in the Middle Ages in the *Modus florum*, produced in Germany in the tenth century; it is represented in France by about ten versions, which differ little from each other.

6. SIMPLE-MINDED JEANNE. (T. 1450 *and* T. 1384) [*p. 347*]

Paul Sébillot: Contes des paysans et des pêcheurs (*Paris, 1881*), *p. 239. Told in 1880 by Joseph Macé, of Saint-Cast, Côtes-du-Nord, a fourteen-year-old cabin boy.*

In most of the twenty-eight French versions of this tale, which is scattered throughout Europe and the Near East, one finds only the following two portions, which form the second and the third parts of the version of our collection.

1. The daughter who has gone to the cellar to draw wine or

---

[1] A name applied to uncultivated minds that are indifferent to beauty, with reference to the reputation that the Bœotians had for being heavy-witted.

[p. 352]

beer (sometimes to the fountain to draw water) is looking for the name to give to the son that she will have one day, can't find one, and is desolate; or else she wails about her imaginary misfortune which will happen perhaps some day with this child; her mother and her father join her and are desolate with her.

2. Her suitor or her husband comes to look into their prolonged absence and, when he learns the cause, he goes away declaring that he won't come back until he has found three people as stupid as they.

This second part forms a framework in which are inserted stupidities that can vary a great deal from one version to the next. In that of this collection the stupidities observed are: the harvest made head by head, the heat of the sun brought with a wheelbarrow, the castle that someone wants to move (generally it is rather a church that someone wants to move away from a dung pile).

There are many others that are all found in various versions: to take nuts up to the attic with a fork; to step into one's breeches by climbing onto a chair and trying to jump into them; to put a cow on a house so that she can eat a stand of grass which is growing there; to capture rays of sunlight and to bring them back to light the house; to put a pig in an oak tree to eat the acorns; to empty the water of a pond with a basket; to cut a tree down to pick its fruit. . . .

In brief, one can introduce into this tale a great part of the "Numbskull Stories" which are catalogued by Aarne-Thompson in their *Types of the Folktale* as tale-types from No. 1200 to No. 1335, and many others.

7. JEAN-BAPTISTE'S SWAPS. (T. 1415) [p. 352]

Emmanuel Cosquin: Contes populaires de Lorraine (*Paris, 1886*), *Vol. I, p. 155. Collected at Moutiers-sur-Sault, Meuse.*

This tale is known throughout Europe, western Asia as far as India, here and there in the Far East, in North Africa.

I have noted seven French versions.

And recently a French *chansonnier* made a song, set to a lively tune, entitled *Où vas-tu Basile?* which has enjoyed a great success. The hero exchanges his horse for a cow, the cow for a goat,

(402)

SOURCES AND COMMENTARY [p. 355]

the goat for a capon, the capon for a bouquet of violets, and the bouquet for his lady's heart.

8. CIRCULAR TALE. (*Motif* x16) [p. 355]
Collected in 1944 by Jean Drouillet from his mother, Eugénie Drouillet, whose maiden name was Riffet, born at Neuvy-sur-Barangeon, Cher, in Sologne in 1879. She got the tale from her mother, Octavie Riffet, who was born at Theillay, Cher, in 1851.

There exists a whole cycle of similar stories which Stith Thompson calls in his *Motif-Index:* "Stories which begin over and over again and repeat," (Motif Z 16).

These stories are quite varied and are the delight of children, who tell them to one another, and students who embellish them and make thereof a "saw." It is thus that the little folk story of this collection took the following form fifty years ago among students who had added local color:

"It was in the deep caverns of the high mountains of Calabria. Three brigands were seated on a stone. Suddenly one of them said to the oldest: 'Beppo, you who know how to tell stories, tell us one.' And Beppo began in these words: 'It was in the deep caverns of the high mountains of Calabria . . .'"

And to terminate this last note of this book, I cite a "saw" that has been entertaining students of the lycées and universities:

Ah! It was a very touching ceremony! Everybody was crying. The captain of the firemen himself cried in his helmet. Soon the helmet overflowed and a drop fell on a peach stone. The stone germinated and the tree grew and bore fruit. The king's son came by; he saw this fruit, and he picked some, and ate some, and he died. His father, who loved him a great, great deal, had a magnificent funeral for him. Ah! It was a very touching ceremony! Everybody was crying. The captain of the firemen, etc. . . .

FOLKLORE OF THE WORLD
An Arno Press Collection

Almquist, Bo, editor. **Hereditas.** 1975

Arewa, Erastus Ojo. **A Classification of the Folktales of the Northern East African Cattle Area by Types.** 1980

Bassett, Helen Wheeler and Frederick Starr, editors. **The International Folk-lore Congress of the World's Columbian Exposition** 1898

Beck, E.C. **They Knew Paul Bunyan.** 1956

Budge, Ernest A. Wallis, translator. **Egyptian Tales and Romances.** 1931

Campbell, Charles Grimshaw. **Tales from the Arab Tribes.** 1950

Carpenter, Inta Gale, editor. **Folklore of the Calumet Region.** 1977

Carpenter, Inta Gale. **A Latvian Storyteller.** 1980

Childers, J. Wesley. **Motif-Index of the *Cuentos* of Juan Timoneda.** 1948

Christiansen, Reidar Th. **Studies in Irish and Scandinavian Folktales.** 1959

Dawkins, Richard M. **Forty-Five Stories from the Dodekanese.** 1950

Degh, Linda. **People in the Tobacco Belt.** 1975

Delarue, Paul. **The Borzoi Book of French Folk Tales.** 1956

Dorson, Richard, editor. **America Begins.** 1950

Dorson, Richard, editor. **Studies in Japanese Folklore.** 1963

Eberhard, Wolfram. **Minstrel Tales from Southeastern Turkey.** 1955

Elwin, Verrier. **Folk-Tales of Mahakoshal**. 1944

Elwin, Verrier. **Tribal Myths of Orissa**. 1954

Flowers, Helen L. **A Classification of the Folktales of the West Indies by Types and Motifs**. 1980

Georges, Robert A. **Greek-American Folk Beliefs and Narratives**. 1980

Gizelis, Gregory. **Narrative Rhetorical Devices of Persuasion in the Greek Community of Philadelphia**. 1980

Hardwick, Charles. **Traditions, Superstitions, and Folk-Lore**. 1973

Kirtley, Bacil Flemming. **A Motif-Index of Polynesian, Melanesian, and Micronesian Narratives**. 1980

Klein, Barbro Sklute. **Legends and Folk Beliefs in a Swedish American Community**. 1980

Klymasz, Robert Bogdan. **Ukrainian Folklore in Canada**. 1980

Köngäs-Maranda, Elli Kaija. **Finnish-American Folklore**. 1980

Mattfield, Julius. **The Folk Music of the Western Hemisphere**. 1924 and 1925

Meñez, Herminia Quimpo. **Folklore Communication Among Filipinos in California**. 1980

Parry, Adam, editor. **The Making of Homeric Verse**. 1971

Penzer, Norman Mosley. **Poison-Damsels and Other Essays in Folklore and Anthropology**. 1952

Perry, Ben Edwin, editor. **Aesopica**. 1952

Rooth, Ann Birgitta. **The Cinderella Cycle**. 1951

Sébillot, Paul. **Légendes et Curiosités des Métiers**. 1895

Stern, Stephen. **The Sephardic Jewish Community of Los Angeles**. 1980

Taylor, Archer. **The Black Ox**. 1927

Teske, Robert Thomas. **Votive Offerings Among Greek-Philadelphians**. 1980

Thigpen, Kenneth A. **Folklore and the Ethnicity Factor in the Lives of Romanian-Americans**. 1980

Winner, Thomas G. **The Oral Art and Literature of Kazakhs of Russian Central Asia**. 1958